Marcus

A Writer's Theatre
George Devine and the English Stage Company
at the Royal Court 1956–1965

Herbert Lang Bern
Peter Lang Frankfurt/M.
1972

ISBN 3 261 00719 2

Marcus Tschudin

A Writer's Theatre

George Devine and the English Stage Company
at the Royal Court 1956-1965

European University Papers

Europäische Hochschulschriften
Publications Universitaires Européennes

Series XIV
Anglo-Saxon language and literature

Reihe XIV   Série XIV
Angelsächsische Sprache und Literatur
Langue et littérature anglo-saxonnes

Vol./Bd. 3

Marcus Tschudin

A Writer's Theatre
George Devine and the English Stage Company
at the Royal Court 1956-1965

Herbert Lang Bern
Peter Lang Frankfurt/M.
1972

To my parents

CONTENTS

page

I   Preface   11

II   A Short History of the Royal Court before 1956   15

III   George Devine: A Short Account of his Life and Work 1910-1956   23

IV   The Foundation of the English Stage Company   35

V   George Devine as a Producer at the Royal Court 1956-1963   43

VI   George Devine as an Actor at the Royal Court 1956-1965   51

VII   George Devine as an Artistic Director of the Royal Court   63

VIII Ann Jellicoe: The Sport of My Mad Mother   69

IX   John Arden: Serjeant Musgrave's Dance   99

X   N.F. Simpson: One Way Pendulum   133

XI   Arnold Wesker: The Kitchen   159

XII   John Osborne: Luther   183

XIII Conclusion   217

XIV   Gaskill and After: Outlook   219

Annotations   221

A p p e n d i x   277

Record of Productions 1956-1969

How Profitable is the Royal Court?   292

Bibliography   293

C 17M 3P

List of Abbreviations

Sport	Ann Jellicoe, The Sport of My Mad Mother. In: The Observer Plays, Faber & Faber, London 1958 (pp. 157-217).
New Version	Ann Jellicoe, The Sport of My Mad Mother. New Version. Faber Paper Covered Editions, London 1964.
Shelley	Ann Jellicoe, Shelley, or The Idealist. Faber & Faber, London 1966.
Musgrave	John Arden, Serjeant Musgrave's Dance. Methuen & Co. Ltd, London 1960.
Pendulum	Norman Frederick Simpson, One Way Pendulum. Faber & Faber, London 1960.
Kitchen	Arnold Wesker, The Kitchen. Jonathan Cape, London 1961.
Luther	John Osborne, Luther. Faber & Faber, London 1961.
Taylor	John Russell Taylor, Anger and After. A Guide to the New British Drama. Methuen & Co. Ltd, London 1962.
Theatre at Work	Charles Marowitz/Simon Trussler, Theatre at Work. Playwrights and Productions in the Modern British Theatre. Methuen & Co. Ltd, London 1967.
Haymann/Arden	Ronald Haymann, John Arden. Contemporary Playwrights Series, Heinemann, London 1968.
Haymann/Osborne	Ronald Haymann, John Osborne. Contemporary Playwrights Series, Heinemann, London 1968.
Purdom	C.B. Purdom, Harley Granville Barker. London 1955.
MM	Raymond Mander/Joe Mitchenson, The Theatres of London. New York 1961, London 1963.
S.E.	Oscar James Campbell/Edward G. Quinn (ed.), A Shakespeare Encyclopaedia. Methuen & Co. Ltd, London 1966.
ESC	English Stage Company. A Record of Two Years Work. London 1958.
ESC 58/59	English Stage Company 1958-1959. London 1960.

Ten Years	Ten Years at the Royal Court 1956/66.
TRF	George Devine, "The Right to Fail". In: The Twentieth Century, February 1961, pp. 128-132.
BBC	George Devine 1910-1966. Broadcast on BBC-3 on December 4th, 1966. Compiled and narrated by Leigh Crutchley. Produced by Robert Pocock.

I PREFACE

Today, sixteen years after its start in 1956, the achievement of the English Stage
Company at the Royal Court Theatre London is undisputed. Despite some valuable
efforts from other sides, the theatre in Sloane Square remains the place where the
modern British drama was given its first great chance; where John Osborne's <u>Look
Back in Anger</u> shocked comfortable audiences into a new awareness of what drama
could be; where drama was put into touch with contemporary life again, after many
years (Eliot's and Fry's plays are excepted) of drawing-room comedies, musicals,
revues, revivals and thrillers.

This book is an attempt to present and evaluate the achievement of the English Stage
Company at the Court between 1956 and 1965; that is to say, during the period in
which George Devine was its artistic director.

Many articles and even books (1) have been written about the Royal Court; about the
angry young authors and their plays. The gossip columnists had their share, too.
In 1966, when the idea of this thesis was first discussed between Prof.Dr.Rudolf
Stamm and me, it appeared already clear that it was of little use to produce yet
another book of author biographies and abstract analyses of plays.

The existing studies are concerned with the plays and playwrights at the Court, even
with the productions. But I have not yet come across a study which tries to examine
the productions in comparison with the text of the plays and with the principles established by the English Stage Company at the time of its foundation. The following questions seem to me to have been neglected: What has been done to an author's original
script? What has happened to it during its transformation into a performance? Has
it been faithfully realized by the director? Have the actors and the designer joined
their forces to get the best out of the play? It is the aim of this thesis to answer them.

Moreover, I want to pay tribute to the man who did more than anybody else to make
a new British drama possible; the man whose name is inseparably connected with
the Royal Court: George Devine. In the chapters III, V, VI and VII I try to provide
a short sketch of his life and activities before 1956, of the influences he was exposed
to and the ideas he developed, and to show how these became visible in his work as a
director, actor and manager at the Court - for which the productions discussed in
chapters VIII to XII stand as characteristic examples.

To bring a performance to life in a later description is an almost impossible task.
It seems even more presumptuous if an author tries to describe and evaluate productions that he has not seen himself. I perceived this problem as soon as I started
collecting the material, but by then I was so fascinated by my subject that I decided
to risk the task by using all the available sources, such as newspaper reviews, pho-
tographs, prompt-books, tapes, interviews.

It was also necessary to restrict drastically the number of productions to be discussed here. It was hard indeed to choose among the 150 plays staged at the Court during the time in question. I finally chose five productions which, I am convinced, are representative for the work that has been done by the English Stage Company. The inclusion of further productions would have led to similar results, and would only have been feasible at the expense of precision and detail. I have also avoided to write about that pièce de resistance of every book on the new British drama, Look Back in Anger. Dozens of articles have been lavished on this play (2), every fibre of it has been dissected, and I did not feel the urge of enriching this literature by another (and probably superfluous) essay.

In dealing with my five productions I have endeavoured to be as exact as possible. I first discuss the text of each play and then proceed to compare its contents and form with the stage production. If beyond that I have succeeded in conveying a glimpse of the fascination that sparked from those productions into the audience some years ago, all the better.

Most of the material presented was collected in the summer of 1967 and the autumn of 1968, when I spent altogether five months in London. I had the opportunity of working in the press office of the Royal Court - hundreds of press cuttings were read, interviews arranged and prepared, often under difficult circumstances. I visited dress rehearsals and productions at the Court to gain insight into methods of direction and acting; I talked to authors, directors, actors and designers.

In preparing this thesis I have been greatly helped by most of the authors and directors whose work is examined in it, and also by Jocelyn Herbert, who designed the sets of four of the five productions analyzed. I am deeply grateful for their assistance, without which this book could not have been written.

My particular thanks go to William Gaskill, artistic director of the Royal Court, who allowed me to come and go as I pleased, helped me in tracing people and furnished me with valuable information; to the authors Ann Jellicoe, John Osborne, N. F. Simpson and Arnold Wesker; to the directors Tony Richardson, John Dexter, Lindsay Anderson, Michel Saint-Denis, Glen Byam Shaw, Keith Johnstone and Jane Howell; to the actors and actresses Peggy Ashcroft, Joan Plowright, Robert Stephens and Colin Blakely. I am further indebted to Miss Jennifer Aylmer of the British Theatre Museum for details of the history of the Court before 1956 and for allowing me to use various scripts; to Mrs. Lena Cope in the press office of the Royal Court, who assisted me in every way imaginable; to Mrs. Harriet Mennie-Devine, who helped me with the chapters concerning her father; to Ronald Bryden, drama critic of The Observer, for informations about some productions; to Professor John Russell Brown of the University of Birmingham, who sent me two articles about George Devine which it would have been difficult to get otherwise; to Leigh Crutchley and the BBC London, who allowed me to read the script of a radio programme on George Devine; and to the staff of the University of London Library, who were kind enough to let me examine the original typescripts of The Kitchen and One Way Pendulum. Miss Elizabeth M. Akers helped me untiringly in correcting and typing the different drafts. I am especially grateful to Prof. Dr. Rudolf Stamm, who encouraged me throughout, always found the time for a discussion and by his helpful and stimulating criticism guided me safely to the conclusion.

M. T.

II A SHORT HISTORY OF THE ROYAL COURT BEFORE 1956

In the year 1870 a theatre called the New Chelsea was opened on the South side of Sloane Square. This building had been a dissenting chapel, and was turned into a theatre through the initiative of Arthur Morgan and B. Oliver, who were to become its first managers. In the course of the same year its name was changed into Belgravia (1).

The productions staged here on the first night presented a sensational mixture indeed; there were songs, drama and even ventriloquism to draw a full house:

"Drama, comedy, farce, ballet, and burlesque, with a strong company, comprised the amusement on the first night ... Miss Patty Goddard and Miss Julian were also on the list; and the original drama of Mabel, the plot of which is simplicity itself, two honest people being suspected of dishonesty, and the honour being established before the curtain falls, was furnished for giving the perfect theatrical air to the bill ..." (2)

After a "drastic reconstruction" (3) under the supervision of the architect Walter Emden had taken place at the end of 1870, the theatre, under the new management of Marie Litton, assumed the name Royal Court, reopened in January 1871 and had a great success with W.S. Gilbert's burlesque The Happy Land. In 1881, under the directorship of John Clayton, again alterations were made on the building (4).

Four years later, in 1885, a successful period started with a series of farces by Arthur Wing Pinero. The Magistrate, The Schoolmistress (1886), and Dandy Dick (1887) had exceptionally long runs and attracted large audiences.

In 1887 improvements were made in Sloane Square. The Royal Court Theatre was to be demolished. It closed on July 22nd. John Clayton, the manager, decided to build a new theatre not far from the original building of 1870. The second Royal Court was designed by Walter Emden and W.R. Crewe and opened on September 24th 1888 (5).

There is a critical account of the building in The Builder of November 29th 1888:

"The decoration is not much better than theatre decoration usually is, and the large vases and fronton (we borrow a French word for what we have no precise English for) with nothing behind it, which forms the centre feature of the skyline of the façade, belong to the most commonplace order of architectural accessories. The worst point, architecturally, is the manner in which the drum of the octagonal dome over the centre part of the auditorium hangs in the air in front of the gallery. Nothing could look more unarchitectural and inconstructive." (6)

It was a three-tier theatre, with a gallery rising behind the upper circle (7). There were seats for 642 people. In the years between 1888 and 1921 further structural alterations were made, along with redecorations (8).

In 1934 the Royal Court was sold to a cinema company for £ 7,500. It was damaged in November 1940, when Sloane Square Station was bombed, and it remained derelict for about twelve years. In 1952 it was completely renovated by Robert Cromie, for the London Theatre Guild.

When the English Stage Company moved into the Royal Court in 1956, new changes were carried out on the building:

> " ... a completely new colour scheme of interior decoration has been introduced and an apron stage constructed, turning the lower boxes into stage doors, with balconies above. The old rehearsal room of the theatre is now used as a restaurant for the club premises incorporated in the theatre ... " (9).
>
> *

The first play to be produced at the second theatre designed by Emden and Crewe was Mamma!, a farcical comedy by Sidney Grundy (10), preceded by Hermine, a one-act play by Charles Thomas. The management of the theatre was shared by Mrs. John Wood and Arthur Chudleigh, a team-work which lasted until 1891. Among the plays produced under their management Pinero's The Cabinet Minister, (1890), The Weaker Sex, and The Late Lamented (1891) made the theatre famous.

On January 20th 1898 there was the first night of Pinero's Trelawny of the Wells, which saw 135 performances (11).

In 1899 Dion Boucicault joined Arthur Chudleigh in the management, and, after a short interval, during which H.T. Brickwell and Frederick Kerr directed the Court and Martin Harvey produced his great success A Cigarette Maker's Romance (1901), the theatre was taken over by J.H. Leigh, who presented some plays by Shakespeare, in which he himself acted together with his wife.

*

It was at this moment that the name of Harley Granville Barker (12) appeared for the first time in connection with the Royal Court:

> "After another Shakespeare Representation at the Court, Leigh was dissatisfied with what was being done, and Thyrza Norman (13) was told by William Archer, to whom she went for advice, to get the young Granville Barker for the next play ... Barker produced the third play, The Two Gentlemen of Verona, on 8 April 1904, Barker playing Speed ... The production and Barker's performance were both much praised ... " (14)

Already during those first contacts with the Court Barker had definite plans and ideas:

> " ... for this production (15) J.E. Vedrenne joined Leigh as business manager. Barker in conjunction with Vedrenne persuaded Leigh to allow them to present special matinées of Shaw's Candida, from this began the famous management which was to remain at this theatre until June 1907." (16)

These matinées proved successful. The Vedrenne-Barker management started its work at the Court on October 18th, 1904. It was a collaboration of a pure business-man, primarily interested in money, with an artist, who wanted to give something new to the theatre.

The productions were based on a kind of short run system. New plays were tested in matinées. If successful, they were presented in evening performances for about four or six weeks, then taken off and later revived if it seemed worthwhile to do so (17). But although Vedrenne and Barker took great trouble in order to attract new playwrights to their theatre, Bernard Shaw was the only outstanding author at the Court. His endeavours to persuade Rudyard Kipling, G.K. Chesterton, and Joseph Conrad to write for the theatre remained without response. But John Galsworthy tried his hand as a dramatist and made his reputation with The Silver Box. It was produced by Barker, who also directed all the plays put on with the exception of those by Shaw, who produced his own.

Harley Granville Barker devoted special attention to the acting. This is how he expressed his sense of its importance:

> "The art of the theatre is the art of acting, first, last and all the time". (18)

He gave the first impulses in England to the school of what is called "natural acting" (19). The main point of his theory consisted in the so-called underacting. He under-acted himself and demanded the same of his company (20). Shaw did not wholly agree with this style:

> "This method was successful in works of a domestic realistic nature when the audiences had the illusion that they were sharers, not spectators of the drama. But the plays of Shaw, like those of Shakespeare, demand flamboyant acting, and here Barker's method failed ... The great thing about the Court Theatre, however, was the allround excellence of the acting; there were no stars: the cast was a team." (21)

The plays were carefully and painstakingly rehearsed by Barker. He wanted his actors to think about their parts and to feel them, not to learn their lines mechanically (22). Hesketh Pearson gives us some details of Barker's methods as a director in rehearsal:

"Barker then provided a brief biography of the character in the play, from which it appeared among other things, that his childhood had been unhappy, that his father had been an enthusiastic golfer, that part of his life had been spent at an unhealthy spot on the coast of South America ... This sort of thing was done by Barker merely to stimulate the imagination of his actors, with the result that his productions conveyed a sense of intimacy and naturalness that was new to the stage." (23)

Together with the careful production of a play went his respect for an author's text. Nothing shows this better than the almost overscrupulous note which the Court managers inserted in the programme of Shaw's Man and Superman, presented in May 1905:

" ... Messrs. Vedrenne and Barker beg leave to explain that the acting version of Man and Superman now presented has been prepared solely by the author. None of the omissions by which he has brought the performance within the customary limits of time have been made or suggested by the managers. They do not regard a complete performance, occupying both afternoon and evening, as impossible or unacceptable. But as Mr. Bernard Shaw designed the play from the beginning so as to admit of the excision, for practical stage purposes, of the scene in which John Tanner's motor-car is stopped in Spain by brigands, of the philosophical episode of Don Juan in Hell, and of the disquisition on the evolution of morality as a passion, they feel that they can present the rest of the play as a complete comedy in three acts without injury to the artistic integrity of the work, or violation of the author's wishes, which have been unconditionally complied with on all points." (24)

But despite this devoted work, despite this close collaboration of directors, actors, and writers, there was a force against which the Court under Vedrenne and Barker had to battle. This force were the critics. The greater part of them did not show any appreciation of the artistic efforts that were made there. For some reason or other they did not back the Court:

" ... the critics did their best to belittle the Court Theatre productions from the start. With the notable exceptions of Max Beerbohm and one or two others, they received every play as if it had been specially written to annoy or shock them. They had been used to dramas that dealt with murder, adultery and artificial theatrical situations; their intelligence had become numbed; and they could not respond to anything novel ... " (25)

Among the plays presented between the years 1904 and 1907 were John Galsworthy's The Silver Box, St. John Hankin's The Charity That Began at Home and The Return of the Prodigal, and Elizabeth Robins's Votes for Women! Plays by Shaw staged during that period, in which his reputation was made, included John Bull's Other

Island (26), You Never Can Tell, Man and Superman (27), Candida, Major Barbara, Captain Brassbound's Conversion, and The Doctor's Dilemma. Then there were the three Greek plays by Euripides, Hippolytus, The Trojan Women, and Electra, in the translations of Gilbert Murray (28), and two plays by Granville Barker himself, The Voysey Inheritance (29) and Prunella (30), which he wrote in collaboration with Laurence Housman. Among the plays by foreign authors produced at the Court were Arthur Schnitzler's In the Hospital, Gerhart Hauptmann's The Thieves Comedy, Ibsen's The Wild Duck and Hedda Gabler, and Maeterlinck's Aglavaine and Selysette. On the whole, thirty-two plays by seventeen authors were put on and over a thousand performances given (31).

Hesketh Pearson summed up:

> "It was a pity that the Vedrenne-Barker management ever left the Court Theatre, where, though their success was on a modest scale, the work they did had an unparalleled effect on public taste and dramatic art. But Vedrenne wanted to make more money, and Barker's ambition was to reach a wider public by producing plays for which the stage at the Court was too small." (32)

The results of the Vedrenne-Barker period are impressive. New playwrights such as John Galsworthy, John Masefield, St.John Hankin, and Barker himself were discovered and introduced to the English theatre. Shaw's position was strengthened and his work made widely known and famous. Important foreign authors were presented to the London public; the Greek drama was approached in a new way through the verse translations by Gilbert Murray. Moreover, there were vital impulses to the arts of acting and production, and Barker's refusal to let a "star" dominate the stage caused people to come to the theatre in order to see a play and not just an actor or actress displaying themselves. An outstanding achievement indeed, considering the fact that the management lasted for only about three years.

*

After this climax in the history of the Court (Granville Barker and Vedrenne moved to the Savoy Theatre in 1907), the house in Sloane Square received many famous visitors. There was a London season by the Abbey Theatre Company from Dublin in May 1910, and in 1913 and 1914 the Irish National Theatre took the stage. Frank Benson's production of Shakespeare's A Midsummer Night's Dream was staged at Christmas 1915. There was now, however, no firm line in the Court's policy:

> "The Court was often used by amateurs and play-producing societies and apart from the special seasons, was more often than not closed during the decade which followed the Vedrenne-Barker management." (33)

After the First World War J.H. Leigh sold the theatre. J.B. Fagan became its manager in 1918 and produced, among other plays, Shakespeare's The Merchant of

Venice and Twelfth Night. George Bernard Shaw's Heartbreak House had its London first night here in October 1921. This was followed by a number of Shakespearian revivals, and in 1922 there was a season of plays by John Galsworthy presented by J.T. Grein and Leon M. Lion.

New life came into the Royal Court when Barry Jackson and his Birmingham Repertory Company took it over in 1924. Jackson began his work with an enormous task: he produced Shaw's "play cycle in five parts" Back to Methuselah, showing one part each night from February 18th to 22nd. This was followed by The Farmer's Wife by Eden Phillpotts, which scored a tremendous success with 1329 performances, lasting from March 11th 1924 until January 1927. Jackson and his company proved their original ideas and their theatrical zest with two Shakespeare productions: Macbeth and The Taming of the Shrew were both done in modern dress (34).

After this interlude with Barry Jackson the Macdona Players performed several plays by Shaw in 1929, 1930 and 1931. The School for Husbands, staged in 1932, was the last play to be presented at the Court for a long time to come. The theatre was closed.

Having been turned into a cinema in 1934 (35) and closed again in 1940, it was finally reconditioned and restored as a theatre by Alfred Esdaile, who is still in the council today, and the London Theatre Guild. It reopened on July 2nd 1952 with The Bride of Denmark Hill by Lawrence Williams and Neill O'Day. Further plays produced during that year were Shakespeare's The Comedy of Errors and The Long Mirror by J.B. Priestley. In 1954 Laurier Lister presented an intimate revue Airs On A Shoestring, which ran for two years and ended in March 1955, after 772 performances. Nothing remarkable is to be said about the following productions (36), but on February 9th 1956 the Brecht-Weill version of The Beggar's Opera entitled The Threepenny Opera was produced - for the first time in London.

In April of the same year the English Stage Company under the artistic direction of George Devine took over the Royal Court and started its régime with a production of Angus Wilson's The Mulberry Bush, which had its first night on April 2nd.

*

Our brief survey shows that the Royal Court Theatre had a chequered history indeed. In the mid-eighties of the last century Pinero's plays led the theatre to a first period of significance and success. This "Pinero-epoch" lasted until early 1898. The second, more important event was the Vedrenne-Barker era from 1904 to 1907, when the little theatre in Sloane Square became a dramatic centre, the influence of which on the entire British theatre can hardly be overestimated.

Barry Jackson provided some fresh wind from 1924 onward. His work at the Court provoked the last controversies before the theatre was transformed into a cinema, which was bombed.

In 1956, the English Stage Company moved in. Once more there was a spirit of enterprise and revolution; once more there was an angry young man as Shaw had been fifty years before; once more the Royal Court became a theatrical centre (37).

There were further alterations of the building after 1956, as we have mentioned before (38). Some of the most radical changes and redecorations were made in 1964, when the theatre was closed and the English Stage Company embarked on a West End season. It all cost a lot of money, but generous donations helped to transform the house into an attractive theatre. Here is the impression of the reporter of the West London Press:

> "New seating arrangements, more space in the foyer, and a bar at the rear of the stalls ... All are included in £ 35,000 improvements carried out during the past six months to the Royal Court Theatre, which reopens on Wednesday ... plush carpeting provided by the Rank Organisation, and other red carpets in the auditorium given to the English Stage Company by the British Nylon Spinners.

> There have been a number of gifts, in fact. The stage curtain is donated by Cumberland Silk Mills ... Patrons of the stalls will have a better view of the stage because of the raking of the auditorium.

> Lighting is improved by the use of boxes by the wings. There are improvements, too, to the dressing rooms ..." (39)

The Arts Council contributed £ 15,000; the London County Council £ 2,500; and the Chelsea Borough Council expressed its sympathy by giving 200 guineas and additional help with the rates. Chairmann Neville Blond (40) and his wife donated £ 5,000 (41). A journalist of The Stage gave further details about the building:

> "In the bar itself, a long row of double windows gives a clear view of the stage, yet cuts out noise from either side.

> A new floor has been fitted on the stage and a new grid system overhead, and with two rows of seats which may be removed to provide room for an orchestra pit if required, the total seating is now 428, only ten less than formerly. The paintwork in the stalls and on the proscenium arch is in a dark shade of brown, but the dress and upper circles and the roof of the theatre are in a light cream shade brightening the interior without making it look clinical ... The entire theatre is now extremely attractive and can at least bear comparison with those in the West End ... those noisy customers who used to vent their spite on a play by clattering noisily up the rear staircase, will find their efforts baulked by the solid wooden door at the foot, an innovation which will earn the gratitude of long-suffering stalls patrons." (42)

The new and ninth season of the English Stage Company started immediately after the completion of the renovations with the first night of John Osborne's Inadmissible Evidence, which took place on September 9th 1964.

III GEORGE DEVINE: A SHORT ACCOUNT OF HIS LIFE AND WORK 1910-1956

George Alexander Cassidy Devine was born in Hampstead Garden Suburb, London, on November 20th 1910. Not much is known about his early years before he went to Oxford in 1930. His daughter, Harriet Mennie-Devine, says:

> "My father was not much given to personal reminiscences, and he never talked about his early childhood, which was a particularly unhappy time".
> (1)

George Devine's father, also called George and christened Georgios, was one of many children born in Manchester of an Irish father and a Greek mother. All the children were given Greek names: Henrikos; Minos, who became a clergyman and was known for some reason as "the poet-preacher of Vere-Street"; Alexandros, headmaster of Clayesmore School, Winchester; Pericles, who was taken to Greece by his father where they both died. Georgios Devine was a bank clerk working in the Tax Department. He had a passion for the theatre, attended it frequently, showed a special interest in musical comedies and was himself an amateur actor. He apparently had an affair with a young actress, and when this ended unhappily he took a holiday on the Isle of Wight. There he met Ruth Cassidy, a young lady on vacation from Canada. They were married within a week. The marriage was not successful. The young wife felt far from her family and her friends, and soon after George Devine was born his parents separated. His mother removed him from their Hampstead family home, and he spent the early part of his life alone with her in a cottage in the New Forest.

When he was old enough, his father sent him to Clayesmore, the minor public school at Winchester in Dorset, of which his uncle Alexander Devine was the headmaster. His uncle looked after him, was interested in him because he was an only and lonely child and took him to France and on many holidays. George loved France and learnt to speak French perfectly. When he was sixteen his uncle became ill, and for a time he became unofficially the deputy head of Clayesmore School, which rather disconcerted some of the parents.

Obviously influenced by his father, George Devine took an early interest in the theatre. Amongst his earliest reading was an enormous collection of theatre programmes which his father kept carefully in special albums (2). There was about George's education a constant if faint atmosphere of stardust and stage air, which fascinated him and which developed in him an intense and lasting attachment to the theatre.

His father did not mind his being attracted by the stage, but he remained realistic in deciding about his son's future, so he sent him to Oxford to get a degree, which was to provide him with a good background in case a career in the theatre should fail.

George Devine went to Oxford in 1930. He read English at Wadham College and apparently was a well-known figure around Oxford - he always wore a large black Homburg hat, a long black overcoat and carried a silver-topped ebony cane. And his thoughts were never far from the theatre. In 1932 he became president of the Oxford University Dramatic Society (O.U.D.S.), and soon afterwards he invited John Gielgud to direct Shakespeare's Romeo and Juliet for the society. Gielgud accepted. He suggested a team of three women, who called themselves Motley, to design the set and the costumes: this was their first proper commission. The custom at that time was to invite professional actresses to act in the O.U.D.S. productions, and George Devine did not shrink from asking Peggy Ashcroft to play Juliet and Edith Evans to play the part of the Nurse (3). They both accepted. The late Christopher Hassell played Romeo, Terence Rattigan one of the servants and Devine himself Mercutio. Edith Evans was fascinated by his abilities as an actor, as her following statement shows:

> "I remember him when he played Mercutio in Romeo and Juliet. The moment he opened his mouth one knew he knew how to speak the Shakespearean words, he knew what it was about, which told me at once the man was a genuine actor. He did not have to learn, he knew how to do that." (4)

John Gielgud, the director, remembered that production, too. Here is his opinion about twenty-two years old George Devine as an actor:

> "George was very good as Mercutio, but a bit solid, and one never kind of thought that he was that kind of romantic actor or that he would become a 'dashing juvenile', as we say. He was a character actor, and a very good one, too, and a brilliant comedian." (5)

This production was the highlight of George Devine's period in Oxford. For him it was a decisive start; it had a great significance for him because he got in touch with the professional theatre and made friends with John Gielgud as well as Peggy Ashcroft and Edith Evans, and it strengthened his intention to make his way in the theatre.

Later, in 1932, when his three years in Oxford were over (6), George Devine went immediately to London, joined the Motley group and became their General Manager. But this did not satisfy him: at the same time he started his career as a professional actor at the Old Vic where he was cast for a number of rather inappropriate parts and had no great success, though he was always looked upon as a young actor of great intelligence and interest. To begin with the jobs were few and far between, and at times he was very depressed by this. He made his professional debut in April 1932, when he played Salanio in The Merchant of Venice at the St.James's Theatre. His parts at the Old Vic in 1933 (7) included Lucius Septimus in Shaw's Caesar and Cleopatra, Lord Worthington in The Admirable Bashville, and Moses in Sheridan's The School for Scandal. Later he played in John Gielgud's productions of Hamlet (1934), in which he acted Bernardo as well as the First Player, and of Romeo and

<u>Juliet</u>, in which he played Peter (1935). Laurence Olivier recalled Devine's Peter:

" ... George was playing Peter very funnily indeed, this time
obviously a good comic, I had not suspected this before ... We
had marvellous fun in the company ..." (8)

The same year saw Devine in Michel Saint-Denis's production of <u>Noah</u> by André
Obey, where he played the roles of The Bear and The Man, and again with Gielgud
in Chekhov's <u>The Seagull</u> in 1936, in which he took the part of Shamrayev.

After a short interlude during which he worked with the Russian director Theodore
Komisarjevsky, who had a certain influence on him as far as his unconventional
treatment of Shakespeare plays was concerned, he was again associated with John
Gielgud and was with him in his 1937 season at the Queen's Theatre in Shaftesbury
Avenue.

On September 6th 1937 Gielgud opened the season with Shakespeare's <u>Richard II</u>.
George Devine could be seen in the part of the Gardener, while Gielgud took the
title role in a cast which included Michael Redgrave and Peggy Ashcroft. In <u>The
School for Scandal,</u> Devine played Moses as he had done four years before at the
<u>Old Vic</u>; and he was a remarkable Andreij in Michel Saint-Denis's production of
Chekhov's <u>Three Sisters</u>. Saint-Denis still remembered this performance and
thought that Devine acted very well (9).

The Gielgud season ended with the memorable and successful production of <u>The
Merchant Of Venice</u>. Devine played Launcelot Gobbo among an awe-inspiring star
cast (10).

This then was George Devine's career as an actor between 1932 and early 1938 in
collaboration with John Gielgud, in Shakespearean and other classic plays. But he
was not content with this. He did not only want to act. He wanted to give to the
theatre something more: he wanted to teach. To follow Devine's way in this field,
we have to go back again to the year 1931 when he was still at Oxford.

*

During Devine's Oxford days a vital encounter between him and a great personality
of the theatre had taken place. Michel Saint-Denis, the French director, had come
to London with his <u>Compagnie des Quinze</u> in 1931. They presented <u>Noah</u> by André
Obey and an adaptation of Shakespeare's <u>The Rape of Lucrece,</u> both in French. They
had started at the Arts Theatre, but in consequence of their revolutionary productions they were soon playing to full houses and moved to the Ambassadors and later
on to the New Theatre. It was during these performances that George Devine met
Saint-Denis for the first time, and that their friendship, which was to be so important for Devine, was formed.

What was it that Michel Saint-Denis offered the London theatre audiences at that time, and what was revolutionary about it?

The Compagnie des Quinze was a group of actors who had been working with Copeau. Most of them were between twenty-six and thirty-five years old, but there were also a few older members. The most striking qualities of this group were its technical skill and its aversion to realism. Each of the actors could sing and dance. They brought very unrealistic scenery to London, whereas theatre scenery in England at that time was almost entirely realistic. In their The Rape of Lucrece the changes of the sets took place in full view of the audience (11). In some of the scenes pantomime and improvisation were made use of to an extent which took the audience completely by surprise. The text of Noah by Obey is written for movement and rhythm, and the group did justice to it. Action was predominant. The conventions of the theatre were changed or disregarded. It was something completely new for the English spectators. Michel Saint-Denis recalled:

"The London audiences had never seen anything like this before. First we had a one week or two weeks contract, then a five weeks contract, and all the theatre people came to see us ... I remember the reaction of the audience in our performance of The Rape of Lucrece: after the second act, in which you see the rape, there used to be complete silence after the curtain had fallen. It was a long and deep silence, followed by tremendous applause ..." (12)

No wonder that George Devine was very much impressed by Saint-Denis's methods. The carefulness of the productions, the skill of the actors struck him. This experience showed him that there were still many methods of production, which perhaps could be usefully transferred to England. He realized that the friendship with Saint-Denis could give him something which in turn he would be able to give to the British theatre. John Gielgud summed up the impact Saint-Denis made on George Devine:

"When he met Saint-Denis I think his whole landscape changed ... he was enormously taken by his magnetism and his fascination and his charm, and soon after they began to work together ..." (13)

After Devine had played in an English translation of Noah himself, under the direction of Saint-Denis (14), they both decided to start an exciting enterprise: a school for actors.

*

It was founded in Islington in 1936, and it was called the London Theatre Studio. Saint-Denis was the director, George Devine the manager and Michel's right hand. In establishing and running this school they tried to do something which they felt was lacking in the British theatre, and which had been part of the success of the Compagnie des Quinze: they were after a new and more satisfying way of acting. Michel Saint-Denis described the work at the school and the ideas they were trying to realize there:

" ... we were terribly rebellious to the conditions of the modern theatre, and we were conscious that we were rebellious, but at the same
time we were in it. We never intended a school for the sake of a
school. We did the school because we wanted to work in a certain
direction, and we were after a kind of untheatrical truth, a truth to
the bone, for which in particular we tried to use the mask, because
the animation of the mask depends on the inner truth ..." (15)

The terms "truth to the bone" and "inner truth" with their implications recall the
theories which Konstantin Stanislavsky worked out in the first decade of the 20th
century, and which he taught at his Moscow Art Theatre (16).

The idea of the masks at the London Theatre Studio originated in George Devine.
He found out that they were an important help for the new pupils training to become
actors at the school, because with the aid of the masks they lost their embarrassment
and felt freer and more courageous in expressing what they wanted to express. The
fact that their faces were hidden made them feel more secure. Devine realized that
this was an effective way of giving the young actors confidence in their own abilities.
As Laurence Olivier said:

"And then he put the masks off and he would say: 'you see, it's only
the mask that makes it easy and it's only not the mask that makes it
difficult ...'" (17)

As this example shows Devine was a practical teacher. He was not given to lengthy
theoretical explanations. He always tried to show a useful way to the young people,
to make some concrete suggestion with the help of which they could work and improve themselves. In this Devine was similar to Saint-Denis. They both knew how
to guide their pupils towards satisfying results. Still today Laurence Olivier has a
high respect for Saint-Denis and the work he did with Devine at the London Theatre
Studio.

George Devine was also technically proficient. He was an expert in stage lighting
and actually worked the switchboard at all the shows which were put on at the school
(18). He was very much interested in all the technical problems of the stage (19).

The school lasted for four years and was closed when the Second World War broke
out (20). Now, for an interlude of six years, the war took the stage.

*

In 1938 George Devine, who during his period with Saint-Denis at the London Theatre Studio had continued to work as General Manager for the designer team Motley,
married one of its members, Sophie Harris. Motley were now doing well and they
all lived in a large studio in St. Martin's Lane. In the same year Devine directed
a professional company for the first time (21), and early in 1940 he produced Re-
becca by Daphne du Maurier at the Queen's Theatre and Shakespeare's The Tempest

at the Old Vic (22), the latter play jointly with Marius Goring. With another production of his, Shaw's The Millionairess, he went on tour.

Then the war came. Devine was convinced he would not be passed fit as his eyesight was bad and as he was supposed to have a weak heart, but to his surprise he was passed A1. He was so proud of this that he went off to his training on Salisbury Plain quite happily. In 1942, shortly before his daughter Harriet was born, he was sent to India and Burma, where he spent the rest of the war and was twice mentioned in dispatches while serving with the Royal Regiment of Artillery (23). The war was a crushing experience for him. When he went to India Devine had pitch black hair. When he came back, it was snow white (24).

*

When George Devine returned from the Eastern battlefields in 1946, his interest in the theatre was as intense as it had been before the war. Again he met with Michel Saint-Denis, and they decided to embark on a new bold venture: after their experiences at the London Theatre Studio from 1936 to 1939 they wanted to build up another school where young people could be trained for the theatre as actors, directors, and designers. Devine and Saint-Denis asked Glen Byam Shaw, the actor and director, who had just staged Antony and Cleopatra earlier in 1946, to join them in the formation of the Old Vic Theatre Centre. Shaw agreed, and the enterprise was started. Michel Saint-Denis was the director of the Centre, Glen Byam Shaw the head of the School, and George Devine became the director of the so-called Young Vic, a company which presented plays for schoolchildren. His work with the Young Vic Company gave him the opportunity and the satisfaction of teaching young actors again. His daughter wrote:

> "My father always loved teaching and working with young people, and one of the happiest times was when he was running the Old Vic School and the Young Vic Company ..." (25)

With this company Devine produced Thomas Dekker's The Shoemaker's Holiday (1947), Shakespeare's A Midsummer Night's Dream (1948), Goldoni's The Servant of Two Masters (1949), and Beaumont and Fletcher's The Knight of the Burning Pestle (1950). During his work with Saint-Denis at the Old Vic School Devine developed some important ideas, which represented in nuce the conspicuous principles he was to follow later on. Michel Saint-Denis noticed them:

> "Devine had a clear view of what he wanted to do in a production. He was attentive to all the details, and very faithful to the text. He was very conscientious, and there was nothing glamorous about his work. He took immense trouble to understand a play and to find out what the author meant." (26)

It is exactly this great respect for an author's text, this extreme carefulness in producing a play (27), which were to characterize his later work at the Royal Court

Theatre (28).

At the same time George Devine taught at the <u>Old Vic School</u>, which was developing into a promising training ground for young actors and actresses. The school was run in close contact with the <u>Old Vic</u>; its founders wanted to be attached to a "live" theatre. Saint-Denis, Shaw and Devine wanted to prepare actors, designers, and directors for their future careers. They were willing to give a complete training to those who were eager to work in the theatre. The school was to provide hard professional teaching for young talents.

A lot of pantomime work and improvisation was done. Devine was highly interested in everything connected with this, especially with comic improvisation. He generally led these particular classes himself or together with Saint-Denis - they were, as the latter said himself, "the sensitive part of our teaching" (29). There was an "animal improvisation class", where all the actors had to act an animal. There were speech and diction classes. There were movement classes, where the actors had to express everything with their bodies, without any use of words. In the style classes they were taught the essential habits of different periods; they were taught how to wear costumes, how to interpret the manners of the respective period. There were dancing classes. In special speech classes the actors were taught to speak under difficult circumstances and appalling physical conditions: they were asked to make themselves heard against noise and wind, after running and dancing, while being out of breath. There were studies of the texts, lectures on the history of the theatre. The actors had to go through a real theatrical education. It was a thorough training within which there was no room for compromises and carelessness. The actors were expected to take their task seriously and to devote themselves wholly to their work (30).

George Devine was obviously the "clown" of the triumvirate of directors. Conducting his comic improvisation class in masks he tried to release the actors' imagination and to use their initial embarrassment for a comic effect. The training with masks he had already applied with success at the <u>London Theatre Studio</u> before the war. Joan Plowright, one of his first pupils, remembered her teacher:

> "I found my feet at the school with George. With him I felt the freest.
> He was plump and friendly, zestful, and did things with relish. He
> loved the old Music Hall of England, had an earthy sense of humour
> and adored old famous comedians ... In this school you were trans-
> formed from a gifted, confident amateur to a gifted, confident and
> apparently unself-conscious professional ..." (31)

Devine believed that a perfect technique is essential for every actor, but that finally it must not show but remain hidden. He was an especially good teacher of comedy acting and had an extraordinary understanding for his pupils. At the school he used to relieve the tension during the exhausting training by shouting at the actors across the stage, not nastily, but in a friendly way that had not a destructive but an encouraging effect.

The Old Vic School was responsible for the training of many outstanding artists: among the actors James Maxwell, Alan Dobie, Avril Elgar, Joan Plowright, Prunella Scales, Dilys Hamlett, Powys Thomas (32); among the directors Frank Dunlop and Caspar Wrede. The school helped them to start remarkable careers and gave them a theatrical polish which was above average. All the actors who have attended these memorable courses are still today grateful for the things they were taught, and for the thorough coaching they experienced there.

But the Old Vic School, despite its great reputation, did not last long. It was closed in 1951, after an existence of only about five years. It appears difficult today to say what it really was that led to the closing of the school. There are many evasive and contradictory explanations. Some say that it was shut because of financial reasons only (33). Harriet Mennie-Devine remembered:

"I was too young at the time to fully understand what was happening, but I remember the tense and unhappy atmosphere, the conferences, the pressmen continually at the door, the phone always ringing." (34)

In the opinion of Leigh Crutchley (35) the school was closed "because it was found to be an appendage, of which the directors of that time were embarrassed" (36). All this, however, does not sound very convincing, although Leigh Crutchley is somewhere near the truth. Most probably the Old Vic School came to an end because the board of the Old Vic Theatre did not like the policy of its directors. They approached in turn Glen Byam Shaw, George Devine and Michel Saint-Denis and offered each of them the sole directorship over the other two, on condition that the instructions of the board would be obeyed. With this unfair proposition the triumvirate flatly refused to agree, and with a heavy heart they decided to break up their enterprise (37). It was a great shock for the team, who had devoted their time and their abilities to the school, and the one who suffered most from this shock was George Devine. It was hard, almost impossible for him to accept the fact something he had put his entire enthusiasm into was on the point of vanishing. The event affected him physically: he visibly lost weight. As Peggy Ashcroft said:

"It was as though something that he had absolutely directed his whole attention and idealism towards had been broken up, and for the time being he was at a loss, I think, and found it difficult to know where to start again building in the theatre, because he really wanted to give something to the theatre, to create something other than just acting or even production ..." (38)

Michel Saint-Denis went back to France where, in 1953, he started to work in the Centre Dramatique de l'Est at Strasbourg. Glen Byam Shaw joined Anthony Quayle as co-director of the Royal Shakespeare Theatre. George Devine was at a loose end; another stage in his career had finished.

*

There followed a time span of about four years during which George Devine was drifting along without any real sense of purpose. He felt lost and cut off from the theatre. It is true that he acted and produced quite a lot between 1952 and 1955; in Stratford-on-Avon, in London, for the television; but it was not really what he was looking for.

In 1952 he directed Ben Jonson's Volpone at Stratford, and also tried his hand at opera in producing Eugene Onegin at Sadler's Wells the same year. He staged Shakespeare's The Taming of the Shrew twice at short intervals in 1953 and 1954 at the Shakespeare Memorial Theatre, first with Marius Goring and Yvonne Mitchell, then with Keith Michell and Barbara Jefford in the leading parts (39). In 1953 he also directed King Lear in Stratford, King John at the Old Vic, and the opera version of Romeo and Juliet by Sutermeister at Sadler's Wells. The 1953 Lear production saw Michael Redgrave in the title part; Harry Andrews played Kent and Yvonne Mitchell Cordelia. The cast for King John included Richard Burton as the Bastard, Michael Hordern as the King, and Fay Compton as Constance (40).

In 1954 he staged A Midsummer Night's Dream at Stratford and then directed the world premiere of William Walton's Troilus and Cressida at Covent Garden, which scored a notable success (41).

In 1955 George Devine again produced Shakespeare's King Lear, this time at the Palace Theatre, with a Stratford company. He himself played Gloucester. It was, according to its star, John Gielgud, "little short of disastrous" (42). The production had a rather exotic character owing to the designs by the Japanese sculptor Isamu Noguchi. The audience reacted with "horrified expressions of dismay" (43). This, however, did not prevent Devine from taking the production on a European tour. Later in 1955 he staged The Magic Flute at Sadler's Wells.

George Devine also worked as an actor during that period. His parts included George Tesman opposite Peggy Ashcroft in Ibsen's Hedda Gabler (1954) (44), and Dogberry in Much Ado About Nothing in 1955 (45).

*

This, in broad outline, was George Devine's experience after the suppression of the Old Vic School. His activities in these years show a certain aimlessness. He appears to have been hunting after something he was not able to find. Stratford, Sadler's Wells, Covent Garden, the Old Vic, the Duke of York's Theatre were just stations on his way, and one gets the impression that he was trying hard to realize something which had been at the back of his mind for a long time; that he was looking for a place where his ideas for the theatre could materialize. Already during his period with Saint-Denis he had been obsessed with the thought of changing the face of the British theatre. He wanted to confront the audiences with new plays by new playwrights. Michel Saint-Denis knew about these plans:

"George Devine found that the English theatre was late in developing

and that there was something in the postwar generation that was not
expressed but should be expressed ... The plays had to have value
from the literary point of view and from the theatrical one. The
tendency was not important ..." (46)

Here again we have principles to which Devine was to adhere in his later work at
the Royal Court.

George Devine was now forty-five years old, and he had given a lot to the British
theatre and had learnt a lot about it. His student years at Oxford had brought him
into vital contact with professional theatre people, notably with John Gielgud, in
whose company he had made his way as an actor. His close teamwork with Michel
Saint-Denis both before and after the war, in the London Theatre Studio and at the
Old Vic School, had developed his talent of working with and teaching young pupils
and furnished him with deeper insight into the methods of acting and producing.
Saint-Denis was also an important influence on Devine as far as ideas about décor
and presentation were concerned - the performances of the Compagnie des Quinze
had been a breakthrough. In his work with Saint-Denis and Glen Byam Shaw Devine
was able to indulge in his passion for experiment. But he was not only an original
theorist. He was a thoroughly practical man besides, as his proficienoy in stage
lighting and his work as a manager for Motley proved.

So Devine had had a comprehensive theatrical training and an astonishingly varied
career. He had been a solid, average actor, a sound producer, a good teacher and
manager, and a skilful lighting specialist. He loved each one of these occupations,
he devoted himself to them, but none of them satisfied him completely. What he was
looking for was a place where he would be able to turn all his abilities and his rich
experience to the use of the British theatre. It hat to be something similar to the
London Theatre Studio, a place that belonged to him, and where writers, actors,
directors and designers would find ideal conditions for working, learning, and ex-
perimenting. His daughter felt this urge in her father:

"Though his free-lance period was the time when I remember my
father most clearly being at home, his most warm and amusing and
fatherly, the desire for his own theatre, his own company, was
always in his mind." (47)

Joan Plowright corroborated:

"There was a rumour of a new theatre George tried to found. He
longed for new writers and new material, for work relevant to
contemporary life." (48)

George Devine had not found the right track yet.

But the seed out of which his plans and ideas were to be fully developed and realized
had already been planted two or three years before. In 1952/53 George Devine had

met Tony Richardson, a young director, who was then doing a television adaptation of a Chekhov short story (49). Richardson asked him to act in it. He confirmed the impression we have gained about Devine's situation at that point:

> "It was a transitional time for George. He was searching for something, he wanted to do something for new plays." (50)

Together they had the idea of a season of Brecht and other authors neglected in Britain. Above all, however, they were eager to discover new playwrights and new plays. They decided to hire a theatre for some time and to see how it would develop. They approached the Royal Court. But their plans collapsed for financial reasons. Today we can say it was a good thing they collapsed, because Devine and Richardson were three years too early with their intentions. There was no Mr. Osborne ready with Look Back in Anger at that time (51). But various contacts were established, and some important people knew about the fresh ideas that were being hatched in two adventurous brains, while in the West End the star festivals continued to occupy the stages.

Richardson and Devine remained in constant touch with each other over the next three years. In 1955/56, finally, the great moment came. The time was ripe. For George Devine the most exciting period of his life was to begin with the formation of the English Stage Company.

***

IV THE FOUNDATION OF THE ENGLISH STAGE COMPANY

Before we set about our task of dealing with the foundation of the English Stage
Company in this chapter, it is perhaps useful to take a brief survey of the plays
that were shown in the London theatres around 1950.

If we study the production lists of some of the London theatres in the late forties
and early fifties we are inclined to agree with what Penelope Gilliatt wrote in an
article about the situation of English drama and theatre at that time:

> " ... the country with the greatest body of dramatic literature in
> the world possessed a theater that had turned into a stuffed flunkey.
> At that time there wasn't a contemporary English play worth discussing.
> The available choices came in two broad categories, generally described
> by salespeople in theater-ticket agencies as 'entertaining' and 'some-
> thing to think about' ... " (1)

There were a lot of revues and musicals (2), many of them longrunning successes;
there were thrillers (3); and there were drawing-room comedies (4), preferably
by Terence Rattigan, J.B. Priestley, and Noel Coward. Now and then there was
a play by Christopher Fry, T.S. Eliot (5), or George Bernard Shaw. And, of course,
there were Shakespeare revivals, presented mostly with a cast including as many
star actors as possible.

But on the whole there were hardly any plays related to contemporary events and
problems. There were no young playwrights who expressed opinions and feelings
about a rapidly changing Britain in their works. To say it more accurately: the
playwrights probably existed, but nobody was interested in their plays. The West
End and the theatre managers in general preferred to stage safe middle-class plays
by safe authors, which entertained large audiences and brought in a lot of money
(6); plays which spread the soothing certainty among the spectators that their country was still the proud Britannia, as unshakeable as ever. The elegant and witty
conversation inside stylish drawing-rooms rose above the cracking in the beams of
a crumbling empire.

*

There were people, however, who felt dissatisfied with this British theatre, going
on as if cut off from the world; people who had the strong wish to connect it with
contemporary life again, and who were of the opinion that it should be more than
mere entertainment. As we have pointed out at the end of the preceding chapter (7),
George Devine and Tony Richardson were among those people. Although their first
attempt to hire the Royal Court Theatre had proved abortive because of financial
difficulties and the undecided attitude of the owner, their initial idea of trying to
present new plays stayed with them. They waited for their chance.

At about the same time the poet Ronald Duncan (8) had started a festival in Devon, and during the work he did there, in collaboration with Lord Harewood, they both developed plans of doing something for the English drama, comparable to what the English Opera Group had achieved for the opera. Duncan had begun to assemble a company with the intention of producing his own plays. His mind was set on a revival of the poetic drama. He wanted to rent a theatre and promote his own work. But somehow the whole enterprise lacked vitality and a resolute approach.

*

At this critical moment, when two independent groups were groping for a similar aim, the business man Neville Blond appeared on the scene. He had a pronounced inclination for the theatre and wanted to use some of his money to promote activities which would give new impulses to the British drama. He was approached by the Duncan group. However, he was not quite convinced by their plans. He imagined something more definite on a larger scale, professionally organized and on a permanent basis. Suddenly there were greater possibilities, but no equipment for their realization.

Oscar Lewenstein, who at that time was managing the Royal Court, knew about George Devine and the plans he had worked out together with Richardson. A continuation of their project was proposed. Many discussions followed, and Devine agreed to take the post of an artistic director of the new company, on condition that a permanent theatre could be found (9). The two groups came together at last and were ready to start their adventure. Out of their alliance with Neville Blond arose the possibility of creating the English Stage Company.

*

It was difficult, indeed, to find a theatre for the newly formed company. At first the intention was to hire the derelict Kingsway Theatre and to redecorate it. This idea was eventually abolished, and finally, in November 1955, the founders succeeded in taking a lease of thirty-four years on the Royal Court Theatre (10). Tony Richardson recalls the atmosphere in which those events took place:

> "It was a period of tremendous excitement and exhilaration because we felt we were doing something new. We were up against all the forces of the establishment, and we were looking all the time to do new things in design, to find new sorts of actors and above all to find new plays. And George was absolutely at the centre of all this, with an incredible grasp of the complexities of this sort of theatrical organization ..." (11)

*

The plans for the first season were largely those which had been formulated by George Devine before. Young writers, who had something to say about contemporary life, were to be encouraged to put their energies into the theatre; new plays were to be produced; and, as the company was to be run as a non profit-making organization (12), they were to be presented without regard to the financial success. The dramatist was to be put first, although it was made clear that young actors, directors and designers of promise should be promoted as well. As George Devine expressed it:

> "Ours is not to be a producer's theatre or an actor's theatre; it is a writer's theatre." (13)

Devine wrote on these ambitious plans:

> "We want to encourage good writers who have not yet written for the theatre ... It is a mistake to take for granted that there are no new plays being written, and to put one's efforts into the classics. We want to find a contemporary style in dramatic work, acting, décor and production. We hope to present exciting, provocative and stimulating plays ... And we want to attract young people ... " (14)

The plays were to be presented in a repertory system (15). Two plays at least were to be performed each week. At the Royal Court the young playwright was to find a company which was ready and eager to accept unconventional work. Dramatists were to be given the opportunity of attending rehearsals of their own plays - a great novelty - in order to strengthen their experience in stage technique, and to show them how a manuscript was transformed into a performance:

> "I want ... dramatists to look upon the Court as a workshop, and have invited them to come to any rehearsals, not only of their own plays but of other people's." (16)

Team-work between author, director and actors was to be stressed. And something very important for the future appeared in the statement made by George Devine in an interview for the New Statesman and Nation:

> " ... and when I asked him (17) if he had any particular theory of acting which he was seeking to develop in his company, his answer was in terms of catching the author's style and giving that its full weight." (18)

This remark shows Devine's intent to remain true to his respect for an author's text, a conception he had developed during his work with Michel Saint-Denis at the London Theatre Studio and the Old Vic School (19). No "English Stage Company style" was propagated to be applied indiscriminately to every play, but every play submitted and accepted was to get the production that served it best and that was most appropriate to the author's intentions. Special attention was to be paid to a writer's individual style. The plays were to be produced as simply and honestly as possible. No attempts were to be made at clever production tricks to make a play more attractive. Everything was to serve the play, the actors were to be directed accordingly, and the director was not to be allowed to falsify it.

These then, in short, were the main ideas that were put forward and that defined the basis of the Royal Court's policy. A provisional company of about fifteen actors was engaged, which was to be completed by guest-players according to the demands of the individual plays (20).

The next step was up to the dramatists. They, who had always bitterly complained about the lacking interest of managements in new and contemporary work, were now offered tempting conditions which gave them the opportunity of proving that they were serious. Neville Blond challenged them:

"This will be a playground for them to show what they can do." (21)

The reaction of the press to this daring enterprise was immediate and positive. Most of the newspapers welcomed the spirit which had come to the Royal Court Theatre, and they were quite enthusiastic that some fresh ideas were to be introduced into the London theatre:

" ... Mr. Devine hopes to present there 'a repertory of modern plays' - not classics, which is a welcome change!" (22)

A journalist in The Sunday Times reacted similarly:

"Modern English plays which concern themselves with current problems, political or social, are rare. It is for this reason that the debut tomorrow week of the English Stage Company has become one of the most eagerly awaited events of the present season ..." (23)

In a lengthy article in the New Statesman and Nation, entitled "A Writer's Theatre", T.C. Worsley came to the same conclusion:

"What promises to be one of the most exciting and important events in the English theatre for a great many years, takes place in Easter Week. This is the opening on Easter Monday of the newly founded English Stage Company's season ... Not since the famous Court Theatre season of the nineteen hundreds has anything so adventurous and so full of promise been planned and executed ... This is something quite new in the English theatre ..." (24)

The Times greeted the enterprise with an unusually vivacious article, and encouraged (as did other newspapers) the audience to back it:

"The prospects of English dramatic authorship could scarcely be darker; yet this very Easter gilds them with a ray of hope as

bright as it is solitary ... despairing young playwrights must
have rubbed their eyes in astonishment when they read what are
to be the aims of the new enterprise ... Here, on paper as yet
but with substantial financial backing, it is understood, is a
theatre formed to the desire and needs of the young writer. We
must all hope that the dreams and the reality will be brought
into accord; and the audience has a part to play which may be
well worth playing. " (25)

The author of an article in the periodical <u>Plays and Players</u> dealt with the state of
English drama and saw a real chance for an improvement:

"Despairingly theatre-lovers in this country have been aksing
for years where our new dramatists are to be found. Season after
season almost every serious play London has seen has come from
Paris or, less frequently, New York, while our own writers have
been represented by mechanically constructed thrillers or pot-
boiling comedies ... The blame for this sad state of affairs has
been variously distributed ... But whatever the cause, there has
certainly been little encouragement of new talent.
At last, however, with the formation of the English Stage Company,
there are glimmerings of hope. This company ... has as its chief
aim the fostering of new dramatists. Five of its first six productions are the work of British writers ..." (26)

George Devine stood on the threshold of an exciting undertaking, of which nobody
knew exactly what it was going to be. He and his company were looked upon with
considerable expectations; the eyes of nearly everybody genuinely interested in the
British theatre were directed towards Sloane Square. The first productions were
rehearsed; an advertisement was published in <u>The Stage,</u> encouraging young writers
to send in their plays. Devine and his colleagues waited for promising scripts to
arrive.

*

The first production, <u>The Mulberry Bush</u> by Angus Wilson (27), was presented by
the English Stage Company on April 2nd 1956. It was directed by George Devine
himself, and the Royal Court was completely booked up for the opening night. The
play, in fact, had already been performed in England, by the Bristol Old Vic Company. It was not a very extraordinary start, but nevertheless a sound production of
a good play. Already in this first performance the thoroughness of Devine as a producer and his dedication to a play could be noticed clearly. The experiences he had
collected during his period with Saint-Denis bore fruits. Lindsay Anderson (28), a
director who later on worked at the Royal Court in close association with Devine,
remembered that evening and explained what it was that had struck him particularly
about it:

" ... the whole feeling of the play and the production which was
direct and honest and done with a very great intelligence and
respect for text, and had altogether a kind of feeling and relationship to people as I knew them that I didn't generally experience in the theatre. And there was also what I think was very
important: a kind of wholeness about the presentation. Not merely was it an intelligent play well acted, but it was the whole design, the whole look at the stage, the whole feeling of the evening
had a kind of integrity about it which to me is very much a part
of George as an artist in the theatre ... " (29)

*

The Mulberry Bush was an impressive beginning, although not financially, but it
was not really what Devine and his company had in mind and outlined in their plans
for a future policy. The reaction of the press wavered between goodwill, shoul-
der-patting and slight disappointment. Derek Granger in The Financial Times was
very careful and obviously resolved to give the Royal Court team as much courage
as possible:

"Mr. George Devine's production makes this altogether an admirable start to a most admirable venture. " (30)

Kenneth Tynan in The Observer moved on similar ground:

"The English Stage Company embark with this production on a repertory season of new plays. I wish their enterprise too well to em-
barrass it with further criticism. " (31)

The reviewer of The Spectator mixed goodwill with critical advice:

"And so, while I wish the English Stage Company every possible
success, I hope that it will never fall into the error of supposing
that the theatre can be revived merely by pumping dramatized
novels into it. " (32)

Harold Conway in The Daily Sketch judged the production somewhat more severely,
entitling his article "Mulberry Bush Gets So Boring":

"I hope Lord Harewood and his colleagues will choose more
discerningly. We want original plays. It isn't quite enough to
watch Chekhov being chased around a mulberry bush. " (33)

Among the critics who were predominantly sceptical and negative, Philip Hope-
Wallace in The Guardian (34) spoke about "a rather diffident start", and R.B.
Marriott, paying his tribute to "a courageous enterprise", expressed his view in
The Stage as follows:

"All the more pity, therefore, that the first play ... in spite of
its basic distinction, is so disappointing." (35)

Nearly the same could be read in The Sunday Express:

"So it is a pity that the first play ... is a straight flat disappointment." (36)

Alan Dent, in the News Chronicle, summed up the controversy and in giving the
following comment said something that turned out to be a real prophesy:

"You will be very foolish - foolisher than ever - if you miss seeing
The Mulberry Bush ... because it has had what is called a 'mixed
reception' from the critics ... Angus Wilson's play is, in short,
the precursor of good and exciting things to come." (37)

The exciting thing came. After a generally acclaimed production of Arthur Miller's
The Crucible, directed by George Devine and presented on April 9th 1956, the bomb-
shell exploded. A playscript arrived at the Royal Court, and Devine and Tony
Richardson knew at once that this was the thing they had been looking for, that here
they had something on their hands which they had always wanted to stage. The play
was written by a certain John Osborne; its title was Look Back in Anger.

*

V GEORGE DEVINE AS A PRODUCER AT THE ROYAL COURT 1956-1963

The main task that lay ahead of George Devine, after he had been elected Artistic Director of the English Stage Company, was the organization of the Royal Court. Devine was intended to be the guiding spirit who was to hold all the strings with a firm hand. But as a universally trained man of the theatre he was not prepared to restrict himself to the function of an organizer. He was eager to continue his work as an actor and as a producer as well.

George Devine's productions for the Court were staged between the years 1956 and 1963. Altogether he directed seventeen plays; fourteen on his own, three in collaboration with a co-producer (1). We shall try in this chapter to observe what leading principles Devine followed as a producer, and whether there are any connections with his former work during his years with Michel Saint-Denis. It may be useful to quote some of the principles he had in mind when setting out to produce a play. In an interview with Peter Thipthorp in The West London Press (2) Devine said:

> "Rule Number One ... Don't produce a play unless you really
> believe in it. Otherwise you don't produce the play - you produce
> your own ideas ... Rule Number Two ... Don't try to impose
> ideas on to actors. Give them the framework and your conception
> of the play and help them to use their own contribution within that
> framework ... Rule Number Three. Don't try to show off how
> clever you are, because that is not what you are for ... A pro-
> ducer should never give them (3) the impression that they are
> putting over his conception ..."

The principles formulated by Devine in an interview with Harold Downs are extensions of these "rules":

> "To see the performance of a play through the mind's eye of the
> playwright is to strengthen enormously its appeal ... I am very
> much more interested in content than in form. I do not think any
> play is really worth producing if it is not a play of ideas ... Pro-
> duction and performance in combination should interpret the play.
> Literally, the play's the thing, and everything should be subordi-
> nated to the play. Producer and players reveal and emphasize
> artistically the play's true meaning. One method of production is
> to rely upon simplicity in presentation. Scenery and costumes
> are essentials, but secondary, and should be made to serve the
> play as it is presented by the actors and actresses. Get the
> interpretation of the play clear cut and soundly based, and the
> rest not only follows, but also helps ..." (4)

We shall now take a brief look at some of Devine's productions at the Court and endeavour to show how these ideas were applied in them.

Because of a certain lack of precision in most of the statements of Devine's colleagues whom we interviewed about his productions (admiration for his achievements, especially after his death in 1966, tended to blur the critical judgment), we were forced to rely almost entirely upon the reviews published in the press. In order to arrive at a fair evaluation and at the greatest possible objectivity we have tried to take into account as many reviews as we could get hold of. The opinion formed about any production examined is based on the comparison of at least twelve articles dealing with it (5).

Respect for the text and the intentions of the author and careful procedure in producing a play (6) could be noticed in almost all of Devine's productions at the Court. Here are some extracts from reviews putting forward this characteristic quality:

> " ... his direction of the play ... is ... directly in sympathy with what Miller conveys with words". (The Crucible) (7) " ... directed ... with a ... maximum of attention to the words". (Major Barbara) (8) " ... direction cleverly brings to view the subtlest shades of meaning". (Major Barbara) (9) "He began with the text and wove his actors into it". (Rosmersholm) (10)

Indeed, the critics who accused Devine of being negligent of the text are very few in number. In the 234 reviews considered we could only find two (11).

Very rarely did Devine - a logical consequence - cut the text. The only play to be cut substantially was Jean-Paul Sartre's Nekrassov:

> " ... Devine has cut the original text pretty freely and has certainly improved it for English stage purposes, though one effect of the cutting is to alter the balance of the jokes, distributed with seemingly careless impartiality between Left and Right ... " (12) "Since its production at the Edinburgh Festival this ... play ... has been shortened by a good half hour". (13)

But this was an exception. Basically, Devine had an aversion to alterations of an author's text. He only cut upon mature consideration and often after long discussions with the author himself. Sometimes the effect of this reluctance was that the plays lasted too long and suffered from dragging passages and lack of drive. This slowness was frequently commented upon. The following quotations may serve as a proof:

> " ... production is on the slow side ... " (Nekrassov) (14). "It plainly needs cutting by at least a third ... it is the job of producers to be ruthless. Another third wants shredding". (Live Like Pigs) (15). " ... would be twice as effective if the producers ... had taken out at least half an hour's dialogue". (Live Like Pigs) (16). "Perhaps if George Devine had directed the thing so that it moved at slightly more than a funeral pace ... something

might have come across ..." (<u>Cock-A-Doodle Dandy</u>) (17).
" ... production moves slowly, too slowly I think ..."
(<u>Rosmersholm</u>) (18).

It would be wrong to say, however, that this slowness pervaded all of Devine's productions. Reading the reviews, one comes across the characterizations "pith and pungency" (19), "genuine swing" (20), "verve" (21), "speed of direction" (22), "lively" (23) (<u>Nekrassov</u>); "racy production" (24), "verbal speed and punch" (25) (<u>Major Barbara</u>); "spasms of vigour" (26) (<u>End-Game</u>); "pace and impact" (27), "bustling production" (28), "immense zest" (29) (<u>Cock-A-Doodle-Dandy</u>); "smooth and swift" (30) (<u>Platonov</u>); "pacing near perfect" (31), "pace right" (32) (<u>Happy Days</u>).

This occasional slowness of George Devine's directing had also positive aspects: straightforwardness, honesty, and an exceptional aversion to cheap tricks, gimmicks and empty gags (33). This simplicity in presenting a play - which had nothing to do with simplification - can be observed in almost all of Devine's productions. The working out of a clear line, the perceptive interpretation of an author's text with regard to the details (34) were the first steps Devine took before realizing a production. Already during his association with Michel Saint-Denis, Devine had taken immense trouble to understand a play (35). In the press these characteristics found the following echo:

> "Produced ... with almost Calvinist austerity and intensity ..."
> (<u>The Crucible</u>) (36). " ... direction ... is economical, taut as a
> bowstring ..." (<u>The Crucible</u>) (37). " ... directed ... with a
> minimum of fuss ..." (<u>Major Barbara</u>) (38). "There were no
> tricks in Mr. Devine's production of this fascinating, elusive,
> nervous play". (<u>Rosmersholm</u>) (39).

In the reviews examined we found a single critic reproaching Devine with using "tricks" without any relation to the character of the play (40).

Devine's love of simplicity could also be felt in the sets for his productions. He worked closely together with his designers. Scenery was not just to be background decoration or something to look at. It had, like everything else, to serve the play and if possible to enhance its meaning and effect. Perhaps the most ingenious designer at the Court, who became famous through her work there, was Jocelyn Herbert (41). With her ability of designing with the simplest means a set of the greatest evocative power she agreed with Devine's principles of production (42). A few excerpts from some reviews describe this functional use of scenery under Devine:

> " ... a bed of nails would have been a luxury in this comfortless
> décor ..." (<u>The Crucible</u>) (43). "Motley's setting is simple to the
> point of severity ..." (<u>The Crucible</u>) (44). "The settings by Motley
> contribute considerably to the general effect, as well as to many a

significant detail. For once at least in the London theatre this
season we have settings which are an integral part of the drama,
and not merely background or chic decoration". (Rosmersholm)
(45). "Jocelyn Herbert's set excellently captured the futility inherent in the play ..." (Happy Days) (46) "Jocelyn Herbert's
dilapidated throne-room, a mud-daubed chamber with self-sealing
doors, beautifully intensifies the metaphor of the palace and kingdom as a projection of Berenger's mind". (Exit the King) (47).

George Devine was experienced in casting a play, a faculty probably acquired during his years at the London Theatre Studio and the Old Vic School. He knew how to
bring together the right actor and the right part and was not afraid of taking risks
and giving demanding parts to promising actors without great experience. By as-
signing tasks to them that were possibly somewhat beyond their scope he tried to
bring out the best in them and to spur them to special achievements. His encouragement of young actors appeared clearly in his production of Wycherley's The
Country Wife, a play which was put on especially for Joan Plowright (48). As Devine
has formulated it:

"Here in the Royal Court we are casting actors out of their range
... We are giving them a chance to do things they have never done
before. It is a wonderful opportunity". (49)

Although he could rely on a great many actors of reputation, such as Gwen Ffrangcon-
Davies (The Mulberry Bush), Michael Gwynn, Rosalie Crutchley (The Crucible),
Peggy Ashcroft (The Good Woman of Setzuan, Rosmersholm), Robert Helpman
(Nekrassov), Alan Webb (Major Barbara), Jack MacGowran (Endgame), Eric Porter
(Rosmersholm), Rex Harrison (Platonov), Brenda Bruce (Happy Days), Alec
Guinness, Googie Withers (Exit the King), he never made a play a star performance.
He favoured team-work, gave weight to the minor parts, and did not permit the ap-
propriate interpretation of a play to be distorted by a star actor or actress. Every-
thing had to be kept in proportion. The forces in the cast had to be balanced against
each other, and all had to serve the play (50). Here are a few press comments on
these points:

" ... where players and dramatist were in true league, the night
sped along ..." (Major Barbara) (51). "What also helped to make
this revival particularly memorable was the consistently high
level of acting from every member of the cast. There are three
good excuses - Barbara herself, Andrew Undershaft, and Lady
Britomart Undershaft - for turning this play into a star-vehicle
and making nonsense of it. Joan Plowright, Alan Webb and
Frances Rowe did not, most commendably, take these excuses
and the smaller parts were all executed with such care and
respect for the play as a whole ... splendid teamwork ..."
(Major Barbara) (52). " ... minor performances which in
George Devine's production are all well kept in the atmospheric

picture set by Motley". (<u>Rosmersholm</u>) (53). "George Devine's
production remains essentially a triumph of teamwork ... "
(<u>Rosmersholm</u>) (54)

Of course, Devine was not infallible in casting. He who takes risks is bound to
make mistakes. Various critics thought that certain parts were miscast in some
of his productions; that actors, in consequence of inadequate guiding by the producer, misinterpreted a play or falsified its characters; or that the acting was
incompetent. The following passages provide a few examples:

> "Two main parts, that of the editor and that of Nekrassov, quite
> misfire in performance ... Robert Helpman hasn't, quite simply,
> the comedian's touch; his voice is too heavy, he isn't nimble
> tongued enough, he doesn't have the trick of comic timing."
> (<u>Nekrassov</u>) (55). "Joan Plowright has a brave try at Major
> Barbara ... but for her two moments of crisis she simply lacks
> the range or the stage presence necessary ..." (<u>Major Barbara</u>)
> (56). " ... many of the other parts, large and small, are played
> with practically no sense of style, timing, conviction or under-
> standing". (<u>Cock-A-Doodle Dandy</u>) (57). "It is here, in the ab-
> sence of the wildness beneath the intelligence, the explosiveness
> beneath the competent nurse and housekeeper, that I felt Dame
> Peggy's performance falling short ... " (<u>Rosmersholm</u>) (58).
> "A voice without a trace of sonorousness and as flat, hard and
> inflexible as a steel girder ..." (<u>Happy Days</u>) (59).

It is possible that some controversial interpretations must be attributed to Devine's
principle of not imposing ideas on to actors, but of letting them act with a great
deal of freedom within a given framework. And we must always bear in mind that
the critics on whom we rely, were not infallible either. They often contradict each
other, and their views leave plenty of room for discussion. It is probably true,
however, that Devine's respect for the actor could be a drawback when his opinion
as a producer clashed with the one of an actor with a strong personality. Another
criticism expressed by the reviewers and Devine's colleagues concerns his interpretation of certain plays and the kind of production devised for them. His production of Brecht's <u>The Good Woman of Setzuan</u> - by the way the first professional
staging of a Brecht play in England - resulted in a great mixture of styles, because
the actors did not know anything about the "alienation technique" demanded of them.
In England this sort of acting was virtually unknown at that time, so that it proved
impossible to create a consistent style in this production (60). Devine had met Brecht
in Germany while touring the Continent, and in his effort to do justice to the author
he proceeded extremely carefully, with the result that the production in the end made
a somewhat academic impression (61). In <u>Nekrassov</u> Devine was reproached with
weakening the play's satire by escaping into cheap slapstick comedy and farce, and
letting the actors indulge in guying (62). In the case of Sean O'Casey's <u>Cock-A-
Doodle Dandy</u> some of the critics accused him of an unimaginative, dull and pedestrian approach (63). In <u>Rosmersholm</u>, a generally acclaimed success, Devine's

handling of the ending did not satisfy two or three reviewers. His dislike of melodrama and sense of balance may have been the reason here (64). As regards Major
Barbara and Rosmersholm, two critics thought that Devine was too anxious to keep
the plays in their period (65). In Platonov he was blamed for gliding into burlesque,
of aiming at laughs only, and of destroying the tragedy in the play by farcical treatment (66). Although he was a good friend of Beckett's, and the author had been present at the rehearsals, Devine's interpretation of Happy Days (67) was judged a failure, while in Exit the King his lack of response to Ionesco's wit was criticized, as
well as the heaviness of the production in general (68).

On the other hand, Devine's sense of style, his imaginative approach, his percep-
tiveness and attention to the details were underlined in dozens of reviews. So was
his ability of making everything in a production work for the general effect (69). As
to his attitude to theatrical effects, he was thoroughly capable, despite his sound
aversion to sheer brilliance, of creating gripping scenes. Among those which stuck
in the critics' minds were the flick-knife fight between Col and Blackmouth (Alan
Dobie and Robert Shaw) in Live Like Pigs (70), the scene in the Salvation Army
shelter in Major Barbara (71), the exorcism scene in Cock-A-Doodle Dandy - a
production in which Devine made use of a rather complicated stage machinery:

> " ... lightning flashes and sudden darkness descends, chairs
> dissolve beneath drinkers, roofs rise off the tops of houses and
> right themselves again". (72)

Another memorable scene was the ending of Exit the King, in which Devine, together with Jocelyn Herbert, was successful in evoking exactly the atmosphere
demanded by Ionesco in his stage directions (73). T.C. Worsley experienced this
final moment on the stage as follows:

> "He (King Berenger) is alone, and slowly the walls of his palace
> dissolve into nothingness, into a grey light, the king himself
> dissolves and we are left with the throne and the greyness. It is
> a highly effective and theatrical moment, admirably managed by
> the scene designer ... and the director ..." (74)

*

George Devine was neither an extraordinary nor an ingenious producer. He was a
careful, conscientious, scrupulous one, who tried to give to each play the production which brought out its meaning most clearly and forcibly. He never pushed
his way into the foreground. He was a humble man, more humble than he need have
been (75). His respect for the text sometimes resulted in his being almost too much
in awe. When he started to rehearse a play, he tended to make a plan and stick to
it. But he was always open to suggestions (76). In discussions with the author, the
designer and the actors he modified and changed this plan, until everything was in
balance (77). His teamwork with Jocelyn Herbert became famous - her love for
simplicity coincided with Devine's ideas and found a striking expression in her sets

for the production of Beckett's Happy Days (78).

His training under Michel Saint-Denis became evident in his careful preparation of scenery and costumes. His work as a producer was, as his colleagues say (79), always sound, though not as imaginative as it could have been. But his rich pre-war experience enabled him to create interesting productions again and again. Joan Plowright stressed this experience:

> "George showed a great deal of comic invention as a producer
> (80). His intellectual appreciation of a text was equalled by his
> practical knowledge of every facet of the theatre, and of the
> problems of acting. Many of the young directors do not have
> this practical knowledge; sometimes they cannot put their ideas
> through to the actors. George could: he had gone through the
> whole mill". (81)

Devine allowed his writers to make mistakes. If he wanted something in a text to be cut and the author did not agree, he let him have his will so that he could see the mistake on the stage himself and learn from it. He believed that the artist must have the right to fail - it was essential for his development (82). He also gave young actors and actresses like Joan Plowright (83), Robert Stephens (84), Kenneth Haigh (85), Alan Bates (86), Mary Ure (87), Frances Cuka (88), Alan Dobie (89) and others real chances to develop their abilities.

If we look at the seventeen plays Devine produced for the Court we see that among the English classics he staged Wycherley, Shaw and Shakespeare (90), among continental classics Chekhov and Ibsen; among well established foreign authors Brecht, O'Casey, Miller, Sartre, Beckett, Ionesco; among English poets and novelists temporarily turned playwrights Angus Wilson, Ronald Duncan and Nigel Dennis. Finally, among new English dramatists, he staged John Arden and Ann Jellicoe, which may not seem much considering the fact that it was the proclaimed aim of the English Stage Company to concentrate on new British plays. But perhaps, as Tony Richardson said (91), Devine did not feel near enough in age any more and left the production of new plays to his younger men, such as Richardson himself, Lindsay Anderson, John Dexter and William Gaskill. The latter gave a further reason:

> "An artistic director tends to do plays which are 'safe'; he is
> forced into a position of doing less experimental work. This
> happened to George". (92)

Most of the productions Devine staged at the Court met with a mixed reception from the critics, with the exception of The Crucible, Major Barbara, Rosmersholm, and Exit the King, which received predominantly positive notices. If we look at the principles Devine had formulated at the beginning of his enterprise (93), we notice that he lived up to them to an impressive degree. Nearly every play staged, with the possible exceptions of Nekrassov and The Sport of My Mad Mother, can be called a play of ideas. Respect for the author's intentions (94), subordination to the play, clarity and simplicity in presentation, team-work between actors, designers and producer, carefulness and honesty: these were the pillars on which Devine's work rested.

*

So George Devine had become thoroughly involved in the Royal Court. Not only did he devote himself to his theatre by managing it and by producing plays for it. He also brought his whole experience as an actor into the English Stage Company and did not spare himself in taking parts.

Devine appeared thirteen times as an actor in productions at the Court. Five of them he directed at the same time. We shall try to work out some of the most important characteristics of the actor Devine in 1956 and after. Again we were forced to rely on newspaper reviews to a relatively high degree, as many of the statements made by the friends of his whom we interviewed were of a rather vague and uncritical nature. Fortunately, many of these statements are - in the essential points - in agreement with the opinion of the critics.

In the present chapter we shall study five parts played by Devine between 1956 and 1965. Some of the remaining eight productions in which he acted will be dealt with collectively in a summary fashion (1).

*

The first part George Devine took after the formation of the English Stage Company was the one of Deputy Governor Danforth in Arthur Miller's play The Crucible, which had its first night on April 9th 1956. The author describes this character as follows:

> "Danforth is a grave man in his sixties, of some humour and
> sophistication that does not, however, interfere with an exact
> loyalty to his position and his cause ..." (2)

He is a man who on the one hand is ready to listen to the evidence of the people caught up in the trial, but who despite this attitude shows a maddening obstinacy, and whose "loyalty" cannot hide a severe lack of insight (3). Moreover, in his disposition the intellect often appears as dominated by dangerous emotions, and there are moments when his attitude borders on insane fanaticism (4), and when he is just as much involved in the general superstitious atmosphere as most of the other characters (5). Severity and a feeling of duty are strangely mixed up with the irrational forces in him. Judging from what the critics wrote in their reviews Devine succeeded in presenting a man of these very qualities. It was the irrational element in Danforth which struck the reviewer of The Times in his representation of the character:

> "Here Mr. George Devine plays the judge not as a man of fine
> legal integrity but as a man with a good share of the credulity
> and intolerance that has swept Salem. The result is immensely
> to strengthen the final scenes of the story ... She (6) ... stages

an extraordinary pretence of witch seeing which could only
deceive a judge as blended with superstitious fear as the people
he has come to judge. Mr. Devine presents just such a man,
and his presence makes us feel ... that the whole shocking
affair could have come about in this and in no other way". (7)

This element in Devine's acting as well as in Danforth's character obviously es-
caped the attention of the critic in The Stage, who stressed another aspect of the
part which is, as we have seen, certainly there, though not to such a degree as the
reviewer saw it. It may be necessary to say that he was the only one (8) to interpret Devine's performance in a way which casts a predominantly positive light on
Danforth:

"George Devine ... plays with fine sincerity the part of the
Deputy-Governor ... always gives the impression of a faithful seeker-for-truth ... " (9)

A counter-statement to prove that Devine did not overstress the "fine sincerity" in
Danforth (which would have been falsifying the part) can be found in the review of
the Daily Sketch, where different qualities are placed in the foreground:

" ... the judge's role, well as George Devine acts it, is too
fanatical for belief ... " (10)

Paul Grahame in the Daily Worker came to a conclusion which seems to sum up
the elements of the part and to show that Devine achieved a fine balance between
them in his characterization:

"George Devine is the tight-lipped representative of rough
justice and gives an extremely subtle portrayal of a bigoted
judge who applies his own tests and is not fundamentally
dishonest within the limits of those tests. " (11)

On the whole it appears that Devine caught the essential characteristics inherent in
the part, that he gave them their appropriate weight and kept them in the right proportions. He brought to life a part which demands the careful synthesis of opposite
attitudes (12).

*

George Devine's admiration for the work of Samuel Beckett (13) found expression
in his production of Endgame (14), which he staged in October 28th 1958, and in
which he played the part of Hamm. The author was present at the rehearsals.

As to his outward appearance, Devine corresponded almost exactly to the directions given by Beckett (15): he wore a black dressing-gown, a black cap adorned
with leaves, a necktie, and dark glasses. A blanket was spread over his knees, a

whistle hung from his neck, and he was equipped with an iron-shod cane. He had thin, white, ungroomed whiskers and sat in a large armchair mounted with brass studs.

From opinions heard (16) and reviews read it seems that Devine missed the stylized, bitter, cruelly sharp acting of the play adopted by Roger Blin and Jean Martin in the original French version a year before at the same theatre. Instead he tried to transfer the performance into a somewhat more human atmosphere:

> "George Devine told me he preferred the less stylized dress and
> was emphasizing the localized, domestic setting. 'The thing is not
> to frighten people off by making them think this is something fan-
> tastic; it is not. It is a dramatic experience, a very poetic, and
> funny, illustration of one side of all of us'." (17)

The effect of the playing of Hamm by Devine (and of the other three actors as well) in consequence of this conception brought about a more limited interpretation of the play; it lost to a certain extent its possible claim of being an utterly pessimistic, generally valid representation of human life. The critic of The Times experienced it as follows:

> "The producer ... appears to have persuaded Mr. Beckett to
> let him bring the creatures of the play to within closer reach of
> sympathy ... treating master and servant less as automatons
> and more like human beings, and letting a little humour into
> their laconic exchanges ..." (18)

If Devine's conception may have somewhat softened the original acidity of the play it certainly did not try to render it harmless by making Hamm an amiable character. His own perception of the play's meaning and the presence of Beckett made him act the hard, cruel and desperate, yet tragic Hamm as the author intended him:

> " ... Devine is only following his author's intentions in directing
> this one (19) as sombrely as possible. He plays the blind, paralyzed
> Hamm, himself, with a hard harshness allowing himself only a rare
> glint of humour, dry as a raw medlar." (20)

The reviewer of The Stage noticed some other elements in Devine's acting which belong also to the character as presented in the text:

> "It is excellently cast, with George Devine a convincing mixture
> of peevishness and pathos as the helpless Hamm ..." (21)

Harold Hobson in The Sunday Times was above all impressed by the three long and revealing monologues Hamm speaks (22); the first the story he tells about a "man crawling towards me, on his belly ..." whom he offered to take into his services (23); the second concerning his recollection of the people he could have helped and saved (24); and the third in which he asks a last favour of Clov who is about to leave him (25).

Other positive evaluations, though somewhat vague, of Devine's playing of this part, were given by the critics of The Morning Advertiser (26), The Sunday Times (27), and The Daily Sketch (28).

Adverse critism of Devine's Hamm was mainly concerned with his "humanizing" the role - the very fact which the critic of The Times judged positively. Possibly the character of Hamm is falsified by such a procedure. There is certainly an uncanny and frightening note about him, and Milton Shulman missed this in Devine's performance when he wrote the following passage in The Evening Standard:

> "George Devine makes a majestic mountain of cynical despair of
> Hamm, but one felt at times that his resigned aplomb should oc-
> casionally have been shot through with hints of terror." (29)

That the terrifying aspect of the characters in the play came through only spasmodically in the performances is also implied in Alan Brien's statement in The Spectator:

> "George Devine as Hamm and Jack MacGowran as Clov have
> isolated moments of comedy and terror and farce and intensity
> ..." (30)

The predominance of resignation over terror can also be guessed from Kenneth A. Hurren's opinion in What's On in London:

> "George Devine appears as the chair-ridden despot, and I thought
> at first that he was going to enliven the evening with an imperson-
> ation of a former Conservative Prime Minister, but the promise in
> his first few sentences was not fulfilled and his performance, on
> the whole, turned out to be rather doleful ..." (31)

Michel Saint-Denis thought that Devine "was not very good in Endgame" and missed the uncomprimising aggressiveness of the original French performance (32). Alan Dent in the News Chronicle (33) reproached Devine with being "much too slow in his delivery" - a criticism which, if it was justified at all, recalls the occasional slowness of Devine as a director (34). Despite these critical remarks it seems that the impact of the play as interpreted by George Devine and the other three actors remained considerable, in spite of Devine's reluctance to go to the extreme limits of the possibilities offered by the play (35). His liking for subdued effects, balance and understatement made itself felt in this part again. However, the critic of The Times thought that "the impression of a world beheld in a terrifying nightmare remains" (36), and a reviewer in Time and Tide wrote:

> "Congratulations are due to George Devine and Jack MacGowran for

handing this bitter pill unjammed to us ..." (37)

In any case, the director and actor Devine obviously came to an agreement with the author Beckett. Consequently his performance must be taken as one possible interpretation of both Hamm and the play.

*

The part of Johann von Staupitz, Vicar General of the Augustinian Order, in John Osborne's Luther, was one of the most memorable realized by George Devine at the Court. The reason for this successful performance may be that the stage directions suggest certain similarities between this figure and Devine's own character. Devine may have felt invited to identify himself with this fatherly vicar, as his own attitude towards his young dramatists was fatherly. It could even be that Osborne, who had and still has deep admiration for Devine, thought of him when he was creating the part; and according to several statements by close colleagues Devine was best in those roles with which he could identify himself (38). Here are the stage directions referring to Staupitz:

"He is a quiet, gentle-voiced man in late middle age, almost
stolidly contemplative. He has profound respect for Martin,
recognizing in him the powerful potential of insight, sensitivity,
courage and, also heroics that is quite outside the range of his
own endeavour. However, he also understands that a man of
his own limitations can offer a great deal to such a young man
at this point in his development, and his treatment of Martin is
a successful astringent mixture of sympathy and ridicule." (39)

All the critics who wrote on the Court production of the play found extremely positive words for Devine's achievement. As to the quietness and wisdom the part demands (in contrast to the compulsiveness of Luther), Devine was to a high degree able to convey these features. The critic of The Sunday Telegraph put it like this:

"George Devine, serenely articulate and gently probing, is the
mouthpiece for most of the insights into Luther's psyche - a
brilliant exercise in quietism ..." (40)

The passage in Plays and Players dealing with Devine's characterization of the part goes even further in its positive assessment:

" ... George Devine's Staupitz, in its certainty and its quietude
the best thing that I have seen the doyen of Sloane Square do ..."
(41)

Similar qualities of Devine's performance are stressed in the review of The Morning Advertiser:

"George Devine arrestingly underlines the wisdom and tolerance
of John Staupitz ..." (42)

The steadying, appeasing, harmonizing character of the part of Staupitz as opposed
to the protesting and temperamental "angry young man" Martin seemed to be made
to measure for Devine, and maybe Anthony Cookman in The Tatler sensed the parallel between Devine as Staupitz and Devine the manager of the Royal Court when he
wrote the following sentence:

" ... George Devine is a knowing old priest who makes himself Luther's patron ..." (43)

Among the critics who judged Devine's playing of the part positively but generally
and without the mentioning of details were those of the West London Press (44),
Time and Tide (45), St. Martin's Review (46), The Daily Telegraph (47), and The
Stage (48). In Staupitz George Devine had found a part which suited his own character and gave him great opportunities to show his qualities as an actor.

*

Tony Richardson's production of Chekhov's The Seagull (49) provided Devine with
the part of Jevgenij Sergejevich Dorn among a cast which included Peggy Ashcroft,
Vanessa Redgrave, Peter McEnery, Peter Finch, Rachel Kempson, Mark Dignam,
and Paul Rogers. Devine had acted in this play before: in John Gielgud's production
of 1936 he played the part of Shamrayev. Doctor Dorn was another character which
Devine seized upon with enthusiasm, because again there are traits in the part which
were comparable to some of his own (50). The resignation and the subdued disappointment hidden under the charm and the apparent happiness of the doctor called
for a fine balance of forces standing in opposition to each other in a single person.
A similar task had been faced by Devine in the figure of Danforth in The Crucible
(51).

To tell from the reviews and from the reports of many of Devine's colleagues (they
all remembered his Dorn and were still enthusiastic about him), he succeeded impressively in conveying the shades of this complex character. This was Bernard
Levin's opinion in The Daily Mail:

"And above all, there is Mr. George Devine's faultless Dorn.
The butterfly-doctor, eternally prescribing valerian drops,
making his peace with his unsatisfactory life, is an easy part
to do, a fiendishly difficult part to do well. Mr. Devine balances
it between thoughtlessness and hopelessness, and strikes
golden fire again and again." (52)

B.A. Young's praise in The Financial Times sounded equally unstinted:

"George Devine's Doctor Dorn, the complete provincial

sophisticate with his hummed snatches of Gounod and Brahms
(French and German accents impeccable, of course), is beautifully observed ..." (53)

C.B. Mortlock in the City Press came to the same conclusion and hinted at the way
the doctor's disguising his real condition was brought out by Devine:

"George Devine's portrayal of the middle-aged doctor, alone
among the characters in professing to be content with his lot,
is perfectly judged ..." (54)

But there were also critics who thought that certain characteristics in the spectrum
of the doctor's qualities as presented by Chekhov were missing in Devine's performance. As Philip Hope-Wallace in The Guardian wrote:

"George Devine's Doctor Dorn has the right sort of gravity but
too little of the much spoken of charm ..." (55)

Ronald Bryden saw one fault not so much in Devine's acting but in Tony Richardson's
conception of the play, which he accused of being too cold in its approach:

"What's missing is the emotion, self-indulged, febrile,
destructive, which was Chekhov's spectacle and subject.
Without it, there is no room for George Devine, as Dorn,
to bring into the doctor's ironic observation the dramatist's
embracing compassion for a species which could have grown
like the trees, but cut them down to cage itself in the madness of cities ..." (56)

In spite of this criticism, admiration for Devine's achievement and his elucidation
of this demanding part prevailed. Harold Hobson in The Sunday Times was especially impressed by the last words of the play - "Konstantin Gavrilovich has killed
himself" - which are spoken by Doctor Dorn. It is a sentence that may easily lose
its effect if not conveyed with the command of an actor who is able to strike the
people on stage as well as in the auditorium:

"I have never felt this so strongly at any previous production
of 'The Seagull'. After the doctor's dreadful declaration Arkadina
the actress, the novelist Trigorin, the old landowner Sorin, their
friends and their dependants will go on living, flirting, recalling
past triumphs, regretting lost opportunities, writing new books.
But on Thursday George Devine spoke the words with such accurate
timing, the curtain came down so perfectly on cue that one realised
with an almost physical shock that anything that might happen to
them afterwards was of no importance. " (57)

Some critics maintained that this was one of the best parts George Devine had acted during his whole career (58), and people like Peggy Ashcroft (59), Robert Stephens (60), Michel Saint-Denis (61), John Gielgud (62), William Gaskill (63), and Tony Richardson (64) were of the opinion that Dorn as played by Devine was an achievement which rose high above the general level of an actor's competence. It seems to be one of the parts by which Devine the actor will be remembered for a long time.

*

Baron Von Epp in John Osborne's A Patriot For Me was the last part in George Devine's acting career. In this role, presiding the notorious drag ball scene at the beginning of Act II, where all the participants are men dressed up as women, Devine was given an opportunity to make use of his strength as a comedian. Disguised as Queen Alexandra, in a red wig topped with a small diamond crown, adorned with a pearl necklace and earrings, flashing rings over the elbow-length gloves, he became the majestic centre of the ballroom crowd:

"With George Devine, dressed as a dominating dowager and
ruling over these twittering males with the biting, corrosive
tongue of an ageing queer, this is a moment of magnificent
theatre." (65)

Again Devine presented a delicate mixture of different attitudes; he was witty, detached, nasty, amiable, self-confident and in command of every situation. This is how the reviewer of The Scotsman saw him:

"Reigning over this gathering is a baron dressed as a dowager,
and played with clowning, feminine coyness, gentle humour, and
teasing malice by a queenly George Devine. A more hilariously
skilful role Mr. Devine can never have played." (66)

A critic in the Middlesex County Times noticed the varying shades Devine gave to the character as well:

"The play's great centre piece, though, is the half-hour Act Two
ball scene with George Devine marvellously witty and bitchy and
dignified as the ageing, transvestite Baron who acts as host ..."
(67)

Devine did not slide into cheap comedy - a danger which is certainly there in this part - but he shot the fun through with sharpness and an ambiguous malignity. As John Holmstrom in Plays and Players wrote:

" ... it gives a splendid opportunity to George Devine as the robed
and tiara'd Baron(ess) von Epp, snapping like a bossy old salmon
and forcing us to admire his tough determination that standards
shall be maintained, in or out of camp." (68)

In any case these remarks show that George Devine did not fall into the trap of singling out one effective trait in the character of Von Epp. He tried to get out as many variations as possible in order to present a personality as iridescent as suggested by the text. The reaction of the audience was perhaps too onesided, and, to judge from the impression recorded by Kenneth A. Hurren in What's On in London, refused to see the darker elements under the amusing surface:

> " ... George Devine, whose appearance as the hostess of the
> ball elicited such ecstatic squeals from the audience the night
> I was there that I feared he would have to be smuggled out of
> the theatre. " (69)

The critics of the Daily Mail (70), the Yorkshire Post (71), The Stage (72), the Bolton Evening News (73), and The Spectator (74) reacted very positively to Devine's characterization but contented themselves with more general remarks of praise.

The career of George Devine ended abruptly while he was playing this very part. On August 7th 1965 he collapsed after acting in the drag ball scene and was ordered to take a rest. He never really recovered. He had only six more months to live.

*

The other parts acted by Devine at the Court were the Old Man in Ionesco's The Chairs (75), Father Golden Orfe in Nigel Dennis's Cards of Identity (76), Pinchwife in Wycherley's The Country Wife (77), Frederick Compton in Dennis's The Making of Moo (78), Undershaft in Shaw's Major Barbara (79), Van Putzeboum in Coward's Look After Lulu (80), The Man at the End in Wedekind's Spring Awakening (81), and Mr. Shu Fu in Brecht's The Good Woman of Setzuan (82). In The Chairs Devine was confronted with a part quite different from what he had done before. Already in the years with Saint-Denis he had developed a special liking for Ionesco (83). He was partnered by Joan Plowright, who was still more remote from her part as far as the age demanded was concerned, but, to judge from what the critic of The Guardian said, they had both studied their roles intensely:

> " ... Miss Plowright and George Devine show an acute and
> sympathetic observation of the mannerisms of the very old
> ... " (84)

In The Sunday Times Harold Hobson drew attention to the "ballet of chairs and doors" (85) which took place in Jocelyn Herbert's set consisting of unceasingly swinging doors all the way round the stage:

> "Joan Plowright and George Devine not only give in it superb
> performances, but in their management of the chairs themselves
> they bring off a feat of physical dexterity which would gain a round
> of applause in a circus ring. " (86)

There was criticism as well. The reviewer of The Scotsman drew parallels with the productions staged in 1957:

> " ... George Devine, who, especially, had perfected his
> technique for the part since the last time. Yet somehow
> lines were less audible ... " (87)

This criticism of Devine's diction seems rather surprising, as he directed his special attention to this particular point (88). It may have been the deliberate result of his interpretation of the part.

Tony Richardson, the director, was most impressed by the extraordinary understanding that existed between Devine and Joan Plowright - a fact which emerged as a result from their former teacher-pupil relationship at the Old Vic School (89). Joan Plowright had great difficulties in the beginning to "find" her part, and it was Devine's merit that after some nerve-racking rehearsals she found the strength to play her role at all (90). In the opinion of Ronald Bryden (91), whom we interviewed in the autumn of 1968, ten years after this production of The Chairs, the Old Man as played by George Devine (in a crumpled jacket and waistcoat, an ill-fitting collar and tie, and with a white moustache), was among his best achievements (92).

As Father Golden Orfe, the "whisky priest" in Cards of Identity, Devine managed to render a lengthy speech effectively - Dennis's plays of ideas were something he responded to (93). In his own stylized production of The Country Wife he once more - as in The Chairs - gave a notable performance together with Joan Plowright. In Look After Lulu he was able to exploit his qualities as a comedian (94) - the comic field was one of his specialities since his days at the Old Vic School (95).

*

In order to say anything conclusive about George Devine the actor we have to bear in mind that he could not devote his entire work to the acting. His task as a manager, the constant organizing and his directing did not leave him much time for the study and the polishing of a part. On the other hand, he enjoyed acting very much, and he made something elaborate of his roles when he found the time.

Devine was not an outstanding actor (97). He was quiet, meticulous and understating, tried to serve the play and did not seek to go beyond the limitations of his part (98). Sometimes, in his effort to do justice to the text and the intentions of the author, he tended to be slow (Endgame); and every now and then he had a too theoretical approach to his roles and remained "slightly intellectual" (99). His preference for subdued effects and balance often prevented him from realizing the more exciting possibilities of a part - in Endgame he somewhat neglected the demoniac aspects of Hamm's character.

But he was a good and sound actor in the right part (100). As soon as he relaxed he was able to come to an impressive achievement. This was especially the case with parts he could identify himself with (Dorn in <u>The Seagull</u>, Staupitz in <u>Luther</u>). He had also the gift of conveying a whole range of different features in a single character and so of rendering it as complex as the author intended it (Danforth in <u>The Crucible</u>, Von Epp in <u>A Patriot For Me</u>), and his strength as a comedian resulted in some fine and personal interpretations (Pinchwife in <u>The Country Wife</u>, Father Golden Orfe in <u>Cards of Identity</u>, Van Putzeboum in <u>Look After Lulu</u>, Von Epp). He was a solid actor who approached every part with the same seriousness. His principles as an actor, formed during his years at the London Theatre Studio and at the Old Vic School, largely coincided with his convictions as a producer: they culminated in the firm belief that everything should be subordinated to the play. The play was not to serve the actor, but the actor the play.

VII GEORGE DEVINE AS AN ARTISTIC DIRECTOR
AT THE ROYAL COURT 1956-1965

Besides discovering dramatists, besides producing and acting, Devine's tasks as
a manager were manifold. One of the most important was the building up of an
audience.

From their start in 1956, Devine and his company had the intention of attracting
a new and young audience. By their policy of presenting new and unconventional
work they hoped to raise that part of the theatre-going public which up to then had
been dissatisfied with the British theatre - an interested and intelligent audience
that did not look on the theatre as a mere entertainment. Devine formulated this
hope one month after the opening at the Court:

> "The theatre should be more than just the aftermath of a good
> dinner. I want to see people so involved in the play and its
> subject that they are prepared to stand up in their seats and
> fight about them. This is an exciting time in which to live.
> The theatre should reflect it ..." (1)

But he had to learn that it is difficult to fill the theatre-goers with enthusiasm for
something new. It proved very hard to recruit a "permanent" audience ready to back
the adventurous policy of the English Stage Company by coming to the plays regularly. In 1958 Devine published a few truths about the audiences, which did not seem
to be of age yet:

> "The regular audience at the Royal Court itself is still regret-
> tably small. Far more people in London support the English
> Stage Company as an idea rather than buy seats at the box
> office, except for obvious successes. There is a lamentable
> lack of theatrical interest amongst the potential audience of
> such a theatre. In a recent case of the presentation of an
> experimental play, a pall of doubt cast on the play by the
> critics, resulted in such poor attendances that it had to be
> withdrawn from the repertory. We still have to create an
> audience that will feel some sense of responsibility towards
> a certain kind of work being done. There is in London an
> apathy towards exciting new work until it has received the
> approval of the pundits, intellectual or social, which compares
> unfavourably with Berlin, Paris or New York." (2)

Despite the formation of the English Stage Society (3), a "supporters' group",
which gave its members the right of attending the Sunday Night Productions without
Décor, as well as the advantages of priority booking and reduced prices, things had
not changed much by 1962, as Devine's statement in The Guardian indicates:

"Apart from about a thousand people there is no regular public
to support us through thick and thin. To pay our way we have to
achieve 'rave notices'." (4)

Devine tried hard to build up an audience. He had the idea of contacting schools
and bringing school children into the Court, where they could gain insight into the
work being done at a theatre and were shown round by directors, actors and authors.
By this he hoped to interest the young people at an early age and to infect them with
an enthusiasm for the theatre that would last through their lifetimes. The plan
seemed to be successful, as the following report shows:

"Most of them seem to have been thrilled, and some have written
to tell us that it's given them a totally different idea of what the
theatre means. One boy said that it had not only affected his feelings about the theatre, but about life in general, to see a group of
people working together in this dedicated way ... Now I'm going
to try to organize one visit a week. If we could get 500 of them
round the theatre in a year, that would eventually build up into
something quite formidable. What we ought to do is to send a team
round the schools to show them how theatre works and what it is,
but we've got too much on our plate here as it is. Yet the theatre
must explore this field. Middle-aged playgoers come to a play
if it's successful, or if they think they' re going to get a kick out
of it. But if you're going to make the theatre a part of your life
- if you're going to be demanding, to take an attitude, to be critical - then you need formation and that, I think, ought to start in
schooldays." (5)

This proves that the Company took pains to educate a critical audience. Although
all these endeavours had relatively meagre results, due to indifference and apathy,
they succeeded in stimulating at least some interest in the work of Ann Jellicoe,
John Arden, N.F. Simpson and Arnold Wesker (6). John Osborne had a good start
owing to the fact that part of Look Back in Anger was broadcast on television, and
that Laurence Olivier acted in The Entertainer.

*

But where, under the circumstances, did the Court get its money from? After all,
the house seats only 407 people, and even if completely booked up, it yields only
about £ 340. By the financial exploitation of transfers, film and television rights
connected with Osborne's plays, and by a few classical revivals which turned out
to be hits with the public, the Court managed to cover its expenses. Additional help
came from the Arts Council, which, after a very cautious start (£ 2,500 in 1956),
gave £ 8,000 in 1961 and 1962, and increased its allowance to £ 20,000 in 1963 and
1964, and to £ 32,500 in 1965. Donations from the London County Council, the
Chelsea Borough Council, from business organizations and private individuals provided further sources of income. As Tony Richardson said, " ... there was always

very little money around but somehow overall it did work ..." (7).

*

If the promotion of young playwrights was the main occupation of the Court, it was by no means the only one. Just as important was the constant looking for and training of directors, actors and designers. Devine wanted the Court to be a workshop for them (8), a place similar to the London Theatre Studio and the Old Vic School.

It is impressive to see that many now famous actors or actresses of the younger generation, among them Joan Plowright, Wendy Craig, Frances Cuka, Rita Tushingham, Albert Finney, Peter O'Toole, Robert Stephens, Alan Dobie and Nicol Williamson, were discovered at the Court. They were brought up in an atmosphere of team-work, and expected to work seriously in the smallest parts. Beyond this, we must not forget that before 1956 dialect and regional accent were seldom heard on the London stage. There was the concept of the "beautiful voice", and accents were only allowed in minor parts or comic characters. The Court did much to change this: its introduction of many young actors from the provinces, mainly the North, tumbled the old rules and made room for a more contemporary style of acting (9). Regional accents could be heard in Ann Jellicoe's The Sport of My Mad Mother, John Arden's Serjeant Musgrave's Dance, Arnold Wesker's The Kitchen, and perhaps most strikingly in Luther, Albert Finney speaking his part in his Lancashire dialect (10).

In 1963, an Actors Studio attached to the Court was opened at the Jeanetta Cochrane Theatre, through the initiative of the designer Jocelyn Herbert. It was run under the general supervision of George Devine, and William Gaskill was appointed its first director, followed by Keith Johnstone. Between 1963 and early 1966 fourteen terms took place (one term lasting about six to eight weeks) and about 250 actors attended the various courses organized there:

> "The courses have included 'method', improvisation, comedy,
> mime, movement, speech and mask work, and have been largely
> in the hands of Doreen Cannon, Claude Chagrin, George Devine,
> William Gaskill, Keith Johnstone, Yat Malmgren, Helen Montague,
> Jennifer Patrick and Marc Wilkinson." (11)

Special stress was laid on the improvisation work, "after the example of Commedia dell'Arte" (12). The "mask work" reminds us of Devine's experiments together with Saint-Denis before the war. By teaching at the Cochrane Studio Devine was able to work with young people again, a task he had always been particularly fond of (13). He taught comedy, tragedy and comic mask work himself, thus continuing some of his former endeavours in close connection with the Royal Court. Together with the Court itself the Studio combined into a workshop, in which an intense and rewarding theatrical training was practised.

*

Many attempts were made, too, to form a permanent company of actors at the Court (14). It proved economically impossible. Originally Devine and Tony Richardson wanted to assemble a group of actors to be supplemented, as the need arose, with new people. But this idea was eventually abandoned. Instead it was agreed that the best actors and actresses should be found for each play staged. Richardson explained this decision:

> "When you are doing new plays it is impossible to have a permanent
> company. The demands regarding the actors are too different. The
> authors themselves of course want the best cast for their plays. " (15)

So we have to consider "English Stage Company" as the name of an organization that puts on new plays. It does not mean a company of actors like the Royal Shakespeare Company or the National Theatre Company.

The original plan of playing in repertory (16), too, could not be sustained, and this for similar reasons. If a theatre wants to remain flexible and to present new plays on short notice, it cannot adopt a repertory system.

*

Among the designers working for the Court the outstanding personality is Jocelyn Herbert. Her sets for the four productions examined in the chapters VIII, IX, XI and XII (17) and for many others prove that she is one of the truly imaginative designers who are able to combine in their work simplicity, visual beauty and great evocativeness (18) and who designs scenery not for the sake of spectacle but in the service of the play (19). Probably influenced by the sets of the Berliner Ensemble (20), she developed an unmistakeably personal style. Other designers trained by the English Stage Company include Stephen Doncaster, Alan Tagg, Sean Kenny, Richard Negri and John Gunter (21).

*

George Devine died from a heart attack at his home in Chelsea on January 20th, 1966, at the age of fifty-five. He had been ill since the summer of 1965, when he collapsed while playing in Osborne's A Patriot For Me (22).

In Devine's case it is no exaggeration to say that he ruined himself for the theatre. Perhaps he was one of the last universal men of the theatre in England: actor, producer and manager in one person. As time went on, he found less and less opportunity for acting, which he always loved, and even for producing. Administrative problems, the encouraging and teaching of young dramatists and actors took more and more of his time and energy. His daughter, Harriet Mennie-Devine, remembered the change in her father:

> "He changed from a large, rather untidy man, full of laughter, to
> a thin elegant serious one who had little time to laugh, to relax and

to be himself." (23)

The constant wear and tear of the running of the Court, together with the ruthlessness towards himself in his work, finally proved too much for him. "He worked
like a maniac", Jocelyn Herbert said (24) - and in this she was confirmed by Robert
Stephens (25) and William Gaskill (26). But he had to pay the price for this relentless dedication to the theatre. When he announced his retirement as an artistic director in January 1965, it became clear that the physical and psychical burden had
become too heavy for him:

> "When a man begins to feel that he is part of the fixtures and
> fittings it is time he left. I am deeply tired. The weight of this
> edifice is driving me into the ground up to my neck." (27)

His ten years at the Court meant a lot, perhaps everything, to George Devine. Here
his passionate effort to change the face of the modern British theatre bore its fruits
(28). The Royal Court became the centre from which a new theatrical life spread in
England. Devine wanted problems of today treated on the stage by young dramatists,
he wanted theatre as an art and not as a mere entertainment. And he wanted a theatre atmosphere of work and not of making money. He never imposed his ideas on
others, but found ways of helping all those that were in contact with him. His readi-
ness for discussion and his broadmindedness (29), his steadying and protecting influence earned him the deep respect of colleagues and pupils (30). John Osborne recalled the atmosphere created by Devine:

> "What was wonderful about George in the way he treated all the
> writers in that theatre was that you never got the sense that you
> were being judged at that time. You always felt if he took you
> seriously - and you felt if you were being produced at that theatre,
> you were being taken seriously - he looked at you in some historical
> sense. He saw you as part of a tradition or some sort of continuity,
> and you felt that your life was being scrutinized sympathetically
> and from a long term point of view, so that you felt always that
> what happened to that particular production or what was wrong
> with it or what you had failed to do didn't matter, because it was
> all done in terms of the rest of your life. And this is one of the
> wonderful things that he had this genius for of giving you a sense
> of time, and a time to relax in which to work, which in my expe-
> rience I think is quite unique ..." (31)

In some notes to an unwritten book Devine expressed some of his central ideas about
the theatre, and we notice that the Royal Court stands as the impressive realization
of his theories:

> "You should choose your theatre like you choose a religion. Make
> sure you don't get into the wrong temple. For me the theatre is
> really a religion or way of life. You must decide what you feel the

world is about and what you want to say about it, so that everything in the theatre you work in is saying the same thing. This
will be influenced partly by the man who is running it, and the
actual physical and economic conditions under which he works.
... For me, the theatre is a temple of ideas and ideas so well
expressed it may be called art. So always look for quality in the
writing above what is being said.
This is how to choose a theatre to work in, and if you can't
find one you like, start one of your own. A theatre must have
a recognisable attitude. It will have one, whether you like it
or not." (32)

***

VIII ANN JELLICOE: THE SPORT OF MY MAD MOTHER

"It hits them here" (a resounding
slap on the diaphragm) "rather
than here" (a tap on the forehead).
Ann Jellicoe in an interview published in London Life, October 6th
1965.

Ann Jellicoe, born in Middlesborough in 1928, wrote The Sport of My Mad Mother,
her first full-length play, for the Observer play competition of 1956. It won third
prize - together with Norman Frederick Simpson's A Resounding Tinkle and an
Australian play (1) - and what was even more important, a production at the Royal
Court Theatre. It was staged there on February 25th 1958. The author, who had
always had the ambition to produce plays, shared the direction with George Devine.
In this fact we notice the tendency typical for the Court: the great respect for the
authors and their intentions as expressed in their work (2). The restless, unpredictably reacting Ann Jellicoe was given the chance to direct her own play.

*

In order to convey an impression of the characteristics of The Sport of My Mad
Mother and the particular problems connected with its production, I quote a few
sentences from Ann Jellicoe's preface to the printed text of the revised edition (3):

"'The Sport of My Mad Mother' was not written intellectually
according to a prearranged plan. It was shaped bit by bit until the bits felt right in relation to each other and to the whole.
It is an anti-intellect play not only because it is about irrational
forces and urges but because one hopes it will reach the audience
directly through rhythm, noise and music and their reaction to
basic stimuli.
The play is written to be acted: nothing is put into words that
cannot be shown in action. Very often the words counterpoint
the action or intensify the action by conflicting with it ... the
people in the play ... betray their real feeling either by what
they do, or by the very fact that they need to assume a mask
... We create rituals when we want to strengthen, celebrate or
define our common life and common values, or when we want
to give ourselves confidence to undertake a common course of
action. A ritual generally takes the form of repeating a pattern
of words and gestures which tend to excite us above a normal
state of mind: at the climax of the rite the essential nature of
something is changed (e.g. the mass, a marriage service, the
bestowal of diplomas, etc.) This play proceeds by rituals because
the insecure and inarticulate group of people who figure in the

play depend on them so much ..." (4)

This sounded all very extraordinary, new and strange to audiences and readers at that time. In her Production Note Ann Jellicoe makes the following points with regard to the performance:

> "The verses and poems should be spoken, chanted or distorted
> according to the needs of character and situation. They may be
> pointed or emphasized by FLIM on his instruments as necessary.
> FLIM sits downstage and with one, or several of his instruments
> makes sounds (not strictly music) rough or sweet, discordant or
> harmonious, rhythmical or arhythmic. These sounds heighten
> scenes of extreme excitement and may also stimulate or give a
> cue to the action.
> The stage comes forward to meet the audience and there is no
> precise architectural detail to mark where the stage ends and
> the auditorium begins. The main acting area is down stage." (5)

In these lines we see clearly that Ann Jellicoe tries to get through to the audience by means which, in 1958, were quite exceptional on the British stage. The barrier between actors and spectators is broken down, and the audience is confronted not with ideas and polite conversation, but assaulted by sound and the musical and rhythmical qualities of language. Intellect and cool reason give way to emotion and irrationality.

What did George Devine, the co-director, think of the play? The lines he wrote for the programme shed some light upon his attitude:

> "The play is about people. People of today. The grown-ups play
> with atom bombs, the Kids with knives and guns. Fear dominates
> the world - fear of 'them', whichever side you are on, fear of
> surprise, of violence and death. Humanity looks for a leader, for
> the security of a dynamic personality, for the warmth of compan-
> ionship, however silly or irresponsible the consequences. This
> is so, particularly of the young.
> The dramatist here attempts to show a group of young people in
> such a world, who are, at the same time, a microcosm of all
> people. Knowledge and science are trying to put order in the
> chaos, to discover 'how people tick', to take on the responsibili-
> ty for humanity. In the play the American Caldaro takes on this
> task. In so doing he comes up against his match in the Australian
> girl Greta, an irresponsible 'life force'. The play sets up this
> conflict in a series of episodes strung together with the apparent
> inconsequence of real life. The aimlessness, the violence, the
> cruelty, the need for security of the young people are the raw
> material with which the dramatist demonstrates this conflict
> ..." (6)

In this note George Devine makes his remarks about what, in his opinion, is the subject-matter of the play. Ann Jellicoe, in her preface, talks about the methods with which she tries to convey this subject-matter to a theatre audience. We shall now undertake the task of examining how The Sport of My Mad Mother was realized on the stage. First of all, however, we shall focus our attention on the text itself.

*

One of the first stage directions takes up and puts into effect some of the ideas mentioned in the preface:

> "FLIM brings on stage a drum, motor-horn, triangle, cymbals, washboard, etc., which he arranges on a stand at one side of the stage." (7)

This assembly of instruments is an important factor for the realization of the author's plan, namely to "reach the audience directly through rhythm, noise and music ..." (8)

The passages in which Ann Jellicoe turns theory into practice and in which rhythm, sound, ritual and gestic impulses play a predominant part are arresting and have a notable power of involving the reader (and the audience) in their movement:

> "PATTY. Catch me -
> CONE. Catch me.
> FAK. Catch me.
> CONE. Catch me, Patty-paws, who'd ever have thought?
> PATTY. Oh, give over.
> CONE. Give over.
> FAK. Give over.
> PATTY. Give over. Give over.
> CONE. Give over, sweetheart." (9)

The initial challenge by Patty - "catch me" - which implies some sort of provoking gesture combined with a retreating movement or with running away is taken up by Cone and then by Fak, who join in the game. Patty, however, gets bored by their reaction and tries to stop them with an uninterested remark ("give over") involving, perhaps, a casual declining hand-gesture. Cone and Fak continue their game as before by repeating Patty's words. This time her reaction changes. She gets clearly irritated and tries to silence them. Her "Give over. Give over" has an urging and alarmed ring about it. Cone's answer is on the playful, appeasing level again. By the repetitions a tension is created, and the rhythm has something hypnotizing about it, from which Patty seeks to escape.

A different employment of speech rhythms appears in the following example, where rhyme is used as an additional means of heightening the impact. It is a light-hearted interchange of lines similar to a nursery rhyme between Cone, Fak and Patty:

```
"CONE &      If you see a big fat woman.
FAK.         Standing on a corner humming.
             That's fat Jessie.
PATTY.    Is that so.
CONE &       If you see her in the pictures
FAK.         With a bag of dolly mixtures
             That's fat Jessie.
PATTY.    Is that so." (10)
```

A few moments later the ritual use of two words and the rhythm arising from their
repetition are driven to such a pitch as to make one of the characters, Patty, virtually break down. Her resistance is shattered by the ruthless impact of sounds. She
turns to the audience for help; to an audience which is in this moment - at least to
some extent - in the same situation as herself:

```
"CONE.    Dolly?
FAK.      Dolly!
CONE.     Dolly!
FAK.      Dolly.
CONE.     Dolly.
FAK.      Dolly.
```

> CONE and FAK have hypnotized each other. PATTY tries to get
> away and in so doing draws them on to her.

```
FAK. (at PATTY). Dolly.
CONE. (at PATTY). Dolly.
FAK. Dolly.
CONE. Dolly.
FAK. Dolly.
PATTY. Shoo.
FAK. Shoo.
PATTY. Shoo.
CONE. Shoo.
FAK. Shoo. Shoo.
PATTY. Shoo. Shoo.
CONE. Shoo. Shoo.
```
> PATTY screams.
```
PATTY. (to audience as if drowning.) Help! Help me! Help!" (11)
```

Cone and Fak - as the stage direction indicates - hypnotize each other by their repetition of the word "Dolly". As Patty wants to leave, they turn towards her and fling
the same word at her. The missing exclamation or question marks seem to suggest
that the repetitions - unlike in the beginning - have become mechanical and uncontrolled. Patty tries to weaken and resist the impact of the sound "Dolly" by using
the sound "Shoo", which is generally used to make somebody go away. But she is
beaten at her own game, as Cone and Fak (as in the "catch me" episode) absorb the
sound. Patty's last defense consists in a scream; she sees her only rescue with the

spectators who, however, feel just as helpless and paralyzed.

A scene in which violent action and onomatopoeic sounds blend into a theatrically thrilling unity is found shortly afterwards. Patty, Cone and Fak move threateningly round Caldaro, shouting words which operate as "valves" for some sort of accumulated emotion (12). Rationality, personified in Caldaro, stands against irrationality and is defeated. Caldaro sees himself in the middle of a tumult of sound and movement and tries to get the gang under control. But in vain. The excitement created by the sound of words finally releases itself in physical violence: Caldaro is knocked down. The scene is effective and not without brutality:

> "PATTY. Bim! Bam!
> CONE. Bang! Bang!
> FAK. (bringing out his gun). Yak! Yak! Yak! Yak!
> PATTY. Boo boo boo boo!
> CONE. Yak! Yak!
> CALDARO. Control. Control.
> FAK. Yak yak yak yak!
> PATTY. Tcha! Tcha! Tcha!
> FAK. Yay Yak yak yak!
> PATTY. Tcha tcha tcha tcha!
> CALDARO. making a great effort to collect himself and
>   dominate them. What are you trying to do?
>   <u>CONE behind CALDARO gives him a sharp blow at the
> base of the skull - unseen by the others.</u>
> Ah!
> <u>CALDARO collapses forward against FAK who is sent staggering away firing
> his gun wildly. Caldaro falls and is still.</u> " (13)

This wild scene is followed by a calmer counter-movement. The whirlwind is over. Audience and readers are allowed to recover from the emotional impact of the preceding scenes. In an almost motionless interlude Caldaro tries to analyze the situation, to come to grips intellectually with a phenomenon which remains incomprehensible and uncanny to his rational outlook. He fails to do so; he just feels helpless opposite forces which are beyond his control:

> "CALDARO. What is this? What is this? I don't get it ...
> I like to understand things and I don't understand this ... It's
> like some nasty joke ... it's like spitting in your eye ... kind
> of nasty and weak and dangerous ... " (14)

But action is resumed soon: to the rhythmical language which pushes the emotions of the characters towards a climax, movement in the form of a ritual dance is added:

> "<u>FAK wraps up CALDARO in newspapers and makes a parcel
> of him.</u>

```
DODO.  No No No No
       Throw Throw Throw Throw
       So So So So
       Blow Blow Blow Blow
       Crow Crow Crow Crow
       Doe Doe Doe Doe
...
DODO.  Tootle tootle tootle toot.
       Tootle tootle tootle toot.
FAK.   Got a penny for the guy.
       Got a penny for the guy.
```

FLIM picks up the rhythm. The rest pretend to be playing instruments.

```
DODO.  Tootle tootle tootle toot.
       Tootle tootle tootle toot.
CONE.  Bang bang Bang Bang
---
```

CONE, FAK and PATTY begin to dance round CALDARO as round a
totem: bellowing words at the head wrapped in newspaper." (15)

Rhyme, rhythm and movement combine with the sound of words nonsensical or isolated from their context. Dodo indulges in all kinds of childish associations and her
pleasure increases with the amount of similar sounds she is able to find. There is
sheer delight in the sound of words, and the others join in. The scene comes to a
wild close again:

```
"PATTY.  Wow wow wow wow wow wow wow wow
FAK.     Guy guy guy guy guy guy guy guy
CONE.    Bang bang bang bang bang bang bang bang
```

CONE, FAK and PATTY begin frenziedly to tear the paper from
CALDARO.

```
CONE.   Ah! Ah! Ah! Ah!
FAK.    Ah! Ah! Ah! Ah!
PATTY.  Ah! Ah! Ah! Ah! (16)
```

The repetition of one-syllable-words and contrasting vowels excite violent action;
the rhythm accelerates, the final tearing off of the newspapers replaces vocal expression, and ultimately dammed-up emotion breaks forth in a series of short,
breathless interjections, which counterpoint the action (17). One gets the feeling
that without the possibility of uttering sounds Cone, Patty and Fak would burst with
inner tension and pressure (18).

In this first scene all the important aspects of Ann Jellicoe's method can be found.
The spectator is attacked by sound, movement, rhythm, violent action. He does not
get a message which he can grasp with his intellect. Instead he is called upon to

distil a meaning for himself from the way he is emotionally involved.

The second scene of the first act does not begin with words. The stage is in complete darkness. Then light, movement and noise, and later the sound of exclamations, prepare the spectators for the events to come. Here is the beginning of the scene:

"Black-Out, FLIM and DODO on stage. Enter CALDARO, PATTY and FAK who run about the stage with lighted sparklers weaving patterns in the dark.

CALDARO. Ha ha! Whew! Whew!
PATTY. Whew! Whew!
FAK. Ain't it pretty?
PATTY. Christmas! Christmas!" (19)

Soon afterwards there is the scene in which the members of the group try to give Patty a permanent wave. With much noise they prepare their work as amateur hairdressers. In this scene the rhythm of the language becomes more and more forceful and intense; the printed instructions read from the bottle with the lotion accumulate towards a frenetic incantation; a chorus of alternating voices produces a truly captivating effect by means of repetition and variation. Patty takes the part of the precentor:

"PATTY. Take a section the size of a curler.
CALDARO, DODO AND FAK. Take a section the size of a curler.
PATTY. Thoroughly saturate with the lotion.
CALDARO, DODO AND FAK. Thoroughly saturate with the lotion.
PATTY. Fold an end paper over and under.
CALDARO, DODO AND FAK. Fold an end paper over and under.
PATTY. Wind it firmly to the root of the hair.
CALDARO, DODO AND FAK. Wind it firmly to the root of the hair.
CALDARO, DODO, PATTY AND FAK.
　　　　　Take a section the size of a curler
　　　　　Thoroughly saturate with the lotion
　　　　　Fold an end paper over and under
　　　　　Wind it firmly to the root of the hair." (20)

Fascination with their own game spreads among the characters of the scene. Rhythm grips them (21), the pronunciation of the words becomes syncopated, the chorus abbreviates the recurring words and creates a new rhythm, the movement becomes faster, the sounds drift towards another climax:

75

```
"CALDARO.   Careful not tò sit ìn draughts.
 FAK.       Sec.
 DODO.             Sat.
 PATTY.                  Pap.
 FAK.                          Wind.
 FAK.       Use nò metàl with the lotion.
 DODO.      Sec.
 PATTY.            Sat.
 CALDARO.                Pap.
 DODO.                         Wind. " (22)
```

The instructions are not taken as instructions any more but just as a start for developing new sounds which result in a new game. In the end again scraps of words
are ejaculated to release the inner tension which has become unbearable (23). The
whole scale of vowel sounds is run through; moreover the final lines show a riotous play with words which are shouted as soon as they cross the mind. Caldaro,
Patty and Fak seem to have wild associations, urged on by the fun of the game:

```
"FAK and PATTY.    Sec sat pap wind!
                   Sec sat pap wind!
 CALDARO. Pour the rinse in! Pour the rinse in!
 CALDARO, PATTY and FAK.
                   Pour the rinse in! Pour the rinse in!
                   Sec! Sat! Sick! Sock! Pip! Pap!
                   Pop! Pup! Pep! Pump! Pimp! Pamp! Wind!" (24)
```

After these extraordinary events the audience is hardly given time to recover:
there follows a grotesque dressing-up scene with masks and disguises. It is linked
with a cross-examination (25) by which the gang tries to dominate Caldaro and to
rob him of his security and superiority. Greta makes her surprising entrance and
strikes terror into Dodo (26). The rest of the gang is still afraid of Caldaro. They
need masks and disguises in order to cover up their insecurity and to experience a
feeling of being masters of the situation (27). This method of the gang really works:
Caldaro fails to penetrate the masks and is lost as soon as the human faces are hidden from his sight. Just as the others are afraid of faces, he is afraid of masks.
What is security to the group makes him insecure.

The cross-examination itself is constructed out of the same elements which we have
encountered in previous scenes. By means of word repetitions rhythmical patterns
are formed, which assume a threatening quality. This procedure has an unnerving
effect on Caldaro, who - in a last effort - tries to dominate the situation by telling
Cone to take his mask off: the mask in front of which he feels helpless:

```
"CONE.  Caldaro.
 CALDARO. Yes?
 FAK. Where you from, Caldaro?
 CALDARO. The U.S.
```

PATTY. What part of the U.S.?
CALDARO. Illinois.
CONE. What town in Illinois?
...
CONE. How d'you get your cigarettes?
CALDARO. What?
FAK. How do you get your cigarettes?
CALDARO. From a friend.
CONE. Who? ... What's his name?
FAK. Why won't you give us his name?
PATTY. Afraid?
CONE. Afraid to get mixed up?
CALDARO. This is stupid. Stupid! For heaven's sake, Cone,
        take off that silly mask." (28)

But he is in the power of the gang now. In the confusion of language brought about by Cone, Fak, Patty and Greta, Caldaro desperately tries to grasp a sense in order to strike back with his intellectual faculties. He loses the battle because they fight with different weapons. They use words as sounds and stimuli to break his resistance while he clings to the meaning. By letting his questions hang in the air they slowly drag him into their rhythmic word-net and drive him into a corner so much as to leave him on the verge of a nervous breakdown:

"CONE. The shoemaker ---
CALDARO. What?
PATTY. You deny ---
CALDARO. Shoe? Shoe?
PATTY. --- Said you ---
FAK. --- Get it out ---
PATTY. Say you ---
CALDARO. No shoe ---
PATTY. Said ---
FAK. Get ---
CONE. Get ---
GRETA. Mother born Pittsburgh.
CALDARO. Mamma!" (29)

The rhythm becomes more and more breathless and overpowers Caldaro. We can compare this scene to the one earlier in the play (I, i, 168-169) where Patty undergoes a similar experience: unable to bear the impact of sounds any longer she cries out for help.

Although the members of the gang seem to have gained the upper hand over Caldaro, they are not able to defeat him completely. He defends himself by escaping into silence. This is exactly what the others cannot stand. By not answering their questions Caldaro maintains a sort of superiority, which keeps him out of their reach. This fact leads up to another violent scene:

> "CONE. Why don't you answer?
> CALDARO. Because I won't submit to this degradation.
> FAK. Eh?
> CONE. Degradation!
> PATTY. Yawooerl!
> CONE. Degradation! Yoweooh! Yoweeoh!
> PATTY. Yawooerl! Yawooerl! Ugh! Ugh!
> FAK. Whaow! Aherooigh! Aherooigh!
>> Screaming with anger, PATTY, CONE and FAK fall upon
>> CALDARO. FAK picks up the gun and raises it to club
>> CALDARO.
> GRETA. Stop. " (30)

Caldaro's refusal to answer triggers something off in Patty and the two boys. They fly into a rage at his determined statement involving such a high-faluting word as "degradation". First they instinctively try to divert their fury into sounds, to fight the unknown and to get rid of their anger by shouts and exclamations of a frightening, elementary character reminding us of wild animals or Red Indians dancing round some totem. But this time it is not enough: they attack Caldaro and see the last solution in an act of physical violence. Greta prevents them with a single word. She is the person everybody in the gang is afraid of. The ending of Act I, ii provides the audience with a special surprise. In the last moments, when an approaching, not clearly defined danger spreads insecurity and anguish among the group, Greta remains quiet and detached and when she finally gets up, she is seen to be pregnant (31).

Act Two takes up the atmosphere of danger conjured up at the end of I, ii. The uncanny and terrifying aspect of an empty street with all its possibilities of violence is stressed by some indistinct figures who whisper stanzas of a haunting rhythm; a rhythm which renders the oncoming movement of something dangerous and the sound of echoes in the emptiness:

> " ... FLIM picks up a rhythm on the percussion. A spot begins to
> burn brightly down on to the stage. Around and beyond the spot
> are figures that cannot quite be seen.

> THE FIGURES almost whispering

> ...

>> Empty. Empty. Empty. Empty.
>> 'Lone on the street.
>> Alone on the street.
>> Hear your steps as you walk the street.
>> Hear your steps alone alone on the empty street.
>> Empty. Empty. Empty. Empty. ..." (32)

Immediately afterwards, Cone addresses the audience directly. Threatened as he feels, all he is able to do is to utter some imperatives and short sentences evoking an atmosphere of danger and terrible events, which everybody is exposed to. The audience becomes involved in Cone's fear and anguish. They are invited to identify with the state of mind he finds himself in: a sense of all-pervading peril and terror is created.

> "CONE. You don't know. You don't understand. Think! Think!
> Behind you - behind your head. As you turn your head there's
> something behind you ... behind your eyes. Think! Feel it in
> your bones. In your joints. In your blood as it runs through
> your body. It's all about you. You can feel it on your neck, it
> breathes and rustles past. Too dark to see but you can feel it.
> It thickens the air. It bumps against you like moths at night.
> Soon it will swell bulbous and enveloping."(33)

The atmosphere of panic is increased as Dodo comes running in, frightened out of her wits. Fierce movement and brief interjections mingle. The missing exclamation marks in Dodo's refusal of Caldaro's help seem to point out that Dodo is almost consumed with fear:

> "Enter DODO running. CONE catches her by the coat and swings
> her round and round, letting her go and catching her again.
>
> DODO. Oh. Oh.
> CONE. Ha ha. Done. Done done done. Ha ha.
> DODO. Hurt.
> CONE. Ha ha.
> DODO. Hurt - Greta.
> CONE. Hurt?
>   Exit CONE
>   Enter CALDARO.
> CALDARO. Dodo! Dodo!
> DODO. Oh ...
> CALDARO. Why ---
> DODO. No.
> CALDARO. Dodo - it's me - Caldaro.
> DODO. Go away ... I'm dead ... I'm dead ... go away ..."(34)

As before, these scenes full of movement, noise and suggestive rhythmical word-patterns are followed by some calmer moments. Caldaro is exasperated about the state of things. He still tries to lead the rational forces to their victory over destructive emotions, fear and insecurity and to cope with the events he is not able to understand. His calm interlude after the preceding outburst provides an effective contrast (35):

> "CALDARO. They fall asleep so easy ... they just let go ...
> they feel safe - well, I guess they're as safe with me as that
> fantastic woman. ... They just give up the bother of looking

after themselves. ... Why does she do her hair like that? ...
What is she? ... Ranging around like a scorpion - lively as a
viper. ... I've got to find out, I've got to - why have I got to?
... I mean have I got to - to understand - to find out? ... I
wish I knew what all this was about - I wish I knew. ... If I
understood I could get things clear - organized. ... If you get
things clear you know where you are - what you're up against
..." (36)

Unexpectedly the scene changes. After Caldaro's lonely considerations the place of
action is shifted to a schoolroom; Greta assumes the part of a teacher. Patty and
Fak are puzzled at first, but after Cone has taken up the cue they enter into the game
without asking many questions. Greta seems to be accepted in any form of superiority (37).

Out of this unconventional teacher-pupils play arises the first really serious confrontation between Caldaro and the emotional Greta. In a tense dialogue consisting
of one-word-sentences the elementary battle between Greta and Caldaro is fought
out; a verbal war in which he tries to dominate her by opposing to her examples
destructive counter-examples. Greta's images are taken from nature, whereas
Caldaro hits back with mechanical devices invented by the human intellect in order
to control nature. Only in the last two lines Caldaro turns to using animal examples:

"CALDARO. Come here!
GRETA. What!
CALDARO. Come here to me!
GRETA. What, me?
CALDARO. Very well. I'll come and get you.
GRETA. Tree.
CALDARO. Axe.
GRETA. Bird.
CALDARO. Gun.
GRETA. Water.
CALDARO. Dam.
GRETA. Fire.
CALDARO. Sand.
GRETA. Worm.
CALDARO. Sparrow.
GRETA. Hawk.
CALDARO. Eagle. " (38)

But in the end he proves unable to get her under his control. He is repelled and
fascinated by her at the same time:

"CALDARO. Who are you? Who are you? Extravagant, tempestuous,
exultant, instinctive, audacious, magnificent ---" (39)

For a change, real moments of fun and comedy occur in a later scene when Cone, jealous and revengeful, tries to persuade Fak to betray Greta and nearly succeeds in doing so. Ann Jellicoe uses the same linguistic devices as in other scenes (especially in the cross-examination which we have mentioned before), namely repetition, elliptical sentences and pronounced rhythm. But for once these devices are put into action not to evoke an atmosphere of danger, fear, or threat, but to create comic effects (40). I think it worthwhile to quote this scene extensively:

"FAK. You mean I could be ...
CONE. You could be.
FAK. King of the Teds!
CONE. King of the Teds!
FAK. King of the Teds!
CONE. (to the audience). Meet the King of the Teds! ...
         The King of the Teds ... who else is as sensatio-
         nal, as strong, as stupid.
FAK. Tony Curtis the second.
CONE. All the fellers who've had a bash. All the fellers
         with cigars and girls and gats.
FAK. King! King! King Fak! I'll put bloody south London
         in fear of Fak - I'll - I'll --
CONE. Look.
FAK. What?
CONE. That.
FAK. Her?
CONE. Get outside.
FAK. I get outside.
CONE. Find one of them.
FAK. I find one of them.
CONE. Tell 'em she's here.
FAK. I tell 'em she's here ... tell them she's here?
CONE. They'll break the place to get her and then they'll
         break her and that'll be that about that.
FAK. I get outside, I find one of them ... I tell him she's
         here ... (his knees knocking) what? ... What?
CONE. What's the matter?
FAK. 'Fraid of what she'll do." (41)

Fak is drawn into Cone's sinister plan and his automatic repetitions show that he is about to surrender to the latter's influence. Cone talks him into believing himself to be a strong man, a "King of the Teds". The anticlimax comes immediately after Fak's imagination has run wild and reached a peak ("I'll - I'll ---"). But he fails to live up to his own fantastic image. During his last summing-up of Cone's instructions the possible consequences are dawning on him: he shrinks back from fear of Greta's counteractions. The reason why this passage has such an amusing effect is that in this case the stylistic means of repetition is used to show a "big man made stupid" (42). The tension of the cross-examination scene, for instance, is relaxed here. It is of a different kind: we wonder whether Fak will be persuaded by Cone or not. In the course of the dialogue Fak loses status. We tend to laugh at people who lose status.

After this passage of a different mood we are back to violence once again. Cone attacks Greta with onomatopoeic words expressing brutality, supported by strong images. He departs in a fury:

> "CONE. ... He'll wreck you! Break! Rip! Crack! Tear! And it'll
> be you! I'll tell Pampinato and he'll destroy you. The sky'll be
> black and purple and the blood'll knot in the veins and it'll be you!
> You! I'll destroy you! I'll destroy earth! I'll destroy everything!
> And it'll be you! You! You! You! You!" (43)

A few minutes later Greta is completely carried away in an exalted moment which makes her appear some sort of super-human force. In an ecstatic speech she sees herself as the centre of the world and as the meeting point of its elemental powers. She provokes Caldaro and nearly suffocates him by her overpowering presence. He loses his nerves and experiences extreme terror and weakness opposite Greta who assumes, in his reaction, fantastic and bestial qualities. Caldaro's speech abounds in contradictory gestic impulses and horrified exclamations:

> "CALDARO. Ah! Down! Down! You're pulling me - an abyss - a
> howling - howling - a pit - a raging emptiness - a waste of howling
> - Ah! Falling! Falling - catch me! Hold me - let me - let me - your
> skin - it feels like scales, like fish scales, your skin is crawling.
> Under my hand - putrefaction! Horror. My hand through your shoulder
> see! To the elbow - rottenness! Find a bone, a clean bone - break it.
> Disperse it. Scavenge. Burn! Burn!" (44)

A few instants later the audience witnesses the extraordinary scene in which Greta gives birth to a child. Even this event is not free from violence: it is introduced with machine-gun fire, and the spectators are kept at bay by Flim. Destruction and creation are in juxtaposition (45). The audience is not only threatened from the stage, but also from the auditorium. The spectators find themselves in the middle of the action, and violence surrounds them:

> "FLIM. ... <u>Calling up into the auditorium</u>. Got 'em covered, Joe?
> VOICE FROM REAR OF STALLS. Yeah boss.
> FLIM. Got 'em covered, Garry?
> VOICE FROM REAR OF DRESS CIRCLE. Yeah boss." (46)

The following stage direction brings this dramatic episode to its end:

> "<u>INFANT cries from behind the sheets</u>. ... <u>The sheet falls to
> reveal GRETA and a small white bundle</u>." (47)

With this "coup de théâtre" the play finishes. The close relationship between actors, stage and audience is maintained to the very last lines when Flim once again turns to the people in the auditorium with a rather rough invitation to leave the theatre. The last impression of the spectators is one of violence: the final tableau with Greta and her baby provides a puzzling and effective contrast (48).

*

" ... I was interested in piling up patterns of sound and releasing them ... ", Ann Jellicoe wrote with regard to The Sport of My Mad Mother (49). She wanted to write a play in which she could use this particular conception of language. After having decided about the stylistic means, she started looking for people "who would talk like this" (50). She found them among London's teddy boys and girls. "I used to wander about and to watch them" (51).

This is a play about a group of young people whose home are the streets and backyards and who are loosely organized under the leadership of Greta, an Australian girl. Caldaro, an American of Italian origin, is established as a counterpoint to the members of the group and is clearly intended to represent the forces of intellect, reason, and helpful understanding. He believes in the good and is not free from sentimentality. The gang, on the other hand, is governed by irrational forces. The play shows the conflict between Caldaro and Greta, who throughout is associated with violence, cruelty and destruction. The battle between these two opposite powers goes on and fluctuates; neither Greta nor Caldaro are able to completely master their respective opponents.

As a motto to her play Ann Jellicoe used the title of a Hindu hymn: "All creation is the sport of my mad mother Kali" (52). Greta seems to correspond to Kali, the Indian goddess of creation and destruction. She is a contradictory character: in the ending of the play, when she gives birth to a child, she becomes "creative" instead of "destructive" and obviously, as the last lines indicate, becomes aware of a new and hitherto unknown task. There is a feeling of an equilibrium gained after a long fight. "In the burlesque extravaganza of the last few moments we may find the clue to her (53) conclusions ... ", wrote George Devine (54). We may. I do not know which clue Devine found for himself. That Greta's elementary wildness and uncontrolled behaviour should suddenly become transformed and perhaps changed by the duties of motherhood seems somewhat pedestrian a conclusion. It is also very hard to decide what the "baby" represents. The only fixed impression is that at least for some moments the conflict between opposite forces is brought to an end.

Apart from this battle Greta-Caldaro the play provides scenes with people who use language in the way Ann Jellicoe describes in the prefaces to her New Version and to her later play Shelley (55). They use this kind of repetitive, rhythmical, ritualistic language to accompany everyday and also extraordinary actions: a tag, a sort of soldier or war game, the application of a permanent wave. They use it in order to attack an enemy force and instinctively take the words at their sound value with the aim of breaking a resistance (cross-examination scene, soldier game).

They use it to give themselves confidence in their own actions, to build a wall of sounds behind which they feel safe. They use it to get rid of accumulated emotion (newspaper scene and I, ii, 192). The repetitions can assume a threatening quality (cross-examination) or result in amusing moments (betrayal scene between Cone and Fak). It is, in short, a language which in its use of rhythm and sound is especially suitable - although it is a stylized language - to express the feelings of people who have difficulties to communicate and to make themselves understood clearly (56). We can experience a similar phenomenon with children, whose repetition of words while for instance playing in the street with other children gives them some sort of self-confidence hard to explain. They trust in the sounds as a protective force. We ourselves tend to repeat words either when we feel insecure, or when we want to insist on something and try to break a person's resistance. As Ann Jellicoe says:

> "This play proceeds by rituals because the insecure and inartic-
> ulate group of people who figure in the play depend on them so
> much." (57)

Both scenes of Act One are alive with these mainly exciting and stimulating speech rhythms. Ann Jellicoe makes an impressive attempt at getting "through to the audience by rhythm, noise and music" (58). In Act Two this rhythmical conception of language is abolished to a considerable extent, with the effect that the grip on the reader's or spectator's emotions is released and his intellectual faculties come into play more and more. And now it appears that, as John Russell Taylor points out, "the play is lost to us" (59). In the first act the reader is held in spite of his bewilderment, but in the second act he is subject to the magic of sounds to a much lesser degree and notices that the statement of the play is much less forceful than before. What with Caldaro's lengthy monologue (60) and the dialogue between the members of the group it starts dragging. As Ann Jellicoe says herself:

> "I have always been dissatisfied with the last act (61) ... It does
> not have these patterns, and it is not well written so it appears
> boring ..." (62)

But on the whole the author has succeeded in presenting impressively the life among a group of homeless teenagers. We experience a kind of basic, raw existence in a place of action which might be any large city - a place of action on which there arises a conflict between the irresponsible, anarchical Greta who is up against all the rules, and the world reformer Caldaro who believes in the victory of the rational over the irrational forces and in friendship among human beings. Around Greta, who as their leader gives them a certain feeling of security in a world full of danger, just because she is so rough, and around the intruder Caldaro revolve Dodo, Fak, Patty and Cone with their outbreaks of violence, their fears, their dreams of security and their longing for warmth (63). "They fall asleep so easy ... they just let go ... they feel safe ..." as Caldaro once says (64): in sleep they are able to forget their anguish and their insecurity. The ending of the play does not bring a solution, but a momentary suspension: we are left to think about the issue ourselves.

Out of strangely fascinating patterns of language there emerges an atmosphere which envelops the life of the group: an atmosphere of violence, fear, insecurity and terror, occasionally flashed through with childlike fun and lighthearted games. This is the feeling that overcomes the reader and spreads among the audience, and it is this feeling that gives us an idea of what the play is about. Ann Jellicoe has transformed her material into a highly theatrical play which demands a new approach from the audience. What is so theatrical about it is the way the author is able to produce moods in a crowd. She succeeded in controlling basic emotions by rhythm and thus by art, and realized her theories in a way which shows her impressive command of theatrical effect.

> "The theatre is a medium which works upon people's imagination
> and emotion - not merely their intellect. And I am trying to use
> every possible effect that the theatre can offer to stir up the au-
> dience - to get at them through their emotions ... I write this
> way because - the image that everybody has of the rational,
> intellectual and intelligent man - I don't believe it's true. I think
> people are driven by their emotions, and by their fears and inse-
> curities." (65)

*

Reading this play one certainly gets the impression that Ann Jellicoe has created something very original, extraordinary and new in drama writing. To a large extent this was also the opinion of the audience and the critics, whether they liked the play or not. Looking for quite a time for examples in English literature where word patterns of this kind and language of a similarly incantatory character would be used, I found some interesting parallels in the lyrical work of Thomas Stearns Eliot (66). One of the most striking resemblances occurs in <u>Sweeney Agonistes</u> where sounds play an equally predominant part:

```
"DORIS:        He is a funny fellow
          He's like a fellow once I knew
          He could make you laugh.
DUSTY:            Sam could make you laugh:
          Sam's all right
DORIS:            But Pereira won't do.
          We can't have Pereira
DUSTY:            Well what you going to do?
TELEPHONE:        Ting a ling ling
                  Ting a ling ling
DUSTY:            That's Pereira
DORIS:  Yes that's Pereira
DUSTY:            Well what you going to do?
TELEPHONE:        Ting a ling ling
                  Ting a ling ling
DUSTY:            That's Pereira" (67)
```

Here an everyday conversation revolving round a person called Pereira and the
ringing of a telephone develop a nervous rhythm which catches the undecidedness of
the two people speaking. The ending is a frightening mixture of laughter and death
which is expressed in sounds denoting the uncanny and the threatening knock at the
door:

> "You dreamt you waked up at seven o'clock and it's foggy
>   and it's damp and it's dawn and it's dark
> And you wait for a knock and the turning of a lock
>   for you know the hangman's waiting for you.
> And perhaps you're alive
> And perhaps you're dead
> Hoo ha ha
> Hoo ha ha
> Hoo
> Hoo
> Hoo
> KNOCK KNOCK KNOCK
> KNOCK KNOCK KNOCK
> KNOCK
> KNOCK
> KNOCK" (68)

The first series of quick knocks and the three final knocks - as the one-word-per-
line-printing shows they occur at greater intervals - drive expectancy and the feeling of danger to their climax. Rhythm and sound combine and create a dense atmosphere of menace.

It is interesting to know that Ann Jellicoe remembers having read <u>Sweeney Ago-
nistes</u> at school and having been fascinated by it as well as by Eliot in general. As
she herself said (69) the poem might have been an influence on her. She is not really conscious of it, however. The comparison indicates at least that the technique
of her play belongs to a certain tradition which also includes characteristics of the
English nonsense poetry, and that her work does not stand in front of us completely
rootless. What she did was to push this style to an extreme. She had the courage to
build up large parts of a play with it. This is her achievement, and this was the
challenge the Royal Court met by presenting <u>The Sport of My Mad Mother.</u>

*

According to the author's stage direction "There is no precise architectural detail
to mark where the stage ends and the auditorium begins" (70). Although the stage
of the comparatively small Royal Court Theatre is separated from the auditorium
by a proscenium arch, there arises no feeling of two isolated rooms sharply cut
off from each other (71). Consequently the author's claim could be fulfilled to a
certain degree, although a completely open stage would have been the ideal place
for the action.

The scenes which for their effect rely on speech rhythms, sound and repetition proved exciting and captivating on the stage. In the "catch me" scene (72) Cone and Fak followed Patty like bees, teasing and echoing her round the stage and thus confusing her. This, as well as the orchestrated "fat Jessie" passage (73) was a new and stirring experience for the audience of 1958, and they could not help being arrested by the author's handling of language.

The "Dolly-Shoo" scene (74) was played with a fine observation of the text. After Cone's and Fak's initial "Dolly"-exclamations the repetitions assumed an automatic quality and became uncontrolled. The actors ejaculated them as if they had taken drugs, with heads shaking and eyes half closed, their bodies intensifying the word "Dolly" (75). When Patty tried to get rid of them by her "shooing", they just switched from the sound "Dolly" to the sound "Shoo". Their means of expression remained the same. The whole scene impressively built up to that final desperate scream of Patty. The scene in which Fak, Cone and Patty pass round Caldaro assaulting him with sounds implying beating and shooting (76) was done in a way which Ann Jellicoe described as "jokey-frightening" (77). The sounds flung at Caldaro became louder and louder, until at their peak they were replaced by the violent physical action when Caldaro is knocked down by Cone. At the Court this was done with a savage drive which shocked part of the audience considerably: they could see exactly how Caldaro received the blow; Patty standing at the left side of the stage, Fak near the centre, Caldaro further right in front of him, with his back towards the audience, and Cone at the extreme right.

In the "newspaper scene" (78) the sounds produced by Dodo, Cone, Fak and Patty had the effect of a spell and resulted in fascinating moments on the stage. The actors enjoyed themselves and imagined themselves a jazz band, as indicated in the stage direction. In the end their dancing round Caldaro was accompanied by accelerating ejaculations as is suggested in the text, and they built up to the breathless exclamations which go with the tearing off of the newspapers.

The beginning of Act One, Scene Two worked well in performance; the actors ran about the stage whooping, the sparklers went up one by one and created an effective atmosphere in the dark auditorium (79).

One of the most expressive scenes in the Court production was the "perm scene" (80). It overpowered the audience to such an extent that they simply could not resist the impact any longer. The action of the permanent wave given to Patty by the members of the group became a real ritual. The chorus with Patty as a leader got into an exciting swing, words were exclaimed in a syncopated way, the scene became more and more riotous, the sounds flooded the audience irresistibly; joy, fun and swinging sound enveloped the action. The last line culminated in the strongly accentuated word "wind". This "perm scene", as Ann Jellicoe said herself, "stopped the show and always proved very effective on the stage" (81). The force of it caught the audience every time. It was one of the moments in which the intentions of the playwright were realized most successfully: to get through to the spectators by rhythm and noise, to make them respond emotionally instead of intellectually

(82). Kenneth Tynan in <u>The Observer</u> was impressed as well:

> " ... the scene where they give their resident doxy a homeperm,
> chanting the instructions on the packet as if they were part of a
> sacred rite - ... unforgettable ... " (83)

The "dressing up and masking scene" (84) introducing the "examination scene" where Greta mixes among the rest of the group, unnoticed, provoked a row between director Ann Jellicoe and co-director George Devine (85). Devine was of the opinion that Greta, who should not be noticed by the group but by the audience, would fail to make any impression on the spectators by her appearance. Ann Jellicoe said she would. She was right. The audience gasped at Dodo's unexpected and horrified discovery that there is a sixth person on the stage all of a sudden. Greta's first entrance, therefore, was rendered most effectively.

The "examination scene" (86) itself worked successfully. Ann Jellicoe thought it one of the most impressive of her production (87). It was frightening, and an atmosphere of menace spread in the auditorium. The feeling that Caldaro was getting trapped, that the interrogation was closing on him grew overwhelming. The fact that Caldaro is caught in the gang's net was forcefully intensified by the way Ann Jellicoe let the actors move. Caldaro stood in the centre of a triangle at the corners of which were Patty, Fak and Cone. Caldaro looked towards Cone. Fak spoke behind him. Caldaro turned round to Fak. Patty crossed in front of Caldaro and so attracted his attention. While Caldaro was looking at Patty, Cone spoke behind him. Caldaro turned towards him, at the same time Fak crossed in front of Caldaro, and the same process was repeated several times. The final confusion of Caldaro and his loss of nerve was in this way carefully prepared by sound and movement.

The outbreak of violence in the scene where Greta beats up Cone was directed with straightforward ferocity (88). It was done "sadistically, brutally, revoltingly" (89). Greta appeared as an indomitable, wild force breaking any resistance within her sight.

The opening of Act Two with the haunting "empty street" ballad (90) was delivered by the actors whispering the words across the partially dark stage lighted only by a single spot, and again the feeling of menace became palpable. The following speech of Cone (91), however, could not sustain the tension created. It did not work with the audience. Nobody was urged to look backwards, nobody seemed to feel any menace in the scruff of their necks. Cone did not succeed in involving the audience to such a degree as to draw the reaction from them which the author intended (92). The subsequent scene with the scared Dodo had a better effect (93).

The calm interlude of Caldaro's lengthy speech while Fak, Cone and Patty are asleep, as a contrast to the foregoing actions, was carefully brought out under the author's direction (94). The "schoolroom scene" (95) with Greta as a teacher following it had a rather perplexing effect with its abrupt change of mood.

The "betrayal scene" (96) between Cone and Fak in its counterplay of suggestion and repetition proved exhilarating and extremely successful on the stage. "The audience laughed and loved it" (97).

The surprise effect when Greta gave birth to her child (98), an event accompanied by machine-gun fire, was considerable. Fak and Patty held the sheet behind which the delivery took place, Flim knelt at the left side holding his banjo, and Caldaro rested on the right. The final attack on the audience from all sides enhanced the puzzlement.

*

The Sport of My Mad Mother is undoubtedly a play making high demands upon the actors' physical and vocal resources. The actors at the Court (Anthony Valentine, Jerry Stovin, Philip Locke, Wendy Craig, Sheila Ballantine, Avril Elgar, Paul Bailey) coped with zest, skill and success with their parts, which, at least for the majority of them, presented new problems. They developed a great sense for the rhythmical qualities of Ann Jellicoe's text. As T.C. Worsley in the New Statesman put it:

> "The play - and this is one of its strengths - gives its young cast
> a very large opportunity for the kind of acting that ordinarily our
> actors get little practice in, the kind of acting which is nearer
> mime, and I very much admired their performances. They used
> their bodies as well as their voices most expressively ..." (99)

Even critics and spectators who disliked the play and rejected it admitted that the acting had been excellent (100).

Wendy Craig gave a brilliant performance as the mysterious Australian girl leader of the gang representing some irrational force. Her appearance was very faithful to the stage direction referring to Greta, although perhaps she "should have been great, heavy and ugly" (101), which was not the case:

> "Her hair is long, straight and red; falling from her brow like
> a Japanese lion wig. Her face is very heavily made up and almost
> dead white ..." (102)

A leather jacket, tight-fitting trousers and boots completed Wendy Craig's outfit. She was most successful in bringing out the basic violence, aggressiveness and self-assurance of Greta. Most of the reviewers reacted positively to her achievement. An exception was Milton Shulman in the Evening Standard, who remained unimpressed:

> "Wendy Craig, looking like Hermione Gingold sucking a lemon,
> might represent universal evil to a barber who had to handle her
> hair - but to no one else ..." (103)

The actress had to acquire an Australian accent for this particular role, which she managed to do with the help of tape recordings. As Ann Jellicoe herself said, Wendy Craig tended to forget this accent during scenes which are very demanding both physically and vocally (104). There exist many contradictory opinions, too, about her success in conveying the atmosphere of threat emanating from Greta. She possessed, however, power and vitality, was very energetic (105), and in her best moments - especially in the scenes connected with movement - she came near to what Patty says of Greta early in the play:

> " ... Greta! ... Like spit on a hot plate that's her. Razzle
> dazzle ..." (106).

Jerry Stovin, as her opponent Caldaro, was chosen for this part by Ann Jellicoe herself, but he was, as she admits, miscast. He was not convincing as a believer in rationality and companionship fighting against dark emotional powers beyond his control. Caldaro should give the impression of a strong intellectuality in order to establish a dramatic conflict between himself and Greta. But Stovin was too soft, too weak and did not have the sort of confidence the part demands. Dressed in sober clothes and wearing a tie he at least formed a strong contrast to Greta and the gang by his outward appearance. The stage direction referring to him reads as follows:

> "Enter CALDARO, a young American. He is 5ft. 10 in. tall and
> weighs 130lb. more or less. He has a big nose and a large,
> sensitively shaped mouth. His eyes are large, brown and luminous
> or small, black and glittering according to his mood. His hair is
> dark. His body, like his mind, is strong, sensitive and supple."
> (107)

In the Court production Jerry Stovin failed to live up completely to these standards.

Flim, the comparatively detached character functioning as a link between stage and auditorium (108) was given life by Anthony Valentine. In the original production he had a Beatles haircut, moustache and wore a bow-tie.

Sheila Ballantine gave a remarkable performance as Patty, "a pretty little cockney girl with a lot of make-up round her eyes" (109). She confronted the audience with a magnificently genuine backstreet teenage-girl: equipped with "jigger-coat, bucket-bag and poppet-beads" (110), she put on stage an image of heartbreaking emptiness mirrored in her looks and her whole behaviour, mixed with vanity and bewilderment. Insecurity, cheekiness and a longing for safety were expressed in her glances, although Kenneth Tynan thought that she "constantly verged on revue Cockney" (111).

Fak was most happily embodied by Philip Locke. He enjoyed himself thoroughly in his part, was the freest of any of the actors and "bounced on and off the stage" (112). He was especially good in conveying a sense of the irresponsibility and violence lurking beneath his sluggish, bragging behaviour. Among his most brilliant scenes was the one in which he is tempted by Cone to betray Greta. As the critic of The Times wrote:

> "Mr. Philip Locke, as the most moronic of the Teddy Boys,
> has one delightful moment of utter fatuity when faced with the
> vision of himself as a 'King of the Underworld'." (113)

Derek Granger in The Financial Times was hit by this actor's smile, which in his opinion was

> "... about the most sinister facial expression since Widmark
> (114) first tried to look pleasant as he pushed an old party down
> the stairs." (115)

Paul Bailey, who acted the difficult part of Cone, the almost tragic figure in Ann Jellicoe's play, did not succeed all the way through. "He was good, but too thin, short and wiry - he should have been physically stronger", as the author expressed it (116). He was often too loud, lacked undertones, and according to Kenneth Tynan, who described him as a "sawn-off parody Brando", "especially needed muting" (117). He was good, however, in those scenes where he tried to attract Greta's attention.

Finally, Avril Elgar was just the right actress to personify Dodo. The stage directions concerning her appearance are striking enough, and her first entrance is a truly effective moment (118). None of the important newspapers really appreciated Avril Elgar's performance. She gave herself up to her strange and disturbing part and had total belief in it. As Ann Jellicoe said, "the best acting is self-effacing, and that was the case with Avril, who is a very sensitive actress" (119).

Looking at all these judgments we can say that from the point of view of the acting the production of The Sport of My Mad Mother must be assessed as outstanding. It was the director's skill and the actors' enthusiasm which transformed the text into a theatrical event, into life on the stage.

*

The Sport of My Mad Mother is a remarkable example of "director's theatre". The text of the play is the raw material which offers fascinating possibilities for a transmutation into vigorous theatre. At the same time it demands great abilities of the director (120).

We are justified in saying that almost the entire responsibility of the play's production rested on Ann Jellicoe's shoulders. As she declared herself, George Devine gave her very much liberty (121). He attended one rehearsal in four, on an average. The same fact is stressed by Devine himself: "Ann Jellicoe has conducted her own rehearsals - I have only guided them ..." (122).

The striking point about this particular production was that the author, in carefully and intelligently realizing her text on the stage, proved to be an extremely dexterous and successful director. This became especially apparent in the many scenes where sound, rhythmical language and movement predominate (123). Ann Jellicoe was able to hold the actors in a firm grip. The result was a play in which the acting reached a high standard (124).

What can be critized is that the author in the part of the director tended to "play out" certain passages (e.g. the scene where Caldaro has his monologue) (125). The second act, as we have noticed before, drove the performance dangerously near boredom and appeared drawn out; responsible for this is the text which does not have the initial tension any more (126). Kenneth Tynan, in his review in The Observer, had a similar experience (127). Ann Jellicoe's dissatisfaction with her second act made itself felt in her direction: its impact on the stage was weaker than the one of the first act (128). On the whole, however, Ann Jellicoe did full justice to her text and created a production in which clever timing, skilful orchestrating of rhythmical word-patterns, sound and rhyme effects combined into a fascinating pandemonium of violence, fear, strange fun and insecurity among a group of young people.

*

The set of the play was designed by the star-designer of the Royal Court, Jocelyn Herbert. It consisted of little else than a metallic pylon with a lamp on top at the right side of the stage, a vast board constructed of metal sheets of a pinky-grey colour and scribbled on by children left from the centre, and black drapings which surrounded the stage. A few stylized props indicating typical shapes and structures existent in any city and a few chairs were dispersed over the almost bare stage. In a corner, at the left end of the stage, there were a kettle-drum, a drum and two cymbals for Flim.

In the first stages of the production Jocelyn Herbert suggested - rightly, as I think - a more real and mysterious set. The group, after all, is looking for safety and protection, and people who feel threatened tend to hide in some dark and secluded place. Ann Jellicoe, however, insisted on a non-realistic set. Jocelyn Herbert gave in. The author had the last word. The range of sketches the designer produced during the rehearsals show this process from the realistic to the abstract impressively. Afterwards, Ann Jellicoe agreed to Jocelyn Herbert's original proposition. This shows in her text of the New Version, where she gives the following stage direction concerning the set:

"Down behind a back street, a protected corner" (129).

As the author herself said: "The set was far too abstract. It should have been more realistic. It was my fault, not the designer's. It should have been dark, enclosing, and protective. The actors should come in from the darkness." (130)

So the set, although inspired by the author, was completely wrong for the atmo-

sphere of the play. There was no fear and no menace behind it, and it did practically nothing to enhance the general effect ot the production (131).

The costumes were better: they suited the individual characters of the group, came
near to the grotesque in the "masking" and "examination" scenes, and had just the
right touch of shabbiness about them.

*

As has already been pointed out earlier in this examination, The Sport of My Mad
Mother was a new and shocking experience for the greater part of the public - although the audiences at the Royal Court had seen unusual productions before. The
reactions of the spectators differed widely, but on the whole it can be said that the
attitude of the majority was negative. This was partly because the play demanded
a new outlook from their side; they had to reform their ideas about theatrical possibilities, and it is a commonplace to say that this is always a slow process. As
Ann Jellicoe said: "I think the audience of 1958 did not know what to make of it -
they had been used to 'message'-plays" (132). Certain scenes, of course, gripped
the audience, as for instance the "perm", the "newspaper" and the "cross-examination" scenes. But on the whole they failed to respond vividly. Obviously Ann
Jellicoe had been too optimistic in thinking that she could "reach the audience directly through rhythm, noise and music" (133). There were quite a lot of people
who walked out in protest during the performance. Others were not impressed at
all by the events on the stage and did not show a flicker of interest. They sat in
polite silence and waited for the final curtain. The people who did not like the play
gave the following reasons: 1. They felt helpless in the face of words used as sounds,
not as conveyors of meaning, 2. They could not make out what the author wanted to
say, 3. They were bored stiff, 4. They were angry because they had expected something else. Most of them were just unable to respond emotionally to the impulses
coming from the stage (134). They had come to the theatre to relax and to have a
nice evening, not to be presented with "acts of violence which burst open like hot-
house flowers" (135) or to be attacked by noise, rhythm and obtrusive actors. They
were confused by the missing continuity, and a scene change like the one in Act II
(136) was just too much for all those who were used to a rational plot development
within a play. What was especially depressing: on the first night empty rows in the
auditorium yawned towards the stage. The reviewer of the Westminster and Pimlico
News (137) made some critical remarks concerning the audience:

> " ... The severest criticism I have to offer must be levelled not
> at the stage but at the audience. On the night of my visit, when
> the curtain went up, there was only a handful of people in the
> auditorium. After the play had started that number doubled, and
> for the first five minutes the lines were lost in the sound of
> creaking floor boards ... muttered apologies, the rustle of
> programmes and the bumping up and down of tie-up seats ..."

The change came two years later, when the play was revived at the Royal Court under the direction of Jane Howell: the audiences had obviously caught up with the "Jellicoe-technique", and the production became a great success.

*

The critics gave The Sport of My Mad Mother a slightly better reception than the audience. The reviews, however, show no great enthusiasm. Nearly all of them are negative to at least a certain extent. Most of them, on the other hand, admit the acting had been good. In reading some of the reviews one gets the impression that their authors had the vague feeling that Ann Jellicoe had given something entirely new and revolutionary to the British theatre.

Harry Weaver in the Daily Herald entitled his article "How I Envied the Walk-Outs", but paid tribute to the actors'achievement (138). R.B. Marriott's response in the weekly theatre-newspaper The Stage was unequivocally negative:

> " ... This effort by Ann Jellicoe is a pale, poor little scramble
> to put Teddy Boy life on the stage ... The production is about as
> boring and pretentious as the play ..." (139)

Most of the reviews are a mixture of appreciation and rejection. Almost all of the reviewers recognized the dramatist's skill in organizing language, and her feeling for rhythm. Here is the critic of The Times:

> " ... Miss Jellicoe, though she is not without skill in working
> arresting rhythms into the basic English of her dialogue, gives
> us a rather gritty evening of expressionism which sheds no
> special illumination on its theme and is not particularly enter-
> taining ..." (140)

We find a similar reaction in the Northern Echo:

> " ... The idiom of the streets is sometimes poetically caught,
> and use is made of mask and movement. It is a theatrically
> effective piece that does not come off at the deeper levels, but
> which introduces a talented writer ..." (141)

It is comforting to see that practically none of the reviewers challenged the theatrical effect of the play. An extract from the Oxford Mail:

> "London's oddest first night for many a month took place this
> week with the presentation of 'The Sport of My Mad Mother'
> at the Royal Court Theatre ... The play was not strong but
> the evening effervesced with clever theatrical ideas ..." (142)

Alan Brien in The Spectator was positively impressed and employed a far-fetched simile to express his opinion:

94

"The production is not at fault. Miss Jellicoe has devised some
ingenious and spectacular methods of keeping her ideas juggling
in the air like Indian clubs. But the clubs are invisible or else
so hollow and light that they go up in the air and are carried off
by the wind." (143)

Under the title "No Story, No Poetry: Just Fizz ..." John Barber in the Daily Express hid his criticism behind his appreciation for the effectiveness of the play on
the stage:

"This new play fizzes on to the stage like a splash of tonic water
(144). It is sharp, it is bright, and it is full of tiny bubbles ...
The author, 30-year-old Ann Jellicoe, catches brilliantly the
quick, disjointed slang and crude violence of these homeless
youngsters ... A pity: The effervescene did not last the whole
drink through." (145)

The critic of The Sunday Times was taken in by the "perm" and the "cross-examination" scenes (146), but at the same time he made reservations:

"These scenes, with their ritual, rhythmic dances, are very
cathartic, but the phantasmagoria which surround them is often
not emotive enough to escape boredom." (147)

A more precise view of the production was given by Derek Granger in The Financial
Times. He acknowledged Ann Jellicoe's grasp of language and rhythm and her attempt at something new and different, appreciated the acting, but did not hold back
his criticism:

"For one act this is not uninteresting stuff, suggesting partly a
series of Method Actors' exercises loosely strung together and
partly a genuine attempt to employ something of an almost
musical or balletic impact in an entertainment confined to words
... her sense of words ... can create a frequent shuddering
effect from the skilful capture of inarticulate speech rhythms.
It is in the second half that this literate reproduction of pullulat-
ing lower life suddenly defeats its own ends; it is here that we
become uneasily aware that Miss Jellicoe is saying everything
and nothing. Leading nowhere and having neither narrative
tension nor character to sustain it, the evening assumes the
daunting aspect of a rather self-indulgent exercise in which the
words seem to have got Miss Jellicoe by the nose and she herself to have lost almost complete control of her own invention.
What emerges is in no sense a play; it is a promising notebook
of jottings in a rather pretentious performance ..." (148)

It is also quite interesting to look at the titles of the different reviews: many of them

betray their authors' perplexity and uneasiness in the face of a stage event which
shook their ideas about the theatre:

> "Slightly lunatic (149) - Odd Play (150) - Mad? Yes, but it's too
> grim for sport (151) - Miss Jellicoe gives us a kick in the Teeth
> (152) - Almost a Highbrow Crazy Show (153) - Obscurity on
> Teenage (154) - Somebody Isn't Using Aristotle! (155)

The reviewer of the Daily Telegraph put it more clearly: A Ballet in Words about
Crazy World (156).

The Sport of My Mad Mother was - as Ann Jellicoe herself said - a critical failure
(157). The critics did not say no explicitly, but their no was stronger than their yes.
Perhaps Richard Buckle caught the mixed feelings of his colleagues when he wrote
in his article for the periodical Plays and Players:

> "It was an effective curtain, coming at the end of a brave
> experiment ..." (158)

There is perhaps some insecurity on the part of the reviewers in all of these statements. Insecurity in front of something new and off the beaten track.

*

Although The Sport of My Mad Mother turned out a commercial disaster and did not
even cover its expenses during its short run of less than a fortnight, it can certainly
be called an artistic success. This production showed the seriousness and the firm
intent of the English Stage Company to realize the basic ideas and aims which had
been put forward on the occasion of its foundation in 1956. As Ann Jellicoe directed
her play herself it can be taken for granted that her idea of the play-in-performance
found the fullest theatrical expression on the stage - with the exception, as we have
pointed out, of the set (159).

With this production the Royal Court Theatre took a real risk in confronting the
theatre-goers with something entirely new, without regard to commercial factors,
but with regard to artistic criteria only. Ann Jellicoe as well as George Devine knew
what was at stake in presenting a play which does not appeal to the mind but to the
basic emotions; which proceeds by rituals and is written to be acted; the dialogue
of which often reminds us of jazz in its rhythms (160), and which therefore was bound
to shock, annoy and even disgust large parts of the audience.

The Court, in taking the decision of staging this play, did at least three important
things: 1. It introduced a new, promising author and director to the theatre, 2. It
offered Ann Jellicoe the chance to develop and extend her dramatic talents, and
3. It gave the British theatre fresh impulses and drew its attention to new theatrical
forms and possibilities which had been little known before. The Royal Court here
fulfilled its noblest task: to give a chance and a start to a new play which the Com-

pany considered valuable. In doing so it diverged from other establishments that would have shrunk back for financial reasons.

It was a loss for the Court financially - but artistically it was a gain. Ann Jellicoe continued writing for the theatre. Four years later, together with Keith Johnstone, she produced her play The Knack at the Court (161). It turned out a success. In 1965 she had a new drama ready for the same stage: Shelley, of The Idealist (162), which she directed herself again. This would hardly have been possible without the early backing of Ann Jellicoe by the English Stage Company and George Devine. The Sport of My Mad Mother, in retrospect, was a necessary and decisive beginning and a success for the courageous policy of the Royal Court.

*

IX JOHN ARDEN: SERJEANT MUSGRAVE'S DANCE

When his first play, The Waters of Babylon, was staged at the Court in October 1957, John Arden was twenty-seven years old. Born in Barnsley, Yorkshire, he had taken to play-writing while reading architecture at the universities of Cambridge and Edinburgh, and his study of two contrasting groups of human beings in Live Like Pigs, presented at the Court under the direction of Anthony Page and George Devine (1) in 1958, had established him as a promising young playwright. Serjeant Musgrave's Dance was the third play by Arden to be produced by the English Stage Company. It was directed by Lindsay Anderson, and the sets were designed by Jocelyn Herbert. The official first night was on October 22nd 1959.

*

In his General Notes at the beginning of the typescript (2) Arden informs the reader in one sentence about the style and character of the play:

> "This play is not realistic, and the events it deals with are not
> a little improbable."

As to the "meaning" of Serjeant Musgrave's Dance the author felt forced to make some introductory remarks in the printed version of the play. I quote this particular passage in full:

> "I do not think that an introductory note is a suitable place for a
> lengthy analysis of the work, but in view of the obvious puzzlement
> with which it was greeted by the critics, perhaps a few points may
> be made. This is not a nihilistic play. This is not (except perhaps
> unconsciously) a symbolist play. Nor does it advocate bloody
> revolution. I have endeavoured to write about the violence that is
> so evident in the world, and to do so through a story that is partly
> one of wishfulfilment. I think that many of us must at some time
> have felt an overpowering urge to match some particularly out-
> rageous piece of violence with an even greater and more outra-
> geous retaliation. Musgrave tries to do this: and the fact that the
> sympathies of the play are clearly with him in his original horror,
> and then turn against him and his intended remedy, seems to have
> bewildered many people. I would suggest, however, that a study
> of the roles of the women, and of Private Attercliffe, should be
> sufficient to remove any doubts as to where the 'moral' of the
> play lies. Accusations of nihilism seem to derive from the scene
> where the Colliers turn away from Musgrave and join in the general
> dance around the beer barrel. Again, I would suggest, that an un-
> willingness to dwell upon unpleasant situations that do not immedi-
> ately concern us is a general human trait, and recognition of it
> need imply neither cynicism nor despair. Complete pacifism is a

very hard doctrine: and if this play appears to advocate it with perhaps some timidity, it is probably because I am naturally a timid man - and also because I know that if I am hit I very easily hit back: and I do not care to preach too confidently what I am not sure I can practise." (3)

This then is John Arden's view of his own text. In the course of this chapter we shall try to come to an evaluation of Serjeant Musgrave's Dance, and we will see how our results link up with the author's opinion. We shall start with an interpretation of what we think are the most significant scenes of the play, and then compare the text with Lindsay Anderson's production (4).

*

The play opens with three soldiers, Hurst, Attercliffe and Sparky, waiting at a canal wharf. It is a cold, snowy winter evening. Hurst and Attercliffe play cards on top of a drum. Sparky stands nearby on guard, talking and singing. They wait for their sergeant, "Black Jack Musgrave" (5). Already one of their first talks contains a lot of interesting information for the careful reader:

> "ATTERCLIFFE. He'll come on the stroke, as he said. He works his life to bugle and drum, this serjeant. You ever seen him late?
> SPARKY. No. (He sings):
>> When first I deserted I thought myself free
>> Till my cruel sweetheart informed upon me -
> ATTERCLIFFE (sharply). I don't think you ought to sing that one.
> SPARKY. Why not? It's true, isn't it? (He sings):
>> Court martial, court martial, they held upon me
>> And the sentence they passed was the high gallows tree.
> HURST (dropping cards and springing up in a rage). Now shut it, will you! God-damned devil of a song to sing on this sort of a journey!" (6)

According to Attercliffe Musgrave seems to be a man of strict military discipline. The song Sparky starts immediately afterwards provokes a violent reaction on Attercliffe's part, and makes us wonder whether the word "deserted" has anything to do with the three soldiers, especially after Sparky's question "Why not? It's true, isn't it?" and his defiant resumption of the song, which results in an even more furious outbreak by Hurst. All three of them are in some kind of nervous tension, and things become even more mysterious in the following passage:

> "SPARKY (a little wildly). Steady yourself, you crumbling old cuckold. He might laugh, who knows? Well, make a rattling any road. Mightn't he, soldier boy?
> HURST. Are you coming funny wi'me -
> SPARKY. Funny? About him? You don't tell me he don't know what we're at. Why shouldn't he have a laugh at it, if that's how

he feels?

HURST. Arrh, you're talking daft.

SPARKY. Now don't you be nervous, boy: not for you to be nervous.
You're a man and a soldier! Or an old red rag stretched over four
pair o' bones - well, what's the odds? Eh?" (7)

Sparky, gesturing towards the wooden boxes the soldiers have brought with them,
hints at somebody who "might laugh" or "make a rattling". His conclusion that he
does not see any difference between a soldier and "an old red rag stretched over
four pair o' bones" leaves us puzzled: does he refer to something in the boxes? What
is it? But now the bargee and Musgrave enter, and they all prepare for leaving on
a boat along the canal, to the near coal-mining town. From the bargee's answer to
Musgrave's question as to the weather, we can guess for the first time a reason for
the soldiers' arrival in a place that is being slowly closed in by winter: they have
obviously come recruiting. When the bargee warns Musgrave of the hard life and the
wants they are likely to encounter in the town, the sergeant cuts him short in a way
which shows him as a stern military man whose life is insolubly connected with
duty:

> "MUSGRAVE (curtly). It's not material. We have our duty. A
> soldier's duty is a soldier's life.
> BARGEE. Ah, duty.
> > The Empire wars are far away
> > For duty's sake we sail away
> > Me arms and legs is shot away
> > And all for the wink of a shilling and a drink ... " (8)

The bargee reacts in a half serious, half mocking manner: in four rhyming lines he
confronts us with a bitter afterthought about the possible consequences of duty, which
in a way also implies the futility of war in general.

The second scene of Act One opens in the bar of a public house in the mining town.
From the dialogue between Mrs. Hitchcock. the landlady, and the parson we hear
some indistinct remarks about a strike going on in the mines. The bargee confirms
this when he enters, and informs the parson of the news:

> "BARGEE (significantly). Four on 'em, Parson. Soldiers.
> ...
> PARSON (in some alarm). Soldiers! Already? Who sent for them?
> Why was I not told? This could be very dangerous-
> BARGEE. They're not here for what you think, you know. Not yet,
> any road. You see, they've come recruiting. ...
> BARGEE. You're a power, you are: in a town of trouble, in a
> place of danger. Yes. You're the word and the book, aren't you?
> Well then: soldiers. Recruiting. Useful?" (9)

Here he proves to be a sly, plotting fellow who treats the self-conceited parson with

a strange mixture of respect and irony. His three final dry words with their implications make it clear that in the recruiting soldiers he sees a chance for the "town
of trouble".

Now that the idea of the soldiers' coming has caught hold of the bargee and Mrs.
Hitchcock, they suggest that Annie, who works as a serving girl in the pub, should
tell them "what soldiers is good for" (10). After some hesitation she does so:

> "ANNIE. I'll tell you for what a soldier's good:
>   To march behind his roaring drum,
>   Shout to us all: 'Here I come
>   I've killed as many as I could -
>   I'm stamping into your fat town
>   From the war and to the war
>   And every girl can be my whore
>   Just watch me lay them squealing down.
>   And that's what he does and so do we.
>   Because we know he'll soon be dead
>   We strap our arms round the scarlet red
>   Then send him weeping over the sea. ..." (11)

Annie's surprising change-over into a ballad-like rhyme indicates that her emotions
are so directly appealed to that she is constrained to express herself in verse (12).
On the other hand her experiences with soldiers - which she obviously has had, as
she switches from "them" to "we" in the ninth line, and thus identifies herself with
the girls that are laid "squealing down" - were apparently so similar to each other
that this kind of summary does justice to all of them. Out of her lines speaks a sort
of desperate resignation about the destiny of the soldiers, which in a way links up
with what the bargee says about duty earlier on (13). The absurdity of war shines
through again.

Somewhat later Musgrave is told about the strike in the colliery by Mrs. Hitchcock
(14), and soon afterwards the mayor enters, developing his plans in front of the
parson:

> "MAYOR (looking at him sideways). I think we'll use 'em, Parson.
> Temporary expedient, but it'll do. The price of coal has fell, I've
> had to cut me wages, I've had to turn men off. They say they'll
> strike, so I close me gates. We can't live like that for ever. There's
> two ways to solve this colliery - one is to build the railway here and
> cut me costs of haulage, that takes two years and an Act of Parliament,
> though God knows I want to do it. The other is clear out half the popu-
> lation, stir up a diversion, turn their minds to summat else. The
> Queen's got wars, she's got rebellions. Over the sea. All right. Beat
> these fellers' drums high around the town, I'll put one pound down for
> every Royal Shilling the serjeant pays. Red coats and flags. Get rid
> o' the troublemakers. Drums and fifes and glory." (15)

To the mayor the arrival of the soldiers appears very convenient: for him it is a cheap way out of his difficulties. The hard rhythm of his sentences suits the dryness of his calculations. He hides his selfish motives behind a patriotic mask and stresses the glorious aspect of war: "drums and fifes and glory" cover up the dirty realities. The recruiting campaign offers a good chance to get rid of irksome people. The mayor encourages Musgrave to recruit the "best lads" (16) and even goes as far as to propose a list of possibly willing men. The parson has different worries about the stay of the soldiers in his parish, and from Musgrave's answer we see what the latter considers himself to be:

> "PARSON. I want no drunkenness, and no fornication, from your
> soldiers. Need I speak plainer?
> MUSGRAVE. No, sir. There will be none. I am a religious man."
> (17)

Shortly afterwards Annie, scrutinizing Musgrave's face, gives her opinion about him in a four line ballad stanza, and through her eyes, for the first time, we come to see the sergeant differently. Musgrave's reaction to Annie's judgment is somewhat puzzling:

> "ANNIE.   The North Wind in a pair of millstones
>   Was your father and your mother
>   They got you in a cold grinding.
>   God help us all if they get you a brother.
> She looks at him another minute, then nods her head
> and goes out.
> MUSGRAVE (wryly). She talks a kind of truth, that lassie.
> Is she daft?" (18)

In the following conversation between Musgrave and the landlady there is all of a sudden a connection established between the soldiers and the two women in the public house. The sergeant mentions a comrade he once had who was from this very town, and his recollection of the name produces a strange commotion on Mrs. Hitchcock's side:

> "MUSGRAVE. Tell me, ma'am. It sticks on my mind that I once
> had a sort of a comrade came from this town. ... Long, yellow-
> haired lad ... Name of, oh, Hickson, was it, Hickman?
> MRS. HITCHCOCK (astonished and disturbed). Ey, ey -
> MUSGRAVE. What was it now, his name - Billy - Billy -
> MRS. HITCHCOCK (very upset). Billy Hicks, Hicks. Aye, oh,
> strange, serjeant, strange roads bringing you along, I'd not
> wonder." (19)

She informs the sergeant about a fact which sheds some light on Annie's attitude towards soldiers and explains to a certain extent her ballad about their relation with girls, and with Annie in particular. Her relations with Billy Hicks and their consequences seem to have brought about her obvious disillusion:

> "MRS. HITCHCOCK ... He gave her a baby, and he went straight
> off to the war. Or the rebellions, they called it. They told us he
> was killed.
> MUSGRAVE (without emotion). Aye, he was killed. He was shot
> dead last year ... Gave a baby to who?
> MRS. HITCHCOCK (jerks her thumb to door behind bar). Her." (20)

So the two groups, the soldiers and the inhabitants of the town - more precisely
Mrs. Hitchcock and Annie - have come into a strange contact. The dead Billy Hicks
is the link that connects two different kinds of people by means of a shared experience.

Scene three of the first act is set in the churchyard of the town. The three privates,
having been sent on a tour by their sergeant, meet with Musgrave and tell of the
observations they have made while walking through the town. The result is not encouraging. The whole community seems to have formed a conspiracy against the
military intruders: they move in an atmosphere of hostility, which is mirrored in
the soldiers' hard, chopped-off sentences expressing sharply seen details, similar
to photographic snapshots. Their reports sound almost identical:

> "ATTERCLIFFE. Hardly a thing. Street empty, doors locked,
> windows blind, shops cold and empty. A young lass calls her
> kids in from playing in the dirt - she sees me coming, so she
> calls 'em. There's someone throws a stone. -
> ...
> SPARKY. Hardly a thing. Street empty, no chimney's smoking,
> no horses, yesterday's horsedung frozen on the road. Three men
> at a corner-post, four men leaning on a wall. No words: but
> some chalked up on a closed door - they said: 'Soldiers go home'."
> (21)

The sense of being surrounded by hostile inhabitants brings about a crisis in Hurst:
he loses his nerves and demands an account of Musgrave's plans. Here we get the
explanation why Hurst, at the beginning of the play, reacted so violently to Sparky's
song, in which the word "deserted" occurs (22): from him we learn that the four
soldiers are in fact "on the run":

> "HURST (breaking out suddenly). Appropriate? Serjeant, now we've
> come with you so far. And every day we're in great danger. We're
> on the run, in red uniforms, in a black-and-white coalfield; and it's
> cold; and the money's running out that you stole from the Company
> office; and we don't know who's heard of us or how much they've
> heard. Isn't it time you brought out clear just what you've got in
> mind?" (23)

We also learn that Musgrave has stolen money, and what is most important: Hurst's final question shows that the soldiers do not know themselves what their actual purpose in the town is. Obviously they have not come for recruiting, or at least not only for recruiting. In his answer Musgrave confirms the desertion and gives further particulars, from which it appears that Hurst killed an officer. But we do not know anything about the reasons, about the events that led up to these actions, or about the soldiers' intentions in the town. These intentions are a little more clearly outlined in the ensuing dialogue between Musgrave and Hurst: the sergeant apparently considers himself and his men as the bearers of a message which should be delivered to the people - a message coming from God:

> "MUSGRAVE. ... because my power's the power of God, and
> that's what's brought me here and all three of you with me ...
> ...
> HURST (browbeaten into incoherence). ... It's nowt to do wi'
> God. I don't understand all that about God, why d'you bring God
> into it! You've come here to tell the people and then there'd
> be no more war -
> MUSGRAVE (taking him up with passionate affirmation). Which
> is the word of God! Our message without God is a bad belch and
> a hiccup. You three of you, without me, are a bad belch and a
> hiccup ... You don't understand about God! But you think, your-
> self, you alone, stupid, without a gill of discipline, illiterate,
> ignorant of the Scriptures - you think you can make a whole
> town, a whole nation, understand the cruelty and greed of armies,
> what it means, and how to punish it!" (24)

They have come to tell the people something decisive about war, to make them "understand the cruelty and greed of armies ... and how to punish it". In any case, Musgrave's statement suits a reformer rather than a soldier who has come to a town to beat up recruits.

In the meantime the colliers still think that the four soldiers have come in order to break their strike, and they do not hide their hatred when they meet them in the graveyard. Musgrave remains quiet, and from him we get some more precise facts as to their desertion and their arrival in the town:

> "MUSGRAVE. ... 'Cos all that we know now is that we've had to
> leave behind us a colonial war that is a war of sin and unjust blood.
> ... This is particular - one night's work in the streets of one city,
> and it damned all four of us and the war it was part of. We're each
> one guilty of particular blood. We've come to this town to work that
> guilt back to where it began. " (25)

To tell from the sergeant's speech they deserted because they did not agree with that war any more. The "one night's work in the streets of one city" probably refers to some atrocity committed by the soldiers (the murder by Hurst has already been mentioned), which has left them with a feeling of guilt. Musgrave's final sentence explaining the reason of their coming to this town appears rather obscure. But the following passages which are dominated by lengthy speeches of Musgrave reveal a new outlook and confirm that the sergeant sees himself in the role of a herald (26):

> "MUSGRAVE. ... take count of the corruption, then stand before
> this people with our white shining word, and let it dance! ... This
> town is ours, it's ready for us: and its people, when they've heard
> us, and the Word of God, crying the murders that we've done - I'll
> tell you they'll turn to us, and they'll turn against that war!" (27)

We become aware of the missionary zeal in Musgrave's words, which has something uncanny about it. He apparently wants to convert the townspeople into enemies of war. His sentences sound rather self-confident and presumptuous. The word "dance" from the title of the play appears for the first time. A few instants later Musgrave's exaltation even increases: he regards himself and his three men as the direct instruments of God, selected by Him to show the people the way out of inhuman deeds:

> "MUSGRAVE (with angry articulation). We are here with a word.
> That's all. That's particular. Let the word dance. That's all
> that's material, this day and for the next. What happens afterwards,
> the Lord God will provide. I am with you, He said. Abide with Me
> in Power. A Pillar of Flame before the people. What we show here'll
> lead forward forever, against dishonour, and greed, and murder-for-
> greed! There is our duty, the new, deserter's duty: God's dance on
> this earth: and all that we are is His four strong legs to dance it ..."
> (28)

The scene and with it the first act ends with Musgrave praying to God. His prayer shows that he has definitely come to the town as a judge, and that his judgment will be exercised by means of a dance:

> "MUSGRAVE. ... My prayer is: keep my mind clear so I can weigh
> Judgement against the Mercy and Judgement against the Blood, and
> make this Dance as terrible as You have put it into my brain. The
> Word alone is terrible: the Deed must be worse. But I know it is
> Your Logic, and You will provide." (29)

After this first act we know that the soldiers have come to the mining town with an extraordinary purpose. From all we have heard up to now we may assume that they have a message for the people concerning war, and that they want "to work that guilt back to where it began" (30). But we are still not clear about their intentions. Neither are we about Musgrave's scintillating character.

During a lengthy scene in the pub the soldiers succeed in establishing a friendlier contact with the colliers by means of singing and free drinks. Annie makes advances to Hurst, and the constable is attacked by the pugnacious collier. Sparky drops another remark about "rattling, clattering, old bones in a box" (31) and mentions the name Billy (which can only refer to Billy Hicks). At the end of the scene Musgrave warns Annie not to distract his men. Once more he stresses that he is "a religious man" (32), but his statement about duty being destroyed by love has an inhuman ring about it, and points to a character whose sense of duty has become an obsession. Annie does not pay attention to his words. In the following scene in the stable she visits Hurst, looking for a little love and warmth. But he, without a clear reason, dismisses her despite her entreaties. Attercliffe turns her away for equally obscure motives (33), and from his words we learn that Sparky's former allusions (34) were based upon truth and that he has been made a cuckold by his wife. At last Sparky starts speaking to Annie. We become conscious that he is frightened, and that he has "his laugh ... because or else he might well howl" (35). In the meantime Musgrave, sleeping in his brass-bed upstairs, is caught up in a telling dream, while Annie recalls her dead lover Billy:

> "MUSGRAVE (<u>in clear categorical tones, though in his sleep</u>).
> Twenty-five men. Nine women. Twenty-five men. No children.
> No.
> ANNIE (<u>in a sudden uprush</u>). Look, boy, there was a time I had
> a soldier, he made jokes, he sang songs and all - ah, <u>he</u> lived
> yes-sarnt no-sarnt three-bags-full-serjeant, but he called it
> one damned joke. God damn you, he was killed!" (36)

She draws parallels between Sparky and Hicks, who appears to have been a similar character. Her outbreak shows her desperation: since Billy's death she has lost her balance. At the same time Musgrave's nightmare - which must have its cause in the actions carried out during the war he deserted from - approaches its climax:

> "MUSGRAVE. Be quiet. Twenty ... Eighteen ... I'm on duty,
> woman. I'm timing the end of the world. Ten more seconds, sir
> ... Five ... three ... two ... one.
> <u>He lets out a great cry of agony and falls back on the</u>
> <u>bed.</u>" (37)

His exaggerated sense for order, obedience and duty equals everything contrary to these notions with the end of the world. As an answer to Mrs. Hitchcock's soothing words he goes on talking about that final catastrophe, which he would like to encounter "... in control; I mean, numbers and order ..." (38). Apparently already as a young soldier he had been different from the others, cut off from them by some particular quality, which might have been this very obsession with order, logic, duty and numbers (39).

While these events take place in the upstairs room, Sparky decides to free himself from the grip of Musgrave and their strange mission and agrees with Annie to run away with her - "Your life and my life - make our <u>own</u> road, we don't follow nobody" (40). But Hurst overhears their conversation and accuses Sparky of cowardice and desertion. The ensuing struggle comes to a bloody close: Sparky is stabbed accidentally (41). His death occurs surprisingly and unexpectedly (42). Attercliffe is left with the bayonet in his hand; Musgrave, who joins his men in the stable, shows no great emotion and gives orders to bury the body. Annie has nearly gone out of her mind after another death which destroys something that has not even begun. But the excitement is not yet over. Sparky has hardly been carried out when Walsh, one of the colliers, is led in by Attercliffe and Hurst: together with some of his fellow-colliers he has tried to break into the coach-house where the soldiers have locked up their baggage and weapons. For some reason Musgrave hides him in a woodshed before the Constable enters, on the evidence that they "was brothers" (43). And now things start moving with the following announcement of the mayor:

> "MAYOR. The telegraph's working.
> MUSGRAVE. The telegraph!
> MAYOR. Aye, there's a thaw begun. Thank God for that:
> they've mended the broken wire on top of the moor. So I
> sent word for the Dragoons. They'll come as fast as they
> can, but not afore twelve I shouldn't think, so we've got
> to hold this town!
> MUSGRAVE. Six hours, thereabouts. Keep 'em quiet now,
> they may bide. Mr. Mayor, I'll do it for you.
> MAYOR. How?
> MUSGRAVE. I'll do what I'm paid for: start a recruiting-
> meeting. Look, we had 'em last night as merry as Christ-
> mas in here, why not this morning? Flags, drums, shillings,
> sovereigns - hey, start the drum! Top o' the market-place,
> make a jolly speech to 'em!" (44)

The isolation of the town by the snow is broken. A contact to the outside world has been re-established. The mayor has already called in troops in order to suppress the threatening riots of the colliers. And whatever Musgrave is up to, he decides to act as well. Six hours are left before the Dragoons arrive. After all the talk about recruiting he is all of a sudden in a hurry to hold an official meeting - help-ful, as it seems, to the mayor whose problem consists in keeping the people under control until the Dragoons reach the town.

When the curtain opens on Act Three the meeting in the market-square is already in progress (45). Against a background of noise and colour, against the rolls of the drum and the display of the flags the mayor and the parson make their introductory, incisive speeches to convince the men to enlist. Every trick is played by the speak-ers to achieve their aim. The mayor tries to bribe them with money. The parson's speech shows him to be an especially fine example of the type of clergyman who would tear any biblical phrase out of its context if it serves his purpose. Common-place statements and empty drivel combine:

> "PARSON. 'And Jesus said, I come not to bring peace but a
> sword.' ... Therefore, I say, therefore: when called to

shoulder our country's burdens we should do it with a glancing eye
and a leaping heart, to draw the sword with gladness, thinking
nothing of our petty differences and grievances - but all united
under one brave flag, going forth in Christian resolution, and
showing a manly spirit! The Empire calls! Greatness is at hand!
Serjeant Musgrave will take down the names of any men willing,
if you'll file on to the platform in an orderly fashion, in the name
of the Father, the Son and mumble mumble mumble ..." (46)

Arden here shoots very ironical arrows at both the mayor and the parson, who
represent the political and the clerical power by which the people in the town are
governed. But now Musgrave gets the scene under his command. With his speech
about the army he seems to start a real propaganda campaign: he explains the
composition and the working of guns with an uncanny, cold accuracy. But slowly
emotional overtones creep in: when he explains about the Gatling gun his attitude
changes. As before, we become aware of a frightening quality in Musgrave's character. His speech about duty, supported by Attercliffe, who keeps the people in the
market-square covered with the Gatling, and by Hurst, who beats the drum, comes
to its strange and menacing climax. All of a sudden the mystery of the box, which
has been alluded to several times earlier in the play, is solved. All the dark hints
as to its possible contents are justified in the following action:

"MUSGRAVE (at the top of his passion). ... I'm Black Jack Musgrave, me, the hardest serjeant of the line - I work my life to
bugle and drum, for eighteen years I fought for one flag only ...
Look - I'll show it to you all. And I'll dance for you beneath it
- hoist up the flag, boy - up, up, up!
    ATTERCLIFFE has nipped up the ladder, holding the
rope. He loops the rope over the cross-bar of the lamp-bracket,
drops to the plinth again, flings open the lid of the big box, and
hauls on the rope.
HURST beats frantically on his drum. The rope is attached to
the contents of the box, and these are jerked up to the cross-bar
and reveal themselves as an articulated skeleton dressed in a
soldier's tunic and trousers, the rope noosed round the neck.
The PEOPLE draw back in horror. MUSGRAVE begins to dance,
waving his rifle, his face contorted with demoniac fury." (47)

This shocking development makes clear, as we have suspected before, that this
meeting has not anything to do with a recruiting campaign any more. Musgrave
wants to teach the people a lesson they will never forget, and his compulsive dance
under the skeleton indicates that he has to get rid of an enormous inner tension. He
is forced into the dance by some obsession. He wants to express something which
he cannot formulate. Cool reasoning and explanation do not suffice; he has to rely
on the more forceful impact of movement and song:

"MUSGRAVE (as he dances, sings, with mounting emphasis).
Up he goes and no one knows
How to bring him downwards
Dead man's feet
Over the street
Riding the roofs
And crying down your chimneys
... (48)

We still do not know what message exactly Musgrave in his fury, wants to deliver
to his terrified audience. At last the sergeant is ready to make a declaration. He
tells how the soldier now hanging before them as a skeleton had been shot in the
back by snipers on his way back from the opera, and how as a grim reprisal five
people in that town were killed by the revengeful troops, because, as they failed
to find the killers, they considered everybody responsible for the death of their
comrade. The announcement that the skeleton was once Billy Hicks, a local boy,
comes as a shock to the citizens - less to the reader, who has been sufficiently
prepared as to this fact. In a following passage Musgrave expresses his ideas
about the irresistible escalation of physical violence, and he accuses his audience
of favouring the vicious circle despite the warnings they have received:

"MUSGRAVE. ... Now as I understand the workings of God,
through greed and the world, this man didn't die because he
went alone to the opera, he was killed because he had to be -
it being decided; that now the people in that city was worked
right up to killing soldiers, then more and more soldiers
should be sent for them to kill, and the soldiers in turn should
kill the people in that city, more and more, always - that's
what I said to you: four men. one girl, then the twenty-five
and the nine - and it'll go on, there or elsewhere, and it can't
be stopped neither, except there's someone finds out Logic
and brings the wheel round ... You've had Moses and the
Prophets - that's him - (he points at Walsh) - 'cos he told you.
But you were all for enlisting, it'd still have gone on. Moses
and the Prophets, what good did they do?
He sits down and broods. There is a pause. " (49)

In his last sentences he alludes to the inefficacy of the prophets, and reminds the
people of Walsh's attempt to draw their attention to the nonsense of enlisting (50).
And then he comes to his awful conclusion concerning the punitive action following
Billy Hicks's murder. His proposition is terrifying in its cruel simplicity:

"MUSGRAVE (as though to himself). One man, and for him five.
Therefore, for five of them we multiply out, and we find it five-
and-twenty ... So, as I understand Logic and Logic to me is the
mechanism of God - that means that today there's twenty-five
persons will have to be -

In this passage we become fully aware of Musgrave's state of mind. Obviously his intellect and his judgment have been disturbed by the horrible events he and his men have witnessed. He thinks logic the mechanism of God, and himself the executioner of the will of God, but his logic moves on an insane level. He argues with an almost mad logical consistency, and there is evidence in the text that the soldiers' experiences before they came to the town have driven them to the brink of madness (52). Musgrave is apparently of the opinion that his message can only be impressed on the citizens forcefully enough by a further outrageous deed: in order to make them aware of the terror of war, blood and killing he advocates further killing. He offers to start execution with the mayor, the parson and the constable, who have all three supported and encouraged the enlisting and thus made possible further atrocities. But Attercliffe and Walsh refuse to join him in his wild crusade. Musgrave loses his command and Hurst, in a last desperate attempt, tries to convince the colliers of the necessity of eliminating people like the mayor, the parson and the constable, because " ... if you let 'em be, then us three'll be killed - aye and worse, we'll be forgotten - and the whole bloody lot'll start all over again!" (52 a) But Annie, who is only able to repeat her sad story about her Billy, turns the colliers against the soldiers once more with her report about Sparky's death. Hurst, who loses all control, threatens to open fire on the crowd but is prevented by Attercliffe and Musgrave. When he tries to run away he is hit by a bullet fired by the dragoons, who are arriving at this moment. Musgrave and Attercliffe are arrested for robbery and desertion.

> "OFFICER. The winter's broken up. Let normal life begin again.
> BARGEE. Aye, aye, begin again!
> He is handing the mugs to the people. He starts singing,
> and they all join in, by degrees.
>> There was an old man called Michael Finnegan
>> He had whiskers on his chin-egan
>> The wind came out and blew them in agen
>> Poor old Michael Finnegan -
>> Begin agen - ... " (53)

The dance in which they all join clearly signifies that they are subordinating themselves to the fixed, controlled movement of re-established law and order. It is not the personal, emotional dance of an individual that tries to articulate an internal obsession, like Musgrave's, but the uniforming, equalizing form of a dance. Free movement has been reduced to controlled movement. "Normal life" begins again, people return from the brink of disaster and start forgetting; everything is the same as before. Walsh, too, the most intelligent of the colliers, joins in the dance, but reluctantly, with a feeling of bitterness and impotence (54).

The process of thinking, which has set in during Musgrave's terrifying demonstration in the market-square, is quickly abolished again by the people (55). Musgrave has tried to show something with the wrong means and has not achieved anything.

Annie, with Billy's skeleton on her lap, sits among the dancing men, a living accusation in her suffering, which has been brought about by human beings who will never learn.

Act III, ii, in a confrontation of Musgrave, Attercliffe and Mrs. Hitchcock, puts the sergeant's procedure into the right perspective:

> "MRS. HITCHCOCK. ... It's time you learnt your life, you big
> proud serjeant. Listen: last evening you told all about this anarchy
> and where it came from - like, scribble all over with life or love,
> and that makes anarchy. Right? ... Then use your Logic - if you
> can. Look at it this road: here we are, and we'd got life and love.
> Then you came in and you did your scribbling where nobody asked
> you. Aye, it's arsy-versey to what you said, but it's still an anar-
> chy, isn't it? And it's all your work ... But you brought in a dif-
> ferent war.
> MUSGRAVE. I brought it in to end it.
> ATTERCLIFFE. To end it by its own rules: no bloody good. She's
> right, you're wrong. You can't cure the pox by further whoring ... "
> (56)

Mrs. Hitchcock makes clear that it was Musgrave, in his fanatical missionary zeal, who brought anarchy and war into a community. His idea of teaching the people a lesson about the futility of war and violence, good in itself, has been destroyed by his ruthless method. As Attercliffe says: "You can't cure the pox by further whoring" (57). Atrocities cannot be stopped by committing further atrocities.

*

With Serjeant Musgrave's Dance John Arden has written a play containing plenty of material for discussion. The author himself felt that the play caused some puzzle-ment amont the critics and the audiences; as in his earlier plays, The Waters of Babylon and Live Like Pigs, he invited widely divergent interpretations because he did not take sides. As a consequence, in the Methuen paperback edition, he provid-ed a short guide to the meaning of the play (58), the principal points of which agree with our own interpretation.

We can certainly recognize again Arden's aversion to taking sides: the play does not "advocate bloody revolution" (59), but it does not advocate "complete pacifism" (60) either. For Arden the problem is much too complex for a clear-cut and simple solution (61). Set in a town cut off from the rest of the world by winter, Serjeant Musgrave's Dance is a play about the constant presence of violence (62), about its escalation and about an individual's attempt to make his fellow-creatures aware of this fact (63). But Musgrave's mission is doomed to failure because he allows him-self to be carried away by his fanaticism and wants to erase violence by further violence, and because the people fail to see the point he is eager to prove and re-fuse to learn their lesson. Musgrave's desperation may be excused by the slaugther and cruelty he has been forced to witness before he came to the town, but by his twisted conception of the "logic of God" he draws the wrong conclusions. Musgrave and his men are on the brink of madness because of what they have lived through, but it would be too simple to say that the sergeant is just a madman. Despite his feverish determination to accomplish the task he has set himself, despite his repeated references to logic, there is a nagging doubt deep in Musgrave. This is why he takes such a long time to stage his decisive meeting. Only in the final scene in the market-square is he able to approach his real subject: he works himself up, and when his excitement reaches the climax he goes off into the dance which gives the play its title. This dance has to be seen predominantly in relation to Musgrave himself. He is locked up in himself, and the dance is his attempt to break out and to transfer the cause of his inner pressure onto his audience, to externalize his emotions. Musgrave's tragedy is that he does not find a means of establishing a contact, and that at the end of the play, when the dragoons arrest him, he has not achieved anything. The people prefer to return to their former condition, to live under the same corrupt authorities. They are afraid of thinking about the deeper implications of Musgrave's action; they refuse to draw conclusions from what they see and hear during the meeting. They start forgetting the events in the market-square as soon as the dragoons are in command of the situation; they content themselves with considering the whole affair as a "bad bad dream" (64) and are glad to be rid of the responsibility of using their brains. War, violence and cruelty will continue.

And people like Annie, Mrs. Hitchcock, and Private Attercliffe will go on suffering. Annie, who loses her lover in the war, whose life becomes empty, who turns into a prostitute because she does not see any sense in life any more, cannot get out of her hopeless existence. When her slowly developing love for Sparky promises a new life to her, he is killed in a stupid fight, without any compelling reason. In the end, when she is sitting on the stage with Billy's skeleton on her knees, not understanding but suffering, she becomes a tragic figure. Mrs. Hitchcock, the landlady, has lost her belief in the people of the town and has become hard, bitter and scornful, but her reactions in some scenes show that her bitterness is the protection of a compassionate soul.

Attercliffe is the man turned soldier because of the breaking up of his love and marriage; he is totally unfit for the military profession, which he has taken up without thinking of the atrocities involved. He is tormented by the fact that he has killed a girl during a riot and completely shattered by his guilt in the death of Sparky, whose murder he tried to prevent. He is pushed into crime through no fault of his, by a strange concatenation of incidents. Significantly enough, Arden provides him with the final passage of the play - a simple song in which Attercliffe sadly expresses his personal tragedy. Of comparable importance and revealing force is the ballad allotted to Annie in I, ii (65): here the whole idiocy of war is exposed and the real theme of the play concentrated. " ... a study of the roles of the women, and of Private Attercliffe, should be sufficient to remove any doubts as to where the 'moral' of the play lies ...", as Arden said in his Introduction (66). To call it a nihilistic play is definitely absurd.

<u>Serjeant Musgrave's Dance</u> is an impressive drama about the impossibility of stopping cruelty and violence among human beings, which have their cause in the fact that those who are preaching against violence try to achieve their ends by the very methods they condemn, and in the fact that people's stupidity prevents them from grasping the truth about the nature of violence. Arden formulates this predicament: "I think that many of us must at some time have felt an overpowering urge to match some particularly outrageous piece of violence with an even greater and more outrageous retaliation" (67). This is what Musgrave attempts to do. It is perhaps understandable. But it secures the survival of what he stands up against.

Arden's play is not a fast moving one. It builds up very slowly to its climax in the market-square scene. Structurally it cannot be called perfect (68). Ronald Hayman's remark concerning the scene with the dance appears justified to me:

> "Musgrave knows that the Grenadiers are coming, but he still
> hasn't done anything by the time they arrive. This indecision
> could itself have made very good dramatic material if only it
> were shown up as such, but it never comes into focus properly.
> Arden must have been aware that his big scene hadn't resolved
> the confusion because he found it necessary to tack on another
> scene after the climax that ought to have ended the play . . .
> But the discussion only succeeds in making points that have
> been made quite adequately already. " (69)

There is a weakness in this last scene. It comes rather as an anti-climax despite the stressing of personal tragedy in Attercliffe's song.

But this does not weaken <u>Serjeant Musgrave's Dance</u>. Arden is a Yorkshireman, and he has written a very northern play: dark, biting, ironic. It is enveloped by an atmosphere of obsession. Arden appears to be not so much a dramatic but an epic writer; he writes a "packed" kind of language that tends to be literary and sometimes lacks dramatic impulses (70). But his syntax has compelling force; especially in Musgrave's speeches the sentences, separated by commas, follow each other in breathless succession, indicating his inner pressure and tension (71). It is a hard, strong, severe language the characters in the play are speaking; rough as the colliers' work and the winter surrounding them, occasionally relieved by dry humour and accentuated by sarcasm, interspersed by dialectical forms and sentence constructions typical of Northern England, with a rhythm the movement of which slowly accelerates as the play goes on. As to the rhymed lyrical insets and the songs, they serve, as we have seen, as a means to express a particular statement in a concentrated form (72). They are used by characters whose emotional involvement in what they are going to say is so strong that they, perhaps unconsciously, slide into a form that gives emphasis to the experience they want to express. John Arden himself explains his use of prose and verse in the following passage:

> "I see prose as being a more useful vehicle for conveying plot and

character relationships, and poetry as a sort of comment on them. ... I mean, you are writing a scene, for instance, which seems to call for prose, then you get a heightened emotion, and before you know where you are, the prose has become lyrical, and yet it doesn't seem to warrant a change into verse ... I did use verse in the first act, where Annie is asked what she thinks of soldiers, and she goes off into a four-stanza spoken ballad. There she was speaking on a subject which is actually the theme for the whole play; she is also speaking out of an emotional pressure, and therefore can drop into verse without any difficulty at all. " (73)

Prose, verse and song combine to express the idea of the play with great power.

*

If we look for ancestors of Serjeant Musgrave's Dance, we might mention George Farquhar's The Recruiting Officer (1706). Here the motif of recruiting is, of course, not used as a pretence as in Arden's play, but has a central position. Sergeant Kite, in his boastful recruiting speech, and Captain Plume are very eager to beat up recruits; the greatness of England appears to be based on the force of its efficient army, the life of a soldier is presented as glorious, his profession as a chance to win honour. It is a comedy, witty and ironic, entirely without the dark and threatening undertones of Serjeant Musgrave's Dance. Kite's speech does not take that disturbing turn of Musgrave's (74). Nearer in spirit is Brecht's adaptation of Farquhar's play, Pauken und Trompeten (1955). Here the tone is different, more aggressive; England is not glorified any more; war appears as the result of selfish interests; the English army is presented as a meeting place of criminals; the human being stands against the corrupt authorities. But none of the characters in Brecht's play are obsessed with the idea of convincing the people of the absurdity of war - the play as a whole provokes the conclusion that war is absurd. So does Serjeant Musgrave's Dance, but here the central character himself tries to prove this point. Both Brecht and Arden write about cruelty, violence and inhumanity, Brecht suggesting an alteration of the conditions, Arden suggesting the same but also pointing to the possibility of failure.

As to the obsession of Musgrave, his self-righteousness and his religious fanaticism, we feel strangely reminded of James Hogg's novel The Private Memoirs and Confessions of a Justified Sinner (1824), in which Robert Wringhim, convinced by his stepfather that he is one of God's elect human beings, pursues his deeds of violence without scruples against those who are already damned anyway. The doubt which is in Musgrave is also in Wringhim, but with him it develops slowly throughout the action. They both pursue their aims with similar ruthlessness.

We agree with Ronald Hayman when he says that

"Serjeant Musgrave's Dance is, like Mother Courage, a simultaneous demonstration of the idiocy of war and of people's inability to learn how idiotic it is." (75)

Arden's achievement, however, consists in his concentration on the element of violence. In Musgrave's schizophrenic approach Arden tackled the problem of pacifism in a way not to be found in any other English or Continental drama (76).

*

Asked in a interview whether he had "any strong views for or against the proscenium arch stage", Arden gave the following answer:

> "I like an open stage, with the audience in the same room as the stage. The proscenium arch is not a very happy medium for staging the sort of plays I want to write: people tell me I am a cold writer anyway." (77)

As a matter of fact he makes the same demands as Ann Jellicoe in her preface to The Sport of My Mad Mother (78). He favours a close contact between actors and spectators, but as the Royal Court is a theatre with a proscenium arch stage, he had to accept it. Compared to other London theatres, however, the connection between stage and auditorium is rather good (79). The beginning of the play was realized according to the author's stage directions (80). The sound of the howling wind, the subdued colours of the set, the voices of the soldiers eventually dropping in: all this combined produced a feeling of coldness, winter, loneliness. The question why the men in their scarlet uniforms were waiting in those uninviting surroundings suggested itself irresistibly. Their words and Sparky's song generated an atmosphere of expectancy and suspense.

The second scene of the first act had its effects in the pronounced irony of the exchanges between Mrs. Hitchcock, the bargee and the parson. Annie's ballad about the soldiers brought about a change of tone and mood, which led to the disturbing dialogue between Musgrave and the landlady concerning Billy Hicks and Annie. The hostile reaction of the inhabitants to the intruding soldiers was made palpable on the stage in the carefully directed "churchyard scene" (I, iii). Hurst's outbreak and Musgrave's violent reply, during which the plans of the soldiers become somewhat clearer, created a strong tension. It was in this scene as played at the Court that Arden saw a dramatic problem:

> " ... I do think that the general purpose of the soldiers' visit should be made much clearer. The real trouble is that in the churchyard scene, where they explain themselves, there is a tremendous amount of emotion being generated. They are all getting angry with each other, and Musgrave goes off into a religious tirade. The result is that the audience is so busy watching the actors dramatizing their emotions that they aren't picking up the plot information which is being conveyed in the dialogue." (81)

Act II, i started with the gauze curtain down (82). Music, noise, the sound of voices and singing were heard. Then the gauze disappeared, the lights came up, and the scene in the pub was already in full swing. A wild chorus led by Sparky filled the room. It was a memorable realization of what the author describes in his text as "A scene of noise and conviviality, crowded confusion" (83). The quieter episode between Annie and Hurst was accompanied by melancholy accordion music.

The drilling scene at the beginning of II, ii proved of an extraordinary force on the stage. It was performed with strict regard to Arden's detailed directions. The pugnacious collier's dry remark at the end of the "parade" ("I'll tell you what, we're bloody good") (84) really worked as a spell breaker and provoked laughs in the audience.

The stable scene stressed the dramatic change from the tender and quiet moments between Annie and Sparky to his unexpected death. Before the murder Musgrave's nightmare at the back of the stage provided some exciting moments, which had their climax in the sergeant's terrifying cry. The killing of Sparky itself happened at the end of a fight which was quickly and sharply played; it came as the shock Arden intended it to be. After this episode the pace of the actions on the stage was accelerated. The rest of Act II, iii was played at an enormous speed, which culminated in the "general noise, bustle and confusion" (85) demanded by the author.

The suspense created in the final moments of Act II, iii was kept up when the gauze was raised over the scene in the market-square (III, i) (86). It was set in the middle of the stage and introduced by organ music. Hurst's frantic beating of the drum added to the excited atmosphere. Musgrave's speech after the addresses of the mayor and the parson (which were, with due regard to the stage direction, acclaimed by the citizens with very perfunctory cheers) (87), had a relentless grip on the audience and spread, as it went on, a threatening atmosphere. The speed and the urgency increased, and the pulling out of the uniformed skeleton came as the shocking climax of a suspense carefully built up by the nerve-racking combination of "effect" organ music (consisting of a high sustained tune which also accompanied the song and the dance) (88) and maddening drumbeats.

The dance itself was disjointed; a sequence of heavy stamps similar to a kind of parade-ground movement (89) and strongly related to Musgrave's compulsive character. The impression was that of a heavy puppet in motion. The sergeant's dance ended abruptly together with his song, as if cut off. His quiet voice after this outbreak made a deep impression. The prolonged pause (indicated in the text) Musgrave makes after his question "Moses and the prophets, what good did they do?" (90), gave the necessary weight to this important passage. It did not miss its impact: not a single sound, not even a cough was heard in the audience (91).

The final dance of the colliers was also impressively directed. Authorities and citizens formed a ring round the stage by linking wrists with each other. The stamping of their feet, their wild chorus of "Michael Finnegan" led by the bargee, resulted in a depressing image of people evading all responsibility and returning under the so-called law and order symbolized by the measured rhythm of the dance (92). Arden, however, was not completely satisfied with the visual effect:

> "This scene didn't quite work in the theatre - for purely economic reasons. What should be happening in that dance is that the audience should be made conscious of the fact that the town has been taken over by the real military - the Dragoons. Now, because the Royal Court couldn't afford more than two dragoons, this effect was somewhat nullified. Ideally there should be a complete force. If I were able to produce the play in a larger theatre, able to pay an enormous cast of supers, the stage would be full of dragoons and the dance would take place in front of them. Then the impression given would be that even the most sympathetic of the colliers, who nearly sides with Musgrave, has no alternative but to take part in the dance, and that law and order have been re-established by force. Which, if you like, is the natural result of Musgrave trying to establish the opposite by force." (93).

The last moments of the play were marked by Attercliffe's sad song. Musgrave stood with his back towards the audience. When Attercliffe, in the last line, asked his question, the bars of the prison slowly disappeared.

The single acts and scenes were connected and emphasized by strange, disturbing organ music and melancholy accordion melodies composed by Dudley Moore.

*

Serjeant Musgrave's Dance provides parts for fifteen actors. Director Lindsay Anderson took his task of casting the play very seriously. As he said himself:

> "What you look for in casting is temperament and balance of ensemble ... To me casting is 70% of a production ... In the casting intuitively you clarify your ideas about the nature of the play ... We ended with a marvellous cast ..." (94)

The acting, generally, was appreciated by both spectators and the press - even if the play and the production were judged negatively. The critic of the Kensington News found that

> "The cast ... play their parts with a kind of drilled morbidity, as though the tenor of the play had eaten into their bones ..." (95)

The central part of Musgrave was played by Ian Bannen. He spoke with a slight Scottish accent, rolling the r. By a gradation and variation of his voice, which extended from a singing quality over a clear, low, matter-of-fact one to the aggressive and threatening outbreaks, he succeeded in conveying a character who vacillates between madness and control. Bannen was able to speak an everyday sentence in a way that made the audience shudder; his voice brought into play an unpredictable and uncanny element. He let Musgrave's obsession shine through in his muttering as well as in his shouting. Already at the end of Act I, iii he infected his words with an urgency which foreboded strange events. When Hurst challenges Musgrave (I, iii), Bannen made palpable the violence lying underneath his hissed sentences. He brought about a most gripping change of mood in the same scene, when Musgrave explains the soldiers' task in the town (96). He started in a very low voice, almost preaching. In the sentence "God's dance on this earth: and all that we are is His four strong legs to dance it ..." he suddenly, for seconds only, broke out in a frenzy which was frightening and made the audience aware of that unknown dark quality in Musgrave, which is so important and pervades the whole text. Bannen accentuated this vacillation between enforced self-control and emotional outbreaks, between the god-fearing attitude and the fanaticism. In the scene in the market-square he again realized a most effective, almost imperceptible change of attitude: from a cold efficiency during the explanation of the mechanism of a rifle he switched to a more threatening tone while demonstrating the Gatling gun - a change culminating in his passionate speech and his desperate dance. Alan Brien in The Spectator experienced Bannen's achievement as follows:

> "Ian Bannen is the monomaniac sergeant - a soldier stuffed stiff
> with ramrods and guncotton, whose madness shines through only
> in restless eyes which swivel like greased ball-bearings." (97)

Caryl Brahms in Plays and Players elaborates on this impression:

> "And now to the most impressive performance to be seen on the
> stage today ... He (98) is a ghastly grin, an illness in the mind,
> a puritan, a drum-beater - one who abrogates to himself the
> final function of the Lord which is to mete out death. He will die
> with his boots on." (99)

The reviewer of The Stage came to the following conclusion:

> " ... the cast is a very well-chosen one. None are perfectly served
> by the writing, but it is hard to imagine anyone persuading us more
> forcefully than Ian Bannen of the sergeant's grim torments and strug-
> gles ..." (100)

W.A. Darlington's verdict in The Daily Telegraph was equally positive:

> "The play lends itself to vehement acting, and Ian Bannen makes
> him an impressive, tortured figure, roaring his speeches in a
> thick accent ..." (101).

The three soldiers with their different temperaments were well cast. Hurst was given life by Alan Dobie, who played him as an irascible and insecure character, shouting and growling, dangerous and emotional. His scene with Musgrave in the churchyard (102) showed him as the impulsive type who loses his nerves and who, confronted with the stronger personality, "knuckles under" (103). In the stable scene, during the episode with Sparky and the fight which ends in murder, he appeared malicious and threatening.

Donal Donnelly, an Irish actor, took the part of Sparky, and offered an excellent interpretation. Speaking with his native Irish accent, he conveyed a man who talked and moved with an enforced gaiety and had a maddening manner of turning everything into a joke. He also succeeded in making apparent Sparky's anguish and quivering nervousness underneath his boisterous behaviour, his insecurity and misery beneath the smart, exaggerated military surface. The critic of the Westminster and Pimlico News confirms:

> "Donal Donnelly as Pte. Sparky, gaily Irish yet uncomprehendingly
> scared, was the most convincing of the trio of privates. He shared
> one scene, in particular, magnificently with Patsy Byrne, a barmaid
> tortured and tantalising and tortured again." (104)

Ronald Bryden, drama critic of The Observer, was much impressed by Donnelly's performance and thought that the play suffered from Sparky's elimination:

> "Sparky was beautifully acted and most sympathetic on the stage.
> His death tore something from the play." (105)

There was only one instance where Donnelly did not exactly follow Arden's directions. In this he can, however, be excused. The author noted in his typescript that "His (106) songs are not all that well sung" (107). Now Donnelly's were. He sang them dreamily, haltingly (108), wildly and merrily (109), sadly and softly (110); according to simple, beautiful melodies, often recalling Irish folksongs (111). They mirrored Sparky's moods admirably and caught his longing for another kind of life.

Frank Finlay as Attercliffe did justice to a part which was clearly meant by Arden as a calming, balancing element among the soldiers. Finlay adopted a northern accent with dark vowels to act a man who went to be a soldier because he had been left by his wife. His Attercliffe never seemed to recover from that blow - he suffered from the violence around him, did not understand the cruelty, could not come to grips with the fact that he became involved in two murders. The whole of his suffering and desperation appeared in his song at the end of the play.

The difficult and delicate part of Annie was realized by Patsy Byrne. As Lindsay Anderson remarked, she "worked well" (112). She found the right attitude to incorporate a character described by Arden as

> "A big strong-boned girl, dirty and untidy. Harsh-voiced and rude
> in the Northern manner. No feminine charms in the usual sense,
> but by no means unattractive." (113)

With her expressive face she played Annie as the disillusioned, outwardly hard girl that has not lost her ability to love before her hopes are shattered a second time. Her rendering of the ballad on the soldiers (114) was a first highlight: after reciting the first eight lines in a fierce voice, she made a pause, and then, silently, sadly and resignedly, she spoke the line "And that's what he does and so do we" (115). It was a striking moment. In her scene with Sparky in the stable the actress held the audience by her subtle changes of mood: disappointed, hurt and scornful after Hurst's refusal, she broke down miserably and silently crying - to gather comfort and strength again in her awakening tenderness for Sparky. Her realization of Annie's shaken state after the murder, when she is half out of her mind, was a piece of impressive acting. This is Caryl Brahms's comment in Plays and Players:

> "Miss Patsy Byrne ... playing a sex-fed slut, is one to watch; and
> in a part that calls for but cannot get Miss Joan Plowright, might
> well establish a line of Patsy Byrne parts ..." (116)

Now to refer to Annie simply as a "sex-fed slut" betrays a certain lack of insight into this complex character. It is a most perfunctory statement based on a perfunctory study of the part.

Freda Jackson gave a fascinating study of Mrs. Hitchcock, the landlady. Speaking fast and hard in a scornful way, she outdid the parson in Act, I, ii, and by her ready wit had the laughs of the audience on her side. By means of a dry, matter-of-fact tone she presented a woman who has lost her illusions long ago but who, like Annie, suffers underneath her apparent coldness. In her scene with Musgrave and Attercliffe at the end of the play, Freda Jackson let her emotions rise because of Sparky's death and gave particular weight to her explicit statement (117). Caryl Brahms in Plays and Players was impressed:

> "As a raw-boned mainly silent woman behind a law-abiding bar she
> is, in her way, almost as terrifying as the fell sergeant. Set her
> brooding at a window and who could tear their eyes away to the
> procession." (118)

James Bree played the part of the sly, erratic bargee Joe Bludgeon mischievously, unpredictably; with a lurking, intriguing voice and sneaking behaviour - as a man always on the side of the winning party, wavering between servility and impertinence, with a twisted humour. He conveyed the smirking familiarity of a perfidious character always ready to make an insidious joke, a queer comment, always giving the sign for a cheer, a dance, or a chorus. As Lindsay Anderson said, "the bargee was played as a Dickensian grotesque" (119). Sometimes Bree tended to exaggerate the equivocal nature of the character. This was Caryl Brahms's reaction in Plays and Players:

> "He (120) is admirably supported by James Bree, a stubby limping,
> jumpy little fellow of a man, like a chirpy undertaker on the way home,
> malicious as a ferret, gay as a cause so irretrievably lost as to leave

nothing much for tears ..." (121)

The reviewer of The Westminster and Pimlico News was of the opinion that

"A touch of genius hovered about the twisted bargee of James Bree,
providing a fund of humour to relieve the earthy darkness." (122)

Of course, it is open to discussion whether Arden intended the bargee to function
as a kind of "comic relief" - in the text his humour appears rather uncomfortable.

The roles of the parson and the mayor were acted by Richard Caldicot and Stratford Johns. Caldicot very well expressed the self-satisfied haughtiness of the corrupt clergyman imagined by Arden:

"The PARSON is over-conscious that he is the only gentleman in a
very ungentleman-like community. He has no Christian meekness,
and is both aloof and commanding. No 'Parsonical' voice, either."
(123)

Stratford Johns made the mayor the "brisk bullying ... man, with a superficial
joviality and good-fellow heartiness" (124) of Arden's description and spat out his
short sentences with coarse determination.

As to the colliers, Jack Smethurst (Slow Collier), Colin Blakely (Pugnacious Collier), Harry Gwynn Davies (Walsh) did justice to their temperaments (125), Davies
giving his Walsh the right sort of insight mixed with bitterness and resignation (126).
Michael Hunt played the constable as the conceited, inefficient bully he is, and the
dragoons (Clinton Greyn and Barry Wilsher) showed the military smartness and
sense of duty required. The achievement of the cast was summed up in a letter by
John Arden himself:

"To the Cast, 'Sjt Musgrave's Dance'
I am sorry I am not able to be in town to see the last night of the
play, but I hope it is a good one! I am sure it will be - you have
been a splendid company and I am very grateful to you all.
                    Thank you so much,
                            John Arden." (127)

                              *

Before Serjeant Musgrave's Dance Lindsay Anderson had directed three Sunday
Night Productions (128) and one main bill play (129) for the Royal Court. He described how he came to direct Arden's play:

"One day George Devine gave me two plays to read. One of them
was Serjeant Musgrave's Dance. 'Do you think we should do it?'
he asked me after I had read it. 'Yes', I said. So when he asked

me 'Would you direct it?' I couldn't say 'no' any more, of course."
(130)

In building up the production Anderson worked closely together with Arden. They did quite a lot of additional work on the text (131). The author took a real interest in the production and came to practically all the rehearsals. It was "work on the basis of friendship and collaboration" (132), as Anderson expressed it.

The text was considerably cut. The cuts were thought necessary because Arden - as we have seen before - writes a language which tends to be too literary. Anderson's aim in cutting the text was to make it more dramatic. Arden agreed with all the cuts made (133). Their general tendency was to "thin down" (134) the dialogue.

One major cut concerned the passage in Act III, i where Annie, looking out of the window, realizes that the skeleton is her former lover Billy and climbs down by means of a ladder (135). Anderson explained his reasons for eliminating this episode:

> "I cut the whole business with Annie and the ladder in the end, because the reality in that situation is difficult to maintain. To achieve reality is the chief problem of the last act anyway." (136)

He led the actors through the first two acts in a slow rhythm. The author had planned them like that:

> "Well, I think the thing about the early scenes in Musgrave is that it is a play which started in my mind with the last act. When I wrote it, I was roughly aware of what the climax was to be - the soldiers staging a public meeting, apparently a recruiting meeting, which would turn into a protest. In order to make this credible, it was necessary to lay out a number of scenes in which the soldiers showed themselves for what they were, and at the same time all the people in the town revealed enough of their personality to illustrate their attitude towards war. I think what I was doing in Musgrave was using two acts for what is commonly done in one, in most three-act plays." (137)

Several critics found fault with these first two acts on the stage and accused Lindsay Anderson of a monotonous, dragging and pretentious direction. The review in the New Statesman stressed this point sharply:

> "For the timing was far from faultless. Instead of marshalling both scenes and actors so that they moved with the dramatic concentration that Arden's writing ... demands, ... Anderson deliberately slowed everything down. Even the most trivial bits of dialogue were punctuated by those tiny pauses in which the actors turn, or move up stage, or gesture, as though about to embark on some long set speech. The

talk bogged down in endless hesitation. The action, too, dragged
repetitively. I'm sure Mr. Anderson would have no compunction
about decimating a text of Shakespeare. It is odd then that he should
have had qualms about cutting John Arden's play to a manageable
size." (138)

As we have seen, the sarcastic remark concerning the cutting is certainly not justified; the text was cut by the director and the author, and further cutting would
have falsified the play.

The reviewer of The Times Educational Supplement offered similar criticism:

"Pretentiousness, alas, is the chief characteristic of "Serjeant
Musgrave's Dance', but whether this is the fault of the author or
that of the director ... it is not easy to say after seeing the play
once only ... On reflection ... Anderson's elaborate direction
may contribute more to this unfortunate effect than the author's
words: it is relentlessly solemn, remorselessly humourless,
monotonous as to rhythm, and muddled as to meaning. It proceeds at a slow march from the beginning of the first scene
until the end of the last and by its apparent anxiety to load every
single instant with significance succeeds in depriving the whole
thing of intelligibility ..." (139)

This passage is not fair to Anderson's direction and contains exaggerations. The
production was not "remorselessly humourless" - there was irony and humour
wherever Arden wished them to be, and Serjeant Musgrave's Dance is not a comedy.
It was not "monotonous as to rhythm", nor did it proceed "at a slow march from the
beginning of the first scene until the end of the last": if the reviewer had followed
the performance more attentively, he would have noticed that from the end of Act
II to the climax in the market-square there was acceleration of rhythm (140). Whether it was "muddled in meaning" remains doubtful, as the play itself does not present
us with clear results (141).

The slowness of the production was also criticized by T.C. Worsley in The Financial
Times:

" ... direction is deliberate, and at times achingly slow." (142)

as well as by J.C. Trewin in the Birmingham Post:

" ... Anderson ... should also have accelerated his production ... "
(143)

Maybe that Lindsay Anderson, in his effort to give the play its adequate movement,
to create the claustrophobic atmosphere, directed it somewhat too slowly through
the first two acts. But this procedure did not falsify its pace (144). The deliberate

direction looks, as in the case of George Devine, like the result of extreme carefulness and respect for the text. Despite some weaknesses it can be said that Anderson achieved a valid interpretation of the play. The reviewer of Theatre World
characterizes the production as one of those which George Devine propagated in the
beginning of the English Stage Company:

> "From the moment the curtain rose this play held the attention in the
> grip of that special kind of magic found nowhere else but in the theatre
> which, we feel, can only work when actors, author, director and stage
> designer are in complete harmony ..." (145)

*

In designing the set for the play Jocelyn Herbert followed the author's directions
very closely:

> "This play is not realistic, and the events it deals with are not a
> little improbable. Therefore the manner of staging and dressing
> it should be somewhat stylised ... There are no less than six
> separate sets requested, and these must clearly be as simple as
> possible ... There must be no more furniture in the interiors
> than is demanded in the action ..." (146)

The sets were simple, but of great evocative power. They hit the sombre atmosphere of the play admirably (147). It may be that the designer was influenced by
the Berlin Ensemble, which visited London in 1956 (148). This was John Arden's
comment:

> " ... Jocelyn Herbert's sets ... beautifully fulfilled the mental
> picture I had while writing the play. The only reservations I had
> about them were not the designs, but the lengthy scene-changes,
> caused by the Royal Court's terribly cramped backstage conditions."
> (149)

Already the set for the first scene was an exact visual counterpart to what Arden
evokes with words:

> "A canal wharf. Evening.
> HURST and ATTERCLIFFE are playing cards on the top of a
> side-drum. A few yards away SPARKY stands, as though on
> guard ... There is a pile of three or four heavy wooden boxes
> with the WD broad arrow stencilled on them, and a lantern
> set on top." (150)

Some rifles with bayonets fixed on leant against the boxes.

The second scene ("The bar of a public house") (151) was furnished with a minimum of properties too: a wall with a door in it, two typical, ornamented pub glass panes; on the inner side some bottles on the bar directly connected with the wall, two heavy tables, some chairs; all lit by a bare lamp. The churchyard scene (I, iii) was designed with the same economy: two or three gravestones, one in the form of a cross; an iron fence; the twisted form of a willow tree.

The setting for the stable and bedroom scene in Act II, iii consisted of two different levels: downstage from the left side of the stage to about the centre there was a wooden fence, a lantern on top of one of the fence-posts, three mattresses in front. On the right side some stairs with a banister led to Musgrave's room with a brass bed on a higher level. Again Jocelyn Herbert obeyed Arden's instructions exactly:

> "The stage is divided into two distinct acting-areas. The downstage
> area represents the stable, and is supposed to be divided into three
> loose boxes. If it is not practicable for the partitions between these
> to be built, it should be sufficient to suggest them by the three mat-
> tresses which are laid parallel, feet to the audience ... The upstage
> area, raised up at least a couple of feet, represents a bedroom in the
> house. It is only large enough to contain a brass-knobbed bedstead
> with a small table or other support for a candle. The two areas must
> be treated as completely separate. Access to the bedroom area should
> be from the rear ..." (152)

With the stairs the designer introduced a connection which is forbidden in the directions. In agreement with the author the partitions between the boxes were abolished.

The directions for the scene in the market-square gave Jocelyn Herbert the opportunity of arranging a colourful structure:

> "In the centre of the stage is a practicable feature - the centre-
> piece of the market-place. It is a sort of Victorian clock-tower-
> cum-lamppost-cum-market-cross, and stands on a raised plinth.
> There is a ladder leaning against it. On the plinth are the soldiers'
> boxes and a coil of rope. The front of the plinth is draped with
> bunting, and other colours are leaning against the centre-piece in
> an impressive disposition." (153)

The plinth was decorated on the front by gathered drapings; part of the centre piece was covered with a bright Union Jack, two flags stood crossed beneath the gallows-like structure in the centre. Two more flags were on either side of the plinth.

For the final scene in the prison cell (III, ii), five or six iron bars were lowered in front of the preceding scene. By means of a light change the background faded away.

In between the acts and at the beginning a gauze hung from the proscenium arch, screening off the stage from the auditorium. On the gauze there was the sketch of a mining town: houses, a tower with the coal hoisting machinery dominating the scene under a grey sky. By lighting the gauze from the front it was made visible. At the beginning of each act the lights went up behind the gauze, making it vanish; at the same time it was raised, and the scene started.

The dominating colours in all the sets (except the one in the market-square) were subdued: sallow grey and yellow, brown, black, white - a depressing mixture of winter and coal. Alan Brien gives a striking description of the effect:

> " ... nightmare draughtsmanship of the designer Jocelyn Herbert.
> Miss Herbert's world is half Ackerman print, half German silent
> film - remote, yet alive, in the centre of one of those crystal balls
> which foam into a snow storm when you turn them upside down. Her
> patterns are black and white on sepia lit by blotches of colour. The
> scarlet uniforms, the shining rifles, the warm brown bar counter,
> the heavy dark trunks are all solid and three-dimensional, but outside
> and around them is wrapped the thick white blanket of winter ... " (154)

The flaming red of the soldiers' coats were the only bright spots in the drab surroundings. The soldiers wore scarlet tunics and spiked helmets of the "Kipling Epoch" as demanded by the author, and "the details of costume covered approximately the years between 1860 and 1880" (155). The colliers were dressed in dark clothes, which contrasted with those of the soldiers. The breaking in of some strange, violent force into the ordinariness of a community was thus emphasized by the colours.

*

The audiences of <u>Serjeant Musgrave's Dance</u> were often at a loss (156). Their puzzlement may have had a specific reason. Although the Royal Court had confronted them before with two plays by Arden (157), many among them were still used to the traditional "message play" or "Lehrstück", which sets a problem and in the end proposes or, at least, points to a solution. <u>Serjeant Musgrave's Dance</u> can be called a message play; but it does not definitely take sides. Hence the puzzlement. Felix Barker in <u>The Evening News</u> noticed this reaction among the audience:

> "'What on earth is it all about?' the audience was still asking in the
> second interval." (158)

The spectators tried to fight their perplexity by gratefully seizing on the few opportunities for a laugh (especially in I, i and I, ii), which sometimes seemed to be real comic relief for them, a means to loosen the grip the play had on their nerves. Because, whether they understood the proceedings on the stage or not, they were against their will arrested by the atmosphere of the production. It was a strange mixture of insecurity, embarrassment and fascination that held them in some sort of inexplicable tension. There were moments of complete silence in the auditorium (159). It was one of those plays which the audience could not dismiss as bad, although it remained a riddle to the greater part of them. The attendance was anything but satisfactory.

*

It is interesting to see what other playwrights connected with the Court thought about the play and its production. Here are a few of their statements, published on a leaflet distributed during the run of the play. They strike us by their unvaryingly positive contents:

> John Osborne: "The reception of SERJEANT MUSGRAVE'S DANCE is the most irresponsible for some time. John Arden's play has more riches to offer than a dozen successful, dazzling critic-comforters. It is courageous, theatrically adventurous and it has startling integrity. Every empty seat at the Royal Court is a reproach to all of us who pretend to reject the West End mini-product for theatregoers."

> N.F. Simpson: "This is not a play for critics and verbalisers. It's a play for everyone else though. Positive, lucid, truthful, funny, moving, haunting ..."

> Arnold Wesker: "I was gripped. By the end of the third act my heart was thumping from sheer excitement. The acting, direction and sets are superb - the work of a devoted team. Arden stands alone. An extraordinary achievement."

*

The reaction of the press was confused. Many of the critics felt just as irritated as the audiences and condemned play and production. Some of the reviews sound rather as if their authors got angry because they could not grasp the author's meaning. Of the twenty-four reviews considered seven inclined towards a positive judgment, nine gave the production a mixed reception (e.g. by criticizing the play and commending the actors), and eight rejected it fiercely.

The critic of the Sunday Dispatch used adjectives implying irritation, but he was gripped by the last act:

> "Mystical, poetic, symbolical, obscure - only a very sensitive production by ... Anderson saved it from appearing affectation. But then in the last act this strange, perverse play blazed into life with one of the most dramatically powerful scenes I can recall on the stage." (160)

Cecil Wilson of The Daily Mail had a similar impression:

> "Baffling, sprawling, and pretentious though it is, the play has some moments of rare theatrical magic and ... direction is

alive to them all ..." (161)

Significantly enough, the critic of the Evening Standard entitled his review "A noble idea - but it only irritates". However, he appreciated the acting:

" ... an impressive aura of doom and dark destiny. Ian Bannen
... gives a terrifying picture of a blunt, honest man gone berserk
because of the shattering of his humane beliefs.
Alan Dobie, Donal Donnelly and Frank Finlay do impressive work
as bewildered soldiers caught up in an idealistic anti-war protest
that they do not really understand." (162)

The reviewer of The Times starts with some positive remarks about Arden's writing but becomes more and more negative as he goes on. He rather bluntly speaks of "a mass of character defects" without giving one single proof:

"Mr. John Arden can write good realistic dialogue and he has a
special gift for creating an atmosphere which is mysteriously
pregnant with suspense. There is some good dialogue and there
are scenes which suggest powerfully that something important
is about to happen in 'Serjeant Musgrave's Dance' ... These
dramatic virtues unfortunately get smothered in a mass of
character defects, and our final impression is of an inordinately
long-winded and rather foolish play. ... Mr. Ian Bannen as the
serjeant conveys authority but rather spoils the impression by
shouting too much. Miss Freda Jackson has a poor part, and none
of the soldiers gets much of a chance.
Mr. James Bree is given too many chances as a crocked bargee,
and he uses them to introduce teasingly the mannerisms of Ibsen's
Engstrand into situations already sufficiently complicated by the
author's determination to overload the case he is trying to make
against the cruelty of war. One cannot recall a week of worse plays."
(163)

For the critic of the Kensington News the quality of a play obviously depends on a booked-out theatre, a sumptuous set, an everyday dialogue and on light entertainment:

"The first ominous indication was the half-empty theatre; the
second was the starkness of the opening scene; the third was the
arduous dialogue -then it was apparent that we were in for a pretty
stiff dose of morality ..." (164)

Mervyn Jones in The Tribune transferred some of his own bewilderment onto the actors and the direction:

"By far the best thing on the Royal Court stage, where the actors
behave with understandable bewilderment, is the decor by Jocelyn

Herbert. If anything could have rescued the play, it would have been
these clear, eloquent designs. But Lindsay Anderson had killed its
slender chances of life with a production of portentous confusion and
funeral slowness." (165)

War play is dull sermon, the reviewer of the Manchester Evening News writes la-
conically and proclaims that

"As theatre, it never really comes into its own until the third act -
but that is too long to wait ..." (166)

Harold Hobson in The Sunday Times used the opportunity for saying something rather dubious about the general purpose of the theatre:

"Another frightful ordeal. It is time someone reminded our advanced
dramatists that the principal function of the theatre is to give pleasure.
It is not the principal function of the theatre to strengthen peace, to
improve morality, or to establish a good social system. Churches,
international associations and political parties already exist for those
purposes. It is the duty of the theatre, not to make men better, but
to render them harmlessly happy." (167)

But there were some critics who appreciated the play and its production. Philip
Hope-Wallace in The Guardian entitled his review "Something just short of a great
play" and wrote:

"For the best part of three hours it has worked on my curiosity,
and often put that ill-definable spell on my imagination. I think
it is something short of a great play. But wild horses wouldn't
have dragged me from my seat before the end ... The play is
written with an acute sense of language ... It gives the actors
every chance and Ian Bannen in particular, as the fanatical Serjeant, gives a magnificent performance ... Lindsay Anderson
produces with strength and economy in the earlier scenes, which
are beautifully set and lighted ... I wish I could think that the
production brought the audience the maximum help in the last act.
But that this is a highly original and challenging experiment in
drama is not in doubt ..." (168)

Especially impressed by the third act was Felix Barker in The Evening News. He
devoted considerable space to it in order to convey something of the excitement
which for him compensated the "slowness" of the first two acts - a slowness he,
like so many of his fellow critics, was not able to appreciate:

"Only in the last act did the author pull out of the bag a scene as
powerful and dramatic as I can ever remember in the theatre.
This scene was a recruiting meeting in the market square ...

That last scene with its breathtaking change in pace and mood and
the blinding flash of understanding that came with it produced a
tremendous theatrical explosion. I think it justified the use of the
long, long time fuse." (169)

Alan Brien in The Spectator gave a thoroughly positive account of the direction, the
acting and the set:

"I have never seen a play which created its own mad, obsessed,
otherworld so completely as 'Serjeant Musgrave's Dance' ...
The first achievement of ... Anderson ... lies in imparting to
his actors the uneasy sense that free will is simply the opportunity to choose the wrong turning in a bricks-and-mortar maze.
Mr. Anderson's cast are as palpable as the atmosphere that Miss
Herbert has built around them.
The behaviour which Lindsay Anderson has to present on the stage
is, at least superficially, melodramatic - that is to say, the characters' reactions have always to be several sizes too large for their
actions. The mention of a man's name in a pub resounds like a
cannonade. The drop of a trunk on a quayside starts off tremors of
an earthquake. The hoisting of a skeleton to a flagpole is expected
to change the world. Mr. Anderson accepts the melodrama and
even underlines and emphasizes it in the style of a UFA thriller.
He uses an eerie warbling note like that of a musical saw to rivet
our attention to the insanity hovering above his characters. A
sepulchral dissonant organ march ushers in the acts. These are
all, in a sense, Irvingesque devices more fitting to the Lyceum
than the Court, but, amazingly, they work.
Both décor and direction could hardly be more effective ... It is
worth visiting if only for the décor, the direction and the acting.
Almost all the performances have that magisterial, heroic profes-
sionalism that is the one quality still too often lacking among our
good, naturalistic, relaxed young actors today ..." (170)

Serjeant Musgrave's Dance was a production which divided the critics. One can
notice maliciously that in 1966, when the play was revived by Jane Howell in a rather inadequate production (171), many of them changed their minds and called it a
great drama, implying that they had judged it as that in 1959 already. Which does
not correspond to the truth at all (172).

*

Serjeant Musgrave's Dance was a complete commercial fiasco for the Court. The
production ran for about three and a half weeks and twenty-eight performances and
lost more than 4000 pounds. As in the case of Ann Jellicoe's The Sport of My Mad
Mother, George Devine and his colleagues were determined to present what they
had recognized as good and to encourage an author whose talent they considered

worth encouraging. Already a year before, in 1958, Arden's <u>Live Like Pigs</u> had lost more than 4000 pounds at the same theatre. This did not prevent the English Stage Company from championing the playwright further.

During the following years Arden came to be recognized as one of the most important dramatists in Britain. He wrote a whole series of other plays which where performed all over the country (173). Without the constant encouragement by the English Stage Company this development would hardly have been possible. Again the Royal Court lived up to its ambitious aims, and again it achieved a result that justified its efforts. The unflagging backing of John Arden had its effects on the British theatre in general.

***

X NORMAN FREDERICK SIMPSON: ONE WAY PENDULUM

Norman Frederick Simpson, born in 1919 - "a Londoner by birth and inclination" (1) - had his first contacts with the Royal Court in 1957, when A Resounding Tinkle was presented there in a Sunday Night Production without décor (2). In 1958 the revised version of the same play was staged at the Court in a double bill production (together with Simpson's The Hole), and on December 22nd 1959 his One Way Pendulum had its London first night; directed by William Gaskill and with designs by Stephen Doncaster. This production had been given a try-out at the Theatre Royal, Brighton, one week before its official opening at the Royal Court.

*

The play is set in the living-room of the Groomkirby family. The beginning as described in the stage directions is certainly most unusual:

> "When the curtain rises the stage is in darkness. The light comes
> slowly up on three centrally placed weighing machines.
> Number One, in the middle, is large and eye-catching and flamboy-
> antly ugly. On it is an enormous weight.
> Number Two, on the right, and Number Three, on the left, are
> identically small, modest, unpretentious. On them are correspondingly
> smaller weights.
> Pause.
> KIRBY enters with a music stand which he places centrally opposite
> Number One. He adjusts its height. There is no music on it.
> As KIRBY takes up his baton and adopts an appropriate stance, the
> light contracts to isolate Number One." (3)

Kirby Groomkirby, assuming the part of a conductor, embarks on a lengthy singing rehearsal with the three weighing machines; he succeeds with "Number Two" and "Number Three", but his efforts prove abortive with "Number One", the only response of which consists in the sentence "Fifteen stone ten pounds" (4). This flabbergasting hobby of Kirby's is commented on by Robert Barnes, a neighbour of the Groomkirbys, who appears to be a sort of link between stage and auditorium:

> "Works like a slave on this. Every night. As soon as he gets in.
> ... It's a form of escape, of course. Escapism." (5)

The lapidary bits of information he throws out to the audience show him as a detached observer.

After Kirby's triumphant conducting of the "Halleluja Chorus", sung by "countless weighing machines as far as the eye can see" (6) - with the exception of stubborn "Number One" named Gormless (7) - Mrs. Groomkirby, in her ensuing conversation with Barnes, astonishes us yet further by her reaction to her son's activity:

133

"BARNES: Wait till he's got all five hundred of them (8) up to concert
pitch!
MRS. GROOMKIRBY: Well, as far as that goes, if we've got to have
five hundred weighing machines in the house, I'd just as soon they
did sing. Especially if they've got nothing more to say for themselves
than Gormless. ... 'Fifteen stone ten' all day long - it gets a bit
monotonous after a time." (9)

She is not at all outraged at Kirby's preoccupation, but seems to have accepted his
mania, remaining unimpressed and trying to make the best of it. Barnes confirms
his function as a link between spectators and stage when he asks Mrs. Groomkirby's
permission for himself and the theatre audience to enter her house:

"BARNES: I'll bring them in, then, shall I, Mrs. Groomkirby?
MRS. G.: Yes. I suppose they'd better come in if they're coming.
. . .
MRS. G.: ... They'll have to take it as they find it. I haven't got
time to go round scrubbing and polishing for them. ..." (10)

Again Mrs. Groomkirby does not show any great emotion at the frightening prospect
of so many visitors; she just refuses to clean the place for them.

Through Barnes, we get to know another member of the household: Mr.Arthur
Groomkirby, who has his special occupations as well: "he makes a bit of a hobby
of the law" (11). Obviously the communication between father and son is not very
developed, as they are "never speaking to each other from one week's end to the
next" (12). From further book titles read out by Barnes we learn that Mr. Groomkirby is also busy with carpentry:

"BARNES: (moving downstage Left). Well, if he's got ideas about
building Noah's Ark in a room this size, he'll find he's bitten off
a bit more than he can chew.
MRS. G.: (off). As long as we don't have to be knee-deep in shavings
while he's finding out." (13)

Mrs. Mabel Groomkirby faces the inevitable in a resigned manner, and her only
but constant worry concerns the dusting and cleaning involved.:

We are introduced to a further inhabitant of the house: Aunt Mildred, who is pushed
in in a wheelchair. Our suspicions with regard to her prove justified: she, too, has
an absorbing interest. She is obsessed with travelling and devours a travel brochure (14). Her account, interrupted by pauses, of a certain Maud, who has tried
all sorts of vehicles from tricycles and wheelbarrows over rickshaws to camels
and roller skates, culminates in the following dialogue:

"AUNT MILDRED: She was perfectly all right till the police stopped
her that time with Dr. Picklock's ambulance.

Pause. ...
MRS. GROOMKIRBY: ... She was committing a nuisance with it,
Aunt Mildred.
Pause.
AUNT M.: It was only through the kindness of Dr. Picklock that she
had an ambulance to commit a nuisance with.
Pause. ...
AUNT M.: In any case it was empty. ...
MRS. G.: We know it was empty, Aunt Mildred. But she knocked
down Dr. Picklock with it.
Pause. ...
AUNT M.: ... Knocked down a doctor? With an ambulance? How
could she? It's a contradiction in terms! (15)

For the first time we come across the queer logic Simpson is going to use throughout the play: the laughter arises out of a paradoxical situation.

The dialogue between Mrs. Groomkirby and her daughter Sylvia confirms our impression of the lady of the house and makes it clear that she takes the goings on in
her family for granted:

"SILVIA: ... Mi mi mi mi-ing all over the place. He's been on it
now since I don't know when and he still isn't any further.
MRS. G.: (off). He's got to go at the pace of the slowest. You know
that, Sylvia, as well as I do. ... I've got quite enough to do down
here moving your father's stuff about all over the place before I
can get on with anything - without bothering about what Kirby's doing
or isn't doing. ... What with you moaning and Aunt Mildred on all
the time. ...
SYLVIA: I don't know what she's doing there in the first place.
MRS. G.: ... You know perfectly well she got on the wrong train,
Sylvia." (16)

Mrs. Groomkirby has adjusted herself to the whims of her family and established
normality on a level that, for us, is near the insane. But this is not enough. Other
particulars are revealed with regard to Kirby:

"MRS. Groomkirby: ... Did you ring Kirby's bell when you came
down? ...
SYLVIA: I don't know what he wants a bell rung every time for.
MRS. G.: (off). You know he won't start eating till he's heard it."
(17)

It seems, indeed, that nothing can greatly shock Mrs. Groomkirby any more. To
tell from the above passage, Kirby, in training his machines like human beings,
has conversely lost his human traits and has himself developed the characteristics
of a machine with its mechanical reactions: the sound of the cash bell triggers off

the impulse in him to eat. He lives according to Pavlov's theory of the "conditioned reflexes".

While Aunt Mildred remains absorbed in her travel fantasies, Mrs. Groomkirby upbraids Sylvia with the "dirty old skull" (18) on the mantelpiece. Again it appears that she is mainly worried about the skull's being dirty, and not "exactly an ornament to have about the place" (19). Once more the discussion takes an unexpected turn:

> "SYLVIA: ... It's supposed to remind you of death.
> There is an eloquent pause.
> MRS. G.: And does it?
> SYLVIA: (looking up). Does it what?
> MRS. G.: (without looking round). I thought it was supposed to remind you of death.
> SYLVIA: (shrugging). Oh. (Glancing at skull and going back to magazine). Not all that much." (20)

Sylvia, too, seems to have lost her natural responses to a certain extent: the skull does not remind her of death; it has lost its usual connotations.

In the meantime, Arthur Groomkirby has arrived with a handcart "stacked precariously with oak-panelling" (21), while in the living-room Mrs. Groomkirby and Mrs. Gantry - a woman who is invited and paid for eating the left-over food of the Groomkirbys - indulge in an amazing conversation. At first it revolves round the way their husbands earn an income: Mr. Groomkirby and Mr. Gantry fill parking-meters with sixpences, wait in front of them until the "hour's up" (22) and empty them at the end of the month. The following account concerning one Mr. Gridlake, however, delivered by Mrs. Gantry, is even more astonishing. As this passage reveals a typical characteristic of Simpson's style, I quote it in full:

> "MRS. GANTRY: You heard about Mr. Gridlake?
> MRS. GROOMKIRBY: No?
> MRS. Gantry: I thought you might have heard. Had an accident on his skis.
> MRS. G.: Serious?
> MRS. GANTRY: Killed himself.
> MRS. G.: No!
> MRS. GANTRY: Straight into the jaws of death, so Mrs. Honeyblock was saying.
> Pause.
> MRS. G.: What on earth did he expect to find in there, for goodness sake?
> MRS. GANTRY: Showing off, I suppose.
> Pause.
> MRS. G.: You'd think he'd have had more sense.
> Pause.

MRS. GANTRY: He hadn't intended staying there, of course.
Pause.
MRS. G. : In one side and out the other, I suppose.
MRS. GANTRY: That's why he had his skis on sideways, accor-
ding to Mrs. Honeyblock.
Pause.
MRS. G. : I can't think what possessed him.
MRS. GANTRY: Trying to take death in by putting his skis on
the wrong way round!
Pause.
MRS. GANTRY: I feel sorry for Mrs. Gridlake.
MRS. G. : What actually happened in there? Missed his footing,
I suppose?
MRS. GANTRY: I'll tell you what I think happened, Mabel.
MRS. G. : Too confident.
MRS. GANTRY: No. What I think happened was that he went in
all right and then caught his head a glancing blow as he was
coming out. (Pause.) It's easily done. Especially a tall man.
MRS. G. : Stunned himself.
MRS. GANTRY: Stunned himself, and then of course it was
too late.
Pause.
MRS. G. : Instead of allowing for his height. ... " (23)

The beginning of Mrs. Gantry's tale looks like a normal piece of gossip, and Mrs.
Groomkirby reacts like a person listening to gossip. But then, with the figure of
speech "into the jaws of death" (24), the character of the dialogue changes. The
following statements of the two women are so to speak triggered off by that figure
of speech and, taking it at its physical value, Mrs. Gantry and Mrs. Groomkirby
extend it further and further, adding yet another thought until the figure becomes
completely unrecognizable. It is a ruthless pursuit started by Mabel's unexpected
reply "What on earth did he expect to find in there, for goodness sake?" Simpson's
sense of timing gives these statements their special quality: the pauses which interrupt the "extensions" delay the points made, thus rendering them additionally
striking and creating comic effects.

After a short interlude during which we see Barnes and Mr. Groomkirby busily
carrying about and setting up the oak panels, Mrs. Groomkirby puzzles us with yet
another fact concerning her son Kirby - a fact which strikes us as being somewhat
macabre: he likes to wear black clothes and is "always glad of an excuse to go into
mourning" (25). We also learn that Kirby taught himself to make paper and ink, that
he wanted to write a book but "lost the thread of his story" (26), uses the cash register as an egg-timer, does not trust his stop-watch and once wished to be one of
the dogs Pavlov kept for his experiments. His wearing of black clothes, however,
is bound up with a condition:

"MRS. GROOMKIRBY: ... He won't wear his black now unless he's

got somebody to go into mourning for.
MRS. GANTRY: Been killing people, I suppose?
MRS. G.: Not so far as I know, Myra. ..." (27)

Again Mabel Groomkirby remains totally unimpressed by Myra's monstrous insinu-
ation and reacts coolly. Mrs. Gantry comments on Arthur's and Kirby's hobbies:

"MRS. GANTRY: They get very tied up in it, don't they?
MRS. G.: I spend half my time one way and another between
the two of them, tidying up and this, that and the other.
... What I'm dreading is the day he brings the Old Bailey
home for us all to fall over." (28)

Mrs. Groomkirby has hardly formulated her apprehension when Arthur and Stan,
Sylvia's boyfriend, carry in a large panel with the inscription "Build-it-yourself.
Series nine - famous institutions. Number seven Old Bailey" (29). A simple but
striking effect, gained by the immediate and surprising realization of Mabel's
mental image.

Some further recollections by Aunt Mildred relating to her notorious friend Maud
lead over to Mrs. Groomkirby's reaction to the witness box which her husband by
now has built up in the living-room. Her objections are what we expect:

"MRS. G.: What is it? A pulpit or something? Stuck right where
we can fall over it? ... Doesn't he think I've got enough to do
moving his books from one place to another? ... This time we
shall have a lot of jury men tramping all over the carpet every time
we want to sit down to a meal, as well. ... Next thing we know we
shall have the entire Old Bailey or something in here. Collecting
the dust. ... Before we know where we are we shall be having
walls knocked out to make room for it and one thing and another.
..." (30)

She does not simply dismiss the idea as absurd, as any normal human being would.
On the contrary, she at once thinks about the consequences of Arthur's activities.

For a change, Sylvia surprises us with her lamentation that her arms are too short
(they "start so blessed high up") (31), and that therefore she is not able to reach
her knees without bending down. A discussion about apes follows. Act One ends with
Arthur Groomkirby being occupied with his construction work. The furious Stan,
having been compelled to help the father of his girl friend, falls out with Sylvia,
bangs the cash register and brings about a crisis in Kirby:

"KIRBY: I might have been dreaming for all he knew!
...
Might have stopped me stone dead in the middle of an orgasm!
(32)

138

He is completely under the command of his conditioned reflexes and can be steered mechanically like a robot.

When the curtain rises on Act Two, we realize at once that all the worst fears of Mrs. Groomkirby have materialized: the living-room is dominated by the built-up courtroom and has turned into a section of the Old Bailey. This circumstance has rather alarming consequences: as Mr. Groomkirby is trying to dress himself up as a judge and thus to put the finishing touch to his hobby-horse, a real Judge appears, "the Court begins gradually to assemble" (33), and Arthur all of a sudden sees himself in the middle of a trial. His kit is invaded by self-confident professionals; what started as a private occupation surprisingly develops into a public legal procedure. Mr. Groomkirby seems to be so absorbed in his hobby that he is not greatly alarmed by this. The prosecuting counsel, who opens the inquest, connects the examination with the events of Act One (" ... The facts you have heard so far in this case, members of the jury, have been simple enough and I do not propose ..." (34), and it becomes clear that Simpson seizes on the professional jargon of the law as an especially rewarding field for his strange logic and his games with language:

> "JUDGE: ... I see no sign of the jury. Are they here?
> PROS. COUN.: I understand they are, m'lord.
> USHER: ... There is no jury box, m'lord. As yet.
> JUDGE: And no jury either apparently.
> USHER: They are here in spirit, m'lord.
> JUDGE: I see. (He ponders momentarily.) As long as they are
> here in one form or another. ..." (35)

Simpson here satirizes the cliché-ridden formulas of the lawyers, implying that they press any information into an abstract concept without regard to its actual meaning. The judge proposes a hearing without the defendant, who is not yet in Court. The summoning of Mr. Groomkirby as a witness gives Simpson the opportunity of exposing the fussy style of the court:

> "PROSECUTING COUNSEL: The whereabouts of the accused,
> members of the jury, on that vital day when he was allegedly
> elsewhere, tally in every single particular with the where-
> abouts of the only other person who so far as we know was on
> the spot at the time, and who is in the court at this moment.
> The whereabouts of this other person are therefore of paramount
> importance, and I should like to call him to the witness box now.
> ..." (36)

There is a short discussion because Arthur Groomkirby refuses "swearing on the unexpurgated Bible" (37). Eventually he takes the oath on a copy of Uncle Tom's Cabin. Simpson demonstrates his ruthless adherence to logic once more in the following dialogue between witness and judge:

> "JUDGE: ... You are here simply and solely to give the Court

the facts as you know them. Anything more or less than this is not,
and can never be, the truth. You must therefore in your answers avoid
anything which is not to the best of your knowledge factually true.
This is what the solemn undertaking you have given to the Court
means.
Mr. G.: I understand that, m'lord.
JUDGE: And you intend therefore to be bound by this undertaking?
Mr. G.: No, m'lord.
JUDGE: You mean, in other words, that you intend to lie to the
Court.
Mr. G.: That is so, m'lord, yes.
JUDGE: A frank and honest reply." (38)

The strict observance of truth and honesty leads to a perversion of values: admit-
ting his intention to lie, Mr. Groomkirby paradoxically shows himself as a truthful
witness. This makes the Judge call him "a witness of candid integrity upon whom
it would be perfectly proper to place the utmost reliance" (39). Again the court pays
attention to the bare form of the statement only, disregarding its implications.

The trial is carried on with the prosecuting counsel questioning Mr. Groomkirby
about his actions on "the twenty-third of August last year" (40). It remains rather
obscure why he does so. The absurd streak in the dialogue is maintained throughout;
the answers of the witness waver between plain nonsense and insignificance (41), but
they are even outdone by the questions of the prosecuting counsel, which are distinguished by an extraordinarily mad application of logic. The reasoning of the lawyer
seems to be based on the assumption that the words and actions of an individual
should be mistrusted, because millions of other people could have spoken the same
words or performed the same actions. The human individual is opposed to the masses, and in the confrontation loses the credibility of his personal utterances and
deeds:

"PROS. COUN.: Would you also agree, Mr. Groomkirby, that -
confining ourselves to these islands alone - something of the order
of fifty million people could, if the need had arisen, have gone to
Chester-le-Street and interviewed this woman that afternoon?
MR. G.: I should think probably something of that order, yes, sir.
PROS. COUN.: The chances, in fact, were almost fifty million to
one against its being you who did so?" (42)

The ensuing observation of the lawyer is based on the same principle, but this time
the single, definite statement is pronounced suspicious compared with the whole of
language: considering the infinite possibilities of sentence constructions it has practically no chance of ever being used. The individual human being and his form of expression are classified as unimportant. The concept of sheer quantity is used against
them, and respect for them has disappeared:

"PROS. COUN.: And this answer she is supposed to have given you.

Goodness knows the words alone in the English language must be
enough in all their various forms virtually to defy computation -
the possible ways of combining them must be infinite. And yet it
was precisely _this_ combination she hit on." (43)

In the further course of the inquest Mr. Groomkirby gets more and more caught in
the maddening net the counsel throws over him and is driven to the most improbable
statements, even to the point of confessing that he was a masochist at the time of
his notorious interview with Myra Gantry. This provides the impulse for another
telling passage:

"PROS. COUN.: What was it that made you take it up in the first
place?
MR. G.: I was at a loose end at the time, sir.
. . .
PROS. COUN.: You were at a loose end. Would you tell the court,
Mr. Groomkirby, as clearly as you can in your own words, exactly
how loose this end was?
MR. G.: It was worn right down, sir.
JUDGE: (intervening). Worn right down. That tells us very little.
Was it swinging loose? Was it rattling about?
. . .
MR. G.: It was practically hanging off, m'lord.
JUDGE: And this is the end you say you were _at_? This loose end
that in your own words was practically hanging off?
MR. G.: I was pretty nearly at it, m'lord.
JUDGE: You told the Court a moment ago you were at it. Now you
say 'pretty nearly at it'. Which of these assertions is the true one?
MR. G.: It was touch and go, sir.
JUDGE: What was?
MR. G.: Whether I fell off, sir." (44)

As in Mrs. Gantry's story of Mr. Gridlake ("the jaws of death"), the use of a figure
of speech ("to be at a loose end") becomes the trigger for another endless discussion, during which the everyday expression is taken at its physical value. It is elaborated upon until it gets a life of its own; and after having been dissected, it is
brought into connection with Mr. Groomkirby again, with the result that his explanation becomes more and more alienated from his original action and utterly
useless for his defense. The court exhausts itself in purely formal matters, a circumstance which ends in its negligence of the actual facts.

The lights fade out, and the action narrows down to an encounter between the Judge
and Mr. Groomkirby, the former proposing a game of three-handed whist in the
dark room. Before this, another maddening conversation takes place, concerning
the fact that Mr. Groomkirby wears earplugs:

"MR. G.: (reluctantly). I wear earplugs.

Pause.
JUDGE: That perhaps is why you weren't able to hear anything out
there, Mr. Groomkirby.
MR. G.: There was nothing to hear!
Pause.
JUDGE: You were wearing earplugs, Mr. Groomkirby.
MR. G.: It was silent out there, I tell you!
JUDGE: Faulty earplugs evidently.
Pause.
JUDGE: You could be as sure as you like about it as long as
you knew your earplugs to be faulty.
Pause.
JUDGE: But not otherwise, Mr. Groomkirby.
Pause.
JUDGE: Were they faulty?
Pause.
JUDGE: I'm asking you a question! Were your earplugs faulty?
MR. G.: What if they were?
JUDGE: I see." (45)

The simple point that with earplugs in you cannot hear anything and its defiance by
Mr. Groomkirby leads the Judge to a series of questions which, punctuated by pauses, build up to Mr. Groomkirby's refractory counter-question ("What if they were?").
The pauses work as an important device in generating the pestering, inquisition-
like quality of the questions.

The fact that the Judge, at the end of his strange interview with Mr. Groomkirby,
treats the skull on the mantelpiece as a clock by comparing its "time" with that of
his watch and by shaking it as if to set it in motion, brings about a horrified reaction
on Sylvia's part: all of a sudden the skull seems to fulfil its task of reminding her of
death.

Now the real defendant is about to be tried before the court: Kirby Groomkirby. His
offences - foreshadowed by the conversation between Myra Gantry and Mabel Groomkirby in Act One (46) - are summed up by the prosecuting counsel:

"M'lord, the facts, as your lordship is aware, are not in dispute in
this case. The accused, Kirby Groomkirby, has admitted in the
Magistrate's Court that between the first of August last year and
the ninth of April he has been fairly regularly taking life, and since
the case was heard there three weeks ago has asked for nine other
offences in addition to the thirty-four in the original indictment to
be taken into account, making a total altogether of forty-three." (47)

The law obviously was in no great hurry to arrest Kirby for his wholesale murders
- "On the last occasion on which he took a life he was warned by Detective-Sergeant
Barnes that complaints had been lodged and that action would be taken against him if

142

he failed to conform to the law" (48), as the prosecuting counsel informs us. He then tells the court about Kirby's killing methods:

> "He seems to have been using the same technique fairly consistently, m'lord. He tells his victim a joke, waits for him to laugh, and then strikes him with an iron bar." (49)

Barnes, who is ordered into the witness box, appears to be in an especially awkward humour - his reaction to Kirby's murders at the time consisted in a remark to the Groomkirbys running. "It's beginning to add up down at the mortuary" (50). He confirms Kirby's liking for wearing black and explains that "he's been studying what he calls logical analysis, and this has gradually taken the form of looking for a logical pretext for wearing his black clothes" (51). This, in consequence, led him to kill people so that he could go into mourning for them. Kirby's mania made him devise the most crack-brained plans in order to satisfy his desire: it appears from the suggestive questions of the defending counsel that Kirby teaches his weighing machines to sing with the ultimate purpose of shipping them to the North Pole, where, acting as a sort of mechanical Sirens, they could lure people to those regions. These people, by jumping all at the same time, could succeed in shifting the axis of the earth somewhat more towards one side. The consequences of this complicated procedure would indeed be highly advantageous for Kirby:

> "DEF. COUN.: This would very likely bring about quite far-reaching climatic changes, would it not, Sergeant? ... A shifting of the Ice Cap, for instance. ... This might well give rise to a new Ice Age so far as these islands are concerned? ... Would it be true to say, Sergeant Barnes, that he was hoping in this way to provide himself with a self-perpetuating pretext for wearing black? ... By ensuring that for an indefinite period deaths from various causes connected with the excessive cold would be many and frequent?
> BARNES: That was at the back of it, yes, sir." (52)

The far-fetched idea suits Kirby's twisted character, and Mrs. Groomkirby confirms before the court that her son has "always been of a very logical turn of mind ever since he was born ..." (53).We also learn from his mother that he was dressed in black ever since he was a baby. The deadpan answer she gives to the defending counsel's question as to the jokes Kirby tells his later victims testifies to her complete indifference. The fact that her son is a mass killer does not trouble her in the least:

> "DEF. COUN.: ... Would it be true to say that your son, Mrs. Groomkirby, went to considerable trouble over these jokes?
> MRS. G.: He went to very great trouble indeed, sir. He sat up to all hours thinking out jokes for them.
> DEF. COUN.: Can you tell his lordship why your son went to

all this trouble with every one of his forty-three victims, when
there were a number of far simpler methods he could have used?
MRS. G.: I think for one thing he rather took to the humorous side
of it. And for another thing he always wanted to do everything he
could for these people. He felt very sorry for them." (54)

After all this evidence the court is to arrive at a decision. The defending counsel
has his final speech, made up of well-wrought phrases, a strained syntax and an
"elevated" diction. His conclusion sounds like a parody of those defending counsels
who try to get their clients free by every trick and under the most impossible circumstances:

"In my respectful submission, m'lord, this very complex
personality with whom we are dealing is not in any ordinary
sense of the word a killer; he is, on the contrary, a kindly,
rather gentle young man, not given to violence - except in this
one respect - and showing himself to be quite exceptionally
considerate of others even to the extent of arranging, at
considerable personal sacrifice of time and energy, for them
to die laughing." (55)

At last Kirby appears, "drops to his knees facing the Judge" (56), and the latter
prepares himself to pass sentence on the murderer. At first he stresses the fact
that none of Kirby's forty-three victims felt obliged to speak up for the accused,
"notwithstanding the great trouble we are told you went to in furnishing them with
laughing matter" (57). It seems significant that the Judge - who certainly is strongly
in favour of anything logical as long as it is perfectly self-evident - sees the only
"redeeming feature" (58) in Kirby's "desire to find a logical pretext" (59). The
concluding sentence is the very top of twisted logic and crowns the excesses we have
been exposed to throughout the play:

"In deciding upon the sentence I shall impose in this case, I have
been influenced by one consideration, and it is this: that in sen-
tencing a man for one crime, we may be putting him beyond the
reach of the law in respect of those other crimes of which he
might otherwise have become guilty. The law, however, is not to
be cheated in this way. I shall therefore discharge you." (60)

The law is not to be cheated, but in passing a sentence like the one above cheats
itself by its exaggerated regard to empty form. By sophisticated conclusions and
over-subtle theories it cuts itself off from common sense and reality.

One Way Pendulum ends with a playful inclusion of the theatre-audience in the action - a sort of alienation effect:

"MRS. G.: ... Seen all they want, have they?
BARNES: I think they have, yes. More or less. (Edging off.)

144

MRS. G.: ... Day in day out. Gawping. The place isn't your own.
BARNES: (escaping). Back tomorrow about half past seven then,
Mrs. Groomkirby - if that's all right." (61)

His last sentence refers to the audience of the following night, which will intrude,
so to speak, into the Groomkirby household.

The final moments with Mr. Groomkirby in a "Judge's wig and robe" (62) and stubborn weighing machine Gormless are a kind of self-repeal of the play by its author:

"Mr. G.: ... That, members of the jury, is the evidence before
you. ... What weight you give to it is a matter entirely for you.
GORMLESS: (lighting up). Fifteen stone ten pounds." (63)

The audience (or the readers) are invited to form their own judgment on the play.
Gormless's answer is a self-ironical evaluation by the author, breaking to a certain extent the point of any potential criticisn by not taking the dramatist and his
play too seriously.

*

After having read the play one is bound to ask the inevitable questions: What is it
all about? What happens in One Way Pendulum? What is the author getting at? Why
One Way Pendulum? Profound statement or plain nonsense?

In the first act we are introduced in detail to the Groomkirbys, who turn out to be
a very remarkable family. We become acquainted with the various eccentricities of
the members of the family, and we can only agree with Barnes when he observes
that "They've got some crack-brained ideas in that house" (64). Kirby and Mr.
Groomkirby are entirely taken up by their strange hobbies; Mabel Groomkirby with
dusting and worrying about her surplus food being eaten; Aunt Mildred with travelling;
Sylvia with death and the appearance of the human body. Communication among the
family members hardly exists, everybody is just living in his or her private world
(65). They tolerate each other, put up with each other; but this tolerance has a frightening quality about it.

Almost the whole of the second act is concerned with the trial scenes taking place
in Arthur Groomkirby's self-constructed Old Bailey, in which the Groomkirbys are
tried for their partly unnamed offences and Kirby is sentenced for his murders by
an apparently crazy court.

Reading the text of the play we notice that there is no normal plot. The author re-
stricts himself to giving us glimpses of persons and situations without developing
a line of action. What we are confronted with might be compared to a series of
snapshots. Scenes could be taken out and cuts made without any serious consequences
to the play as a whole; in fact this happened when One Way Pendulum was adapted for
television and shortened by about half an hour without losing its character.

So it is not the construction or the movement which distinguish the play or make up its particular effect. Simpson builds up his drama out of small units. One Way Pendulum is held together by gags, puns and startling non-sequiturs (66). The techniques Simpson employs throughout the play can be classed in three main categories: 1. The presentation of mad situations and people's deadpan reaction to whatever happens (67). 2. The almost continuous application of the non-sequitur (68); or as John Russell Taylor put it, " ... wilful discontinuity of the action, and the ruthlessly logical ... exploration of the possibilities inherent in each absurd premise ..." (69). 3. Figures of speech are taken at their physical value and reduced to absurdity by endless elaboration. A joke is not simply allowed to get its laugh but is elaborated beyond the "laughter barrier" - which can be the reason for more laughter or for tedium.

Now what do the events of the two acts and the linguistic acrobatics amount to? Is it just amusing nonsense which Simpson presents in One Way Pendulum? Is it mere fooling around with puns and gags, interspersed with black humour? In any case, John Russell Taylor does not think much of the play. He agrees with the unequivocal judgment of a man of the theatre:

> "Charles Marowitz, reviewing Simpson's latest play, The Form
> ... in Encore remarked unkindly but aptly that 'There is about
> Simpson the odour of civil service levity: the kind of pun-laden
> high-jinks one associates with banter around the tea trolley and
> the frolics of Ministry amateur societies', and this seems to me
> to place him exactly." (70)

I do not think that matters are so simple. It cannot be denied that beneath the mad surface, beneath the games with language, there is a disturbing level. A criticism of a certain kind of life cannot be overlooked. There is a dark side to One Way Pendulum. People are not able to communicate with each other, not even the members of the same family. Their pendulum swings to one side only. It does not swing back: human relationships are gravely disturbed. Responses have become atrophied.

But one day this way of life produces its results. The hobby-horse detaches itself from the human control and overpowers its riders. Arthur Groomkirby's kit-court turns into a real court; living-room and courtroom interlock, and the family is tried by a judge and counsels, who cross-examine them with the same indifference to human relationships as the Groomkirbys breed amongst themselves. For both court and family language is not an instrument for human understanding any more, but an empty pattern of fixed expressions. Their ruthless pursuit of everyday sayings and their elaboration of figures of speech indicate that their gamut of expression is so restricted that they have to cling to self-evident phrases in order to keep up any conversation at all. Language has become a noise to fill the empty space and has lost the ability of carrying meaning. Everything is form without contents. Especially the court has completely lost the sense for the communicative powers of language and is merely interested in its formal aspects.

The coming alive of the courtroom proves that something is wrong with the Groomkirbys, that they have become guilty - perhaps of indifference towards and neglect
of their fellow human beings. Their subjection to the absurd inquest of the court
indicates that they suffer from an undefined guilt complex, and Arthur Groomkirby
lives through a veritable nightmare of guilt during his dialogue with the Judge in the
dark.

The deadness of the Groomkirbys' existence pervades their most ordinary everyday
dialogue and penetrates to the smallest everyday speech units; the talk bogs down in
repetitions, the same words are linked with the same reactions and incidents; each
situation or event has its language pattern to accompany it (71). The feelings of the
characters in the play have become numb (72); they move in the treadmill of their
isolated existences without making an attempt to break out. Beneath the glittering
nonsense Simpson seems to make the point - in a dramatic exaggeration - that our
lives have become so automatic that we remain unimpressed by the most outrageous
occurrences. The human beings are turned into machines, and the machines are
treated like human beings (73). Martin Esslin writes:

> " ... The play portrays a suburban family living so wrapped up
> in its private fantasies that each of its members might be in-
> habiting a separate planet. ... Kirby's Pavlovian self-condi-
> tioning is a key image of the play: it stands for the automatism
> induced by habit on which the suburban commuting world rests.
> ... Habit and social convention are the great deadeners of the
> inauthentic society. To find a social justification for wearing
> black, Kirby turns into a mass murderer. ... One Way Pen-
> dulum portrays a society that has become absurd because routine
> and tradition have turned human beings into Pavlovian automata.
> In that sense, Simpson is a more powerful social critic than any
> of the social realists. His work is proof that the Theatre of the
> Absurd is by no means unable to provide highly effective social
> comment." (74)

Marowitz's and Taylor's opinions seem at least open to discussion. Perhaps they
did not fully grasp all the implications of the play. I think that we should give more
weight to the matter than "fifteen stone ten pounds", and I do not believe that we
can dismiss the play as mere "banter around the tea trolley". Out of gags, puns
and laughter an accusation and a warning materialize. Simpson puts his finger on
our everyday language and shows that it is a language running idle. He succeeds in
making visible the terrifying emptiness beneath the cosy surface of suburban middle-class life. He exposes the existence of its habit-ridden, robot-like people and
clearly advocates a two way pendulum.

As to the structure of Simpson's drama: One Way Pendulum appears to be cut into
two parts. Act One deals with the Groomkirby household, Act Two with the courtroom proceedings. The two parts seem to be fairly independent from each other,
at least at first sight. As a matter of fact the two acts are in closer connection

than could be expected: the courtroom presents the consequences of the behaviour of the family in Act One, the sudden development of an unsatisfactory and inhuman way of life. The structure mirrors situation and consequences in sharp but relevant juxtaposition (75).

*

In mixing nonsense with bitter comments on the situation of man in our time, and in exposing the deflation of language and the growing inability of modern man to communicate with his fellow creatures, Simpson reminds us of Eugène Ionesco. His plays, too, are dominated by the petty bourgeois with his clichés of thought and language, who becomes coordinated and robbed of his individuality within a modern mass society, and whose reactions turn mechanical. In his play La Cantatrice Chauve (1948) Ionesco exposes everyday language as absurd (76); and the "hero" of Les Rhinocéros (1958) struggles for his individuality, which is gradually swallowed by the dumb mass. It is probable that Simpson was influenced by Ionesco's theatre, although he developed his themes in British terms. John Russell Taylor is of the same opinion and traces some further affinities:

> "It is uniquely all of a piece, all written in pretty well the same style, and all based on one principle, the non sequitur. This seems to link it with the Theatre of the Absurd ... but it also links it with such humbler native prototypes as Itma and The Goon Show, even without dragging in Lewis Carroll and the English nonsense tradition (77). And it is with Itma that Simpson's plays seem happiest; certainly compared with the works of Ionesco, who appears to have served to a certain extent as Simpson's model, they look very parochial and unresourceful." (78)

We find parallels to one of Simpson's themes in Sterne's The Life and Opinions of Tristram Shandy (1760), where the main characters are absorbed in their private worlds like Arthur and Kirby Groomkirby:

> "They (79) live together in mutual incomprehension; and so do My Father and My Uncle Toby, that innocent, artless, childlike creation, the old soldier whose civilian life is dedicated to playing soldiers. They are creatures of fixed ideas, obsessively riding hobby-horses they alone appreciate." (80)

So Simpson does not stand isolated with One Way Pendulum and the rest of his work.

*

The fact that throughout the play Simpson's significant pauses were strictly adhered to, made the scenes with Aunt Mildred (I, 20-22) as well as the scene between Mrs. Groomkirby and Myra Gantry (I, 31-34) strikingly effective on the stage. The unexpected development of the conversations in both instances gained their full power by this obedience to the author's planned timing. The pauses worked as tension-builders and gave the passages their peculiar, halting rhythm, which drove the audi ence to a pitch of expectation as to the form of the following afterthought.

A very effective moment occurred when Mrs. Groomkirby speaks the sentence "What I'm dreading is the dav he brings the Old Bailey home for us all to fall over" (81) - a sentence followed by the actual arrival of a panel out of the "build-it-your-self" Old Bailey. The hilarious impression was confirmed by Simpson himself (82).

The opening of the second act was another memorable stage event: the curtain rose on a courtroom suffocating the Groomkirby living-room - a moment which provoked a good laugh among the spectators (83). Laughter and puzzlement mingled when the court began to fill up with judge and lawyers.

Another successful scene was the trial of Mr. Groomkirby. It caused Cecil Wilson to write that:

> "The trial scene, with Douglas Wilmer's poker-faced judge presiding as solemnly as if it all really meant something, was the funniest since 'Alice in Wonderland'." (84)

The nonsensical dialogue worked with astonishing effect, as nothing in the scene diverted the attention from the words. No attempt was made to cover them up by visual tricks. The complete seriousness with which they were spoken added to the hilarious impression. Mervyn Jones thought that

> "The cross-examination of Mr. Groomkirby is the high-spot of the play and a masterpiece of satirical fantasy ..." (85)

The continuation fell rather flat on the stage. The relatively drawn out game of cards in the dark between the Judge and Mr. Groomkirby was puzzling without being funny. The dialogue is somewhat pretentious here. After all the verbal witticisms this episode came as a dull patch. Simpson clearly meant it to have an alarming effect but only succeeded in spreading irritation and boredom. Gaskill recalled the scene:

> "I had a lot of trouble because the actors did not know what the scene meant. In the production it did not work completely successful. People were puzzled, and the argument of the two actors did not get many laughs." (86)

Surprisingly the long speech of the Judge near the end of the play caught the audi ence with its mad logic. Gaskill thought it "a bit too long, but brilliantly delivered" (87), whereas Simpson maintained that "The final speech of the judge was delivered with total verisimilitude; it was not too long" (88).

In any case the contrast between the unusual contents of the dialogues and the unconcerned everyday intonation with which they were spoken, proved really amusing
on the stage.

The production was underlined by straight music arranged by Dudley Moore.

*

As one can understand, the 1959 cast of <u>One Way Pendulum</u> was faced with tasks
quite different from those they had had to tackle before. Simpson's queer humour
and his constant use of the non sequitur demanded a new kind of comic acting. Special attention had to be paid to the pauses. Conventional comic techniques had to be
abolished. Simpson was aware of these difficulties:

> "At the time, the style in which I was writing was something new
> in the English theatre, and actors found it difficult to adjust to a
> kind of playing that nowadays they take in their stride." (89)

Alison Leggatt, who played the part of Mrs. Groomkirby, rose magnificently to the
challenge and gave shape to the matter-of-fact-attitude of the character. Director
William Gaskill spoke of her "wonderful comic technique" and thought her "brilliant", although "sometimes she wanted to decorate her performance with other
comic effects unfitting for Simpson" (90). She gave her voice the right unemotional
tinge. Following Simpson's direction, she took "in her stride most of what happens
indoors, and is only marginally concerned with anything that may happen elsewhere
..." (91). The critic of <u>The Times</u> thought her approach exactly right:

> " ... Miss Alison Leggatt has the art of throwing away the finest
> non-sequitur in the world with a matter-of-fact manner which
> redoubles its intrinsic worth." (92)

According to T.C. Worsley she had " ... an absolutely perfect command of the
comfortable and reassuring intonation in which such clichés are commonly uttered
..." (93), and the reviewer of the <u>Glasgow Herald</u> stressed the same point in different words:

> "Alison Leggatt, the mother, is not the sane element that puts
> the others' lunacy into perspective. Her dead-pan ability to take
> every irrelevance as a matter of course is just the one thing
> needed to warp the balanced judgment of any audience irremedi-
> ably." (94)

She caught the rhythm of Simpson's dialogue, especially in her scene with Myra
Gantry (95), and presented the very image of unconcerned equanimity:

> " ... Alison Leggatt, whose timing and delivery of lines was
> immaculate and inspired. She handled the fiendishly difficult

dialogue as though it were something Pinero had put together in
his little spick-and-span workshop ..." (96)

Another successful performance was the Judge as played by Douglas Wilmer. He
spoke his lines with their desperate logic with extreme gravity and a frozen face,
was "unhurried, sure of himself, and with the instincts - sublimated by his profession - of a stoat" (97). Gaskill was of the opinion that Wilmer delivered the final speech of the Judge admirably (98), and T. C. Worsley in The Financial Times
characterized the actor's facial expression by means of a telling simile:

> "Douglas Wilmer is brilliant as the Judge, looking like a sick,
> sour-faced St. Bernard ..." (99)

Together with Graham Crowden as Prosecuting Counsel Wilmer exposed the whole
court as a dead institution caught in empty forms and blessed with dry brains, and
they both proceeded in "solemn absurdity" (100), uttering the most heartrending
nonsense with an irresistible seriousness. The cast (101) succeeded in adapting
themselves to the atmosphere of the play and realized the important fact that nonsense, in order to operate with its full force, must take itself seriously. The actors subjected themselves to Gaskill's respective guidance ("'Absurd' plays demand
strict guiding of the actors") (102) and "did what I liked" (103). The critic of the
City Press noticed the actors' success:

> "Though the humour of this, to me, extremely funny play is
> essentially verbal, it nonetheless gains enormously in impact
> by the impeccable gravity, timing and characterisation with
> which the cast puts it over." (104)

The author himself praised the actors:

> "Most of the acting was as I wanted it, and some (notably by
> Alison Leggatt and Douglas Wilmer) was exceptionally good
> ..." (105)

*

For William Gaskill, who directed One Way Pendulum, this kind of play was not
something entirely new: already in 1957 and 1958 he had staged Simpson's A Resounding Tinkle (both the Sunday Night and the main bill productions) and The Hole
respectively.

Gaskill emphasized the emptiness of the Groomkirby's existence by setting the first
act in a "two-dimensional" scenery, that is to say he had the furniture and other
props, as well as architectural details, drawn and painted onto the walls in black
and white, creating an unreal atmosphere for the action. The courtroom of Act Two,
on the other hand, was solid and three-dimensional, making palpable the disturbing
change by presenting the fantastic realistically.

Gaskill respected the dominating role of the dialogue in the play and accordingly devoted his special attention to the timing, the gradation and the variation of the speeches. "Dialogue in this play comes definitely before the characters", he remarked (106).

Particular weight was given to the intonation in which the non sequitur dialogue was spoken. Gaskill demanded dry matter-of-fact speaking instead of animated, lively talk. "The lines were spoken with precision and what I can only call stylised naturalism (like Wilde)", as Simpson said (107). It was exactly this precision that caught something of the mechanical quality of the characters' reactions.

Gaskill stressed the importance of following the author's directions concerning the pauses:

> "One Way Pendulum is an exercise in time. It is characterized by
> unusual timing, and Simpson uses his pauses to create comic effects.
> If you do not respect his directions, you most probably do not get
> the laughs, either." (108)

The teamwork between author and director in this production was especially remarkable. Simpson confirms This "joining of forces" himself and acknowledges the usefulness of the director's work:

> "All these plays (109) were done with the closest collaboration
> between Mr. Gaskill and me ... As for the director's function,
> it is obviously essential for any play, but particularly for mine,
> which, because of the rhythmic way I write, have to be 'conducted'
> as much as produced." (110)

Gaskill's production was judged positively by most of the critics. Cecil Wilson in the Daily Mail wrote that "The strange gleam of logic that shines through the lunacy owes much to the gravity of William Gaskill's production" (111), and the reviewer of The Stage noted that "The essence of presenting such a play is, of course, solemnity, and ... production is notable for its masterly matter-of-fact projection of the ridiculous ..." (112). A further proof for the director's adequate approach can be seen in the review which appeared in Punch, maintaining that "It is the seeming normality of the Groomkirby household in William Gaskill's production that is so deliciously disturbing ..." (113). This "normality" was achieved, as we have seen above, by the unemotional rendering of the most absurd lines.

The critic of the New Statesman analyzed the direction and summed up its qualities as follows:

> "But the success of the evening says even more for William Gaskill's
> direction. The young directors at the Royal Court aren't usually
> remarkable for their self-effacement. But Mr. Gaskill, who is cer-
> tainly the most talented of them, has resisted all mannerisms, all

hocus-pocus and all but one of the innumerable temptations to
lapse into the symbolic (114). The result is a production which,
instead of calling attention to itself, gets the best out of the play.
And the best is the wittiest entertainment now in London." (115)

By building up his production in collaboration with the author, Gaskill succeeded in
catching the atmosphere of the play perfectly and in presenting a genuine "Simpson".

*

Stephen Doncaster's task consisted in designing two sets - the living-room of the
Groomkirby family and the courtromm of the second act. In accordance with Gas-
kill's conception (116) he devised a rather stylized "fantasy" set for the first act.
He closely followed Simpson's directions but exchanged "Left" and "Right" (117).
The set for Act Two shattered the other one by erupting into it (118). The upper
part of the courtroom architecture pushed through part of the ceiling and cracked
other parts of it, forcibly illustrating the turn of events and the spreading of Arthur
Groomkirby's kit over the household (119). The Judge sat in a heavily carved, elevated chair with the coat of arms overhead. A table with two chairs stood in front
of the whole structure; the control panel (120) was at its left side, and the cash
register stood on top of a cupboard at the extreme left of the stage, near the door
which led to the hall. The staircase, part of which could be seen when the door was
open, was also not solid but painted. Sylvia's memento mori - the skull - was on a
sort of underdeveloped mantelpiece above a suggested fireplace at the right side of
the stage.

Doncaster's set enhanced the effect of the play by recreating and enforcing in visual
terms the sudden change of atmosphere, and in making apparent the life situation of
a family who is about to become inhuman.

*

The reaction of the audience to the play and its production was sharply divided. Part
of the spectators liked One Way Pendulum, part of them did not. Some remained
indifferent and unimpressed. This discrepancy of response is easily explained by
the fact that in order to appreciate Simpson's way of writing one has to have a very
special sense of humour and a liking for sick jokes. If one has not, one is inclined
to dismiss Simpson's plays as silly and ridiculous. "It takes a trained mind to re-
lish a non-sequitur" (121), as the "author" in A Resounding Tinkle remarks. Asked
about his opinion as to the reaction of the audience, Simpson said:

"People tended either to like it all very much, or to hate it with
quite savage feeling. Much of this was induced by total incompre-
hension." (122)

By 1959, of course, the Simpson technique had already found its admirers and
perhaps did not cause such a shock any more as in his first play, A Resounding

<u>Tinkle,</u> which was presented at the Court in 1957. Simpson explains the effect of his style on the audience:

> "I do not write for a certain kind of people. I write for anyone who can be induced to come and see what I write - though it is true that my plays appeal (not by design on my part) to a sophisticated rather than an unsophisticated audience. I hope in the future to rectify this situation by writing plays that appeal to both." (123)

It is certainly appropriate to say that an intellectual spectator derives more fun from Simpson's games with language and logic. The "unsophisticated" theatre-goer is generally more in favour of a straightforward joke which stimulates him in to a direct laugh, without a quick thinking process in between. <u>One Way Pendulum</u> was so successful with the audiences as to get a transfer to the West End Criterion Theatre. The Court had won a large audience for an unusual type of play. William Gaskill summed up:

> "People still remember the production. It must have caught something at the time - perhaps because it was about middle-class people." (124)

*

The critics, forewarned by Simpson's earlier plays, were not as thunderstruck as they had been one year and a half before, although their reviews were again as different as chalk from cheese. Among the twenty reviews examined somewhat more closely I found nine mainly positive ones, a further nine giving the production a mixed reception, and only two treating it devastatingly. Bernard Levin in <u>The Daily Express</u> entitled his article <u>Lunatic Logic - and it's dazzling,</u> and showed an enthusiastic response to Simpson's style, the acting and the direction, even to the point of risking a daring prophesy:

> "The whole thing is composed of lines which have a kind of appalling inevitability ... and which add up to something so funny that before the end it becomes physically painful to go on laughing. Mr. Simpson's verbal felicities are piled up in a glittering mountain of wit and laughter and observation, and if anything funnier and truer is seen on a London stage in 1960, then 1960 will be a very remarkable year indeed. It is acted with a brilliance worthy of it by (among others) Mr. George Benson, Miss Patsy Rowlands, and Mr. Douglas Wilmer, and produced to perfection ..." (125)

The reviewer of <u>The City Press</u> was likewise struck by the weird humour of <u>One Way Pendulum,</u> as well as by the competent production:

> "For me it was an evening of continuous chuckling enjoyment interspersed with surrender to helpless laughter ... The most

hilarious scene is that in which he (126) is in his own witness box
being cross-examined in a case of homicide, presided over a judge,
brilliantly played by Douglas Wilmer. ... It owes a lot, also, to
William Gaskill's direction. Alison Leggatt, Patsy Rowlands, George
Benson, Graham Crowden and Graham Armitage could not conceivably
be bettered in the leading parts." (127)

Simpson's sense of humour was obviously appreciated by J.C. Trewin who entitled
his article in The Illustrated London News with the punning words Laughter in Court:

"Having often been on the wrong side of the fence, I sympathized
with the people at the Court, who (in my pauses for breath or eye-
wiping) were looking as though they had just seen Banquo's ghost
..." (128)

Criticism of one particular scene occurs in the review which appeared in the New
Statesman. It was the only negative point the critic made:

"It says a great deal for Mr. Simpson's invention that he manages
to keep up the pressure of perverse wit for two long acts. Only once
does the play drag, and that is during the interlude in the dark between Dad and the Judge, when the logical rules of the game are
waived for a flight of rather pretentious symbolism." (129)

The review in The Times exposed one of the undoubted weaknesses of the play and
mirrored the critic's admiration for the actors' achievement:

" ... This trial has some delightful passages. They nearly all
depend, however, on the same joke, as do passages rather less
delightful ... a play wholly composed of non-sequiturs is as
hard to digest as a play wholly composed of puns. We should tire
of the sameness of the joke long before we do if the acting were
less resourceful." (130)

Cecil Wilson in the Daily Mail drew a parallel to Lewis Carroll ("This was the most
comic trial scene since 'Alice'"), but put his finger on a dangerous spot in Simpson's play:

"For me it remained a delirious joy until the author began trying
too hard to be funny and therefore failed." (131)

The shortcomings of the author's technique were also mentioned in Patrick Gibb's
review in the Daily Telegraph:

"The parody of a murder trial which followed, with a literal-
minded but conscientious judge, a witness who regards the oath
as a challenge and a languid prosecuting counsel tying him in

knots, displayed Mr. Simpson's comic observation at its keenest.
That he was able to make it seem funny that the witness should
insist on swearing on 'Uncle Tom's Cabin' instead of the Bible
indicates his talent for turning absurdity to theatrical effect.
By contrast with this brilliant court scene much else seemed
rather flat and one was reminded, as so often with inspired
nonsense, how difficult it is to keep the ball up.
A nicely chosen cast ... played admirably in the straightfaced
manner the piece demanded ..." (132)

The review in The Observer dealt critically with some passages in the play but
showed that the critic was impressed by Simpson's dialogue and its most conspicuous elements as well as with the way the actors realized it:

"The plot has a wild logic which needs experience rather than description, but the very high degree of pleasure to be extracted from
it depends chiefly on a combination of looking-glass dialogue and
admirable acting ... But I see no reason to describe a plot which
cannot convey in synopsis the tickling fantasy, the sustained comic
invention which adorn its deadpan absurdities. ... Douglas Wilmer
as Judge gives one of the best performances to be seen on the
London stage; and as Prosecuting Counsel Graham Crowden presents a lifelike portrait of Sir Gladwyn Jebb.
Some of the comic detail miscarries. There is nothing particularly funny about a prolongued game of three-handed whist in
the dark; and too much is made of an aunt in a wheelchair with a
single joke to her name ... direction is geared to the occasion,
and Stephen Doncaster has provided a décor both witty and pretty
..." (133)

Harold Conway admitted the amusing sides of One Way Pendulum but thought that it
was too long:

"Take ten minutes out of each act and you have the funniest,
most inventive romp seen in London for years." (134)

Simpson's special methods were also stressed by T.C. Worsley in The Financial
Times:

"One Way Pendulum moves forward continuously and builds up to
a splendidly absurd climax ... Produced ... and acted throughout
with a very exact feel for comic timing, this is the funniest play
in London - if it happens to hit your sense of humour ..." (135)

The often puzzling impression conveyed by the dialogue was summarized somewhat
drastically by the critic of the Times Educational Supplement, who entitled his review Comic and Curious:

"And at the end of it the public left the gallery, or the audience the
auditorium, feeling that they had been beaten over the heads with
bladders for 37 hours ..." (136)

As already his title Rather Baffling indicates, Dick Richards of the Daily Mirror
could not make much of the play and identified himself with that part of the audience
who could not either:

" ... though there was dutiful laughter, nobody could quite explain
what he was getting at ... as a play it seemed ridiculous." (137)

The harshest rejection came from the reviewer of the Kensington News. His sense
of humour seems to be on an essentially different level from that of Simpson. He
entitled his article with the defiant words "Mr. Simpson Doesn't Make me Laugh"
(138). There you are.

But on the whole Simpson had convinced the critics, who felt that he had introduced
a category into modern English drama which had been little known before. They
were not unwilling to let themselves be carried away by his strange logic and absurd dialogue, and appreciated his witty results to a relatively high degree.

*

One Way Pendulum belongs to the nine plays staged between April 1956 and April
1963 which made a profit for the English Stage Company. It was transferred to the
West End and later on to the Broadway.

N.F. Simpson's next play, The Cresta Run, was also produced at the Court, in
1965. Keith Johnstone directed it, again in close touch with the author. The play
showed that Simpson was not able to develop his technique any further, and that it
resulted in repetitiousness and tedium. Since then, his career as a dramatist
seems to have been interrupted.

But the merit of the English Stage Company in having furthered and sponsored him
at a time when he had to offer something new to the British theatre, remains undoubted. By their encouragement they introduced something into modern English
drama which without this encouragement would not have had its breakthrough.

***

Arnold Wesker's <u>The Kitchen</u> was (after <u>Chicken Soup with Barley</u> (1), <u>Roots</u> (2), and <u>I'm Talking About Jerusalem</u> (3) his fourth play to be staged at the Court - though a first version of it had already been given a Sunday Night production without décor in September 1959. <u>The Kitchen</u> as performed in 1961 was a different play, as Wesker had rewritten it to a considerable extent. In this chapter we are going to examine the later and final version and its realization on the stage. The play was directed by John Dexter, its set designed by Jocelyn Herbert. The first night with the English Stage Company took place at the Belgrade Theatre Coventry on June 19th 1961. The London premiere at the Royal Court followed on June 27th of the same year.

*

Throughout this play the scene is "a large kitchen in a restaurant called the Tivoli" (4). The action starts at seven o'clock in the morning with Magi, the night porter, lighting the ovens. By and by some of the staff come in: Max, the butcher; Bertha, the vegetable cook; Betty and Winnie, two waitresses; Paul and Raymond, the pastry cooks. Slowly the kitchen wakes up, morning greetings are exchanged, private conversations are taken up. From a talk between Anne, Raymond, Paul and Max we learn a thing or two about a cook named Peter and his character:

> "MAX. He's a bloody German, a fool, that's what he is. He is always quarrelling, always. There's no one he hasn't quarrelled with, am I right? No one! That's some scheme that is, exchanging cooks! What do we want to exchange cooks for? Three years he's been here, three years! ..." (5)

Peter is apparently jealous on account of Monique, a waitress, who seems to be his girlfriend, and we also hear about a fight that took place the night before between him and Gaston, a Cypriot cook. The reasons are obscure and provoke Paul to the philosophical utterance:

> "Who knows? There's always fights, who knows how they begin?" (6)

The impression we get of Peter (who has not arrived yet) is of a man with a rather violent temper.

The atmosphere in the kitchen is still relatively peaceful, but Anne, the coffee and dessert waitress, says:

> " ... You wouldn't think this place will become a madhouse in two hours, would you now. ..." (7)

There is some more chat and gossip, and Dimitri, a young Cypriot kitchen porter, explains why he would not work in a factory despite his technical talents:

> " ... All day I would screw in knobs. I tell you, in a factory a
> man makes a little piece till he becomes a little piece, you know
> what I mean?" (8)

Obviously he looks on the kitchen as a better place. Asked about what happened to
Peter, Dimitri gives a reason which is both convincing and thought-provoking:

> "But you think it was all Peter's fault? They all wanted to fight.
> Listen, you put a man in the plate-room all day, he's got dishes
> to make clean, and stinking bins to take away, and floors to
> sweep, what else there is for him to do - he wants to fight. He
> got to show he is a man some way. So - blame him! (9)

A slight criticism can be discovered in this answer, criticism of a way of living
and working, dissatisfaction with an often dirty and humdrum job, in which a man
becomes stunted and dwarfed.

Alfredo comes in ("An old chef, about sixty-five and flatfooted ... He is a typical
cook in that he will help nobody and will accept no help; nor will he impart his
knowledge. ...") (10), and Monique, asked about Peter's adventure, is ready with
some further details as to the circumstances of his fight - details from which we
learn that Peter appears to combine a choleric temperament with a talent for ex-
tracting himself from unpleasant situations by means of an intuitive coolness.

Activities in the kitchen start moving, little problems crop up, and already another
character, Michael, bursts into the scene. The youthful boisterousness of his first
speech hides his longing for a different kind of existence:

> " ... Look at it ... a lovely sight, isn't it? Isn't she beautiful?
> A bloody great mass of iron and we work it - praise be to God
> for man's endeavour - what's on the menu today? I don't know
> why I bother - it's always the same. ... One day I'll work in a
> place where I can create masterpieces, master bloody pieces.
> Beef Stroganoff, Chicken Kiev, and that king of the Greek dishes
> - Mousaka." (11)

He sees the kitchen as some greedy female monster being kept alive by its staff,
and his final lines betray his wish to escape into a brighter place.

While Kevin, the new Irish cook, is introduced by Hans, a first minor row breaks
out between Nicholas, another young Cypriot, and Bertha (12). Gradually the atmosphere grows heated and begins to thicken. The first conflicts among the staff
flare up but die down again.

As Nicholas is briefing Kevin on the organization of the kitchen, the much talked

160

about Peter arrives at last, and finally all the cooks and waitresses are working. The routine gets into its swing; a steady, unhurried rhythm dominates the scene. Peter, in between, attempts to settle his quarrel with Gaston but does not succeed (13). Again Paul comments on the situation and comes to a half angry, half resigned conclusion as to the goings on in the kitchen. His remark seems to be based on long experience:

> " ... Nobody knows when to stop. A quarrel starts and it goes on for months. When one of them is prepared to apologize so the other doesn't know how to accept - and when someone knows how to accept so the other ... ach! Lunatics! ..." (14)

A complaint about sour soup mixes with Frank's order for twelve chickens; and Max all of a sudden, as if his nerves were at breaking point, shouts at Hans "You're in England now, speak bloody English" (15), protesting that everybody talks in a different language. He thus draws attention to the babylonic confusion of idioms reigning in the kitchen. Peter makes some nasty, perhaps apt comments on Marango, the proprietor:

> "You think he is kind? He is a bastard! ... What kind of a life is that, in a kitchen! Is that a life I ask you? Me, I don't care, soon I'm going to get married and then whisht - " (16)

We understand that Peter's nerves, too, are strained, that he is thoroughly dissatisfied with his work as a cook in such a place.

The staff have their early lunch break, which is marked by their grumbling about the food, by a squabble between Nicholas and Daphne, and an accident of Hans who burns his face with hot water. Those of the staff who crowd round him seem to do so from curiosity rather than other feelings, and Frank, the second chef, is not greatly concerned:

> "FRANK. He'll live. (to the crowd) All right, it's all over, come on. ... No matter how many times you tell them they still rush around. ...
> MARANGO. He's burnt his face. It's not serious, (to CHEF) but it might have been. ...
> CHEF (to FRANK) Much he cares. It interrupts the kitchen so he worries. ..." (17)

The dialogue between Frank and the chef reveals that even they, in their superior positions, share the general dissatisfaction with the work in the kitchen and only wait for their chance to get away from it all (18). Gradually the levels hidden underneath the indifferent surface become visible, and emotions break out.

The lunch Peter, Kevin, Hans and Michael sit down to provides a short pause ("the calm before the storm") (19), which gives them the opportunity for some observations on their work. Peter's remarks indicate that the kitchen has seen many changes among its staff, and that in a way he has given up finding any rewarding moments in his profession. He regards it as a "job" and has apparently resigned to his fate.

Paul talks bitterly about his private life and his involvement in an unhappy marriage, and Hans raves about the beauties of New York, where he has been twice. Peter is convinced that everything depends on hard money:

> "KEVIN. Oh I don't know. You'd've thought it was possible to
> run a small restaurant that could take pride in its food and made
> money too.
> PETER. Of course it's possible, my friend - but you pay to eat
> in it. It's money. It's all money. The world chase money so
> you chase money too. (snapping his fingers in a lunatic way)
> Money! Money! Money!" (20)

A waitress enters to order some fish, but Peter detains Kevin with the sentence "The customer can wait" (21). Frank curses about some special wish of Marango's. In the conversation concerning the problem of capital punishment between Frank, Max and Nicholas, the underlying violence and aggressiveness become palpable; an aggressiveness generated and developed by the insane atmosphere of the kitchen.

In a short interlude Peter implores Monique to divorce her husband but only upsets her with his impatience.
The lunchbreak is over, work is resumed. But now the rhythm changes. It accelerates slowly, but surely:

> "CHEF. Let me see. (Watches KEVIN start to work). All right,
> but quicker, quicker, quicker.
> PETER. Quicker, quicker, quicker, Irishman.
> HANS. Quicker, quicker.
> PETER. Watch him now the Irishman, soon he won't know what's
> happening ..." (22)

Peter and Hans here display a sort of desperate fun which only covers up their own nervousness. The waitresses "appear in greater numbers as the service swings into motion. Queues form in front of first one cook, then another" (23). Orders for all kinds of food pour in at a steady pace. Despite the marked acceleration there is still time for occasional private talk:

> "FRANK. Two roast chicken and sauté.
> CYNTHIA (to HANS). These my veal cutlets?
> HANS. These are your cutlets! Four Kalbskotletts only
> for you baby!
> CYNTHIA. Oh really!
> HANS (to PETER). Wunderbar! Peter look! Wie die geht!

162

Wie die aussieht, die ist genau meine Kragenweite!" (24)

The stress of the work begins to tell in the staccato sentences of the waitresses. Voices cross each other, orders are shouted and confirmed, misunderstandings happen, Kevin burns his fish, communication becomes difficult, time presses, the heat and the exasperation grow:

> "PETER (helping KEVIN). Let's go Irishman, let's go. The next.
> DAPHNE. Two salmon.
> PETER. Right.
> BETTY (to HANS). My veal cutlets.
> HANS. Your veal cutlets.
> PETER. And the next?
> JACKIE (to PETER). Three sardines.
> BETTY (to HANS). Oh come on, lobster-face.
> HANS. What does it mean, lobster-face?
> PETER. And the next?" (25)

Peter is working himself up into a perfect frenzy. When the excitement and the rush approach their climax helpfulness and politeness suddenly disappear; everybody is struggling with his tasks and problems, "in the kitchen it is every man for himself now" (26). Noise, agitation and movement build up to a maddening peak; dialogue turns strictly functional; there is hardly a superfluous word, only Peter finds the time to squeeze in a few personal remarks. The rhythm becomes breathless, orders and their repetition amount to a gastronomic confusion in terms of language:

> "DAPHNE (to FRANK). Two roast chicken.
> FRANK. Two roast chicken.
> WINNIE (to ALFREDO). Two roast veal and spaghetti.
> JACKIE (to MICHAEL). One prawn omelet.
> MICHAEL. One prawn.
> GWEN (to ALFREDO). Two roast beef.
> ALFREDO. Two roast beef.
> ...
> GWEN (to HANS). Four veal cutlets.
> HANS. Four veal cutlets.
> MOLLY (to KEVIN). Me sole, luvvy, where's me sole?
> KEVIN (re-entering). Wait a bloody minute, can't you.
> MOLLY (to KEVIN). Two.
> GWEN (to PETER). Two halibut.
> BETTY (to MICHAEL). Three hamburgers.
> CYNTHIA (to KEVIN). Three plaice. There's no time for breathing here, you know.
> KEVIN. Jesus is this a bloody madhouse.
> MICHAEL. Three hamburgers.
> NICHOLAS. Plates.
> MANGOLIS. Plates.

KEVIN. Have you all gone barking-raving-bloody-mad." (27)

The advance towards a peak is mirrored in the short sentences and the ejaculation of single words. Part One ends when Kevin cannot do otherwise but characterize the kitchen as a "madhouse", as "barking-raving-bloody-mad."

This wild vortex is followed by a calm interlude. The rush is over, the waitresses and some of the cooks have left. The others, exhausted, sit and lie around, relaxing as well as they can. Kevin, completely worn out, thinks about leaving. But Dimitri does not give him much hope of a change. From the conversation between Kevin, Peter and Dimitri it appears that the chances for an escape are not lavish, as conditions are similar everywhere. Relationships between human beings are easily broken.

Peter's construction of a fantastic arch out of dustbins, saucepans, ladles and a broomstick, topped by a flower, is followed by his passionate defense of games and dreams, which clearly points to an indistinct but intense nostalgia in him for another life, for a life in a dream world where he could feel as happy as a child. It is, as a matter of fact, the paradise of childhood Peter is longing for:

> "PETER. This one says games and that one says dreams. You
> think it's a waste of time? You know what a game is? A dream?
> It's the time when you forget what you are and you make what
> you could be. When a man dreams - he grows, big, better. You
> find that silly? ... There is time to dream. Everyone should
> dream, once in a life everyone should dream. Hey Irishman, you
> dream, how do you dream, tell us?" (28)

Peter is thoroughly dissatisfied with his existence, but he does not do anything decisive to change the situation. He is the inefficient weakling, reminding us of some of Eugene O'Neill's characters, who flees from reality into the realm of pipe-dreams: "It's the time when you forget what you are and you make what you could be."

Peter wants the others to talk about their secret wishes and hopes. His invitation meets with disappointing results: Dimitri dreams of a shed where he can build radios and TV-sets, Kevin of sleep, Hans of money, Raymond of women. Nobody seems to have a vision of a full and satisfying life. Only Paul expresses the wish of establishing a real relationship with another human being - "I dream of a friend. You give me a rest, you give me silence, you take away this mad kitchen so I make friends, so I think - maybe all the people I thought were pigs are not so much pigs" (29). In the long story he tells about his neighbour, who is a bus driver, he articulates his depression about the absence of understanding among human beings, about their lack of tolerance and their contempt of friendship. Peter's reaction is immediate: "I ask for dreams - you give me nightmares" (30). The moment of truth comes for Peter himself, when Kevin says "We're waiting for your dream now, Peter boy" (31). But he fails in the attempt. Paul concludes "He hasn't got a dream"

(32), and Kevin compares Peter's ideals with his behaviour in the kitchen:

> "KEVIN. ... He talks about peace and dreams and when I ask
> him if I could use his cutting-board to cut me lemons on this
> morning he told me - get your own. Dreams? See yous!" (33)

Peter is unable to apply his ideas to his everyday existence. His concept of a better world remains vague.

Gradually the other members of the staff come back from their afternoon break. Even Alfredo notices that Peter is in an agitated state and asks for the reasons:

> "ALFREDO. You are not ill, are you?
> PETER. Who knows.
> ALFREDO. No pain nor nothing?
> PETER. No. Alfredo, look -
> ALFREDO. Good! You have all your teeth?
> PETER. Yes.
> ALFREDO. Good! You have good lodgings?
> PETER. Yes.
> ALFREDO. So tell me what you're unhappy for." (34)

Alfredo connects happiness with health and good lodgings. On the other hand he admits that now he is only working "for the money" (35). Peter's lines show that the kitchen oppresses him more and more.

As the work is slowly taken up again, Violet meditates about better times, and recalls that she "once served the Prince of Wales" (36). Kevin considers leaving after his first day and expresses his dislike for Mr. Marango, the proprietor, who is spying on everybody and is always worried about everything, especially his money. "Marango spielt den lieben Gott!" (37), as Peter elaborates.

A further conflict brews when Peter gives two cutlets to a tramp who appears in the kitchen. Marango seems to be obsessed by the fixed idea that everybody is against him and tries to do damage to him:

> "MARANGO (softly). Sabotage. (Pause.) It's sabotage you do to me.
> (sadly taking his right hand out of his pocket, and waving it round the
> kitchen) It's my fortune here and you give it away. (He moves off
> muttering 'sabotage.')" (38)

Slowly the signs of desperation in Peter grow ("A bastard man. A bastard house") (39). He wishes the kitchen to disappear - "Just one morning - to find it gone" (40), but cannot offer anything in its place. The kitchen suffocates him:

> "PAUL. Fat lot of good you'd be if it went - you couldn't even
> cough up a dream when it was necessary.

...
PETER. I can't, I can't. (<u>sadly</u>) I can't dream in a kitchen!" (41)

Working speed is slowly increasing again as the evening draws near. A waitress passes out because of the excessive heat (later we learn that she is pregnant), and Peter and Monique carry on with their futile talk.

But by now Peter is at the end of his tether. As the orders pour in again and Violet, the waitress, tries to serve herself, something snaps in him, and he is not able to restrain himself any longer:

"VIOLET (<u>taking another plate from off the oven</u>). I won't take
orders from you, you know, I ...
PETER (<u>shouting and smashing the plate from her hand for a</u>
<u>second time</u>). Leave it! Leave it there! I'll serve you. Me! Me!
Is <u>my</u> kingdom here. This is the side where <u>I</u> live. This.
VIOLET (<u>very quietly</u>). You Boche you. You bloody German
bastard!" (42)

This is just too much for Peter. The brutal, personal insult by Violet triggers off far more in him than a simple feeling of vengeance towards her. Everything he has held back and under control up to now - frustration, desperation, dissatisfaction, misery - breaks forth like an avalanche. He goes berserk and with a chopper smashes the gas lead. The ovens die down, the kitchen is brought to a stop. Nobody is able to hold him back. He knocks plates off tables and crashes the crockery in the dining room. In his violent outbreak he cuts his arms and hands and, smeared with blood and exhausted, he can be calmed down at last by Alfredo and Hans.

Marango enters, and, looking at the battlefield, asks the monstrous question "You have stopped my whole world. ... Did you get permission from God?" (43). His final speech expresses the problem set by the whole play:

"MARANGO (<u>turning to</u> FRANK <u>and making a gentle appeal</u>). Why
does everybody sabotage me, Frank? I give work, I pay well, yes?
they eat what they want, don't they? I don't know what more to give
a man. He works, he eats, I give him money. This is life, isn't it?
I haven't made a mistake, have I? I live in the right world, don't
I? (<u>to</u> PETER) And you've stopped this world. A shnip! A boy!
You've stopped it. Well why? Maybe you can tell me something I
don't know - just tell me. (<u>No answer</u>). I want to learn something.
(<u>to the kitchen</u>) Is there something I don't know? (PETER <u>rises and</u>
<u>in pain moves off. When he reaches a point back centre stage</u>
MARANGO <u>cries at him</u>.)
BLOODY FOOL! (<u>Rushes found to him</u>.) What more do you want? What
is there more, tell me? (<u>He shakes</u> PETER, <u>but gets no reply</u>. PETER
<u>again tries to leave. Again</u> MARANGO <u>cries out</u>.) What is there more?
(PETER <u>stops, turns in pain and sadness, shakes his head as if to say</u>

166

- 'if you don't know, I cannot explain.' And so he moves right off stage. MARANGO is left facing his staff, who stand around, almost accusingly, looking at him. And he asks again -) What is there more? What is there more? What is there more?" (44)

Marango asks many questions, and he makes many suggestions. The audience is left with them and is called upon to find the answers. Wesker does not make an explicit statement, but the passionate urge of the final question leaves no doubt that there must be "something more". The audience is provoked into finding out what it is, and into doing something about it.

*

"The world might have been a stage for Shakespeare but to me it is a kitchen, where people come and go and cannot stay long enough to understand each other, and friendships, loves and enmities are forgotten as quickly as they are made" (45). Wesker, who at one time worked as a kitchen porter, then for two years as a pastry cook in London and for nine months as a chef in Paris, writes this sentence in his Introduction and Notes for the Producer, and it describes the subject of The Kitchen quite accurately. This is a play about the fragility of human relationships, about the difficulties existing among human beings. In the claustrophobic atmosphere of the kitchen people of different nationality and character clash: the English, Germans, Cypriots, Italians and Irish create a terrifying pandemonium of languages. The relations are strained, always on the brink of conflict. Anything can set off a row. The hurried work. the merciless strain, the heat and the all-pervading nervousness result in everybody in the kitchen being against everybody. Everyone stands alone, struggling with his job, gripped in the relentless rhythm of his occupation, defending himself as well as he can and taking advantage of the others. The mood among the staff is vacillating and unsettled; the violence underneath is controlled with difficulty; nerves and muscles are tense. Only during the quieter moments are friendship and love possible. But none of these emotions lasts long - everybody, more or less, remains isolated.

The Kitchen is - perhaps even more - a play about man's basic dissatisfaction with modern life. The rush in the kitchen represents the rush in our modern world. The staff stand for the human beings who are forced into a mechanical existence day after day, without any hope of escaping from the deadly routine (46). Peter is the main character, and it is through him that we experience this dissatisfaction most powerfully. The everyday turmoil of the kitchen has driven him to a point where he rebels, where he starts fighting back like a trapped animal. A relatively insignificant incident unleashes the catastrophe: he runs amuck and destroys the kitchen. It is the catastrophe after a long period of helpless anger and frustration. The other characters suffer as well, but do not react as drastically. Some are resigned, others are grumbling; all the time we become aware of tiny revolts which, however, are extinguished as quickly as they arise.

Wesker does not propose a definite solution. He rather suggests one. Peter does not know exactly what he wants; he "does not have a dream"; he just feels a passionate urge to escape into another life, another world, far from the madding rush of the kitchen, far from the hotpot of mass society. Wesker questions our whole modern way of life, accentuates the existing uneasiness and appears to advocate a simple but rich life in happiness and all-embracing friendship. He clearly maintains that you cannot fob off a man with work, food and money, and makes the point that man cannot be exploited beyond a certain limit. Even somebody working in a kitchen has a certain dignity which asserts itself in extreme situations.

As a symbol for the human condition today Wesker's kitchen works effectively. John Russell Taylor's criticism is pedestrian in its narrowmindedness:

> "Now, to establish the validity of a parallel like this, it is necessary
> that the realistic level should be self-evidently true and believable;
> there should be no evidence that the truth is being doctored to fit
> the argument. But if one looks at the set-up in The Kitchen there is
> far too much evidence, even to the casual uninformed eye, that
> this is just what is happening here. ... For example, what sort
> of London restaurant serves 1, 500 lunches in two hours every day,
> with waitress service and presumably a seating capacity of around
> 500? ... And as for the suggestion that all the food would be
> cooked virtually to order during the lunch-hour rush, with cooks
> frantically trying to keep up with the demands of the waitresses,
> this is clearly impossible; most of the food would surely have to
> be cooked some time before and kept warm, according to standard
> practice in popular restaurants." (47)

These are futile remarks. Obviously Taylor has never heard anything about dramatic exaggeration or creative overstatement, Wesker, after all, does not present a naturalistic kitchen, but a vision of all kitchens; their essence, so to speak. Whether the details correspond to reality is irrelevant, and so is the question of the manner of cooking and serving. The validity of the parallel is by no means affected by Wesker's procedure: his personal experience of kitchens amounts to the image presented in the play, and this is thoroughly sufficient. Taylor failed to draw the necessary conclusions from a Wesker statement which he quotes only one page later:

> "I have discovered that realistic art is a contradiction in terms
> Art is the re-creation of experience not the copying of it. Some
> writers use naturalistic means to recreate experience, others
> non-naturalistic. I happen to use naturalistic means; but all the
> statements I make are made theatrically." (48)

This is exactly in keeping with The Kitchen. The audience is forced to respond, forced to think about the problems stirred up. All the world's a kitchen: Wesker has found a convincing metaphor for some aspects of our modern life which grow more frightening every day. And he has realized it in a language that has musical qualities about it, that carries within itself the breathless rhythm of a working place gone mad.

*

The Kitchen may be placed in the category of "Lehrstück" with an open ending in the manner of Bertolt Brecht and Max Frisch. It carries a message that has to be discovered and interpreted by the audience - an audience that is in a way made responsible for the situation presented, and challenged to change the conditions. As Frisch wrote in his Diary 1946-1949:

> "As a dramatist I would consider my task fulfilled, if a play would ever succeed in asking a question in such a way that the audience could not live any longer without an answer from this hour - without their answer, their personal answer, which they can only give with their lives themselves." (49)

If The Kitchen does not succeed in asking a question in this way, it comes at least very close to it.

*

The opening moments of the production on the Court stage were such as to set the correct atmosphere for the play immediately and impressively: the night porter lit the ovens, the stage lights came on accordingly, in coordination with the process of the lighting. The noise of the ovens increased gradually until at last a steady roar - which was kept up throughout the play - filled the kitchen and penetrated into the theatre.

The slowly developing crescendo of the action was exciting to watch, and the climax of the whirlwind was breathtaking: the movements of the cooks preparing and handing out the food, the waitresses entering and leaving, together with the nervous rhythm of the repetitious dialogue, built up to an eye-and earcatching confusion. As to the effect of Wesker's language in this scene, Bernard Levin found the following words:

> " ... his dialogue, quite apart from its poetic rhythms, has the quality of the best musical part-writing, reaching its climax in the famous scene in which there are 23 people on the stage, almost all of them talking at once ..." (50)

The unceasing coming and going, blending with the sound of the voices and the insistent roar of the ovens, evoked an artistically controlled inferno. The impression of a terrible heat stamped itself on the spectators:

> "It was hot enough in the auditorium during last week's heatwave. But the heat engendered on that stage kitchen made one feel positively cool in contrast." (51)

Wesker thought that "the final service at the end of part one was very striking" (52). As indicated in the text, the lights faded with the activity at its height. The following interval did not really meet with Wesker's approval (53) - he would have preferred the play to be acted through without any break. In fact this happened in the 1959 Sunday night production. Robert Stephens remembered it and clearly favoured the earlier conception:

> "In 1959, after the first climax at the end of the first act the lights
> faded and came on again, which was very effective ... The interval
> in the second production destroyed the play somehow." (54)

Nevertheless the fundamental change of atmosphere after the interval could be strongly felt all the same. The lights came up on a kitchen which, at least for the time being, had lost its aggressiveness. Peter's building of his arch preceding the dream sequence was a fine episode: after the completion of the structure Peter goose-stepped beneath it, accompanied by the Horst Wessel tune. V.S. Pritchett recalled:

> "The moment when he builds his triumphal arch of bins and saucepans
> on the stoves and goose-steps under them was exquisite: it had an
> absurdity that was at once touching, noble and frightening ..." (55)

Paul's significant tale about the bus driver was played without a single cut and changed the excited atmosphere definitely to a sad and reflective one.

The final catastrophe, when Peter goes berserk, was played downstage, near the auditorium, and managed rather drastically, as can be guessed from the review that appeared in The Scotsman:

> " ... the cook ... slashes his wrists in despair during the dinner
> rush. He stays conscious and everything stops as he holds his
> hands above his head to ease the bleeding ... The kitchen and the
> theatre is horrified into silence. The curtain whispers down. An
> impossible moment, but one I won't forget." (56)

Wesker as well as Dexter were of the opinion that this ending was convincing on the stage, and the author remarked that "the tension at the end of the play was successfully sustained" (57). On the other hand, the critic of The Times wrote that "This final scene, however well meant, manifestly fails to drive home the play's symbolic point ..." (58), and T.C. Worsley thought that " ... it is the sort of ending which is theatrically effective rather than entirely satisfying ..." (59).

The lights faded slowly on Marango's final speech, causing its implications to sink into the spectators.

There was no music in this production, with the exception of a song sung by the Cypriots.   *

In a faithful production of <u>The Kitchen</u>, a close team-work of the actors is all important. Besides Peter (and his case is open to discussion as well) there are not any fully elaborated characters in the play. All the others are more or less sketched. Only for short moments are they allowed to show themselves as human beings with a will of their own, only briefly does the author's searchlight rest on the individual.

The main impression is that of a mass movement in which the individual is swallowed. The single person is just a little wheel in a tremendous and inhuman mechanism. To produce this effect, the acting has to be self-effacing. There is no star part.

The cast complied admirably with these demands and united into a team which could really be mistaken for the staff of a kitchen and a restaurant. The actors accomplished their difficult task of pantomiming over large stretches with zest and success. The reviewer of the <u>City Press</u> noticed their amazing collaboration:

> "Yet it is a triumph of mime by a brilliant team of actors who
> create a superb illusion ... To mention names without men-
> tioning all would be unfair." (60)

The acting was judged as being outstanding by practically all the critics. "The casting of the polyglot staff is excellent", could be read in <u>Punch</u> (61), and the reviewer of <u>The Tribune</u> (62) used the same adjective to describe the acting. Arnold Wesker's reaction to the achievement of the cast extinguishes any doubts as to its quality:

> "By and large the actors did correspond to the <u>Notes on the</u>
> <u>Characters</u> ... Everyone in the cast responded to the excite-
> ment of the play. I think they particularly enjoyed the miming
> of the acts of cooking and preparation for cooking and did this
> so successfully that people were known to have come away
> feeling that they actually saw food on the stage." (63)

Robert Stephens presented Peter as a temperamental character, from the beginning under some inner pressure and on the brink of hysteria, making apparent the nervous sickness under the bustling surface and forced gaiety. He dominated the place with his boisterous behaviour and wore out the nerves of everybody in the kitchen. The conditions on the stage helped him in realizing his part - as Stephens said, "on the stage it was terribly hot - it was as if one really was working in a kitchen" (64). He acted with a "maddening irrespressibility" (65), and his interpretation was appreciated by most of the critics. V.S. Pritchett's reaction in the <u>New States-</u><u>man</u> shows that Stephens united all the vital features of his part:

> "Robert Stephens gave us a German impressive in his cleverness,
> simplicity, weakness, temper, evasion, childish sentimentality."
> (66)

Peter Roberts in Plays and Players saw Stephens's achievement as an important step forward in his acting career:

"After seeing Robert Stephens rather too often I had begun to suspect that he had only one performance - George Dillon. After seeing him in 'The Kitchen', I am glad to say that he has two. The manner is much the same, but the range is broader and, screen success willing, should become broader still." (67)

The reviewer of The Queen was impressed by the way the actor handled the delicate final moments of the play when Peter's nerves break:

"The melodrama is totally motivated, and I was stunned by the way Robert Stephens played it: not upstage and in a fury, as before (68), but downstage, five feet from the stalls, and in a moment of curious practical calm." (69)

The article in Arts Review suggested a negative point in Stephens's performance, which, considering the general noise on the stage and Peter's character, remains disputable:

"Robert Stephens who plays ... Peter, who dominates the kitchen with his bullying ranting tends to play too much at fortissimo so that his running amok with a chopper does not come as quite the climax it ought to be ..." (70)

Kenneth Tynan dragged in the name of Laurence Olivier, but his reasons for criticizing Stephens appear somewhat obscure, as the characteristics mentioned suit Peter well:

"The youthful Olivier might perhaps have made something of Peter; as played by Robert Stephens, he is self-consciously histrionic, trapped in a quicksand and forever drawing our attention to the pathos with which he is sinking." (71)

Arnold Wesker, in any case, considered the part validly acted:

"Robert Stephens' performance was brilliant since as an actor he has this particular talent for recreating that special kind of weakness which manifests itself in aggressiveness." (72)

Director John Dexter (who was satisfied with his cast) called him "extraordinary" (73). Stephens's performance did much to get the message of the play across to the audience (74). Mary Peach in the part of Monique was, to tell from interviews as well as some reviews, not entirely convincing, as she was not quite sure how to interpret the character. From the text Monique appears as a moody girl, unable to make up her mind about whether to break with Peter or not. It remains vague whether her situation has a tragic dimension or whether she is just unsteady and incalculable. Peter Roberts confirmed the undecided attitude of the actress:

> "Mary Peach is suitably curvaceous as the lady troublemaker but does not seem to be sure whether the character is hard and cruel or simply sluttish." (75)

David Nathan in the Daily Herald thought that she was "too much of a lady for her role as the tarty waitress" (76), and Bernard Levin of the Daily Express was of the same opinion:

> "As the waitress who has led the cook the dance that ends so horribly after three years, Miss Mary Peach is far too trim and pretty to suggest the essential sluttishness of the character ..." (77)

The almost total absence of press remarks about the rest of the actors (Peter Roberts was an exception in mentioning Jessie Robins as Bertha, Alison Bayley as Violet, and James Bolam as Michael (78) proves that the cast melted into an inseparable whole which held the machinery of the kitchen in motion (79).

*

Having directed all of Wesker's previous plays at the Court and elsewhere, John Dexter had become a real expert for the staging of this dramatist's work. He took Wesker's direction concerning the cooking and serving as the basis of his production:

> "At this point it must be understood that at no time is food ever used. To cook and serve food is of course just not practical. Therefore the waitresses will carry empty dishes, and the cooks will mime their cooking." (80)

Dexter elaborated this direction in the sense that he did not only make the cooks and waitresses go through their actions naturalistically. He went one step further and stylized their movements by imposing onto them an almost balletic pattern. The bustle of the kitchen was subordinated to the rhythm of a confusing but precise dance, which took on the form of a ritual: a ritual of work. During the rush hour this "ballet" developed into a swirling vortex. This feature of Dexter's production found its due attention in the reviews:

> "Although it is a realistic play John Dexter has directed it in a stylized manner in which one has to imagine the food being served almost nonstop to the 2,000 customers of a large West End restaurant ... Mr. Dexter's manipulation around the tremendous complexities of producing such a continuous scene is admirable." (81)

"Dexter's production has an almost balletic control over the
swirling movement ..." (82)

"John Dexter ... has convinced us that we are watching absolute naturalism while imposing on his almost universally
brilliant cast of 30 a style of highly individual formalism
..." (83)

"Highly commendable was the manner in which ... Dexter
kept the huge kitchen staff weaving in and out like busy ants
in a sort of frenzied ballet, always working against time
..." (84)

"John Dexter's production emphasizes the non-realist implications by means of complex movement and mime which are
balletic in origin ..." (85)

John Russell Taylor corroborates these statements in his study Anger and After:

"John Dexter's production emphasized the symbolic elements
in the play, presumably at Wesker's instigation, by formalizing
whole sections of it - the lunchtime rush, the dream interlude
- almost into a balletic ritual ..." (86)

By this conception Dexter succeeded in stressing the mechanical character of the
work in the kitchen and the staff subjected to it; the very precision of the movements mirrored the deadly automatism of an everyday routine; the staff were caught
in a movement from which there is no escape. This, of course, demanded a high
efficiency in the guiding of the actors - the "kitchen-movements" had to be rehearsed every night before the actual performance to grant a perfect "running down" of
the play.

Dexter took great pains to interpret the musical structure of The Kitchen (which
could be described as crescendo-climax-pause / interlude-crescendo-catastrophe)
in terms of pace and movement. Part One, as we have seen, builds up very slowly
to its climax at the height of the lunch rush. Wesker was aware of the difficulties
here:

"There was no marked change in pace during the performance,
though one of the problems was to sustain the right pace during
the service at the end of part one which had to start slowly and
not get too fast too quickly." (87)

Dexter succeeded in bringing out this slow but continuous acceleration and thus
conveyed the impression of a mechanism gradually turning insane. Kenneth Tynan
commented on this development:

"John Dexter's direction is flawless, rising at the end of the first
half to a climactic lunch-hour frenzy that is the fullest theatrical
expression I have ever seen of the laws of supply and demand
..." (88)

Another problem consisted in the balance which had to be established between the
general noise of the kitchen and the dialogue. Dexter himself admitted that here he
faced some difficulties. Already during the rehearsals he had to fight against the
din on the stage: he used to have a whistle in order to interrupt the activities of the
actors. Asked whether they made themselves understood in all the noise, he answered carefully "I hope so" (89). On the whole he solved the problem satisfactorily, as
he used the front part of the stage as the spot where the conversations took place.
Bamber Gascoigne in The Spectator described the effect achieved as follows:

"At the Court Wesker is lucky in his director. John Dexter conducts
the whirlwind in a well-controlled accelerando, coaxes such good
miming out of his cooks that the lack of edibles becomes food for
art, and even goes some way towards solving the one-conversation-
at-a-time problem. The only free space in his kitchen is at the very
front of the stage. This is where the staff eat; this is where they
come if they want to talk. Anyone speaking to them from the back of
the kitchen has to shout above the roar of the ovens. Ordinary chat
at the back of the kitchen can therefore be carried on unheard ..."
(90)

Richard Findlater, on the contrary, thought that Wesker's dialogue suffered from
Dexter's production:

" ... while its merits are often obscured by the same production's
not-so-brilliant sound effects. Too much of Wesker's dialogue, in
the first act especially, disappears in a welter of broken accents
started against the hot, symbolic stoves which roar throughout the
play ..." (91)

After the exciting events of Part One Dexter gave special emphasis to the following
interlude. He payed due regard to Wesker's pauses and thus created a counterpart
to the previous noisy bustle. The conversations pierced an almost quiet kitchen. Peter's building of his arch turned out an almost ceremonial moment. The critic of
The Queen wrote on the general effect of the interlude:

"But the way John Dexter handles this passage is .. full of lyric
character and pungency. More than any director I can imagine, he
makes it almost possible for the characters to speak the over-
explicit moralising that is the stiffest element in Arnold Wesker's
work; and when the chefs suddenly start to build an absurd, beautiful arch out of saucepans, dustbins, a broom and a carnation, one
realises that he is also better than anyone else at staging the

romantic moments in which Wesker is triumphant ..." (92)

There were also negative reactions to Dexter's conception. J.C. Trewin in the
Birmingham Post complained about the director's deficient knowledge of the stage
conditions:

> "John Dexter guides an intricately bustling production that would be
> better if he would consider all the sightlines at the Court." (93)

The critic of The Independent (Plymouth) obviously did not appreciate the way in
which the director guided the actors' movements:

> "At the Royal Court John Dexter achieves noise and speed but the
> staging of the piece is clumsy ..." (94)

Gerard Fay admitted the effectiveness of two scenes but implied in his criticism
that Dexter's direction lacked an original and lively approach:

> " ... the pastry cooks ... work away neatly all the time and almost
> rouse a little appetite for the dainty gateaux they turn out, all by
> mime. This, apart from the crazy screaming ring-a-roses which
> ends the first act, is the only really imaginative touch in John Dex-
> ter's production - all the cuisine is done mimetically, yet the food
> can be seen and almost smelt ..." (95)

The production of The Kitchen is one of the most striking examples for the close
team-work between author and director which is so significant for the Royal Court.
As with his other plays there, Wesker attended all the rehearsals, and according
to him as well as John Dexter, there was constant discussion while the production
was built up (96) - "there was close collaboration between all of us involved in the
production" (97). This went as far as to cause alterations of and additions to the
original typescript. Wesker mentions some details:

> "There were no major disagreements between Dexter and myself;
> on the contrary the original script was written without the interlude
> and it was Dexter who suggested that some quiet period was neces-
> sary between the morning service and the afternoon service. He
> didn't stipulate what form it should take but he prepared me to
> create the interlude." (98)

A further result of this team-work was the final form of the lunch rush at the end of
Part One. This was actually worked out during the rehearsals. In a note to the
printed version Wesker says:

> "The section dealing with the service starting on p.42 with 'Two
> veal cutlets' is the actual production worked out by John Dexter
> based on what was originally only an indicative framework set out

by me. I wish to acknowledge his creation of this workable pattern.

The pattern of service falls into three stages of increasing speed.
(1) From 'Two veal cutlets,' p.42, to Gaston's 'Max send up steaks
and mutton chops quick, ' p.45, the pace is brisk but slow. (2)
From then on to Peter's cry of 'Too old, too old my sweetheart, '
p.47, the pace increases. (3) From then on to the end of the part,
'Have you all gone barking-raving-bloody-mad, ' the pace is fast
and hectic." (99)

Dexter also denied any serious disagreements and maintained that there were not
any notable cuts made on the original text. All the alterations made were the result
of mutual consultation (100).

The fact of an intense team-work was also expressed in some of the reviews. One of
them appeared in The City Press:

"John Dexter's work as director has a touch of something akin to
genius. He brought the whole astonishing activity to life so realistically that one could feel the heat of the stoves and smell the
food. ... If ever there was team-work on the stage here it is."
(101)

The same conclusion was arrived at by the critic of Theatre World:

"This was one of the most compelling and dramatic of recent
theatre offerings, and an arresting example of author and
production functioning in complete accord ..." (102)

John Dexter's production of The Kitchen was thus in agreement with some of the
most important staging principles of the Royal Court (103).

*

Jocelyn Herbert designed a set which was an impressive visual representation of
Wesker's kitchen. The bare stage extended from the footlights to the very backwall of the theatre - a wall painted in a dirty white and covered with the theatre's
permanent tubing. The kitchen furniture, such as ovens, tin stoves, tables, side-
boards etc., was dominated by white, grey and black tones, which together with
the backwall gave the kitchen an oppressive and desolate appearance. From a metal
frame hung from the ceiling eight strong reflectors spread an almost painfully bright
light and a heat which is suggested by the text. Four more spotlights were mounted
at the backwall and lit the stage from there. Together with the black and white costumes of the cooks and waitresses the colour scheme added to the excitement of the
production: the balletic movements of the actors combined into a dazzling mixture
of black and white.

According to two reviews, however, Jocelyn Herbert was somewhat unfortunate as she (whether by mistake or forced by necessity remains obscure) obstructed the sight of the stage from certain seats by the arrangement of her properties. The critic of The Times drew attention to this circumstance:

> "Jocelyn Herbert designs the kitchen with the sizzling ovens most realistically, but since she has the whole of the stage at her disposal it is vastly inconsiderate of her to unsight sizeable sections of the stalls with two cumbrous buffets, one of them piled high with plates." (104)

W.A. Darlington in The Daily Telegraph confirmed this criticism:

> " ... Jocelyn Herbert's setting hides a good deal of the action from a good many of the audience." (105)

John Dexter declared himself entirely satisfied with the set (106), and Wesker wrote that "Jocelyn Herbert's set, like the production, was excellent" (107).

The scenery evoked a kitchen in the sense of Wesker's text: realistic, yet remote, spreading an atmosphere of inhuman efficiency.

*

Asked about the general reaction of the audiences, Dexter in a lapidary way described it as "good" (108). They especially responded to the strikingly directed rush at the end of Part One. Referring to the impact of the last moments of the play on the spectators, Dexter maintained cautiously that they were "presumably impressed" (109), whereas Wesker was more optimistic in saying that they definitely were (110). The review in The Scotsman confirms this assumption (111). The crescendo movement of the production involved the audience in the action more and more - whether at the end they drew the implied conclusions remains, of course, doubtful.

*

The press reacted positively to a large extent. I have taken into account thirty-three reviews and found twenty-two of them predominantly favourable. Nine critics mixed their praise and blame, and I could discover only two who judged clearly negatively. This is a rather proud record for The Kitchen.

Harold Hobson entitled his article in The Sunday Times "With a Certain Grandeur", and showed himself much impressed by the statement of the play, by its language and its transformation into a stage event:

> "When I saw it at the National Union of Students-Sunday Times Festival eighteen months ago I did not recognise its merits. It was neither badly acted nor badly directed. But its performance

then did not have the sleight-of-hand efficiency in detail of John
Dexter's production at the Court, nor its strong controlled musical flow ... The highstrung lightly handled tension, the speed,
the imagination, and the illicit passion of Robert Stephens's
Peter are the essentials of Mr. Stephens's performance. The
exactness with which he repeatedly spreads out three plates
like a fan might well not be there at all. But, though it is never
obtrusive, this exactness adds, below the level of conscious
recognition, greatly to our enjoyment ... But in the second act
are reaped all the fruits so carefully sown in the first. It is then
that the musical pattern of the play becomes apparent. There is
a long slow movement of considerable beauty, in which the dreams,
the desires, the aspirations of mankind are articulate with melancholy and with hope. This is followed by a swift and violent
conclusion which, developing the charm of Peter into a murderous
hysteria, no doubt expresses another aspect of Mr. Wesker's
judgement upon the nature of Germany. The upshot of the play is
an overwhelming sense of the pity that comes of men's mutual
hatred, a noble and magnanimous feeling of waste. 'The Kitchen'
is even more than good Wesker. It is a good play." (112)

The reviewer of The Times Educational Supplement commended the production and
compared the play to the Wesker trilogy - a comparison which definitely ends in
favour of The Kitchen:

"'The Kitchen', as an event in the theatre, is more impressive
in its totality than any of the plays in the trilogy, which are all
diluted by streams of a raw and adolescent idealism which have
somehow bypassed the transforming process of the creative imagination. This early play is by comparison a mature work of
theatrical art, unweakened by sincerity ... The rhythm of Mr.
Wesker's writing, reinforced by Mr. John Dexter's excellent
production, is hypnotic ... Beside 'The Kitchen' the plays of the
trilogy are a naively self-indulgent and superficial sprawl." (113)

Robert Muller in The Daily Mail also paid tribute to Johne Dexter's achievement
and the realistic impact of his production:

"The play's effortless authenticity is brilliantly brought to life
by John Dexter's production. I have had cause to criticise this
young director in the past: here he is at the very top of his form.
The piece is splendidly visual: the white-hatted polyglot cooks
dart about between the stoves and tables, we are made aware of
the heat, the exasperation, the stealing, the flirtations between
cooks and waitresses, the cruelties of the old towards the young,
the sweat-drenched somnolence after lunch, the accidents, the
outbreaks of hysteria ... Not a scrap of food is actually used on

the stage. Yet so completely persuasive are both dramatist and
producer that we can almost smell the stench ..." (114)

The critic of The Sunday Telegraph described in detail the impression he received
from the first moments of the production and the first part as a whole, and his lines
express admiration for the dramatist, the director and the actors. But he also maintained that Wesker exaggerates the didactic element, and that the first part evokes
expectations which are frustrated in the second:

> "He will not realize that all the clues are there already for us -
> we can feel in bones and nerves that 'The Kitchen' is partly a
> world of nervously hostile nations, and partly a capitalist society,
> and partly agnostic man haunted by fears that God may really
> exist. But once he starts to draw this in diagrams, we cease to
> attend the lesson. The more real and true and unique his kitchen
> is, the less it can be generalized and projected as a scale model
> of universe.
> The first act is half a superb play. It leaves us waiting for the
> threads of drama to start their cat's-cradle of thought and action.
> We wait in vain. We get humour and argument and anecdote. We
> get touching little impromptu dances and frightening outbursts of
> hysteria ..." (115)

Peter Roberts, in Plays and Players, dealt with the director's interpretation and
found positive remarks for it:

> "The first part, with its 30 actors simultaneously engaged on
> individual activities, offers the imaginative director a virtuoso
> display. And John Dexter, who served Wesker well in the Trilo-
> gy, makes the most of the opportunity by rejecting a merely real-
> istic show. All the food preparation, for instance, is mimed,
> and in the swirling close of the first part the movements pass on
> beyond the naturalistic to the stylized. It is a very expert and beau-
> tiful blending of two approaches." (116)

Kenneth Tynan in The Observer was more critical. He wrote appreciatively of Dexter's direction, but with reservations concerning the structure of the play and the
way Wesker handles the ending:

> "This final, self-destructive act is melodramatic and deplorably
> unmotivated ... The production lacks a centre-piece; instead of
> the specialité de la maison, we are fobbed off with spinach." (117)

The reviewer of The Independent (Plymouth), who did not recognize many merits
in Dexter's production (118), thought that "there is too much quarrelling in the play,
and nothing much else" (119); and J.C. Trewin in the Birmingham Post was unable
to see anything more in The Kitchen than "document-stuff", and questioned its

purpose, going as far as to consider it as a negative point in Wesker's career as a dramatist:

> "One should go to the theatre prepared, wherever possible, to appreciate. Even so, there are times when hope flags: this is one of them. Let me say that if it is possible to get any satisfaction from a few minutes of document-stuff, explaining what goes on behind the swing doors of a restaurant kitchen at the rush hour, then no doubt that satisfaction is obtainable here. It seems an odd reason for a visit to the theatre. ... some of us still wonder why the play was staged: it does no good to its author's artistic reputation ... " (120)

On the whole, however, the critics showed themselves impressed by Wesker's play and by Dexter's direction, which realized the text in a way that gripped the emotions of the audience. In any case the arguments of those speaking negatively of the production sound considerably weaker than those of its supporters. The Kitchen left the critics more or less unanimous in their judgments.

*

Like all of Wesker's plays produced between 1958 and 1962 (Chicken Soup with Barley, Roots, I'm Talking About Jerusalem, Chips with Everything), The Kitchen did not cover its running expenses and lost money. But the Royal Court continued to stage Wesker's plays. As a matter of fact it was Lindsay Anderson who discovered Wesker the playwright:

> "Outside the National Film Theatre one evening, he met Lindsay Anderson and showed him POOLS, a short story which Wesker hoped could be made into a film. Nothing came of this but Anderson read THE KITCHEN and CHICKEN SOUP WITH BARLEY and brought Wesker to the notice of George Devine ... Anderson had sent the script of CHICKEN SOUP WITH BARLEY to Devine who passed it along to the Belgrade Theatre in Coventry where it was produced on July 7th (121) under the direction of John Dexter." (122)

The Kitchen and Chips With Everything had their first nights directly at the Court - the latter play eventually transferred to the West End Vaudeville Theatre where it became a success. The Kitchen was also filmed.

Wesker continued to write for the stage. In 1965 The Four Seasons opened at the Belgrade, Coventry. The play was transferred to the Saville Theatre London in the same year. In 1966 Their Very Own and Golden City had its first night at the Court. As director William Gaskill put it, "a sense of responsibility towards the theatre and Wesker" made him produce the play. He considered this further encouragement as a duty (123).

With Arnold Wesker, the Court can pride itself on having introduced yet another young dramatist to the British theatre; a dramatist for whom the examination of social problems stands in the foreground. Without the perspicacity of George Devine and his colleagues, Wesker would have had - so I believe - considerable difficulties in making his way in the theatre.

***

XII JOHN OSBORNE: LUTHER

After <u>Look Back in Anger</u>, <u>The Entertainer</u>, and <u>Epitaph for George Dillon</u>, <u>Luther</u>
was John Osborne's fourth play to be staged at the Court. Before coming to London,
it had been given a try-out at the Theatre Royal Nottingham (1), and its presentation
at the Paris Festival (2), where it had a short run, had been a success for the English Stage Company. Expectation among the London audiences was already high before the first night at the Court on July 27th, 1961. Tony Richardson directed,
Jocelyn Herbert designed the set, and there was a rumour about an outstanding
performance by a young actor called Albert Finney in the part of Martin. And of
course the name John Osborne, ever since the explosion of <u>Look Back in Anger</u> in
May 1956, had still a sound of excitement about it, which made <u>Luther</u> additionally
attractive.

*

The play starts with Martin Luther being received into the Order of the Eremites
of St. Augustine. The scene is set in the Cloister Chapel in Erfurt, in the year 1506.

The atmosphere of this ceremony is conjured up by the solemn language, the elevated diction: the ritual of the church, which receives yet another human being into
its bosom, takes place, accompanied by singing and prayers. (3)

A short interlude consisting of a sharp dialogue between Martin's father Hans and
Lucas, from which we learn that the former neither agres with nor understands
his son's becoming a monk, leads on to the first revelation of Martin's character.
It occurs during a communal confession. While the other monks are busy confessing their petty offences - sheer trifles, such as having left their cells without the
scapular, having made mistakes in psalm singing and having arrived late at the
Night Office - Martin's prayers show that he is tortured by other problems:

> "MARTIN: I am a worm and no man, a byword and a laughing
> stock. Crush out the worminess in me, stamp on me. (4) ...
> I was fighting a bear in a garden without flowers, leading into
> a desert ... I saw a naked woman riding on a goat, and the
> goat began to drink my blood, and I thought I should faint with
> the pain and I awoke in my cell, all soaking in the devil's bath.
> (5) ... I am alone. I am alone, and against myself." (6)

These sentences catch something of Luther's recorded painful struggles to find his
inner peace. He is haunted by dreams, and the carrying out of the most humiliating
work, as cleaning the latrines, does not succeed in bringing him the peace and the
inner security desired. Prayers and fasting do not help. He leads an unappeased
life, tormented by a restless conscience:

> "MARTIN: I confess that I have offended grievously against

humility ... I have not only failed to declare myself to myself
lower and lower and of less account than all other men, but I
have failed in my most inmost heart to believe it. ... But although I fulfilled my task, and I did it well, sometimes there
were murmurings in my heart. I prayed that it would cease,
knowing that God, seeing my murmuring heart, must reject
my work, and it was as good as not done. I sought out my
master, and he punished me, telling me to fast for two days.
I have fasted three, but, even so, I can't tell if the murmurings
are really gone ..." (7)

In the last episode of Act One, scene one, Martin's inner tortures culminate in a
fit, which expresses all the agonizing conflicts he is subject to. Against the unwavering background sounds of the office Martin's cry pierces the air like the cry of
a victim about to be sacrificed:

"MARTIN: Not! Me! I am not!" (8)

It is the desperate scream of a man who fights hard for the peace of his mind and
who realizes that even the rigorous life in the seclusion of a monastery cannot
relieve him, that it is not his vocation to be a brother.

Scene two of the first act begins with a monologue by Martin, in which the impression we have gained of his state of mind is further intensified. Osborne uses a
somewhat drastic metaphor in order to express the spiritual "constipation" Luther
suffers from - he transfers it to the body and makes it appear as a physical illness:

"MARTIN: ... There's a bare fist clenched to my bowels and
they can't move, and I have to sit sweating in my little monk's
house to open them. ..." (9)

The syntax itself mirrors Martin's helplessness and his frantic search for peace
and security: already in I, i the sentences push each other, chase each other,
separated by commas: the repetition of words results in a rhythm which catches
the insecurity within Martin, his trying to come to grips with his obsessions, to
grasp his experiences, to understand them by encircling them with words:

"MARTIN: My bones fail. My bones fail, my bones are shattered
and fall away, my bones fail and all that's left of me is a scraped
marrow and a dying jelly." (10) ... "I lost the body of a child, a
child's body, the eyes of a child; and at the first sound of my own
childish voice. I lost the body of a child; and I was afraid, and I
went back to find it. But I'm still afraid. I'm afraid, and there's
an end of it!" (11)

He understands his situation as a physical destruction and longs to be an innocent
child. His language is interspersed with a crude imagery; it is the language of

somebody desperately starting again and again to define his situation.
The rest of Act I, ii is taken up by a dialogue between Martin, about to perform his
first mass, and Brother Weinand, from which we learn further facts concerning the
former's behaviour:

> "BRO. WEINAND: I only meant the whole convent knows you're
> always making up sins you've never committed. That's right -
> well, isn't it? No sensible confessor will have anything to do
> with you.
> MARTIN: What's the use of all this talk of penitence if I can't
> feel it.
> BRO. WEINAND: Father Nathin told me he had to punish you
> only the day before yesterday because you were in some ri-
> diculous state of hysteria, all over some verse in Proverbs
> or something ... And all over the interpretation of one word
> apparently ... Some of the brothers laugh quite openly at you,
> you and your over-stimulated conscience ...
> MARTIN: It's the single words that trouble me." (12)

Martin makes up sins, but he cannot feel any repentance. He stands apart from his
fellow brothers, he is separated from them, he is on his own. He worries about
passages in the Bible and is obviously looking for the words that will relieve him
from his sufferings. As an answer to Weinand's admonitions he questions the purpose of his being a monk:

> "MARTIN: ... What have I gained from coming into this sacred
> Order? Aren't I still the same? I'm still envious, I'm still im-
> patient, I'm still passionate? ... All you teach me in this sacred
> place is how to doubt ..." (13)

This is the first time that Martin hints somewhat more clearly at his search for
inner peace. He has not found it, he is unsteady and persecuted by doubt. He cannot
find his way to God but is obsessed with his sinfulness and with the conviction that
God does not extend his mercy to him:

> "MARTIN: Forgive me, Brother Weinand, but the truth is this
> --- ... It's this, just this. All I can feel, all I can feel is God's
> hatred." (14)

Although Weinand sternly makes him recite the Apostles' Creed and forces him to
repeat the passage "I believe in the forgiveness of sins" (15), all Martin is able to
reply is

> "I wish my bowels would open. I'm blocked up like an old crypt."
> (16)

He is still constipated by doubt and fear - fear that his sins may never be forgiven, his soul never be saved, and that he will be damned. He has not yet found the word of God that will rescue him from his brooding. For Martin God is the threatening judge, who is angry with him and whose presence he finds hard to endure (17). The second scene ends with Martin speaking the dark and foreboding words which seem to point to a radical change in his life and tremendous events to come:

> "MARTIN: And so, the praising ended - and the blasphemy began. " (18)

Act I, iii takes place in the Convent refectory. The first part consists in a conversation between Martin's father Hans and Brother Weinand. Hans has had too much wine and tries to provoke Weinand by awkward and slightly malicious questions:

> HANS: ... Tell me, Brother - would you say that in this monastery - or, any monastery you like - you were as strong as the weakest member of the team? ...
> BRO. WEINAND: I think my opinion would be that the Church is bigger than those who are in her.
> HANS: Yes, yes, but don't you think it could be discredited by, say, just a few men?
> BRO. WEINAND: Plenty of people have tried, but the Church is still there. Besides, a human voice is small and the world's very large. But the Church reaches out and is heard everywhere." (19)

Hans, with his "weakest member", obviously alludes to Martin. Weinand's answer is the comment of a monk firm in his faith. His remark on the impotence of the single human being, however, is a clearly ironical insertion by Osborne: it will be refuted by Luther's later actions and foreshadows them "negatively".

The passage in the mass where Martin, celebrating it, lost his cue, and which he repeats on his father's demand, is in close connection with his personal problems:

> "MARTIN: (rattling it off). Receive, oh Holy Father, almighty and eternal God, this spotless host, which I, thine unworthy servant, offer unto thee for my own innumerable sins of commission and omission, and for all here present and all faithful Christians, living and dead, so that it may avail for their salvation and everlasting life. When I entered the monastery, I wanted to speak to God directly, you see. Without any embarrassment, I wanted to speak to him myself, but when it came to it, I dried up - as I always have. " (20)

It is highly significant that his memory should have failed him just at the moment when the forgiveness of sins is promised, and the prospect of an "everlasting life" is held out to the people. Now this very forgiveness is what troubles Martin most: he does not trust it with regard to his own person and his own sins. It is as if he felt that real forgiveness cannot simply be obtained, and that it has to be deserved in a different way, for example by speaking to God directly and personally. He explains what he experienced during mass:

> "MARTIN: I don't understand what happened. I lifted up my head
> at the host, and, as I was speaking the words, I heard them as if
> it were the first time, and suddenly -- (pause) they struck at my
> life." (21)

Hans, who still cannot understand why his brilliant son turned to monkery instead of becoming a magistrate or a lawyer, realizes that Martin is in search of something which is vital for him to find unless he wants to spend the rest of his life in never ending struggles. But his view of Martin's behaviour remains negative. He reproaches his son for having cut himself off from mother and father, and for neglecting his duties towards them, to which Martin retorts that he has a right to his own life. Hans, however, perceives his son's disturbed condition (22). We learn that Martin had a strong will of his own since his youth. Martin replies that he had been disappointed by his father, too, when he was a child, but that he had loved him more than his mother, who once beat him for stealing a nut. In the following passage further details are revealed why Martin became a monk, and further light is shed on his complex character:

> "HANS: You know what, Martin, I think you've always been scared
> - ever since you could get up off your knees and walk. You've been
> scared for the good reason that that's what you most like to be. Yes,
> I'll tell you. I'll tell you what! Like that day, that day when you were
> coming home from Erfurt, and the thunderstorm broke, and you were
> so piss-scared, you lay on the ground and cried out to St.Anne be-
> cause you saw a bit of lightning and thought you'd seen a vision." (23)

Practical man that Hans is, he has serious doubts about the reality of that vision during which Martin promised to become a monk if he was saved from the storm. The thought that his son could have chosen the wrong life because of an error troubles him:

> "HANS: I mean: I hope it really was a vision. I hope it wasn't a
> delusion and some trick of the devil's. I really hope so, because
> I can't bear to think of it otherwise. ..." (24)

The meeting of father and son ends in a sad note of resignation and lack of mutual understanding. In the end of the scene Martin seems to be in doubt more than ever. Obviously taking up his father's statement regarding that crucial vision he puts the terrible question:

> "MARTIN: But - but what if it isn't true?" (25)

The first scene of Act II, set in the market place of Juterbög in 1517, belongs entirely to Tetzel, "Dominican, inquisitor and most famed and successful indulgence vendor of his day" (26). The whole scene consists in a long monologue, delivered by Tetzel in the manner of a born demagogue, with a power of attraction similar to the one of the Pied Piper of Hamelin. His language is made up of catch-phrases, suggestive and rhetorical questions; his sentences, direct, pungent and persuasive, do not miss their impact on the common people:

> "TETZEL: Are you wondering who I am, or what I am? Is there anyone here among you, any small child, any cripple, or any sick idiot who hasn't heard of me, and doesn't know why I am here? No? No? Well, speak up then if there is? What, no one? Do you all know who I am? If it's true, it's very good, and just as it should be. Just as it should be, and no more than that! ..." (27)

The crowd in the market square must be totally in the grip of his speech, paralyzed by his voice; he dominates their reactions and anticipates moods and opinions. Further characteristics of Tetzel's language include the use of gestic impulses and mirror passages, as he is praising the value of his letters of indulgence:

> " ... No, don't look round for him, you'll only scare him and then he'll lose his one great chance ... Who is this friar with his red cross? ... I am John Tetzel ... and what I bring you is indulgences. Indulgences made possible by the red blood of Jesus Christ, and the red cross you see standing up here behind me is the standard of those who carry them. Look at it! Go on, look at it!" (28)

He takes the questions out of the mouths of the people and answers them with an irresistible mixture of brutality and sly calculation. He evokes the terrors of punishment after death and is sure of the effect he produces. Again gestic impulses and mirror passages enhance the impression of the moment when the letters are held under the noses of his audience:

> "There is something, and that something I have here with me now up here, letters, letters of indulgence. Hold up the letters so that everyone can see them. Is there anyone so small he can't see? Look at them, all properly sealed, an indulgence in every envelope, and one of them can be yours today, now, before it's too late! Come on, come up as close as you like, you won't squash me so easily. Take a good look. ..." (29)

The gestic impulses are implicit in his commands to those who show the letters and to those who are to look at them: they will result in the letters being held above the heads, with outstretched arms, in the people closing in on Tetzel, and in the craning of their necks. A mirror passage occurs in the showing and the description of the sealed letters.

Tetzel promises forgiveness of sins committed and to be committed, explaining that the money raised by the selling of the indulgences will be used for restoring

St. Peter in Rome. The whole absurdity of a perverted faith is exposed in his evocation of this church and its contents:

> "This great church contains the bodies not only of the holy
> apostles Peter and Paul, but of a hundred thousand martyrs
> and no less than forty-six popes! To say nothing of the re-
> lics like St. Veronica's handkerchief, the burning bush of
> Moses and the very rope with which Judas Iscariot hanged
> himself! ..." (30)

The ending of his speech is a last powerful appeal to the purses of the frightened populace. Nothing is too tactless for Tetzel in order to achieve his purpose: he stands there as the representative of the Pope, in whose power is the bestowal of paradise or hell. Eternal life is a question of the financial resources, salvation can be bought with hard coins, struggles and doubts such as Martin's are a waste of time:

> "For remember: As soon as your money rattles in the box and
> the cash bell rings, the soul flies out of purgatory and sings!
> So, come on then, Get your money out! ... Listen then, soon,
> I shall take down the cross, shut the gates of heaven, and put
> out the brightness of this sun of grace that shines on you here
> today. ..." (31)

And the people pay, understanding that this is the only way to escape certain damnation and to reconcile themselves with God (32).

The dialogue between Martin and Johann von Staupitz, Vicar General of the Augustinian Order, in the garden of the Eremite Cloister Wittenberg in 1517, makes up Act II, ii. Staupitz appears as a likeable and reasonable person, who has sympathy for Martin but whose respect for him does not prevent him from criticizing the tortured monk if it seems necessary to do so:

> "I've never had any patience with all your mortifications. The
> only wonder is that you haven't killed yourself with your prayers,
> and watchings, yes and even your reading too. All these trials
> and temptations you go through, they're meat and drink to you."
> (33)

The conversation turns to Luther's central subject: the problem of man's salvation after death. Talking of his father, Martin sheds some light on the progress of his struggles concerning this question. The crucial notion of "faith" is drawn into the discussion:

> "MARTIN: Anyway, he always knew that works alone don't save
> any man. Mind you, he never said anything about faith coming
> first." (34) ... "My father, faced with an unfamiliar notion is

189

like a cow staring at a new barn door. Like those who look on
the cross and see nothing. All they hear is the priest's forgiveness. " (35)

Martin seems to be desperate that those who look for forgiveness do not really have
any strong faith in God and become slaves of the priests instead of trying to establish
a personal contact with God himself. Staupitz then kindly warns him about preaching
too sharply against the sale of indulgences, although on this point he basically agrees
with Martin, who maintains that "you can't strike bargains with God" (36). Martin
gives two examples of the absurd consequences arising from Tetzel's mercenary methods, and Staupitz dismisses him with some serious advice and encourages him to
act. His last words betray real concern about Martin's engagement:

"STAUPITZ: ... Martin - just before you go: a man with a
strong sword will draw it at some time, even if it's only to
turn it on himself. But whatever happens, he can't just let
it dangle from his belt. And, another thing, don't forget -
you began this affair in the name of Our Lord Jesus Christ.
You must do as God commands you, of course, but remember,
St. Jerome once wrote about a philosopher who destroyed his
own eyes so that it would give him more freedom to study.
Take care of your eyes, my son, and do something about
those damned bowels!" (37)

Staupitz has realized that Luther is on the way to achieving something of far-reach-
ing influence and importance.

Act II, iii shows Martin on the steps of the Castle Church, Wittenberg, in October
1517. He is about to preach the first of his three long sermons in the play, and its
subject is the vital biblical passage Luther discovered - according to the historical
sources - in 1513: the passage that struck him as an enlightenment, with the overpowering conviction that the human being will be justified before God, and consequently be saved, by faith alone - by strong, confident faith in God:

"MARTIN: My text is from the Epistle of Paul the Apostle to
the Romans, chapter one, verse seventeen: 'For therein is the
righteousness of God revealed from faith to faith.' (38)

With powerful language he exposes the trust of the people in the outward splendour
of the church, their craving for visible and tangible divine symbols and the empty
things they are fobbed off with. He shatters the myth of relics and purchased indulgences and confronts the crowd with the futility of what they believe in and wor-
ship: .

"Shells for shells, empty things for empty men ... For you must
be made to know that there's no security, there's no security at
all, either in indulgences, holy busywork or anywhere in this

world." (39)

Martin then speaks about the discovery he made in the Bible: with ruthless consistency Osborne elaborates his metaphor of the constipated bowels and transfers the place of Luther's enlightenment to the lavatory:

"It came to me while I was in my tower, what they call the
monk's sweathouse, the jakes, the john or whatever you're
pleased to call it. I was struggling with the text I've given
you: 'For therein is the righteousness of God revealed, from
faith to faith; as it is written, the just shall live by faith'.
And seated there ... I couldn't reach down to my breath for
the sickness in my bowels ... And I sat in my heap of pain
until the words emerged and opened out, 'The just shall live
by faith.' My pain vanished, my bowels flushed and I could
get up." (40)

The relief of the "constipated" spirit by the salutary impact of the biblical passage is paralleled by the relief of the bodily constipation. Martin stresses the all-important notion of pure faith, and as a confirmation he nails his ninety-five theses against the abuse of indulgences to the door of the Castle Church (41).

In Act II, iv the reaction of Rome to the German reformer's activities becomes apparent: Cardinal Cajetan, General of the Dominican Order, papal legate and the Pope's highest representative in Germany, has summoned Luther to the Fugger Palace in Augsburg. It is the year 1518. Cajetan has obviously been instructed to lecture the young rebel and to lead him back into the Catholic Church. After a few polite introductory remarks characterised by subtle irony, the legate comes to the point. At first he tries to settle the unpleasant affair by treating it as harmless. But Martin does not enter into Cajetan's patronizing tone. He meets the legate with firmness and by his unexpected resistance makes him change the character of the conversation. The easy, smooth politeness gives way to rather impatient correction, accentuated by barely disguised threats:

"My son, you have upset all Germany with your dispute about
indulgences ... However, if you wish to remain a member of
the Church, and to find a gracious father in the Pope, you'd
better listen ... First, you must admit your faults, and retract all your errors and sermons. Secondly, you must promise
to abstain from propagating your opinion at any time in the
future. And, thirdly, you must behave generally with greater
moderation, and avoid anything which might cause offence or
grieve and disturb the Church." (42)

This passage shows clearly that Rome wants to silence the troublesome German monk once and for all and provide him with a safe muzzle. What the catholic authorities like are not thinking believers but uncritical idiots who pay and obey. The

demands formulated by the Pope indicate by their schematic, cliché-like form that
the church itself has acquired a cliché-like inflexibility. The confrontation approaches its climax when Martin maintains that he rests his case "entirely on Holy Scriptures" (43) and that the Pope does not have any power over these. It shows more and
more that Cajetan refuses to see Martin's struggles and remains steeped in a rigid
catechism, unable to grasp the seriousness of Martin's revolt:

> "CAJETAN: ... I'm not here to enter into a disputation with you,
> now or at any other time. The Roman Church is the apex of the
> world, secular and temporal, and it may constrain with its sec-
> ular arm any who have once received the faith and gone astray.
> Surely I don't have to remind you that it is not bound to use reason
> to fight and destroy rebels. " (44)

The legate here speaks as the authoritarian representative of a tyrannical system
which treats its adherents as slaves. Immediately afterwards Cajetan changes his
tactics and once again tries the imploring method (45). As he sees that Martin
stands his ground, he decides to enter into something similar to a discussion and
attempts to startle Luther with the question what he would suggest in the place of
the Christendom which he is "tearing down" (46). Martin's straightforward answer
excludes any compromise:

> "A withered arm is best amputated, an infected place is best
> scoured out, and so you pray for healthy tissue and something
> sturdy and clean that was crumbling and full of filth. " (47)

Cajetan, in a last desperate effort, tries to talk Martin into retracting, by describ-
ing to him the consequences of his sermons against indulgences, which could leave
men "helpless and frightened" (48). But Martin remains hard. The final appeal of
the legate does not have the desired effect:

> "Allow them their sins, their petty indulgences, my son ...
> We live in thick darkness, and it grows thicker. How will men
> find God if they are left to themselves each man abandoned and
> only known to himself?
> MARTIN: They'll have to try.
> CAJETAN: I beg of you, my son, I beg of you. Retract.
>   (Pause)
> MARTIN: Most holy father, I cannot. " (49)

Cajetan realizes that he cannot do anything against a man who is ready to fight and
suffer for a cause he considers just.

In the fifth scene of the second act Pope Leo X. himself enters the action. The scene
plays at his hunting lodge at Magliana in Northern Italy, in 1519. Karl von Miltitz, a
chamberlain, reads a letter to the Pope, in which Martin submits himself to his ho-
liness and at the same time begs him to defend him and his activities against his

enemies. Although he confesses not to be able to retract, he invokes the Pope's protection "in order to quieten my enemies and satisfy my friends" (50). His letter forces a clear decision from Leo (51). The reaction of the Pope to this direct appeal confirms the will of the church to extinguish any awkward resistance to its authority and to stifle any new idea. Leo's verdict is as simple as it is brutal:

> "Write to Cajetan. Take this down. We charge you to summon before you Martin Luther ... And, once you get possession of him, keep him in safe custody, so that he can be brought before us. If, however, he should return to his duty of his own accord and begs forgiveness, we give you the power to receive him into the perfect unity of our Holy Mother the Church. But, should he persist in his obstinacy and you cannot secure him, we authorize you to outlaw him in every part of Germany. To banish and excommunicate him ... There's a wild pig in our vineyard, and it must be hunted down and shot. Given under the seal of the Fisherman's Ring, etcetera. That's all." (52)

The highest representative of the Catholic Church has reacted to Luther's reforming work in a way that does not lack distinctness. In an offhand manner, in well-wrought, high-flown and cliché-ridden phrases, only broken by the drastic image in the end, a man is condemned, who has set about to wake up his countrymen by means of plain German language. Any method is fit for Leo to secure the power of the church, and what is more: his own power.

At the beginning of the next scene (II, vi) the papal bull against Martin has already been issued. Luther preaches at the Elster Gate in Wittenberg, while monks burn the papal decretals. It is the year 1520. Martin's reaction to the measure of the Pope becomes evident in his speach:

> "I have been served with a piece of paper. Let me tell you about it. It has come to me from a latrine called Rome, that capital of the devil's own sweet empire. It is called the papal bull and it claims to excommunicate me, Dr.Martin Luther. These lies they rise up from paper like fumes from the bog of Europe; because papal decretals are the devil's excretals. ... Signed beneath the seal of the Fisherman's Ring by one certain midden cock called Leo, an over-indulged jakes' attendant to Satan himself, a glittering worm in excrement, known to you as his holiness the Pope. You may know him as the head of the Church. Which he may still be: like a fish is the head of a cat's dinner; eyes without sight clutched to a stick of sucked bones. God has told me: there can be no dealings between this cat's dinner and me. And, as for this bull, it's going to roast, it's going to roast and so are the balls of the Medici!" (53)

The final break between him and Rome has occured. Martin's former respect for the Pope has given way to downright contempt and enmity. His language is that of fierce polemics: it is of a terrifying acidity. Faecal expressions abound: "latrine", "bog", "excretals", "jakes", "excrement". Undisguised hatred characterizes his definitions of Leo.

After having thrown the bull into the fire, Martin is near a nervous breakdown. He realizes that he has done something monstrous, of tremendous consequences. He has cut himself off irretrievably from the official salvation, his action is past recall. His prayer mirrors his mental agony: he is alone with himself and God (54).

Act III, scene i contains the decisive confrontation between Luther and Johann von Eck at the Diet of Worms in April 1521, in front of "princes, electors, dukes, ambassadors, bishops, counts, barons" (55). In his plea Martin differentiates and analyzes his publications with honesty and simplicity (56). Of course, von Eck, the official specialist of the church for debates concerning religious questions in Germany, cannot accept Martin's argumentation. For him Luther is the heretic, who has disturbed the peace of the established Church and whose opinions have to be crushed. The Church and the Pope alone define and decide in matters of faith and Scriptures: their despotism is the law to which everybody has to submit (57). Von Eck's refusal of a sincere discussion and his persistence in an inflexible dogma bring about the final crisis in Luther: he perceives that he and the members of the diet move on completely different levels. There is no possibility of their coming to an agreement. His famous last statement shows Martin's unbroken spirit:

> "Since your serene majesty and your lordships demand a simple
> answer, you shall have it, without horns and without teeth. Unless
> I am shown by the testimony of the Scriptures - for I don't believe
> in popes or councils - unless I am refuted by Scripture and my
> conscience is captured by God's own word, I cannot and will not
> recant, since to act against one's conscience is neither safe nor
> honest. Here I stand; God help me; I can do no more. Amen." (58)

The last bit of trust in the representatives of the church is gone in Martin. His firm belief that he is doing the right thing and that God is with him in his actions, give him the strength to follow his way unflinchingly.

When the second scene of Act III sets in, four years have elapsed since the diet of Worms. Against the background noises of the peasants' war, a knight - "fatigued, despondent, stained and dirty" (59) - informs the audience in a long monologue about the events that have taken place since 1521. At first he speaks about the tremendous effect Luther and his work had on the population:

> "A lot's happened since then. ... I tell you, you can't have ever
> known the kind of thrill that monk set off amongst that collection
> of all kinds of men gathered together there - ... he fizzed like
> a hot spark in a trail of gunpowder going off in us, that dowdy
> monk, he went off in us, and nothing could stop it, and it blew up

194

and there was nothing we could do, any of us, that was it -...
Something had taken place, something had changed and become
something else, an event had occurred in the flesh, in the flesh
and the breath- ... I wanted to burst my ears with shouting and
draw my sword, no, not draw it, I wanted to pluck it as if it
were a flower in my blood and plunge it into whatever he would
have told me to." (60)

He compares Martin's revolution to the explosion of blasting-powder - an image
which forcibly illustrates the impact the deeds and thoughts of the reformer had on
the common men. The knight tries to describe what happened, but his language fails
to depict Martin's strange fascination. The only thing that he is sure about is that
Luther changed the times, and that he has power over his countrymen. Speaking to
the corpse of a peasant beside him he then hints at the part Luther took in the peasants' revolution, which was beaten down bloodily by the princes whom Martin even
encouraged:

"If one could only understand him. He baffles me, I just can't
make him out ... who'd have ever thought we might end up on
different sides, him on one and us on the other. That when the
war came between you and them, he'd be there beating the
drum for them outside the slaughter house, and beating it
louder and better than anyone, hollering for your blood ..." (61)

The last remarks - conjuring up a gruesome image of Martin as a wild butcher
beating the drum - refer to Luther's condemnation of the peasants' uproar, and his
approval of the outrageous methods of the princes. In the ensuing dialogue between
the knight and Luther the former reproaches him bitterly for his betrayal of the
peasants, and for his failure to bring "freedom and order" (62) to the lower classes
as well. Luther is caught between the princes and the peasants:

"MARTIN: ... The princes blame me, you blame me and the
peasants blame me --- ... When I see chaos, then I see the
devil's organ and then I'm afraid ..." (63)

He distances himself from a movement which drags his name into the struggle for
the old rights of the peasants, and which endangers his achievements (Luther feared that in the chaos of the peasants' war the devil himself rose against his work,
trying to bring him into discredit with the authorities). The knight still maintains
that Martin has disconnected himself from the common people (64). He hints at
Martin's endeavours to bring Christ into closer contact with the individual human
being. But Luther once more condemns the peasants' action:

"They deserved their death, these swarming peasants! They
kicked against authority, they plundered and bargained and all
in Your name! Christ, believe me! ..." (65)

Of course, he himself "kicked against authority" in Christ's name, but in this movement the revolt has clearly got out of hand, and issues of quite another nature were mixed up with Luther's name.

The ending of the scene shows Martin in a monologue, trying to come to grips with his situation. His re-telling of the story of Abraham and Isaac mirrors his longing for the protecting force of a father (already made apparent in his conversation with his father in I, iii) (66). Once again he throws himself upon God imploring him for his assistance. The scene ends with a dumb-show representation of his marriage to the former nun Katherine von Bora.

The last scene of the play (III, iii), five years later, takes us back to the Eremite Cloister Wittenberg in 1530. The first part, a conversation between Martin and Staupitz, is a sort of summary of Luther's achievement. Some facts are recollected, and Staupitz traces Martin's development since his early days in the monastery:

> "But you're not a frightened little monk any more who's come to
> his prior for praise or blame. Every time you belch now, the
> world stops what it's doing and listens." (67)

After some criticism referring to Erasmus and a lashing remark on the "Defender of the Faith", Henry VIII., their discussion centres on the peasants' war of a few years ago. Staupitz obviously does not completely agree with Martin's role during that time. In his reply Luther sticks to his theory that chaos is connected with the devil, and that any rebellion against the authorities is an act against the will of God. His argumentation seems somewhat illogical with regard to his own case:

> "They were a mob, a mob, and if they hadn't been held down and
> slaughtered, there'd have been a thousand more tyrants instead
> of half a dozen. It was a mob, and because it was a mob it was
> against Christ. " ... For there is no power but of God: the powers
> that be are ordained of God. Whosoever therefore resisteth that
> power, resisteth the ordinance of God": that's Paul, Father, and
> that's Scripture! 'And they that resist shall receive to themselves
> damnation. '" (68)

Staupitz then, rather abruptly, sums up Luther's work, recapitulating his activities of which the preceding scenes of the play only present some conspicuous sections. He ends with a warning referring to Martin's impulsive character (69).

The last moments of the play show Luther carrying his little son in his arms, and speaking to him about his former troubles. His final lines take him back to his almost obsessive child-complex which pervades the whole play and which has its cause in his unsatisfactory relationship with his own father. The exact meaning of Luther's last sentences remains obscure: they might express the hope of a new understanding and awareness of Christ, of a new childlike belief in him among the human beings:

> "You should have seen me at Worms. I was almost like you that day, as if I'd learned to play again, to play, to play out in the world, like a naked child ... A little while, and you <u>shall</u> see me. Christ said that, my son. I hope that'll be the way of it again. I hope so. Let's just hope so, eh? Eh? Let's just hope so. " (70)

In this private scene Luther seems to have gained his inner peace, some hope for the future, by the existence of an innocent child who is his own son.

*

<u>Luther</u> was, after <u>A Subject of Scandal and Concern</u> (1960), Osborne's second at-tempt at historical drama. As in his earlier play, he sticks closely to the historical documents; as other critics have pointed out (71), he follows the sources faithfully and uses the generally known and recorded utterances of Luther, thus giving his text authenticity.

The play consists of twelve single scenes of which three make up the first act, six the second act and again three the third one. It is a kind of "Bilderbogen"-arrange-ment reminding us of Brecht and his "epic theatre". Despite these loosely connec-ted scenes there emerges a fine structure, which, in my opinion, has not been suf-ficiently appreciated by the critics. The play shows Luther progressing from pri-vate drama towards sensational, world-changing significance and in the end once more retreating into the private sphere. Its movement could be represented graph-ically by an ascending curve reaching a peak and then descending again.

The three scenes of Act One deal with Martin's personal struggles and problems, with his sense of guilt and feeling of sinfulness, with his exaggerated obedience to the Rule, his doubts and his strained relation to his father (72). The accumulated tensions in Luther are triggered off by the events of the first scene of Act II, which presents the actual cause of Luther's rebellion: Tetzel's trade with the indulgences. Scene ii of the same act shows that Martin has reacted against Tetzel, and that his revolution has begun, cautiously encouraged by Staupitz. The third scene brings Martin's discovery of the crucial biblical passage about faith, and his most con-spicuous exposure to the world by the nailing of his 95 theses to the church door at Wittenberg: this event takes place in the very middle of the play, at the end of the third scene of Act II. It is the peak of Luther's forward motion, the end point for the time being of his offensive. In II, iv the counter-movement sets in: Rome reacts by calling up Cajetan; Martin's revolutionary force meets with a contrary one but asserts itself. His attack does not crumble. The reaction of Rome becomes more .iolent in II, v: the inimical pressure increases, Martin is threatened with excom-munication. This interplay of action and counteraction reaches a climax in the sixth scene of the second act: the Pope has applied his most drastic measure and has ex-communicated Martin. The latter's reaction is just as violent: the two divergent forces clash directly. The result is the final break of two powers, which occurs at the end of Act II.

Act III, i starts with the Diet of Worms which, although it enables Luther to defend his opinion and to defy authority in public, and although it carries his revolution into a wider audience and makes the theatre and its spectators part of that audience (the theatre becoming Luther's world), remains basically a consolidation of an established position.
The second scene of Act III sheds some light on Luther's part in the peasants' war and reflects his changed attitude towards rebellion: a backward movement becomes discernible which leads to Martin's retreat from the public scene. He returns into the seclusion of his private life in the bosom of his family - a seclusion which is comparable to the one of the first act. The champion retires, the revolution is left to the followers.

This structure reveals a careful and deliberate architecture and proves that Osborne subjected his twelve scenes to a thought-out-plan, and that the overall judgment of "twelve self-contained scenes" (73) is not satisfactory.

There is enough room for criticism, all the same. The first act, in which Luther's character is established and his later actions are prepared, takes up too much room compared to the rest of the play: Osborne needs nearly 32 pages of printed text for these three scenes, whereas the six scenes which form the second act and which present the main stations of Luther's life, are crowded into about 30 pages. Twenty pages are left for the third act, which appears very sketchy and was obviously never worked out carefully. It looks rather like a collection of notes to a last act. Its second scene is completely muddled; one never really perceives Luther's position in the peasants' war, and even with an exact knowledge of the historical facts one can only guess the meaning of the knight's long monologue (74). Staupitz's summary of Luther's achievement in the last scene of the play comes as a surprise if one takes into consideration solely what has been presented in the foregoing eleven scenes: Osborne seems to presuppose a rather complete knowledge about Luther on the part of his audience, who are obviously called up to combine everything they know about the reformer with the material dramatized in the play, thus justifying Staupitz's words. But the gaps in the play itself are too wide to explain this fantastic assessment. If one knows Luther from the play only, one cannot possibly believe that he has achieved all this - in the meantime, as it were (75).

Luther is characterized by recurring word patterns which pervade the play as "leitmotifs". Martin's rebellion is partly explained as an outcome of his unhappy relationship with his father, and his repeated allusions to the state of a child mirror a deep longing for his innocence and protection which he did not experience in his youth. The existence of more than twenty words belonging to this sphere (repetitions of the words "child", "children", "infant", "childish"), especially concentrated in Act I, ii and III, iii, indicate Martin's obsession.

The second pattern is constructed out of the excessive use of words denoting physical illness and defects on the one hand, and relating to the faecal sphere on the other ("constipation", "sickness", "vomit", "fit", "sweat", "bowels", "latrine", "anus", "stool", "excretals", "jakes", "john", "sweathouse", "to break wind", "excrement"), of which there are over forty instances in the text.

The physical infirmities are visible symptoms of an alarming mental and spiritual disquiet, and are used by Osborne to externalize Martin's inner condition (76). The fits are the result of his violent inner struggles, developing from his guilt and sin complex. So are his attacks of sickness. The metaphor of the cramped bowels and the constipation and their healing by Luther's discovery of faith as the saving force is somewhat crude, but elaborated with consistency; although in the end it appears that Martin's therapy by faith does not work completely as his stomach cramps still continue. Perhaps Osborne wanted to express that Martin is still not entirely free from doubt. The parallel of the physical and the mental condition is, despite its blatancy, an effective device.

As to the language of the play, it presents necessarily a mixture of styles, as Osborne intersperses his own dialogue with the language of the historical sources. His own language is the colloquial one of our time; sometimes to such an extent as to verge on the slapdash and slang. This mixture results in often embarrassing breaks of style, as for example in the very beginning, when Martin's father replaces the solemn language during his son's inauguration with sentences such as "You've been sitting in this arse-aching congregation all this time ..." (77) or throws in a remark like "Well, what about this chap Erasmus, for instance?" (78)
As usual, Osborne is at his best in the monologues. Tetzel's speech in the market place (II, i) is a small masterpiece of overpowering rhetoric enriched with mirror passages and gestic impulses. Martin's great sermons are distinguished by persuasive force and urgency. The one he hurls at the people after his excommunication (II, vi) possesses all the characteristics of Osborne's polemical tirades known from his earlier plays, tirades abounding with strong expressions and images and carried along by a sharp rhythm produced by short sentences.

The dialogue is less convincing. For instance, the speeches exchanged between Martin and Staupitz on the one hand (II, ii) and between Martin and Cajetan on the other (II, iv) do not always seem to develop from each other organically; often the individual statements remain isolated from what the dialogue-partner says immediately before (79). Here Osborne's preference of the monologue asserts itself clearly.

Quite often the running dialogue is extended by reported scenes (80). The interest throughout the play remains concentrated on Martin. He is the centre of the play, and the lasting impression is that of a rebel struggling against himself and defying authority as he goes through life. What fascinated Osborne about Luther was the single man standing up against the established powers of his day and defeating them; the "angry young man" attacking the rotten institutions; more successful in his results than Jimmy Porter or Archie Rice, whose revolutions remain confined to the verbal sphere (81). His psychological explanation of Martin's rebellion is not convincing: his personal problems are rendered effectively but do not cogently lead up to his world changing actions. Although <u>Luther</u> is written with theatrical flair and shows qualities in its structure (82), and although the author spices history with the unmistakable Osborne characteristics, it never amounts to great drama. Still, it remains an interesting play about a compulsive character, who involves us in his torments and doubts, and it is this doubt, together with the agonizing insecurity underneath, which make us understand and sympathize with Martin's revolution.

*

At first sight, <u>Luther</u> seems to be a history play and therefore comparable to, perhaps, Shakespeare's Histories; among modern English drama to Robert Bolt's <u>A Man for All Seasons</u>, or, among Continental examples, to Bertolt Brecht's plays. Considered from this point of view, Osborne's play would stand in the line of a well-established category with a great tradition.

But in fact <u>Luther</u> is, as other critics have pointed out, no historical play in the strict sense. Osborne rather makes use of the historical figure and background in order to present a rebel (who could just as well be of our time) up against everything resembling authority. Ronald Hayman sees the situation very clearly:

> "Compared with Brecht's <u>Galileo</u> or John Whiting's <u>The Devils,</u> for instance, Osborne's <u>Luther</u> isn't a historical play at all. In their different ways, Brecht and Whiting both devote a great deal of time and energy and love to recreating a solid historical actuality, and whether the details are accurate or not, the stage is effectively steeped in period atmosphere and filled with a wide-angle view of people doing business, practising their religion, eating, suffering, doubting, fighting. Osborne misses out completely on the social element. And whereas Galileo and Grandier are both presented as products of their period - rebels against it, certainly, but still conditioned by it in the way they think and feel - Osborne starts with what he sees as a neurosis and then perfunctorily sketches in a period background. ... Luther emerges as a rebel against everything, including history." (83)

Hayman also points out a definite similarity to Brecht's <u>Leben des Galilei</u> (1938/39). Galileo, too, is in opposition to the reigning doctrine of his day. But he finally revokes his discoveries and convictions and thus subjects himself to the authorities, betraying truth. Luther comes into a similar situation: although he resists the Pope and breaks with the Catholic Church, he compromises with the authorities during the peasants' war, and in the end retires from the spiritual battlefield:

> " ... both plays end with a scene showing the ex-hero passive in the comfort of a private home with a well-meaning woman there to distract him from his bad conscience with good food. ". (84)

But these similarities to Brecht remain superficial. Osborne isolates Luther and pays little regard to the social and historical conditions surrounding him. He clearly identifies himself - and expects his audience to identify themselves - with Luther, whereas Brecht, on the contrary, wants the audience to keep their distance and to avoid identification with his heroes.

Osborne searched history for a character who would correspond to his own innermost convictions. He found it in Martin Luther, took him out of his period and revived him as a man of the twentieth century. The creator of Jimmy Porter obviously endeavoured to demonstrate that there have always been rebels against authority, and that they were the ones to accompplish the feats mankind admires today. Luther's case appears as a justification of today's revolutions. In the sixteenth-century reformer Osborne recognized a personality exposed to struggles and problems not unlike those of modern man. In this facet lies the originality of the play.

*

Osborne's personification of part of the stage directions proved to be an effective device:

> "NOTE. At the opening of each act, the Knight appears. He grasps
> a banner and briefly barks the time and place of the scene following
> at the audience, and then retires." (85)

The spectators were thus directly addressed from the very beginning and explicitly transferred to the places of action.

Already the first scene announced by the knight was one of those which remained unforgettable to most theatregoers. Tony Richardson's skilful direction turned the scenes in the convent of the Augustinian Order of Eremites (Act I, scenes i to iii) into striking events. The stage was in semi-darkness for almost the whole of the first act. Singing monks with censers moved under an expressionistically distorted figure of Christ on the cross. Clouds of incense spread in the auditorium, the atmosphere of a monastery as experienced by Martin was created and suggested irresistibly. His inauguration was a solemn ceremony in the shadows of the cloister chapel; moving and awe-inspiring. The intensity of religious feeling penetrated into the auditorium. These scenes belonged - wrongly, as we shall see later (86) - to the most effective ones of the production. Almost all of the people interviewed about the performance thought them memorable (87). Direction reached a climax when Martin had his fit in the choir (88). This emotionally charged scene "came off with astounding power", as the critic of The Observer wrote (89). It was gripping to hear Martin's scream emerge from the steady, unwavering chant of the monks, to see him stagger into the light, to see him collapse and writhe on the stage, being shaken by cruel forces tormenting his body and soul.

Martin's confrontation with his father (I, iii) turned out to be one of the best scenes altogether, although there is not anything particularly "stagey" about it. Osborne

planned it as one of the highlights of the play, but as he put it in a letter (90),
"Scene with Hans should have been good but undercast". John R. Wilson in the
British Weekly thought better of it when he remarked that

> "The scene of Father and Son, in Act One, is one of the most
> masterly." (91)

The beginning of the second act, which starts with Tetzel's long monologue, gave
Tony Richardson the opportunity of displaying his ability for effective grouping.
Accompanied by drums, waving banners and boys with cymbals. Tetzel was dragged
onto the stage in a cart, holding a red cross and at once commanding the place with
his dangerously fascinating personality. This scene, with its verbal and visual force
(the audience was directly addressed) was, in Osborne's own opinion, one of the
most impressive of the production.

The fanaticism of Tetzel was contrasted by the following calm but intense dialogue
between Staupitz and Martin (II, ii). This transition was carefully realized in the
direction; the particular quality of the scene at the Court was that it really succeeded in quietening the atmosphere and in shedding light on the problems facing Luther
at the outset of his reforming adventure.

The next scene (II, iii) at the end of which Martin nails his theses to the church door,
brought the first of the sermons which, as Osborne himself thinks, belonged to the
most satisfying moments on the stage (92). Martin's outbursts from his pulpit were
of an astonishing vigour, revealing the rhetoric brilliance of the text. It was here
that Osborne's gift for writing dramatic prose designed for the actor's voice (and
the spectator's ear) became forcibly apparent.

The fourth scene of the second act provided a further highlight: the confrontation of
Luther and Cajetan. This dispute was said to be very effective by some of the critics (93). It made the dramatic clash of the conservative church and the rebel palpable - a clash of oily, diplomatic art and unwavering courage and simplicity, which
was intensified by the visually striking contrast between Cajetan's crimson-red habit and Martin's plain black cowl. R. B. Marriott in The Stage was almost the only
one among the reviewers to speak negatively of this scene:

> " ... the encounter between Cajetan ... and Martin, one of the most
> vital scenes in the play, is disappointing in its impact ..." (94)

Unfortunately he does not state what exactly caused his disappointment. Act II, v
showed Richardson as an inventive director: He gave to the entrance of the Pope
and his hunting party an extraordinary touch by introducing live animals into the
action - three beautiful Afghan hounds (95) and a falcon on Leo's hand - as indicated
in Osborne's text. The appearance of this elegant and snobbish group produced a
strong effect and made visible the forces and mentality Luther - and reformation
with him - were up against. A fine detail of the direction: while Leo was threatening
Luther with excommunication, he at the same time teased his falcon: the hunter and

the falcon against Martin, as it were, symbolized the determination of the church to destroy any rebels. This hunting image was strikingly rounded off by the Pope's final remark: "There's a wild pig in our vineyard, and it must be hunted down and shot" (96). Recklessness and brutality hidden under precious clothes and a smooth face, beneath the elegance a cold decision to wipe out everything trying to oppose the power of Rome - such was the lasting impression of this scene (97). The sixth and last scene of Act II, in which the audience is taken back from the pontifical pomp to Germany and rebellious Luther, came as an effective change. In sharp contrast to the scene witnessed before, the spectactors were confrontend with one that had an almost demoniac quality about it. The stage was in semi-darkness, the red and yellow of the flames flared across the back-projected bull and Martin's white face - a memorable realization of Osborne's stage direction.

Act III, i (the Diet of Worms) was directed with all the splendour suggested by the text. With clever grouping and the help of Jocelyn Herbert's set Richardson achieved moments of theatrical grandeur. The visual impression was supplemented by the sound of trumpets announcing the disputation. The actors did not emerge from the auditorium as is demanded by the stage directions. Nevertheless, author and direc- tor led the audience to the final sentence by building up the suspense and made it grasp the significance of that historical moment by a successfully combined effort. Almost regretfully, V.S. Pritchett in the New Statesman wrote:

> "The dispute at the Diet of Worms is beautifully staged, but it
> is potted and over in a flash ..." (98)

Even more breathtaking than this scene was the way in which Richardson managed the transition to the next one (III, ii): without a break in the action the gauze (99), on which part of the congregation was painted (100), was lit from the back of the stage and thus made transparent. Behind the gauze, the banners of the peasants could be discerned coming through, and as the stage grew brighter, they carried their flags into the foreground, singing "Ein Feste Burg ist unser Gott", (101) brutally and harshly and driving out the magnificently dressed people of the diet (102). The court disappeared, and in a kind of quick-motion technique the whole process of the peasants' war and Luther's becoming involved in it were imaginatively realized. Bamber Gascoigne in The Spectator describes this scene in detail:

> "When he (103) is caught up against his will in the Peasants'
> Revolt, we see this happening on the stage in one of Tony
> Richardson's most brilliant strokes of direction. Luther refuses
> to retract at Worms - a personal stand on behalf of his conscience
> - and the gauze painting of the assembly hall fades away behind him
> to reveal a marching army of peasants. Singing "Ein Feste Burg"
> they come up behind Luther: their ranks pass him and close round
> him until he is no longer visible ..." (104)

In the end of this presentation "dead" bodies on the stage and trailing banners indi- cated the bloody end of the rising. The whole development of the revolution was thus expressed in a theatrically effective form. But probably it did not become sufficiently clear to the spectators what the director tried to convey. "I doubt whether the audience got it", Richardson said (105).

After these exciting events, the last scene was directed calmly and simply, adequately reflecting Luther's final situation and his renunciation of rebellious actions.

The liturgical music and the chants, which were used throughout the production, were arranged by John Addision and taken from contemporary composers, such as Josquin des Pres (it is recorded that Luther expressed a great liking for his music) and Jakob Obrecht.

*

Luther, with its cast of twelve actors and one actress, besides a number of walkers-on (monks, lords, peasants, children), presents considerable problems to the director, and it must be conceded to Richardson that he assembled a cast which, to a great extent, fulfilled the demands of the different roles.

Luther, of course, is the part on which the whole weight of the play and the production rests, and Albert Finney proved capable of not only supporting this weight but also of making Martin a character larger than life. As Richardson said in an emotional evaluation, "he was absolutely superb" (106). The achievement of this young actor was noted with respect and admiration by almost all critics. Something of his spellbinding force is captured in the sentences of the reviewer in Plays and Players:

> "Finney, at all times a compulsive actor, is more than com-
> pelling as Luther. He is Luther. His quiet strong and admi-
> rable performance threw me in a frame of mind to swear that
> had he been born into a springtime world he would have turned
> his back on it as did the early Luther ..." (107)

Finney spoke with his native Lancashire accent and thus in a way re-created in English terms some of the power Luther's German - which was the German understood by the common man - must have had (108). Harold Hobson in The Sunday Times stressed Finney's ability of conveying the whole range of Martin's emotion and was unstinting in his praise:

> "Albert Finney's Luther absorbs Protestantism like a man who
> has swallowed a powerful dose of medicine which in the end may
> do him good, but which at the moment is burning out his liver,
> and making his eyes swivel. Every detail of this sensational
> cure, beginning with frantic adoration of a cruel and defeated
> Crucifix, passing through febrile sermons to an exhausted and
> timorous peace at the end, is presented by Mr. Finney with
> astonishing power. Mr. Finney is as unlikely often to get a
> more tremendous part than this as the part itself is ever to

find a better actor than Mr. Finney." (109)

The reviewer of The Sunday Telegraph points to similar characteristics of the performance and describes his impression in telling images:

> "Towering above them all, a fleshy, clammy, worm-gnawed parody of the agonised saviour which hangs above him, is Albert Finney's Luther. Sick, insecure, cowardly, resentful, ambitious - Mr. Finney draws all his emotions from inside him like buckets from a poisoned well. It is a performance which exhausts, and yet hypnotizes, the eyes like the spectacle of a public flogging ..." (110)

Finney's strength of infusing his Luther with the features inherent in the text, his differentiated performance and his ability of changing moods and emotions, impressed T.C. Worsley in The Financial Times:

> "But as soon as the young Luther comes to the fore we are given in Mr. Finney's finely detailed and beautifully imagined acting the living image of the neurotic anguish of conscience, as the author has conceived it ... Mr. Finney is now visibly growing into early manhood, and it is one of the marks of his extraordinary talent that he can seem to grow before our eyes ..." (111)

V.S. Pritchett, reviewing the production for the New Statesman, mingled criticism with praise and appreciated the actor's rendering of the central sermons as well as his consummate employment of silences and pauses:

> "Finney has not - and perhaps cannot be expected to convey - the bodily coarseness of the German which lent to Luther's obscenities a popular richness and which, as Osborne understood, gave the Reformation its formidable quality of the deeply German awakening of a people through their language. He missed the brutal yet poetic humour of the flesh, so that most of Luther's obscenities had more hatred than nature in them and therefore less power. But the ill, tortured, obstinate, pent-up man, Finney completely caught - the strange morbid appeal of the sick mind and the awkward, searching, extemporary mixture, in his sermons, of sly homeliness and rhetoric. He conveyed Luther's doubting, halting quality, and especially he gave weight to those silences - ugly, fermenting, uncouth, yet touching - that (Osborne brilliantly saw) were of the essence of the character. The sermons, and especially the one that contains the scabrous portrait of the Pope as a "fish's head", were preached by a Doctor of Theology who had not forgotten that he had come up from the common people, who enjoyed the images they enjoyed and knew how to play upon their indignations." (112)

Criticism of Finney's realization of the part remained exceptionally rare. R.B.

Marriott in The Stage was of the opinion that

" . . . much of the acting leaves a lot to be desired. Albert Finney
doubtless does quite well for a young actor who has not before been
called upon to take an exceptionally demanding part in a new play,
but the performance remains superficial. It is from the writing alone,
not from Mr. Finney's acting, that we come to know Martin. " (113)

The critic of the Daily Sketch reacted positively to Finney's overall impact but
critized a minor point:

"All the time Finney is on the stage he is the master. Only when he
is not involved personally in what is happening at that precise second
is he inclined to overact . . . Finney says: 'I feel the bones of this
part . . .'" (114)

Ronald Bryden saw Finney's achievement mainly in his emotional force, which,
according to his statement, sometimes failed:

"The burden was on Finney who relied more on sincerity than
technique. Some nights this did come over, some nights it did not.
It was a very cold production the night I went." (115)

Finney's manner of speaking and the quality of his voice were judged ideal for the
part by the critic of The Observer, along with the actor's own character:

"That thick, glowing voice is ideally suited to the tones of surly
self-justification, and there is something stubborn in Mr. Finney's
temperament that corresponds to the same stubborn something in
Luther's. " (116)

The reviewer of The Morning Advertiser was struck by Finney's compelling force
in the pulpit and sums up the impression produced by Luther's sermons as fellow:

"Albert Finney is consistently successful . . . his sermon deploring
the system of indulgences is infused with all the fury and implacability
of an avenging archangel. Physical weakness and moral strength are
revealed with equal truth . . . " (117)

In any case Finney realized an outstanding and strong performance (118). He caught
the basic characteristics of Luther as displayed in Osborne's text and gave his best
throughout the play, as the subsequent review in the West London Press suggests:

"The energy and concentration put into his part by Albert Finney
takes its toll, for at the end of the performance he seems completely exhausted, almost too exhausted to take the unusual number
of curtain calls the audience demands. " (119)

T.C. Worsley, a careful and perceptive critic, drew the conclusions and saw in Finney's performance one of the great achievements in acting:

> " ... in Mr. Albert Finney the author has found a young actor magnificently able to match the conception. This is one of the really great performances of the last decades. No one who cares about acting should miss it." (120)

Another good performance, although practically confined to one scene (II, i) was given by Peter Bull in the part of Tetzel. He was the living counterpart to Osborne's description of the character:

> "He is splendidly equipped to be an ecclesiastical huckster, with alive, silver hair, the powerfully calculating voice, range and technique of a trained crator, the terrible, riveting charm of a dedicated professional able to winkle coppers out of the pockets of the poor and desperate." (121)

Bull made excellent use of the short span of time during which he commanded the stage, behaved "hugely loud-mouthed" (122) and made the audience feel rotten sinners, completely at his mercy. The reviewer in <u>John O'London's</u> was hypnotized by Bull's personality:

> "Peter Bull as the seller of Indulgences is so terrifying a figure that I was in a mind to buy a few then and there and in the market place, just in case. In one resplendant speech, scene-long, he scolds and coaxes, wheedles, winkles out, pins down, extorts and exhorts with the force and fluency that proves him a master of Barkmanship and ought to make him free of the fairground of the world." (123)

Although Bull stressed the frightening aspects of Tetzel's character, Anthony Cookman in <u>The Tatler</u> gave more weight to the comic side of the scene:

> "Mr. Peter Bull presides with oleaginous fake pity over an amusing representation of a mock auction of Papal guaranteed salvation ... "
> (124)

The critic of <u>Plays and Players</u> compared the actor with Osborne's respective stage directions:

> " ... Mr. Osborne has required exactly those qualities which Mr. Bull, quite terrifyingly, is able to supply together with the wit and declamation that would not discredit a member of the great Comédie Française." (125)

An original characterization of Bull's performance is given by V.S. Pritchett in the New Statesman, who stresses its monstrous qualities:

> "There was Peter Bull as the voluminous Tetzel selling off Indul-
> gences in the curdled words of a TV commercial and in a voice
> which seemed to make his Germanic guts boil in his throat." (126)

Jack Lewis in the Reynolds News thought the performance so good as to stand for
the achievement of the whole cast:

> "Among the fine cast I single out Peter Bull as Tetzel, whose
> market-place sale of the Pope's indulgences was a brilliant
> piece of verbal hypnotism ..." (127)

Peter Bull succeeded admirably in extending the action on the stage to the auditorium and thus involving the audience in the play. They were in his grip during the
entire scene (128).

John Moffatt gave life to Cardinal Cajetan. He was excellent in presenting the mixture of diplomatic politeness, ridicule, intolerance and elusive art of persuasion
in this cunning man of the church. The critic of the Yorkshire Evening Post found
him "suavely fascinating" (129), Anthony Merryn in The Stage "brilliant" (130), and
the reviewer of Plays and Players described him as "steely, subtle, civilised" (131).
W.A. Darlington in The Daily Telegraph judged Moffatt's acting as "a first-rate
small performance" (132), and T.C. Worsley wrote that "John Moffatt manages the
sly Italian excellently" (133). V.S. Pritchett elaborates:

> "There was John Moffatt's weary Cajetan, the Papal legate, who
> brought out the immense difference between the Italian Renaissance
> and crude German nationalism. This part was well-written and ex-
> quisitely performed; it is a key point in the public theme of the
> play." (134)

The critic of John O'London's stressed the sleekness of the character as conveyed
by the actor:

> "John Moffatt's Cardinal, scarlet as sin, is sophistry personified;
> a subtle, smooth and worldly-wise Papal Legate, with a silken
> tongue and a sinister sense of humour." (135)

George Devine's achievement in the part of Staupitz has been rated in a former
chapter (136).

It is certainly true to say, as W.A. Darlington did, that "apart from Mr. Finney's,
the acting chances are not lavish" (137). Luther is essentially a one-man play, and
apart from the central character the actors' possibilities are restricted to two
scenes, one scene or even less. The dominance of Finney is reflected by the reviews, in the greater part of which the rest of the cast (with the exception of Peter

Bull, George Devine and John Moffatt) is practically neglected. R.B. Marriott in The Stage is the only one we found (among 36 reviews considered) to mention Charles Kay in the role of Pope Leo (" ... excellent as the dry, pleasure-loving but astute Pope Leo.") (138); and Bill Owen as Hans, Martin's father, was briefly judged as "a good performance" by V.S. Pritchett in the New Statesman (139). The cast subjected themselves to the demands of the play and unobtrusively gave their best within the limits of their parts (140). The proportions established by the author were obeyed. Finney did not make his part a star performance because of egoistic reasons and at the expense of his fellow-actors, but because the play required it.

*

From the point of view of theatrical effect Luther was probably one of the most striking productions ever staged at the Court. Tony Richardson is no doubt a highly imaginative and intelligent director, with an extraordinary visual sense, a feeling for the realities of the stage, and a highly developed ability to transform a dramatic text into full-blooded theatre. Anthony Cookman in The Tatler perceived these qualities in Luther when he wrote that

> " ... Mr. Richardson's production pounces on whatever is dramatic
> and sets the whole chronicle moving to a beautifully strong rhythm."
> (141)

A large part of the critics paid tribute to the direction and admired the theatrical flourish with which Richardson presented the play. W.A. Mitchell in Press and Journal even implies that the director actually saved the play by his production:

> "In such a range of action we can hardly expect more than a
> 'snippety' play, but there must be marvelling at how Mr. Richardson has disguised the worst of that and produced a piece of theatre
> into which several fine actors get their teeth." (142)

Equally impressed by Richardson's effects was V.S. Pritchett - especially by the linking of the individual scenes:

> "Pictorially, Tony Richardson's production and Jocelyn Herbert's
> costumes and designs were excellent and there were some very
> clever shocks of transition from scene to scene." (143)

Other reviewers spoke about the direction in expressions like "easy-flowing unity" (144), "almost medieval poise" (145), "grouping could not be bettered" (146), "competent and clear" (147), "generally effective" (148), "haunting theatrical moments" (149), etc.
Some slight criticism centred on Richardson's direction of the first scenes of the play, although it is by no means a severe criticism:

"Osborne's Luther starts out as a young monk taking his vows, and Tony Richardson's production and Jocelyn Herbert's striking set evoke the solemnity of the occasion. It is necessary for what follows to fix us firmly in the Centre of Catholic ceremonial, though the production lingers here a little too long." (150)

Robert Muller in The Daily Mail moves along similar lines but shifts the fault completely onto Osborne's side:

"Mr. Richardson has not been able to disguise the fact that all the early scenes in the monastery seem to go on for too long ..." (151)

Surprisingly not one of these admiring critics noticed that in spite of its undoubted effectiveness the production falsified the play to a great extent.

In his effort to stage the play as dashingly as possible, Richardson entirely ignored its inherent rhythm (152). The progress of Luther is, as we have pointed out before, a progress from a private drama towards a world sensation, followed by a recession into private life again. A production that wants to catch this basic movement would, for example, have to set the first scenes at the back of the stage, bringing each following scene further downstage until the theatre becomes the world of Luther (III, i), retreating again with the last two scenes. But this whole process, apparent in Osborne's text, was lost sight of. Richardson directed the early scenes in the monastery much too strikingly and noisily, with endless detail. Tetzel (II, i) had his speech right at the front of the stage, which was theatrically effective but destroyed what came afterwards. Richardson neglected the shape of the play, its structure, for the sake of effect. He saw the play almost exclusively in relation to the single scenes which he examined as to their potentiality for impressive staging, at the same time disregarding their interrelation. He achieved a thrilling production but sacrificed the inherent theatricality of the play. What is surprising is that Osborne, who attended the rehearsals, apparently did not mind the violation of his play and did not interfere. Richardson seems to have convinced him to accept his version.

It was one of the few instances at the Court where the principles established by George Devine were disregarded to at least a certain extent. An ingenious director devised an equally ingenious production, the impact of which was achieved at the expense of the original play. The example shows that even a collaboration between author and director is no absolute guarantee for the faithful realization of a dramatic text.

Thus we cannot agree with the critic of The Observer, who observed that Osborne was "loyally served by Tony Richardson's production ..." (153). He was not. (154).

*

Unlike the director, designer Jocelyn Herbert respected Osborne's stage directions and did what the author wanted. She devised one of her simple sets, combining economy, evocativeness and visual beauty. She designed a permanent scenery consisting of a backwall articulated by a stony-coloured texture, conveying a feeling of interlocking gothic arches. Smaller arches and further architectural details formed the sides of the stage. The floor was laid with paving stones. The reviewer of The Times described this set as follows:

> "On Miss Jocelyn Herbert's bare, formal setting, a square-shaped granite hollow box, a suggestion of gothic arches reaches out into the infinite black sky. This serves as a permanent acting area into which some skeletal element is inserted to indicate the locale." (155)

The design for the first scenes in the monastery was impressive in its simplicity: in the semi-darkness of the stage the emaciated figure of Christ on the cross could be seen, the expressionistically distorted face overspread by a cruel crown of thorns. The image was like an indication of Luther's future fight against the perverted faith of the church, far from a harmonious monastic life:

> "The settings are most effective, particularly that of act one, where a huge figure of a twisted Christ on the cross dominates the stage ..." (156)

The setting for Act II, ii - the meeting of Staupitz and Martin in the garden of the Eremite Cloister Wittenberg - was very simple and suited to the occasion. Against the background of gothic arches the branch of a pear tree was visible. Spotlights projected the shapes of leaves onto the ground, and the sounds of singing birds penetrated the peaceful silence - effects mentioned in Osborne's directions.

The Pope's hunting lodge at Magliana (II, v) consisted of painted cloth draped about a wooden, carved frame, displaying the papal coat of arms and tiara overhead. The snobbish elegance of the scene was enhanced by the use of the colours: rich olive-green, brown, gold and black dominated among the hunting apparels.

Act II, vi ("back to no colour - grey, brown and black dominated") (157) was given the demoniac quality required in the directions (158).

The Diet of Worms (III, i) took place in front of a memorable set, which almost exactly corresponded to Osborne's suggestions:

> "A gold front-cloth, and on it, in the brightest sunshine of colour, a bold, joyful representation of this unique gathering of princes, electors, dukes, ambassadors, bishops, counts, barons, etc. ... The mediaeval world dressed up for the Renaissance.
>
> Devoid of depth, such scenes are stamped on a brilliant ground of

gold. Movement is frozen, recession in space ignored and
perspective served by the arrangement of figures, or scenes,
one above the other. In this way, landscape is dramatically
substituted by objects in layers. ... On one side is a table
with about twenty books on it. The table and books may also
be represented on the gold cloth. ..." (159)

Jocelyn Herbert painted the figures piled up on each other, evoking a primitive
"perspective". The table and the members of the Diet were represented on the
cloth, which consisted of three gauzes hung up like curtains: one on the left side of
the stage, one on the right, and one in the centre, somewhat set back. The magnificent impression of the luminous colours was further intensified by the rich red
and orange of the costumes.
The last two scenes of the play were back to austerity again; especially the set for
III, iii underlined the quietness and even slight resignation of the final moments.

The episodes at the beginning of I, ii and the ones which show Martin alone, carrying a child in his arms (ending of I, ii and III, iii) were realized according to Osborne's directions, with Luther standing in front of a crucifix, within the light-cone
of a strong spotlight isolating him from the surroundings.

The costumes of the peasants were plain, drab-coloured, and formed a strong contrast to the magnificent clothes of their ecclesiastical and secular superiors.

It was the work of a designer who remained faithful to the author and whose efforts
were directed at enhancing the total effect of the play (160).

*

Audience reaction to <u>Luther</u> was to a large extent favourable. The spectators were
impressed by Richardson's imaginative production and their attention was almost
constantly caught by Finney's acting. They were entirely captured by the Tetzel
scene. According to Richardson they were not quite clear about the transition from
III, i to III, ii and - for this the play is to blame - about the contents of III, ii; a scene
which seemed to puzzle them understandably. On the whole, however, they reacted
positively throughout, and the number of curtain calls at the end of each performance
mirrored their enthusiasm.

*

The large majority of the reviews about <u>Luther</u> were unanimous in their praise. It
looks as if the combination of such names as Osborne, Richardson, Herbert and
Finney extorted respect even from those reviewers who had not spoilt the Court
with appreciation before.

Bamber Gascoigne in <u>The Spectator</u> wrote approvingly of the play as well as of the
direction, the design and the main actor:

212

"The seal on "Luther"'s excellence is Osborne's language. No one
in the English theatre can write prose like him, dramatic prose
designed for the voice and the ear, and he has now proved what an
adaptable instrument this prose is ... Space limits the full praise
which is due to Tony Richardson's magnificent direction and to
Jocelyn Herbert's sets ... Albert Finney's performance is superb
... The new British drama, of which the leading author and leading
actor here come together for the first time, has already triumphed
in the domestic foothills. It now makes the necessary and decisive
move up the slopes." (161)

The critic of the quarterly theatre review <u>Drama</u> defended the construction of the
play and its presentation of Luther's character:

"Tony Richardson has produced with a welcome absence of fuss.
I do not understand those who find no real dramatic development
in the play. Its short scenes build an arch of passionate belief
constantly threatened by an earthquake of uncertainty. The language is almost always the equal of its theme; and Luther, unlike George Dillon, Jimmy Porter and Archie Rice, never makes
a frontal assault on the audience's emotions, never sits up and
begs for sympathy - and never for a second loses our respect."
(162)

Concluding his animated review in <u>John O'London's,</u> the reviewer expressed his
enthusiasm with the following sentence:

"I have seen the play twice and read the script once and cannot
wait to go again and tremble." (163)

Harold Hobson found words of praise for the play's structure and called special
attention to scenes II, iv and III, iii:

"In fact, all through the play, as soon as one line of thought or
emotion is presented it is broken off, and another offered, in
relevant and stimulating criticism.

The advantage of this method is that it appeals to the mind; the
disadvantage, dramatically, that it does not, and by design
cannot, develop a crescendo of excitement. But every individual
scene is written with vigour and imagination, the first three of
the four big speeches are very good pieces of rhetoric, the
interview between Luther and Cajetan is silky, subtle and witty,
and when he likes, Mr. Osborne shows that he can use ordinary
dramatic construction as skilfully as any conventional craftsman.
The constant tortures of Luther in his recollections and dreams
of children are beautifully gathered up and banished in the exquisite

final scene." (164)

The critic of The Sunday Telegraph mingled his admiration for Richardson's direction with some slight criticism of the play, but covers it up immediately by his overall impression of the performance:

> "Tony Richardson has surpassed himself as director with a
> production of magisterial grandeur and theatrical pageantry.
> Every stage picture seems to have been cut from a frame in
> the Uffizi and set into motion. Just so should the Afghan hounds
> stand beside Pope Leo. Just so should Tetzel, most bovine of
> all Papal bulls, beetle and belly over the audience. ... It is a
> mistake for Osborne to tell us too much too often in explanation
> of his hero ... We become spectators but never participants
> ... Still it remains a hammer-blow of an evening." (165)

Acknowledging the theatrical force of Luther, the reviewer of the Evening Standard made some - partially justified - reservations concerning Osborne's language:

> "On the purely theatrical level, Osborne has succeeded impres-
> sively. With adroit economy, he has capulated Luther's life into
> a neat string of significant incidents showing us Freudian, par-
> ental, moral, physical and religious motivations for the passionate
> defiance that did so much to sweep in the Reformation ... Much of
> the language spoken by everyone but Luther himself is either wooden
> or banal ... forced colloquialisms ..." (166)

Philip Hope-Wallace (The Guardian) entitled his notice A Masterpiece with Flaws, but commended the direction, the sets, the music, and Finney's acting:

> " ... quite splendidly put on that stage and ... acted with passion
> and strong outline by Albert Finney ... The direction ... and the
> sets ... deserve only unstinted praise. John Addison's music is
> exactly right, and Albert Finney justifies the highest hopes." (167)

Somewhat more critical was W. A. Mitchell in Press and Journal. He accused the dramatist of "pretentiousness" - rather peremptorily - but admitted some of the qua lities of the play:

> "Perhaps someone will be bold enough to suggest that Mr. Osborne
> has added pretentiousness to his shortcomings as a dramatist,
> though there is the risk of being blinded by Tony Richardson's
> brilliant direction and Albert Finney's most moving performance
> in the title role.
> But let us be fair. There are long speeches and brief flashes
> of theatre in 'Luther' showing a sense of beauty and a depth of
> intelligence of which I admit I did not think Mr. Osborne capable..." (168)

214

T.C. Worsley in The Financial Times pointed to flaws in the structure of Luther but appreciated the power of Osborne's statement and its realization by Finney:

"The loneliness of this rebel taking on the whole world and enduring the burden of it is superbly brought out in the pallor and the initial quietness and restraint of Mr. Finney's demeanour ... a restraint that cannot and does not last. But structurally, for the play, this isolation is perhaps a defect, for we haven't felt the rising protest of the masses that is growing behind him, a protest which turns, in a well managed piece of stage production, into the Peasants' Revolt. And so the betrayal of it by Luther which makes Mr. Osborne's ending does not come at us with full effect. But that anguish is what Mr. Osborne has known and felt, and it is the over-riding image that we carry away from the play, compellingly expressed in Mr. Finney's amazingly varied and astonishingly finished performance." (169)

Some criticism of the structure also occurs in V.S. Pritchett's review in the New Statesman. He never doubts Osborne's theatrical abilities but criticizes the author's use of language:

"But it is not the rapid calming down of Luther we object to here or that he solved certain private problems, but the banality of the language. ... Osborne's weakness is that he can make a speech but has not enough pleasure in language to construct a whole life or a whole argument. It is pretty easy to state a case; but his remarkable sense of theatre cannot conceal that his language fails when it is faced by the ambiguity of character or by a situation that goes beyond the obsessive and is, in fact, life itself." (170)

Felix Barker in the Evening News was one of the few who reacted more sharply; he thought that Luther was theatrically deficient:

"The best scene in this play is when Albert Finney's Luther, a lonely friar in a black habit, is standing up to the smooth, worldly dialectics of John Moffatt's crimson cardinal. Here, all too briefly, is the conflict which drama demands and which, on the whole, this play sadly lacks ..." (171)

A negative reaction came from the side of the critic of The New Daily, who made a pun on Look Back in Anger:

"During the later stages of the play I was oppressed by a growing sense of tedium and I can only look back on this Luther in disappointment ..." (172)

This opinion is the extreme opposite of the one expressed in the review in Time and

Tide, the author of which asserted that this production was "among the best ever staged at the Royal Court ..." (173)

Luther did not really divide the critics (as did for instance Arden's Serjeant Musgrave's Dance). It was one of those comparatively rare productions of the English Stage Company which were almost universally acclaimed by them: the "angry young man"'s reputation as a dramatist was enhanced and confirmed, and this thanks to a production which disregarded - if brilliantly - the play's structural characteristics.

*

Luther was one of the few productions between 1956 and 1965 which made a profit for the Company. It was transferred to the West End Phoenix Theatre, and later on presented at the Edinburgh Festival 1961, and proved to be what is called "a successful production" (174).

By the time the play was staged, Osborne (who was then 32 years old) had already become a sort of a "house dramatist" of the Court - in fact, since Look Back in Anger, Epitaph for George Dillon, and The Entertainer, his name had been insolubly connected with the theatre in Sloane Square. It was certain that George Devine and the Company would encourage and promote him again as soon as he came along with a new script. They remained faithful to their intention of giving their playwrights all the help they could. Tony Richardson, who had already directed Look Back in Anger and The Entertainer, built up Luther, too, in close collaboration with the author, the designer and the actors (175) - although in this case the teamwork could not prevent a certain falsification of the original play.

Osborne continued writing for the theatre, and what is more, he kept faith with the Court. Further productions of his plays there included Plays for England (1962), Inadmissible Evidence (1964), A Patriot For Me (1965) in which George Devine joined the cast, Time Present and The Hotel in Amsterdam (1968). Affectionate friendship, based on mutual respect, connected him with Devine, and his constant championship by the English Stage Company remains a fact that will be recorded in theatrical history. John Osborne and the Royal Court Theatre became two inseparable notions in modern British drama.

***

XIII CONCLUSION

It remains for us to attempt a summary of the achievements of the English Stage Company. Even in terms of naked facts and figures this achievement is impressive: between April 1956 and December 1965 about 150 productions were staged, more than fifty of which were Sunday Night Productions without Décor (these figures do not include the numerous revivals and other activities, such as poetry recitals, opera and music programmes, discussions, miming and improvisation evenings). Over eighty new British plays were presented and about thirty-five new writers introduced to the London theatre.

We can see from this that Devine's hopes and plans were realized to an unexpected extent. "It is a mistake to take for granted that there are no new plays being written, and to put one's efforts into the classics ... We hope to present exciting, provocative and stimulating plays ...". he wrote in July 1955 (1). His presentiments proved right: Look Back in Anger cleared the way for a new British drama. In John Osborne's wake a crowd of young dramatists followed, encouraged by his example and by the sudden chance offered them by a theatre that had been started especially for them. As was suspected by Devine, the young playwrights actually existed. What did not exist up to 1956 was a theatre interested in their work. The Court filled this gap. As Tony Richardson said: "It was one of these moments when the right people came together at the right place in the right time" (2). He, George Devine and a few other people sensed a change, created a possibility for the staging of new plays, and their courage was rewarded.

The English Stage Company took their promise to run a "writer's theatre" (3) very seriously. The writer and his work became the centres around which everything else revolved. With the introduction of the Sunday Night Productions without Décor Devine and his colleagues found an effective means to further the young playwright (4). As we have seen from the five productions examined, the authors were present at the rehearsals in all cases (5), and virtually nothing was done to their texts without consulting them. The most conspicuous examples of the author's dominating role are perhaps Ann Jellicoe, Keith Johnstone, Wole Soyinka and Donald Howarth, who directed some of their own plays (6).

Team-work characterized the five productions discussed - team-work among authors, directors, designers and actors in the service of the script. Although this method partly failed in the case of Luther, and although the collaboration between Ann Jellicoe and Jocelyn Herbert in The Sport of My Mad Mother produced an unhappy result (7), the idea was a success on the whole. The close team-work made possible productions the main features of which were imaginative staging, resourceful acting and straightforwardness in presentation (Richardson's Luther may not have been quite in agreement with this last point). The team-work was especially important because it included the author in a kind of steady development: certain directors became involved with certain dramatists, as for instance William Gaskill with N.F. Simpson (8), Tony Richardson with John Osborne (9), John Dexter with Arnold

Wesker (10), etc. It gave the writer a feeling of being looked after, of "belonging" to the Court. Often the directors worked on the scripts together with "their" authors and thus prepared the final stage version (e.g. Anderson and Arden in the case of Serjeant Musgrave's Dance, Gaskill and Simpson in One Way Pendulum and the dramatist's other plays, Dexter and Wesker in The Kitchen and the Wesker Trilogy) (11).

To summarize, we can say that the principles announced in 1956 (12) were adhered to and that the approach of Devine and his associate directors was sound and above all unbiassed. They tried to see every play with fresh eyes and to convey it as presented in its text (13). And this is what makes the specific characteristics of the "Royal Court style" - if we want to speak of such a style at all.

The Court is further remarkable for its extreme loyalty towards its dramatists. Once a playwright had been accepted on the grounds of his dramatic strength, he was encouraged without any reservations, backed through good and bad times, and always given another chance. Artistic quality was the only criterion; the English Stage Company stuck to its declaration to be a non profit-making organization (14) and staged the plays without regard to financial success. By far the greater part of the plays produced between 1956 and 1965 lost money (among the productions discussed The Sport of My Mad Mother, Serjeant Musgrave's Dance, and The Kitchen) (15).

Beyond discovering new English playwrights, the Court did justice to its claims of being a workshop and a school of the theatre by introducing new actors, directors and designers to the British stage. It also confronted the London audiences with foreign plays and continental developments - it was the first theatre in England to stage Brecht professionally, and it put on Beckett, Ionesco, Sartre, Genet, Frisch and Pirandello. The catholicity of its repertoire is truly striking: after Look Back in Anger the Court did not stick to the same kind of play - although this must have been tempting - but produced any play the company considered good (16).

The effects of all this work on the British theatre were manifold. The policy of the Court made other managements aware that it could be worthwhile to support young and unkown dramatists - they became quite eager, too, to discover new talent and to introduce new plays to their audiences (17). The Royal Shakespeare Company at the Aldwych Theatre and the National Theatre Company at the Old Vic, among others, started staging modern plays by young authors beside their preoccupation with Shakespeare and the classics.

Furthermore, the Court methods of producing, acting and above all designing (18) influenced other theatres and the cinema, as people trained under George Devine went to work outside the Royal Court (19).

***

XIV GASKILL AND AFTER: OUTLOOK

In September 1965 William Gaskill, associate director at the Court and the National Theatre, succeeded George Devine as artistic director of the English Stage Company. His appointment was announced at the end of January 1965, some weeks after Devine had made known his retirement. Gaskill, writing about his new assignment after Devine's death, was fully aware of the responsibility of his task:

> "To be left in charge of the Berliner Ensemble on the death of Brecht or of the Moscow Art Theatre on the death of Stanislavsky would be intolerable. The sense of the work of one man having been fulfilled could only make one feel 'What is there left to do?' To be in charge of the Royal Court Theatre at the death of another great man, George Devine, means the responsibility and excitement of carrying on his work. There could be no greater tribute to his unique achievement. Our sense of loss at his death is immeasurable, but there is no sudden stop, only a pause while we who worked with him - writers, directors, actors and designers - remember how much of our creative development we owe to him. He has left behind no dogma, no theories on which to base our work. He has left only the work itself and the need for its continuance." (1)

Gaskill was indeed suited for this post as he had been working with Devine since 1957, and had directed several plays at the Court (2). He was willing from the start to continue Devine's policy: "We shall continue to be always on the lookout for new works of quality, particularly by new writers whom we hope to discover and encourage" (3). Up to now this has been done with some success, if not with the old overwhelming response on the part of the playwrights. Nevertheless, the Court cannot complain about lack of interest:

> "We get about 700 plays a year. All of them are read. I read my colleagues' reports about them, and then I decide whether we will use the play for production or not." (4)

Edward Bond, David Cregan, Christopher Hampton and David Storey have proved the most promising discoveries so far (5). Of the "established" Court writers Ann Jellicoe, N. F. Simpson, Arnold Wesker and John Osborne were staged again (6), with varying success but true to Devine's conception of loyalty (7). The plays are produced according to the principles established by Devine and shared by Gaskill: respect for the text (8), team-work author-director-designer-actors (9), central position of the playwright (10), faithfulness in presentation (11). Gaskill also gave the repertory system another trial but came to the same conclusion as Devine and Richardson earlier on (12).

Besides promoting new talent, the English Stage Company found an additional task in staging the mostly unknown dramatic work of D. H. Lawrence - three of his plays ran in repertory between February and May 1968 (13). This re-discovery of an already classical author was yet another merit of the company.

The Royal Court still holds an important place in the English theatre today, although one might say that much of the excitement of the first ten years is gone. But some of it can still be felt. One goes to the Court with great expectations - knowing that here new drama is presented with enthusiasm (14). Gaskill himself remains cautious and realistic about the role of the Court, and indeed of the role of the theatre in general. "Its main function today is to survive. A really enthusiastic audience for modern works does not exist", he said, "we play for a minority group". And he added:

> "I try to attract young people. Students can book 100 seats each
> night for the price of five shillings. But even then they come to
> see plays which they already know, not to see new ones." (15)

This shows that the problem of the audience has not yet been solved. In spite of renewed efforts to gain a regular public, in spite of the fact the English Stage Society has now something around 4,000 members, a loyal body of spectators is missing. The endeavours of creating one will continue (16).

The work at the Court goes on. "We have to carry on regardless whether the public follows us or not", as Gaskill expressed it (17). This is what George Devine did. Gaskill does not arrange any season definitely, but keeps it flexible - this has the advantage that new plays can be staged on short notice. The Court is up to date; the possibilities for the young dramatist are there as before. The English Stage Company is ready for new work. The stage where the playwright has the right to fail still exists. George Devine's Royal Court Theatre is alive as ever and likely to remain so.

***

I Preface

1) Cf. Bibliography and articles quoted throughout the thesis.
2) E.g. Jean Bailhache, Angry Young Men, Les Langues Modernes, Bd. LII,1958; Louis Bonnerot, John Osborne, Etudes Anglaises, Bd.X, 1957; The Observer Profile: John Osborne, The Observer, 17.5.1959; Jacques Vallette, Lettres Anglo-Saxonnes: La Société Anglaise et le Théâtre de John Osborne, Mercure de France, 1958; Norbert Mennemeier, John Osborne, in: Das moderne Drama des Auslandes, Düsseldorf 1961; John Russell Taylor, Anger and After: A Guide to the New British Drama, London 1962; A.E. Dyson, Look Back in Anger, Critical Quarterly, Bd. I, 1959, pp. 318-326; Jean Selz, John Osborne et Jimmy Porter, Les Lettres Nouvelles, Nr. 61, 1958, pp. 908-911; Samuel A. Weiss, Osborne's Angry Young Play, Educationel Theatre Journal, Bd. XII, 1960, pp. 285-288; Horst Oppel, John Osborne: Look Back in Anger, in: Das moderne englische Drama, ed.by Horst Oppel, Berlin 1963, pp. 317-331; Marianne Kesting, John Osborne: Dramatisierte Autobiographie, in: Panorama des zeitgenössischen Theaters, München 1962, pp. 211-214.

II A Short History of the Royal Court before 1956

1) In their book The Theatres of London (London 1961; second revised edition 1963) Raymond Mander and Joe Mitchenson give a precise account of the early days of this theatre: "In 1818 when Sloane Square was still an open space, simply enclosed with wooden posts connected with iron chains, a dissenting chapel was built on ground on the south side ... The chapel fell into disuse and in 1870 was converted into a theatre called the New Chelsea, which opened on April 16, the same night as the Vaudeville Theatre." (pp. 151-152. This book is subsequently referred to as MM).
2) MM, pp. 152-153.
3) MM, p. 153.
4) "The theatre was again completely altered and a new porch added under the supervision of Alexander Peebles." (MM, p. 153).
5) Cf. MM, p. 154. "The front of the new theatre was of stone and red brick, freely treated in the Italian Renaissance style. The entrance was panelled in oak and had a painted ceiling. The interior was decorated in Empire style." (MM, p. 154).
6) MM, p. 154.
7) MM, p. 154.
8) Cf. MM, p. 154.
9) ibid.
10) From the French Les Surprises du Divorce. Cf. MM, p. 151.
11) Cf. MM. p. 155.
12) 1877-1946.

13) Leigh's wife.
14) C.B. Purdom, Harley Granville Barker. London 1955, p. 19. Subsequently referred to as Purdom.
15) The Two Gentlemen of Verona.
16) MM, p. 155. Already in April 1903 Barker, in a letter to William Archer, had proposed "to take the Court Theatre for six months or a year and to run there a stock season of the uncommercial drama". Cf. Purdom, p. 18.
17) "We have opposed to the long-run system the short-run system. It has many disadvantages, perhaps, but it keeps the plays fresh ... I think we can claim that the plays are more value now both from a business and an artistic point of view than they would have been had they simply been run callously to the fullest limit of their popularity." (Barker during a dinner at the Criterion Restaurant, 7.7.1907; cf. Purdom, p. 64). Cf. also Rudolf Stamm, Geschichte des englischen Theaters. Bern 1951, p. 382.
18) From an article, "Actors", in: The Twentieth Century, February 1961, p.133. "That Barker was deeply concerned about acting, though he never treated himself as an actor-manager, was shown throughout his life. Acting was made the basis of all his work, not only as producer, but also as dramatist, and as critic of drama he looked upon plays from the actor's standpoint ... " (Purdom, p. 23).
19) K.S. Stanislavsky, at about the same time (1907 onward) taught a comparable kind of acting at his Moscow Art Theatre.
20) "A stock company was engaged which included then, or later, Lewis Casson, Norman Page, Edmund Gwenn, Trevor Lowe, C.L. Delph, Frederick Lloyd, Allan Wade, Dorothy Minto, Hazel Thompson, Amy Lamborn, and Mary Barton, each of whom was paid £ 3 a week ... " (Purdom, p. 36).
21) From a broadcast by Hesketh Pearson which was carried by the BBC to mark the fiftieth anniversary of the Vedrenne-Barker management of the Court Theatre. Also published by the BBC in its journal The Listener. Reprinted under the title Harley Granville-Barker at the Court, in the programme of the Court's production of Barker's The Voysey Inheritance in 1966, from which this quotation is taken. This article is subsequently referred to as Voysey programme 1966. "The inherent fault in Barker's stage method was under-statement, underemphasis, a tendency even towards what seemed to be inarticulateness, so that the rhythm appeared to go underground. That is what aroused Shaw's fury, for it was the opposite of what he rightly considered appropriate to the stage." (Purdom, p. 41).
22) Again a parallel to Stanislavsky's teaching. Cf. chapter III, p. 27.
23) Voysey programme 1966. "Barker had the teaching ability and the technical knowledge of the stage, for he was himself an actor and was able, when necessary, to demonstrate what the play demanded of the player. He never adopted type-casting, and each player was expected to use his brains ... Every actor in every part was expected to give his best, and Barker spared no effort to develop even the smallest character to the full extent required by the play. The leading character was never treated as a star part ... The work of individual actors was limited by, and was not allowed to go beyond, the requirements of the play as a whole. Thus the stage had life at every moment, and the play had

full justice done to it. There was never anything mechanical ... or merely
clever in any of his productions. He was always able to get from his players
acting that had life and interest, even when the play had a trivial theme, but
he was limited by the theme, never seeking to transcend it ..." (Purdom,
p. 68). Cf. also Lewis Casson's statement in Purdom, p. vii.

24) Purdom, p. 38.

25) Voysey Programme 1966.

26) "...It was, indeed, an admirable production, insufficiently rehearsed, judging
from what some of the critics said, but the sheer brilliance of the dialogue, and
Shaw's success in getting what he wanted from the players, made it an outstanding event. The crowded theatre was amazed and delighted, and the Vedrenne-
Barker management was put firmly upon its feet ..." (Purdom, p. 29.)

27) "With Man and Superman the Vedrenne-Barker management reached its high-
water mark, to be touched again, but never exceeded. The casting of the play
was superb ... Barker, made-up to look like Shaw, and Lillah McCarthy as
Ann Whitefield, gave performances that no subsequent production ever approached ..." (Purdom, p. 39).

28) "The Greek plays were the Court's greatest stage innovation, but Barker did
not solve, either then or later, the problem of the chorus." (ibid., p. 54).

29) "For two years Barker had been working on a new play, The Voysey Inheritance,
which was at last given its six matinées, starting on 7 November (1905). This
was a notable event, for the play was hailed as a masterpiece of the new drama,
and was given a perfect production by the author ... With this work Barker established himself as a leading dramatist of his time, as well as its outstanding
producer and an attractive actor ..." (Purdom, p. 47).

30) "The critics and first audiences were disconcerted to find no Christmas entertainment, but a pathetic, almost tragic fantasy, not without a touch of bitterness." (William Archer, in Purdom, p. 30).

31) 26.4.1904: Candida by Shaw (31 performances); 18.10.04: Hippolytus by Euripides (20); 1.11.04: John Bull's Other Island by Shaw (121); 15.11.04: Aglavaine and Selysette by Maeterlinck (6); 23.12.04: Prunella by Barker/Housman
(48); 28.2.05: The Pot of Broth by Yeats (9); In the Hospital by Schnitzler (9);
How He Lied to Her Husband by Shaw (9); 21.3.05: The Thieves Comedy by
Hauptmann (9); 11.4.05: The Trojan Women by Euripides (8); 2.5.05: You
Never Can Tell by Shaw (149); 23.5.05: Man and Superman by Shaw (176);
26.9.05: The Return of the Prodigal by St. John Hankin (19); 17.10.05: The
Wild Duck by Ibsen (6); 7.11.05: The Voysey Inheritance by Barker (34);
28.11.05: Major Barbara by Shaw (52); 16.1.06: Electra by Euripides (20);
6.2.06: A Question of Age by R.V. Harcourt (2); The Convict on the Hearth by
F. Fenn (2); 27.2.06: Pan and the Young Shepherd by M. Hewlett (6); The
Youngest of the Angels by Hewlett (6);20.3.06: Captain Brassbound's Conver-
sion by Shaw (89); 25.9.06: The Silver Box by Galsworthy (29); 23.10.06: The
Charity that Began at Home by St. John Hankin (8); 20.11.06: The Doctor's
Dilemma by Shaw (50); 8.1.07: The Reformer by C. Harcourt (8); The Camden
Wonder by J. Masefield (8); 5.2.07: The Philanderer by Shaw (8); 5.3.07:
Hedda Gabler by Ibsen (7); 9.4.07: Votes for Women! by E. Robins (23);
4.6.07: Don Juan in Hell by Shaw (8); The Man of Destiny by Shaw (8). (From

Desmond MacCarthy, The Court Theatre 1904-1907, London 1907, p. 124 and pp. 125-169).

32) Voysey programme 1966. "No theatrical enterprise of this century has left a deeper mark upon the theatrical history of London than the Vedrenne-Barker management at the Royal Court Theatre in the first decade of the century ... The management lasted under three years at the Court ... but it brought into being elements that transformed not only the acting and production of plays upon the London stage, but also changed public attitude to the theatre. Its success was due to the collaboration of dramatists and actors, which is the necessary condition for theatrical achievement on the highest level ..." (Purdom, p. 26).

33) MM, p. 156.

34) "Barry Jackson's disastrous experience with a modern-dress version (of Macbeth) produced by H.K. Ayliff at the Court in 1928 may have been attributable less to a fire in the dress circle the night before opening or the scenery collapse during the first week than to the difficulty of presenting the drama convincingly in contemporary dress ..." (Maureen Grice, in: Oscar James Campbell and Edward G. Quinn, A Shakespeare Encyclopaedia, London 1966, p. 487. Subsequently referred to as S.E.).

35) Cf. p. 16.

36) The Burning Boat, musical by N. Phipps and G. Wright; Uncertain Joy by Charlotte Hastings; From Here and There, revue; Sun of York by O. and I. Wigram; Suspect by Edward Percy and Reginald Denham; Let's Make an Opera by Benjamin Britten and Eric Crozier.

37) The fact that it was the Royal Court Theatre which the English Stage Company took over was a mere accident; it could have been any other theatre. It is therefore not proper to speak of the revival of a tradition; the parallels to the Vedrenne-Barker management are interesting but pure coincidence.

38) cf. p. 16.

39) September 4th 1964.

40) Cf. chapter IV, p. 36.

41) Figures from the West London Press, 4.9.64.

42) 3.9.64. A further interesting alteration was carried out in 1969: "Expansion plans at the Royal Court Theatre to be announced on Tuesday by William Gaskill, artistic director of the English Stage Company, will include news of "The Theatre Upstairs", a new studio theatre, seating eighty, at the top of the Royal Court, which opens on February 24." (The Sunday Times, 9.2.69).

III George Devine: A Short Account of his Life and Work 1910-1956

1) Letter to the present writer, 12.11.68. Much of the information about George Devine's youth was given in this letter, and in a second one dated 27.11.68.

2) Cf. Laurence Thompson's article "Can this man save the British Theatre"? in News Chronicle, 8.10.57.

3) Peggy Ashcroft remembered: "... George was elected president the next year, and then he asked me to go down and play Juliet and he invited John Gielgud to

direct it. It was John's first production in fact in the theatre." (from <u>George</u> <u>Devine 1910-1966.</u> A programme broadcasted on BBC-3 on December 4th 1966. Compiled and narrated by Leigh Crutchley, produced by Robert Pocock. Subsequently referred to as <u>BBC</u>).

4) <u>BBC.</u>
5) <u>BBC.</u>
6) "I don't think my father did take his degree at Oxford - I believe that he was unable to complete his full time there because 'the money ran out' - either his father or his uncle was paying and couldn't continue - I'm very vague about this I'm afraid." (Harriet Mennie-Devine in a letter to the present writer, 27.11.68).
7) Then under Lilian Baylis.
8) <u>BBC.</u>
9) Interview with the present writer, 24.8.67.
10) Peggy Ashcroft as Portia, Alec Guinness as Lorenzo, John Gielgud as Shylock. Other parts were acted by Michael Redgrave, Anthony Quayle, Harcourt Williams, Glen Byam Shaw, Gwen Ffrangcon-Davies and Rachel Kempson.
11) A reminiscence of Elizabethan conditions.
12) Interview with the present writer, 24.8.67.
13) <u>BBC.</u>
14) Cf. p. 25.
15) <u>BBC.</u>
16) "'An actor who disregards the wise creative feeling and is a slave of senseless stage habits', Stanislavsky writes, 'is at the mercy of every chance, of the bad taste of the audience, of some clever stage trick, of cheap external success, of his vanity and, indeed, of anything that has nothing whatever to do with art'. No part, in fact, can be really successful unless the actor <u>believes</u> in it. The actor must believe in everything that is taking place on the stage and, above all, he must believe in himself. But he can only believe in what is true. He must, therefore, always be aware of truth and know how to find it, and to do that he must develop his artistic sensibility for truth. And Stanislavsky makes it clear that what he means by truth is the truth of the actor's feelings and sensations, the truth of the inner creative impulse which is striving to express itself. 'I am not interested in the truth outside me', he declares. 'What is important to me is the truth in me, the truth of my attitude towards one scene or another on the stage, towards the different things on the stage, the scenery, my partners, who are playing the other parts in the play, and their feelings and thoughts.'" (from <u>Stanislavsky on the Art of the Stage.</u> Translated with an Introductory Essay by David Magarshack. Faber & Faber, London 1967; pp. 21-22).
17) <u>BBC.</u>
18) Confirmed by Laurence Olivier (<u>BBC</u>) and Jane Howell (interview with the present writer, 15.8.67). Cf. <u>Plays and Players,</u> March 1956 ("Personality of the Month").
19) Michel Saint-Denis, interview with the present writer, 24.8.67.
20) Among the actors who went through the school were Peter Ustinov and James Donald; among the designers Jocelyn Herbert and Alan Tagg. Alec Guinness, Laurence Olivier, John Gielgud and Michael Redgrave went as guests and used

the school as a "refresher course". Jocelyn Herbert, who later on worked
with Devine at the Royal Court, remembered: "In 1936 I met George at the
Studio ... I saw plays by the Compagnie des Quinze in Paris when I was young
... Saint-Denis started the London Theatre Studio, and I wrote to him and asked whether I could train as a designer. Michel looked at my drawings and
took me on". (Interview with the present writer, 18.9.68).

21) Great Expectations, adapted from Dickens, at the Rudolf Steiner Hall.
22) "The Tempest was the last Old Vic production before the bombing in 1940
forced the company to the provinces and later damaged part of the theatre. The
production struck the emotional tone appropriate for the time, with the ascetic
Prospero of John Gielgud especially effective in the reconciliation and farewell
scenes. Jack Hawkins acted Caliban and Jessica Tandy, Miranda, under the
direction of George Devine and Marius Goring." (Maureen Grice in S.E.,
p. 860).
23) Cf. The Times, 21.1.66. Also mentioned by Glen Byam Shaw in a letter to the
present writer, 8.4.68.
24) Jocelyn Herbert, interview with the present writer, 1.8.67; Harriet Mennie-
Devine, letter to the present writer, 12.11.68.
25) Harriet Mennie-Devine, letter to the present writer, 12.11.68.
26) Interview with the present writer, 24.8.67.
27) Here the influence of the Compagnie des Quinze is obvious. Cf. p. 26.
28) Cf. chapters V and VI.
29) Interview with the present writer, 24.8.67.
30) The work done at the Old Vic School resembles once more Stanislavsky's
teaching. Joan Plowright confirmed "There was quite a bit of Stanislavsky-
teaching at the school." (Interview with the present writer, 16.10.67). In
Stanislavsky's Moscow Art Theatre there were language-, grammar- and
literature-classes; there were classes for dancing, fencing, gymnastics,
pronunciation, diction etc.
31) Interview with the present writer, 16.10.67. This interview with her provided
much of the material presented in this chapter about the Old Vic School.
32) Alan Dobie, Avril Elgar and Joan Plowright appeared in some of the Royal
Court productions after 1956.
33) Michel Saint-Denis, interview with the present writer, 24.8.67.
34) Letter to the present writer, 12.11.68.
35) Compiler of the BBC-programme about George Devine. Cf. annotation 3.
36) BBC.
37) This information was given to me by Jocelyn Herbert, on September 18th 1968.
38) BBC.
39) Cf. S.E., p. 848. In an emotional and vague statement Tony Richardson called
them both "marvellous productions" (interview with the present writer, 5.10.67).
40) Cf. S.E., p. 425.
41) Cf. The Daily Telegraph, 21.1.66.
42) Cf. S.E., p. 435.
43) Cf. S.E., p. 435.
44) "One of his best performances, I think" (Harriet Mennie-Devine, letter to the
present writer, 12.11.68).

45) This performance was mentioned by Peggy Ashcroft, 5.8.67., and Joan Plow-right, 16.10.67, both in interviews with the present writer.
46) Interview with the present writer, 24.8.67.
47) Harriet Mennie-Devine, letter to the present writer, 12.11.68.
48) Interview with the present writer, 16.10.67.
49) Curtain Down, original title An Actor's End.
50) Interview with the present writer, 4.10.67.
51) Cf. Richardson's statement in BBC.

IV The Foundation of the English Stage Company

1) In: Life Magazine, 13.6.66, entitled "A Decade That Destroyed 'A Stuffed Flunkey'".
2) Adelphi Theatre: "In 1950 Jack Hylton ... began a series of revues, featuring broadcasting stars, which were to be the main attractions for the next six years." (MM, p. 20). Apollo Theatre: revue For Amusement Only (1956). Cambridge Theatre: Cecil Landeau revue Sauce Tartare (1949) and its sequel Sauce Piquante (1950). The Coliseum: Annie Get Your Gun (1947-50), Kiss Me Kate (1951), Guys and Dolls (1953), Can-Can (1954). Comedy Theatre: Slings and Arrows (1948). Criterion Theatre: Intimacy at 8-30 (1954). Drury Lane Theatre: Oklahoma! (1947), Carousel (1950), South Pacific (1951), The King and I (1953). Garrick Theatre: Better Late (1946), As Long As They're Happy (1953), revue La Plume de ma Tante (1955). The London Casino: revue Over the Moon, by Vivian Ellis (1953). New Theatre: Vivian Ellis's musical version of J.B. Fagan's And So To Bed (1951), I am a Camera (1954), The Remarkable Mr. Pennypacker (1954). Palace Theatre: Zip Goes A Million (1951). Piccadilly Theatre: A Girl Called Jo, musical version of Little Women (1955). Prince of Wales Theatre: Touch and Go (1950); afterwards the theatre was devoted to variety and Folies Bergère style revues. Shaftesbury Theatre: Pal Joey (1954), Wonderful Town (1955). Royalty Theatre: Kismet (1955). St. Martin's Theatre: Penny Plain (1951), Small Hotel (1955). Saville Theatre: Love From Judy (1952), Cecil Landeau's revue Cockles and Champagne (1954). Strand Theatre: Sailor, Beware! (1955). Vaudeville Theatre: musical Salad Days (1954) (All examples from MM).
3) Ambassadors Theatre: The Mousetrap by Agatha Christie (1952, still running). Fortune Theatre: The Hollow by A. Christie (1951). Savoy Theatre, The Spider's Web by A. Christie (1954). Vaudeville Theatre: Murder Mistaken (1952). Westminster Theatre: Dial M for Murder (1952). Winter Garden Theatre: Witness for the Prosecution by A. Christie (1953).
4) Apollo Theatre: Flare Path by Terence Rattigan (1942), Private Lives by Noel Coward (1944). Duchess Theatre: The Linden Tree by J.B. Priestley (1947), The Deep Blue Sea by T. Rattigan (1952). Globe Theatre: Nude With Violin by N. Coward (1956). Haymarket Theatre: Waters of the Moon (1952), A Day by the Sea (1953) both by N.C. Hunter. Lyric Theatre: South Sea Bubble by N. Coward (1956). Phoenix Theatre: Quadrille by N. Coward (1952), The Sleeping Prince by T. Rattigan (1953). All examples are taken from MM.

5) Aldwych Theatre: <u>The Dark is Light Enough</u> by Fry (1955). Globe Theatre: <u>The Lady's Not For Burning</u> by Fry (1949). Lyric Theatre: <u>The Confidential Clerk</u> by Eliot (1953). Phoenix Theatre: <u>The Family Reunion</u> by Eliot (1956).

6) "The writer has on the whole had a raw deal from the stage in the past; and even now, however genuinely anxious the commercial managements are to find new plays, the conditions under which they work operate against the original writer. If they do find an original play on which they are prepared to take a risk, they can only afford to do so when they have secured one or other of the crowd-drawing stars to give them a second line of defence. The protracted delays and frequent frustrations which this involves often ends in sickening writers with the whole business ..." (T.C. Worsley in the <u>New Statesman and Nation</u>, 24.3.56). "Managements say that the serious plays submitted to them by British dramatists are not worthy of being staged, indignant authors complain that managements refuse to consider their excursions into the field of significant drama, while certain progressive opinion holds that the routine realism of our existing theatrical conventions does not exert any great appeal for writers of imagination." (<u>Plays and Players</u>, March 1956). "Britain, characteristically, was approaching a slough of isolation. The encroaching economic miseries, accelerated by the Crash in 1929, produced in Europe and America a militant theatre of the Left wing; England recessed into a theatre of elegant refuge ... England's <u>theatre of refuge</u> lasted through the second world war and well into the peace. It produced great classical revivals, and great players to match ... A development which seemed at one time full of promise was the <u>poetic drama</u> of W.H. Auden, T.S. Eliot and Christopher Fry. This began as a theatre of commitment and declined into a theatre of compensation: Lovely words, in the late Forties, in lieu of butter." (<u>The Sunday Times</u>, 28.5.67, p. 25. Quoted from a supplement entitled "The Sunday Times Guide to the Modern Movement in the Arts: 4 Theatre").

7) Cf. chapter III, pp. 32-33.

8) Born 1915.

9) Cf. also John Russell Taylor, <u>Anger and After</u>, <u>A Guide to the New British Drama</u>. London 1962, p. 34. Subsequently referred to as <u>Taylor</u>.

10) Cf. <u>Taylor</u>, p. 35. "The English Stage Company announced yesterday that it has bought the Royal Court Theatre, Sloane Square, London, and plans to start plays there early next year." (<u>Sunday Pictorial</u>, 20.11.55.).

11) <u>BBC</u>.

12) "This venture is privately financed with no possible hope of financial gain." (Devine in <u>The Daily Express</u>, 3.4.56). Surplus money was to be used for further productions.

13) <u>New Statesman and Nation</u>, 24.3.56.

14) <u>The Stage</u>, 28.7.55. "We are not interested in the sort of play in which all actors have to do is crawl from one piece of Chippendale to the next." (Ronald Duncan, in <u>Manchester Evening News</u>, 20.2.56). "We are not going in for experiment for the sake of experiment ... We are not avant garde, or highbrow, or a coterie set. We want to build a vital, living, popular theatre which, in time, will develop an approach and an acting-style of its own." (Ronald Duncan in <u>The Stage</u>, 10.5.56.)

228

15) "Playing in repertoire ... means that the public will be able to see several plays in a week, and actors will be able to keep their work constantly fresh by appearing in different parts. That is, of course, an ideal, long accepted in the classical theatre, but there has been no serious long term attempt in England to sustain it with modern plays since Granville Barker's seasons before the first world war." (Devine in The Stage, 1.3.56.)

16) Daily Telegraph, 19.3.56. Out of this conception of the Royal Court as a workshop for dramatists originated the idea of the so-called Sunday Night Productions without Décor, by means of which the young and inexperienced author can see his play in performance - without a set and costumes, to keep down the expenses - but staged under professional conditions and presented in front of an interested and critical audience (only members of the English Stage Society have the possibility of attending these productions). Cf. chapter VII, p. 241, annotation 3. "There were a lot of new writers about 1957, and there was a real need for a place where new work could be seen. This is why the Sunday Night Productions had a very important function." (William Gaskill, interview with the present writer, 18.9.68.)

17) Devine.

18) 24.3.56.

19) Cf. chapter III, p. 28.

20) "Mr. Devine ... has got together a permanent company headed by Michael Gwynne, Rosalie Crutchley and Rachel Kempson, and this will be re-enforced as the need arises by guest players ..." (New Statesman and Nation, 24.3.56.)

21) Manchester Evening News, 23.11.55.

22) Stratford-on-Avon Herald, 9.12.55.

23) 25.3.56.

24) 24.3.56.

25) 31.3.56. A similar challenge to the audiences appeared in the New Statesman and Nation (24.3.56.): "Only two things remain for success. First to find an audience, and secondly to find the writers. By an audience I do not mean just an adventitious collection of customers. I mean a loyal body who are also prepared to take their share of the risk by patronizing the theatre regularly and from the start. Playgoers complain often enough of the dearth of interesting new plays. Here is the chance for them to prove that they really want them ..."

26) March 1956, article entitled "Nursery for Drama".

27) Born 1913.

28) Born 1923. Film maker and critic 1948-58. Films include (among others) O Dreamland, Thursday's Children (with Guy Brenton), Every Day Except Christmas, This Sporting Life, If ....

29) BBC. The loose syntax of the statement may be explained by the fact that Anderson spoke spontaneously onto a tape.

30) 3.4.56.

31) 8.4.56.

32) 6.4.56.
33) 3.4.56.
34) 4.4.56.
35) 5.4.56.
36) 8.4.56.
37) 6.4.56. "Sound the trumpets! Beat the drum! There is great news for the Eng-
    lish theatre. In London, last week, there was launched a pioneering enterprise
    which is devoted - believe it or not - to staging serious plays by living authors
    ... Instead of putting the star or the scene-painter first, as is common in the
    West End drama, they proclaim their intention of founding a 'writer's theatre'
    - where the dramatist will no longer be treated as a second class citizen,
    where the play will be of prime importance ... But the importance of all this
    seems, at the moment, to have escaped some newspapers, who have allowed
    their critics no more than the usual meagre inches; and some critics have lim-
    ited themselves to registering with weary detachment, their disappointment at
    the first of the English Stage Company's plays - Angus Wilson's 'The Mulberry
    Bush' ... But the important thing is that he - and many writers like him -
    should be given the chance to learn by experience and to go on learning; and
    this can only be supplied in London by theatres like the Royal Court. Its suc-
    cess depends, in the last resort, on you. The Royal Court needs and deserves
    the support of everyone interested in the theatre now - not in a few months
    time. Stir yourself and book a seat ... " (Richard Findlater in The Tribune,
    13.4.56).

V George Devine as a Producer at the Royal Court 1956-1963

1) The Mulberry Bush by Angus Wilson (2.4.56), The Crucible* by Arthur Miller
   (9.4.56), Don Juan and The Death of Satan by Ronald Duncan (15.5.56), The
   Good Woman of Setzuan* by Bertolt Brecht (31.10.56), The Country Wife* by
   Wycherley (12.12.56), Nekrassov by Jean-Paul Sartre (17.9.57), The Sport of
   My Mad Mother by Ann Jellicoe (directed together with the author, 25.2.58,
   cf. chapter VIII), Major Barbara* by Shaw (28.8.58), Live Like Pigs by John
   Arden (directed together with Anthony Page, 30.9.58), Endgame* by Samuel
   Beckett (28.10.58), Cock-A-Doodle Dandy by Sean O'Casey (17.9.59), Rosmersholm by Ibsen (18.11.59), Platonov by Chekhov (directed together with
   John Blatchley, 13.10.60), August for the People by Nigel Dennis (12.9.61),
   Twelfth Night by Shakespeare (18.2.62), Happy Days by Samuel Beckett (1.11.
   62), Exit the King by Eugène Ionesco (12.9.63). The dates refer to the official
   first nights at the Court. In the productions marked with an asterisk Devine
   also took part as an actor.
2) 15.6.56, also in Westminster and Pimlico News.
3) The actors.
4) Amateur Stage, June 1956, title "Look and Learn". "... there are basically
   two kinds of direction, There's the kind that imposes a strong personal stamp
   on the play, the stamp of brilliant people like Joan Littlewood and Tony Guthrie
   and Peter Brook. I think that in one way we suffer from the lack of that stamp

at the Royal Court. If I did all the productions and said 'Right, THIS is the way we produce plays', then we might do better at the box office. But I don't believe that this kind of direction is very fertile for the dramatist, and what we're trying to do here is to practise the other kind - which attempts to get the best out of each particular element in a production and make them work together in realizing the play." (Devine in The Right to Fail, in: The Twentieth Century, February 1961, p. 129. Subsequently referred to as TRF). "We have established a method of presentation of our own, based on a dramatic rather than decorative attitude. The more meaningful the play, the more truly dramatic the dialogue, the more truly theatrical the acting, the less production 'gimmicks' and fanciful decor are required." (Devine in English Stage Company - A Record of Two Years Work, London 1958. Subsequently referred to as ESC). "Personally I do not set out to create new styles. I select work to do which pleases me and try to create the reality intrinsic in these plays ... In my theatre I select plays which have, in my opinion, contemporary relevance and see that they are presented in a manner consistent with the style of the author, without any gimmicks or fashionable faking." (Devine, Realism in the Theatre, an interview with Laurence Kitchin, 1964. A leaflet in the Royal Court press office). "... I wouldn't say that the director is the author's servant. That's too strong. I don't think that an author really knows what he's written, in theatrical terms, when it comes to interpretation on the stage. It all seems so obvious to him that he can't understand why the actors shouldn't see it at once. It's usually there in the lines, of course, but somebody has to discover that and interpret it to a group of people, while being completely faithful to what the author basically felt. That somebody is the director." (Devine in TRF).

5) The Mulberry Bush: 12 reviews. The Crucible: 13. Nekrassov: 21. Major Barbara: 24. Live Like Pigs: 24. Endgame: 17. Cock-A-Doodle Dandy: 19. Rosmersholm: 30. Platonov: 27. Happy Days: 30. Exit the King: 17.

6) Cf. chapter IV, pp. 37-38.

7) Daily Worker, 16.4.56.

8) The Sunday Times, 31.8.58.

9) Kensington News, 26.10.58.

10) The Spectator, 27.11.59. "George Devine's production drives all Shaw's points home ..." (Major Barbara; News Chronicle, 29.8.58.). "... it gives due shape and emphasis to the speeches ..." (Major Barbara; The Stage, 4.9.58). "Mr. Devine has given him (Shaw) the floor, without distractions ..." (Major Barbara; Punch, 10.9.58). "In his production Mr. George Devine has taken the play's subtitle (A Discussion) to heart; its three acts are essentially conversation pieces and nothing has been done to disguise this." (Major Barbara; The Times, 29.8.58). "... production is faultlessly in period ..." (Major Barbara; Evening News, 29.8.58). "It may be that George Devine's direction carries conscientiousness and deliberation too far ..." (Rosmersholm; What's On in London, 27.11.59). Other, more vague statements to the same effect are to be found in The Morning Advertiser, 24.10.60: "... perceptive direction ..." (Platonov) and The Sunday Telegraph, 4.1..62: "... dedicated direction ..." (Happy Days).

11) "... the director, also appears somewhat out of sympathy with his text." (Exit the King; The Sunday Telegraph, 15.9.63). "George Devine has not taken the

old master too seriously ..." (<u>Cock-A-Doodle Dandy</u>; <u>The Financial Times</u>, 8.9.59).

12) <u>The Times</u>, 20.8.57.
13) <u>News Chronicle</u>, 18.9.57.
14) <u>The Times</u>, 20.8.57.
15) <u>The Financial Times</u>, 1.10.58.
16) <u>The Times</u>, 1.10.58.
17) <u>New Statesman</u>, 26.9.59.
18) <u>The Stage</u>, 26.11.59. "... a production as heavy-handed as its fun ..." (<u>Nekrassov</u>: <u>Sunday Express</u>, 22.9.57). "A night scene in which they (Sailor Sawney and Big Rachel) endeavour to glorify their way of life goes on too long ..." (<u>Live Like Pigs</u>; <u>Theatre World</u>, November 1958). "... one ached for the curtain to come down ten minutes before it did ..." (<u>Live Like Pigs</u>; <u>The Financial Times</u>, 1.10.58). "... a sprawling play, which needs cutting and tightening ... The production needs pace and drive ..." (<u>Live Like Pigs</u>; <u>The Stage</u>, 2.10.58). "...the play, in George Devine's production, seems to move a little too slowly ..." (<u>Rosmersholm</u>; <u>The Observer</u>, 22.11.59). "It could still easily bear a little more shredding." (<u>Platonov</u>; <u>The Financial Times</u>, 14.10.60). "... slow first act ..." (<u>Platonov</u>; <u>The Star</u>, 14.10.60.) "It is much too long, too full of infertile pauses ..." (<u>Happy Days</u>; <u>The Observer</u>, 4.11.62). "The play which is a single act of one and three quarter hours becomes slow in the middle." (<u>Exit the King</u>; <u>Northern Echo</u>, 28.8.63). "... the company play it at greater speed but it is still too long." (<u>Nekrassov</u>; <u>Western Independent</u>, 22.9.57).
19) "Since its production at the Edinburgh Festival this Jean Paul Sartre play ... has been shortened by a good half hour. It has therefore gained considerably in pith as well as pungency ..." (<u>News Chronicle</u>, 18.9.57).
20) "The middle scenes now go with a genuine swing." (<u>Western Independent</u>, 22.9.57).
21) "Last night's production ... impressed by its verve and pith ..." (<u>Bristol Evening Post</u>, 18.9.57).
22) "... the interest is maintained by the skill and speed of George Devine's direction ..." (<u>The Stage</u>, 19.9.57).
23) " ... the present production is notably lively in attack ..." (<u>The Financial Times</u>, 18.9.57).
24) <u>Bristol Evening Post</u>, 29.8.58).
25) "... direction obtains the verbal speed and punch proper to Shaw ..." (<u>The Observer</u>, 31.8.58).
26) "George Devine ... has done his best to make up for the play's monotony by introducing spasms of vigour into the acting." (<u>Daily Telegraph</u>, 29.10.58).
27) "George Devine ... concentrates in his production on pace and impact ..." (<u>The Financial Times</u>, 8.9.59).
28) <u>Daily Mail</u>, 18.9.59.
29) "He has directed ... with immense zest ..." (<u>Western Independent</u>, 20.9.59).
30) "... the progress of the play is smooth and swift." (<u>The Morning Advertiser</u>, 24.10.60).
31) "George Devine's pacing of this play seemed near perfect." (<u>The Guardian</u>,

2.11.62).

32) "Mr. George Devine directs, and gets the pace right." (Daily Mail, 2.11.62).

33) Cf. chapter IV pp. 37 - 38.

34) "Where this production (Rosmersholm) by George Devine is outstandingly successful is in the excitement with which it invests the dozens of tiny incidents that Ibsen so cunningly wove into his momentous story. From this point of view the second act of the play becomes one of the most exhilarating experiences one can have in a theatre." (The Sunday Times, 22.11.59).

35) Cf. chapter III, p 28.

36) Evening Standard, 10.4.56.

37) Daily Worker, 16.4.56.

38) The Sunday Times, 31.8.58.

39) The Spectator, 27.11.59. "For the discretion and the beautifully lowpitched but intense concentration of the whole performance the director ... may claim much of the credit." (Rosmersholm; The Financial Times, 19.11.59). "... producing the play with simplicity and tact ..." (The Crucible; The Spectator, 20.4.56). "The production is ... concise, clear ..." (Major Barbara; The Stage, 4.9.58). "... deft, bright, clear production ..." (Major Barbara; Plays and Players, October 1958). "Even the scene in the Salvation Army shelter, which offers more scope for visual action, is handled with the barest minimum of movement." (Major Barbara; The Times, 29.8.58). "... it is without fuss or strain and on the whole unfolds the play smoothly and well." (Rosmersholm; The Stage, 26. 11.59). "... purity of conception ... spare but concentrated acting ..." (Rosmersholm; The Stage, 26.11.59). "The production ... is a good and clear account of the essentials ..." (Platonov; Plays and Players, December 1960). "... directed it with an unexaggerated straightforwardness, letting the obvious comedy take care of itself and the melodrama raise laughs if it must, and not burlesquing the anxieties." (Platonov; The Stage, 20.10.60). "... rigid economy of gesture." (Major Barbara; The Times, 29.8.58).

40) "George Devine ... too often relies on obvious and perfunctory tricks of staging which temporarily distract the audience but add little to the meaning of the play as a whole." (Alan Brien in The Sunday Telegraph, 15.9.63, about Exit the King).

41) Cf. chapters III and VII.

42) Cf. chapter VII.

43) Evening Standard, 10.4.56.

44) The Times, 10.4.56.

45) The Stage, 26.11.59.

46) Liverpool Daily Post, 2.11.62.

47) The Times, 3.9.63. "... Sean Kenny's perfectly apposite design..." (Cock-A-Doodle Dandy; The Tribune, 25.9.59). "... Richard Negri is responsible for the décor which is ... evocative ..." (Platonov; The Financial Times, 14.10.60). "The sets ... have some evocative power ..." (Platonov; The Guardian, 15.10.60). "... Jocelyn Herbert's set, a bare blazing arena of scorched grass, has the atmosphere of a primitive altar." (Happy Days; The Times, 2.11.62). "The set, designed to represent the senile mind of the king with its crackling walls and decaying flags, plays almost as integral a part in the play as any of its lesser characters." (Exit the King; The Guardian,

13.9.63).

48) "We were keen on her," (Tony Richardson, interview with the present writer, 4.10.67).

49) From an interview published in the West London Press and the Westminster and Pimlico News, 15.6.56).

50) Cf. chapter II, pp. 17-18. Harley Granville Barker moved on similar ground.

51) Illustrated London News, 13.9.58.

52) Plays and Players, October 1958.

53) The Guardian, 20.11.59

54) Daily Mail, 6.1.60. This review was written after the production had been transferred to the Comedy Theatre. "With the arrival of the third act one was accustomed to looking out for the minutiae of the production, particularly as they appeared in the small parts. Sensibly Mr. Devine has not satirized them out of existence." (Major Barbara; The Times, 29.8.58). " ... in spite of their ugliness, there is power and truth about the principal characters. And brilliant-ly captured by a cast including Wilfrid Lawson, Anna Manahan, Madge Brindley and Alan Dobie, these qualities alone make compelling theatre ..." (Live Like Pigs: The Star, 1.10.58). "If Dame Peggy's performance were to dwarf all the others in this production we could hardly complain. But miraculously it does not for, as Rosmer, Eric Porter nearly matches her sensitivity and, as Kroll probing sadistically into the mystery of Mrs. Rosmer's death in the millrace, Mark Dignam is convincingly hateable ..." (Rosmersholm; The Star, 19.11.59). "... an evening studded with delightful character performances ..." (Platonov; Evening News, 14.10.60). "... all these are good performances, though none is superlatively so. But it may be that a level of something more than adequacy serves this play better than an Edith Evans-like cadenza of accomplishment ..." (Platonov: Plays and Players, December 1960). "Mr. Harrison's superbly risky performance is enhanced by the vivid support of Rachel Roberts, Elvi Hale, Graham Crowden, Ronald Barker and George Murcell." (Platonov; The Obser-ver, 16.10.60). "Brenda Bruce, peaked and wan but resilient to the last, sus-tains the evening with dogged valour, and ends up almost looking like Beckett; she is self-effacingly partnered by Peter Duguid ..." (Happy Days: The Obser-ver, 4.11.62).

55) New Statesman and Nation, 28.9.57.

56) The Tribune, 5.9.58.

57) The Stage, 24.9.59.

58) Drama, Spring 1960.

59) Scene, 17.1.63. "It is a pity, however, that some of the supporting performances are of a lamentably inadequate standard ..." (The Crucible; Plays and Players, May 1956). "Instead of a quicksilver nihilist, Mr. Helpman presents a rather staid and confused Harlequin: underplaying the politics, overdoing the vocal japes ... Harry H. Corbett's crusading editor ... is a ponderously wild cari-cature, missing half the serious fun ..." (Nekrassov; The Observer, 22.9.57). "The big disappointment of the production was Miss Joan Plowright's Barbara. Hitherto we have seen her chiefly in parts calling for little straight playing. Her present part does make this demand, and Miss Plowright gives a reading that is

merely adequate. One became conscious of plummy delivery and excessive
blinking; but for much of the time one forgot she was on the stage." (Major
Barbara; The Times, 29.8.58). "The rest - even Robert Shaw - subside into
leering rhetoric. By itself overplaying is forgiveable: slow overplaying is not."
(Live Like Pigs; The Observer, 5.10.58). "His (Devine's) difficulty lies largely, I suspect, in the casting. O'Casey calls for the tongue-happy actors of
the old Abbey Days; and here he doesn't always get them." (Cock-A-Doodle
Dandy; The Financial Times, 18.9.59). "... Wilfrid Lawso 1, who has been
muttering on the London stage for many years and has now reached total inau-
dibility ..." (Cock-A-Doodle Dandy; The Irish Times, 19.9.59). "I am sur-
prised that the producer ... permitted P. Magee such eccentricity as Brendel
that hardly any contribution was made by this character ..." (Rosmersholm;
Socialist Leader, Glasgow, 28.11.59). "... the rest of the cast, including Rex
Harrison as Platonov, go deeper and deeper into mock-burlesque." (Platonov;
Punch, 19.10.60). "Miss Brenda Bruce tackles Winnie's enormous monologue
with intelligence and emotional warmth, but the demands of the language defeat
her; instead of building up a poignant musical fabric, she presents merely a
pendulum sequence of moods that add up to nothing." (Happy Days; The Times,
2.11.62).

60) Robert Stephens, interview with the present writer, 14.9.67. Peggy Ashcroft,
who played the leading part in this production, was of a different opinion: "We
found the style during the rehearsals. In the end it became a very fine production." (Interview with the present writer, 5.8.67).

61) According to Tony Richardson (4.10.67) and Robert Stephens (14.9.67).

62) "... the cutting edge of 'Nekrassov' is somewhat blunted by George Devine's
production, which overweights the play's farcical exaggeration at the expense
of its satirical extremism..." (The Observer, 22.9.57). "The shafts of wit
were replaced by sledge-hammer blows; sly nudges became hefty digs in the
ribs." (Daily Sketch, 18.9.57). "All this is played on the slapstick level ..."
(Evening Standard, 18.9.57). "Mr. Harry Corbett, as the editor, hasn't learnt
the lesson (or is this the director's fault? that the figures in farce must take
themselves seriously. Guying the part for us, as Mr. Corbett does, simply
destroys it; there are traces of this fault everywhere in the production." (New
Statesman and Nation, 28.9.57).

63) "George Devine, it seems to me, has staged it against its natural flow and
atmosphere. Realistic staging, and then not particularly imaginative, goes
against the fantasy and poetry of the play, and the movement seems stiff and
cramped." (The Stage, 24.9.59). "... rather uninspired production ..."
(Times Educational Supplement, 9.10.59). "... unimaginative production,
which tries to force this delightful fantasy into a realistic straightjacket."
(Plays and Players, October 1959).

64) The critic of Time and Tide (28.11.59) was of the same opinion: "... failing
a little I thought at the end by not producing quite enough temperament and exaltation for the final steps. But it may be that both she (Peggy Ashcroft) and
the producer ... deliberately choose the least melodramatic way of handling
the scene, so as to keep it all of a piece with the fascinatingly 'true' and candid revelations of the earlier scenes ..." "I at least feel that the final moments

need a poetic afflatus which is missing." (<u>The Guardian</u>, 20.11.59).

65) "... production is good and the play is very well acted, although it would be no disadvantage if less effort were made to keep the style in period. Shaw can be played hard, fast, and clear, without muzziness and without any attempt at antique charm ..." (<u>Times Educational Supplement,</u> 12.9.58). "But what Mr. Devine's admirable production ... then proceeds to prove is that the play is so firmly bogged down in its own era that our sole pleasure lies in our understanding of the various technicalities involved ..." (<u>Rosmersholm</u>; <u>Times Educational Supplement,</u> 4.12.59).

66) "... the producers throw up the sponge half way through and opt for cheap guying." (<u>Northern Echo</u>, 15.10.60). "The play ends in tragedy. But so firmly has our mood of hilarity been established by the farcical treatment of Platonov's dilemma that even his death cannot be taken seriously." (<u>New Statesman</u>, 22.10.60). "Gradually the company slant these melodramatic utterances more and more towards burlesque ..." (<u>The Times,</u> 14.10.60).

67) "... she (Brenda Bruce) and her director ... see Winnie as a brave little woman fighting against tremendous odds, whereas she is a happy woman. This is not a play about how to be happy though half-buried, but about how one is happy because half-buried. It calls for radiance, not heroism." (<u>The Sunday Times,</u> 4.11.62). "... production failed to throw any light on this singularly obscure and uncommunicative piece." (<u>The Stage,</u> 8.11.62).

68) "... production ... treats the play as if it had been written by Beckett - emphasizing its sombre static qualities and disregarding its invitations to gaiety." (<u>The Times,</u> 3.9.63). "... a lot of the comedy in 'Exit the King' ... fails because of George Devine's heavy production." (<u>The Stage,</u> 20.9.63).

69) "The actors, and the 24 carat Victoriana of the sets and clothes, all contribute to the solid authenticity of George Devine's production." (<u>Rosmersholm</u>; <u>Yorkshire Evening Post,</u> 21.11.59).

70) Scene 10.

71) Act II.

72) <u>The Financial Times,</u> 18.9.59.

73) Quoted by J.C. Trewin in his review in the <u>Illustrated London News</u>, 28.9.63.

74) <u>The Financial Times,</u> 13.9.63.

75) William Gaskill, interview with the present writer, 2.10.67.

76) "The productions were built between many people. There was experimented on a scene, we threw in ideas. George would have ideas which he would be willing to adjust. He would pick up something which suddenly emerged during rehearsals and of which he had not thought before. He would not force actors when he saw that his idea was out of their scope." (Joan Plowright, interview with the present writer, 16.10.67).

77) "... He's George Devine, sitting in his shirtsleeves in the front row of the stalls, looking as if he has just come in contentedly from gardening. Stuck about the stage are little vertical sticks indicating the position of scenery, and suggesting a course marked out for a dinghy race ... Variations are offered, while George Devine ponders. Then he climbs on the stage, pipe in mouth, and begins to push the characters gently about, an arm there, a pace to the right there, with the air of a sympathetic window-dresser not quite satisfied with his display. He

stands back critically, and once the mass is deployed irons out the individual problems." (Eric Keown in Punch, 3.10.56, in an article entitled "At the Rehearsal").

78) "George had admiration for Ionesco, but for Beckett he had complete admiration. He was not as truthful to Ionesco as he was to Beckett." (Michel Saint-Denis, interview with the present writer, 24.8.67).

79) William Gaskill, 2.10.67; Tony Richardson, 4.10.67; Lindsay Anderson, 26.9.68.

80) Already at the Old Vic School he had guided a comic improvisation class. Cf. chapter III, p. 29.

81) Interview with the present writer, 16.10.67.

82) "He would put the case to you for cutting out the things that made people yawn, but ultimately he would stand by your judgment. Because he thought that was what mattered. Your private wound was more important than somebody else's public satisfaction." (John Osborne about Devine in an interview with Kenneth Tynan, The Observer, 30.6.68).

83) The Crucible, The Country Wife, Major Barbara.

84) The Crucible, The Good Woman of Setzuan.

85) The Mulberry Bush, The Crucible.

86) The Mulberry Bush, The Crucible.

87) The Crucible.

88) Live Like Pigs, Endgame.

89) Live Like Pigs.

90) Twelfth Night was put on in order to give young actors a chance to try their hand at Shakespeare. There was no scenery at all in this production.

91) Interview with the present writer, 4.10.67.

92) Interview with the present writer, 2.10.67.

93) Cf. p. 43.

94) Most strikingly to be seen in The Sport of My Mad Mother, which he let the author direct herself, under his supervision. Cf. chapter VIII. It is interesting to see how deeply Devine's ideas and personality influenced the young directors who worked at the Court during those years. What unites Lindsay Anderson, William Gaskill, John Dexter and also - with reservations - Tony Richardson (if we consider their productions dealt with in this thesis) is their devotion to their work, their carefulness towards the text, their aversion to tricks and gimmicks. Sometimes it even seems that Devine's shortcomings as a producer (e.g. the occasional slowness of some of his productions) were adopted by them to a certain extent. "This place is a sort of school, after all, with different talents and points of view - as different as Tony Richardson, Bill Gaskill, John Dexter and Lindsay Anderson. But they do share a certain attitude towards the author." (Devine in TRF, p. 129).

VI George Devine as an Actor at the Royal Court 1956-1965

1) The productions were selected with regard to a) the material available and the amount of information obtained about them, b) their distribution over the nine

years during which Devine acted at the Court. His Danforth in <u>The Crucible</u> (1956), Hamm in <u>Endgame</u> (1958), Staupitz in <u>Luther</u> (1961), Dorn in <u>The Seagull</u> (1964), and Von Epp in <u>A Patriot For Me</u> (1965) will be examined in greater detail.

2) Arthur Miller, <u>Collected Plays</u>. London 1958. Act III, p. 286. Subsequently referred to as <u>Miller</u>.

3) "... I sought to make Danforth, for instance, perceptible as a human being by showing him somewhat put off by Mary Warren's turnabout at the height of the trials, which caused no little confusion. In my play, Danforth seems about to conceive of the truth, and surely there is a disposition in him at least to listen to arguments that go counter to the line of the prosecution. There is no such swerving in the record, and I think now ... that I was wrong in mitigating the evil of this man and the judges he represents." (<u>Miller,</u> p. 43).

4) Cf. <u>Miller</u>, III, 295.

5) Cf. <u>Miller,</u> III, 304; III, 307; and III, 308.

6) Mary Ure as Abigail.

7) 10.4.56.

8) Of the twelve critics whose reviews we examined.

9) 12.4.56.

10) 10.4.56.

11) 16.4.56.

12) " ... George Devine, who also gives the most dynamic performance of the evening ..." (<u>The Star</u>, 10.4.56). "Mr. George Devine's firm and aggressive performance ..." (<u>The Sunday Times,</u> 15.4.56). "There is great tension in the trial scene itself, thanks mainly to a weighty and compelling performance by George Devine ... " (<u>What's On in London</u>, 20.4.56). " ... several of the cast must really polish up their control of their diction. They have an admirable example in their director ... of the kind of clarity, force and command which comes from good articulation ... " (<u>New Statesman and Nation,</u> 15.4.56).

13) Cf. chapter V. p. 237 annotation 78.

14) English version by the author.

15) "In a dressing-gown, a stiff toque on his head, a large bloodstained handkerchief over his face, a whistle hanging from his neck, a rug over his knees ... " (Samuel Beckett, <u>Endgame</u>, Faber Paper Covered Editions, London 1964. Translated from the original French by the author; p. 12. Subsequently referred to as <u>Endgame</u>).

16) E.g. Michel Saint-Denis, interview with the present writer, 24.8.67.

17) Ronald Hastings in <u>The Daily Telegraph,</u> 27.10.58.

18) 29.10.58.

19) play

20) <u>The Financial Times</u>, 29.10.58.

21) 30.10.58.

22) "I had been listening entranced to George Devine's magnificently rich delivery of three great speeches in Samuel Beckett's 'End-Game' ... " (30.11.58).

23) Cf. <u>Endgame</u>, pp. 35-37.

24) Cf. <u>Endgame</u> p. 44.

25) Cf. <u>Endgame</u>, p. 51.

26) "George Devine ... contributes a striking portrait of the sharp-tongued mis-
anthrope ... " (6.11.58).
27) "There is nothing, I think, positively wrong with George Devine's Hamm ..."
(2.11.58).
28) "The four players, headed by George Devine, put over their author's lines ...
skilfully, often movingly ... " (29.10.58).
29) 29.10.58.
30) 7.11.58.
31) 7.11.58.
32) Interview with the present writer, 24.8.67.
33) 29.10.58.
34) Cf. chapter V, pp. 44-45.
35) In retrospect W.A. Darlington wrote: "I shall not easily forget his playing of
Hamm ... craggy and defiant in the fact of imminent destruction." (The Daily
Telegraph, 21.1.66).
36) 29.10.58.
37) 8.11.58.
38) Robert Stephens (14.9.67), Tony Richardson (4.10.67), Ronald Bryden (24.9.
68); all in interviews with the present writer.
39) John Osborne, Luther. Faber & Faber, London 1961; II, ii, 52.
40) 30.7.61.
41) September 1961.
42) 14.8.61.
43) 16.8.61.
44) "... fine performance by George Devine as Staupitz ... " (11.8.61).
45) "... especially good performances by George Devine ... " (10.8.61).
46) "I particularly liked George Devine as the sympathetic Augustine Vicar-Gene-
ral ... " (September 1961).
47) "... a cohort of good actors, including Mr. Devine himself, contribute to a
generally effective production ... " (28.7.61).
48) "There is a notable study of Staupitz ... by George Devine ... " (3.8.61).
49) Translated by Ann Jellicoe.
50) "George's performance in The Seagull was so good because he identified with
this part. The part was very much like George." (William Gaskill, interview
with the present writer, 2.10.67).
51) Cf. pp. 51-52.
52) 13.3.64.
53) 13.3.64.
54) 20.3.64.
55) 13.3.64. Harold Hobson's review in The Sunday Times (15.3.64) implies a
contrary opinion: "Mr. Devine's Doctor, the only person in this Russian country house who is, or thinks he is, satisfied with life, is a most pleasingly and
teasingly composed portrait of hedonistic serenity ... "
56) New Statesman, 20.4.64.
57) 15.3.64.
58) "George Devine gives one of his most accomplished performances as Dorn
... " (The Stage, 19.3.64). "George Devine as Dorn gives one of the finest

performances of his career, delicate, subtle and relaxed ..." (<u>Plays and Players</u>, April 1964).

59) 5.8.67.
60) 14.9.67.
61) 24.8.67.
62) <u>BBC</u>.
63) 2.10.67.
64) 5.10.67. All except Gielgud in interviews with the present writer.
65) <u>Evening Standard,</u> 1.7.65.
66) 5.7.65.
67) 23.7.65.
68) September 1965.
69) 9.7.65.
70) "There is an imposing performance from Mr. George Devine as a splendid queen of a Baron at a transvestite ball ..." (1.7.65).
71) " ... George Devine as a baron dressed up as the queen makes the most remarkable and amusing performance in London so far this year." (1.7.65).
72) " ... George Devine magnificent as a baron in full diamond-radiant, tiara drag ..." (9.7.65).
73) " ... superb performance of George Devine, resplendent in wig, jewels and enormous gown, as the baron ..." (31.7.65).
74) "Mr. George Devine, as a domineering dowager bejewelled like Widow Twankey in the finale, is quite radiant." (7.7.65). "Devine was superb." (Robert Stephens, interview with the present writer, 14.9.67).
75) 14.5.57; 5.8.57; 18.6.58 (this production is examined here); 4.8.58.
76) 26.6.56.
77) 12.12.56.
78) 25.6.57.
79) 28.8.58. Devine took over the part from Alan Webb.
80) 29.7.59.
81) 21.4.63; 19.4.65.
82) 31.10.56. The dates refer to the first nights.
83) Cf. chapter V, p. 237, annotation 78.
84) 20.6.58.
85) Tony Richardson, 5.1.67, Interview with the present writer.
86) 3.8.58. " ... I doubt whether even George Devine and Miss Plowright, without Mr. Richardson's highly disciplined hand, could have peopled an empty stage in such a manner ..." (<u>Plays and Players</u>, August 1958). " ... the old couple in a frenzy of meaningless activity bringing in more and more chairs for people who aren't there while doors swing open and shut and a terrifying background of <u>musique concrète</u> rises to a real inferno of claustrophobia." (The Tribune, 27.6.58). "The crescendo of 'The Chairs', in particular, is wonderfully done. The fetching and arranging of the chairs, of more and more chairs, the ringing bells, the guests pouring in, the noise of the greetings, the pace becoming faster, the excitement rushing to its climax, and then being suddenly relaxed in momentary exhaustion ..." (<u>The Sunday Times,</u> 22.6.58).
87) 20.6.58.

88) Cf. p. 238, annotation 12.
89) Cf. chapter III, p. 29.
90) "George coaxed me back and gave me confidence again when I lost my nerves during the rehearsals." (Joan Plowright, 16.10.67, interview with the present writer).
91) Now drama critic of The Observer.
92) 24.9.68, interview with the present writer.
93) Tony Richardson, 5.10.67, interview with the present writer.
94) "Mr. George Devine booms with magnificent stupidity as the duped godfather ..." (The Times, 30.7.59).
95) Cf. chapter III, p. 29.
96) Robert Stephens, 14.9.67, interview with the present writer.
97) "George was never impressive a lot as an actor. The best things he did were Von Epp in A Patriot For Me and the Old Man in The Chairs." (Ronald Bryden, 24.9.68, interview with the present writer).
98) A parallel to the ideas of Harley Granville Barker. Cf. chapter II, pp. 222-223 annotation 23.
99) Tony Richardson, 4.10.67, interview with the present writer.
100) "He was a very fine actor, given the right part." (W.A. Darlington in The Daily Telegraph, 21.1.66).

VII George Devine as an Artistic Director of the Royal Court 1956-1965

1) The Stage, 10.5.56.
2) ESC.
3) "The English Stage Society was formed to support the work of the English Stage Company at the Royal Court Theatre and in particular to help the Company in its policy of encouraging and fostering new talent. By means of the Sunday night series of 'Productions Without Decor' the new dramatist is given an opportunity of seeing his play produced under professional conditions, being presented to a specialised and critical audience. These Sunday nights are only open to members of the Society, who thus play an active and critical part in the development of new talent. Membership of the Society, however, extends beyond the 'Productions Without Decor'. Facilities include the purchase of seats at reduced prices for dress rehearsals of regular productions, priority bookings at the Box Office, and discussions and presentations of interesting experimental work in other fields such as music and dance are among the Society's other activities." (The official text of the English Stage Company, printed in their theatre programmes).
4) 2.4.62.
5) TRF, p. 131.
6) "At the beginning there was an enormous resistance to the Court; it was called 'dungheap' and a place where 'ghastly plays' were put on ... The Court made the audiences more discerning." (Robert Stephens, interview with the present writer, 14.9.67). Cf. chapter VIII, pp. 93-94; IX, 127-128; X, 153-154; XI, 178.

7) <u>BBC.</u>

8) Cf. chapter IV, pp. 37-38.

9) Cf. chapter IV, p. 37. "Before 1956, 'ordinary' people on the stage were sort of a comic relief. The plays dealt with kings and dukes and nobles. This changed. Literate men and women from non-class origin emerged. This called for a new kind of actor, for a new style of acting. It was a change of manners and society which changed the style of the acting." (Joan Plowright, interview with the present writer, 16.10.67).

10) Cf. chapter XII, p. 204.

11) <u>Ten Years at the Royal Court 1956/1966.</u> A brochure; p. 31. Subsequently referred to as <u>Ten Years</u>.

12) ibid.

13) Cf. chapter III, p.28.

14) Cf. chapter IV, p.38.

15) Interview with the present writer, 5.10.67. William Gaskill was of the same opinion: "It is more expensive to have a steady company, and one is more flexible without." (Interview with the present writer, 18.9.68).

16) Cf. chapter IV, p.37.

17) Cf. pp. 92-93; 125-127; 177-178; 211-212 respectively.

18) "The problems of décor are always complicated in the case of a repertory which involves the keeping on hand and the storage of a number of sets. This problem Mr. Devine is solving by a new system which he wittingly christens 'essentialism', the audience will be called on to use their imaginations." (T.C. Worsley in the <u>New Statesman and Nation,</u> 24.3.56). Jocelyn Herbert made an art of this necessity.

19) Cf. chapter IX, p. 125.

20) ibid.

21) Stephen Doncaster designed the sets for, among other plays, <u>The Crucible,</u> <u>Epitaph for George Dillon,</u> <u>One Way Pendulum</u> (cf. chapter X, p. 153. and <u>That's Us</u>; Alan Tagg those for <u>Look Back in Anger,</u> <u>Live Like Pigs,</u> <u>The Long and the Short and the Tall,</u> <u>The Knack</u> and <u>Plays for England</u>; Sean Kenny those for <u>Sugar in the Morning,</u> <u>Cock-A-Doodle Dandy</u> and <u>Altona</u>; Richard Negri those for <u>Nekrassov</u> and <u>Platonov</u>; John Gunter those for <u>Shelley,</u> <u>The Cresta Run</u> and <u>Saved.</u> "Such an enterprise must be informed throughout with a spirit of adventure, of challenge, of jumping off the deep end, of the 'right to fail', without which no art can develop. Actors, actresses, directors, designers, musicians, photographers, poster artists - these have all been chosen from the same viewpoint. An immense amount of talent has been attracted to the Court, passed through it, and been absorbed by the theatre at large. It is, in the classical sense, a 'school of the theatre'," (Devine in <u>The Guardian,</u> 2.4. 62).

22) Cf. chapter VI, p. 59.

23) Letter to the present writer, 12.11.68.

24) Interview with the present writer, 1.8.67.

25) Interview with the present writer, 14.9.67.

26) Interview with the present writer, 18.9.68. Devine was appointed C.B.E. for services to the theatre in 1957.

27) <u>The Daily Mail</u>, 6.1.65. "It was a sad occasion, this year's annual English Stage Company Luncheon at the Savoy ... The sadness came from the news that the father figure of the whole organisation, George Devine, is to depart. He said that not for a minute did he believe that now there were a National Theatre and a Royal Shakespeare Company operating in London the Royal Court's job had been overtaken. On the contrary, he felt that the 'creative eccentricity' of an organisation like the Court needed more than ever to be preserved. But the burden of overseeing the company had pushed him into the ground till he felt like Winnie in 'Happy Days' - up to his neck in it and going down. The Royal Court venture was born of passion and enthusiasm and now that he had become satiated with the business of running it, he had to hand over to someone else./ It was a sad decision, a sad speech and for the Royal Court it will mark a sadder day than perhaps they guess if another balancing father figure can't be found. There aren't many of them about." (<u>Plays and Players</u>, February 1965).

28) "The Royal Court was born out of passion and enthusiasm, and this sort of madness must be there if it is to perform its function today." (Devine, <u>Evening Standard</u>, 1.2.65).

29) "You could talk to him about any idea, however crackbrained." (William Gaskill in <u>The Observer</u>, 10.1.65). "He was ahead of everyone of his time and generation in the theatre. He was the only one with a vision of a theatre for new writers and young people." (Tony Richardson, ibid.).

30) "When people speak of a creative artist, I suppose they imagine Michelangelo struggling away at a block of marble. I think of George Devine struggling with his own talent and that of his fellow workers to make a new and exciting theatre." (Gaskill, in <u>Plays and Players</u>, March 1966).

31) <u>BBC</u>. "Just to be a director by itself, producing one play here and one play there, isn't enough. You should try to create conditions of work, perhaps even by starting your own company or running your own theatre." (Devine, <u>TRF</u>, p. 130). " ... we have begun to find the way to create conditions wherein new drama can grow and thrive." (Devine, <u>ESC</u>). "But Mr. Devine's aims are long term: to establish a climate in which dramatic writing can flourish." (<u>The Times</u>, 19.3.58).

32) <u>Ten Years</u>, p. 2.

VIII Ann Jellicoe: The Sport of My Mad Mother

1) Richard Beynon, <u>The Shifting Heart</u>.
2) Cf. chapters I, III, IV, V, VI.
3) Ann Jellicoe, <u>The Sport of My Mad Mother</u>. New Version. Faber & Faber, London 1964, paper covered edition. Subsequently referred to as <u>New Version</u>. The text used for the analysis of single scenes and the original production is taken from <u>The Observer Plays</u>, Faber & Faber, London 1958, pp. 157-217, which represents <u>The Sport of My Mad Mother</u> in its first version. This text which was also used for the original production is subsequently referred to as <u>Sport</u>.
4) Preface to the <u>New Version</u>, pp. 5-6.

5) Sport, p. 158.
6) Quoted from the programme of the play.
7) Sport, I, i, 159.
8) Cf. New Version, p. 5.
9) Sport, I, i, p. 163.
10) Sport, I, i, p. 163.
11) Sport, I, i, pp. 168-169.
12) " ... the words they used were meaningless sounds to release emotion ... the characters were incapable of understanding their own motives ... verbal rhythms used in an obvious, musical way ... " (Ann Jellicoe, Shelley, or The Idealist. Faber & Faber, London 1966; pp. 13 ff. Subsequently referred to as Shelley).
13) Sport, I, i, pp. 169-170.
14) Sport, I, i, p. 171.
15) Sport I, i, pp. 175-176.
16) Sport, I, i, 176.
17) Cf. preface to the New Version, p. 5.
18) " ... I was interested in piling up patterns of sound and releasing them ... " (Ann Jellicoe, Shelley, pp. 13ff.). "For instance, there is a scene in my play where Caldaro is knocked out, and the Teds stand him on his feet, wrap him up in newspaper, cavort round him, chanting until they get to a pitch of ec- stasy when they tear the newspaper off him. Now in this action there are hardly any words that make sense - there is nothing which your intellect can take in. If you sit watching and say 'What does this mean? What does this mean?' you're not going to get anywhere; but if you allow yourself to be excited by the visual action and the gradual crescendo of noise underlining this, you may begin to appreciate what it's about ... " (Ann Jellicoe, in: John Russell Taylor, Anger and After. A Guide to the New British Drama, London 1962, p. 67. Subsequent- ly referred to as Taylor).
19) Sport, I, ii, p. 178.
20) Sport, I, ii, pp. 183-184.
21) "The play is written to be acted: nothing is put into words that cannot be shown in action. " (New Version, p. 5).
22) Sport, I, ii, 184-185.
23) Cf. p. 74.
24) Sport, I, ii, 185. "We create rituals when we want to strengthen, celebrate or define our common life ... or when we want to give ourselves confidence to undertake a common course of action ... This play proceeds by rituals because the insecure and inarticulate group of people who figure in the play depend on them so much. " (New Version, pp. 5-6).
25) Cf. Sport, I, ii, pp. 187-192.
26) Cf. Sport, I, ii, 186-187.
27) " ... they betray their real feeling ... by the very fact that they need to assume a mask ... " (New Version, p. 5).
28) Sport, I, ii, pp. 187-188.
29) Sport, I, ii, p. 191.
30) Sport, I, ii, p. 192.

31) On the stage Greta wore a large leather jacket which made her formless, so this change could be shown convincingly.
32) Sport, II, p. 194.
33) Sport, II, p. 195.
34) Sport, II, p. 195.
35) Cf. I, i, p. 171.
36) Sport, II, p. 199.
37) Sport, II, p. 200.
38) Sport, II, p. 201.
39) Sport, II, p. 201.
40) " ... almost inadvertently I had found that I could write comedy (I'm thinking of the scene where Cone tries to persuade Fak to betray Greta) ..." (Ann Jellicoe, Shelley, pp. 13ff.)
41) Sport, II, p. 207.
42) Ann Jellicoe, interview with the present writer, 20.9.68.
43) Sport, II, p. 209.
44) Sport, II, p. 215.
45) Cf. Sport, II, p. 215.
46) Sport, II, p. 216.
47) ibid.
48) Cf. Sport, II, 216-217.
49) Shelley, pp. 13ff.
50) Ann Jellicoe, interview with the present writer, 20.9.68.
51) Ann Jellicoe, interview with the present writer, 20.9.68.
52) New Version, p. 3.
53) The author's.
54) Programme note.
55) Cf. p. 244, annotation 12.
56) "Now, my play is about incoherent people - people who have no power of expression, of analysing their emotions. They don't know why they're afraid; they don't even know that they are afraid. So they have to compensate for their fear by attacking someone else; they're insecure and frustrated, and they have to compensate for that by being big, and violent." (Ann Jellicoe; Taylor, pp. 67-68).
57) New Version, p. 6.
58) New Version, p. 5. "When I write a play I am trying to communicate with the audience, I do this by every means in my power - I try to get at them through their eyes, by providing visual action; I try to get at them through their ears, for instance by noises and rhythm ..." (Ann Jellicoe; Taylor, p. 69).
59) Taylor, p. 67.
60) Sport, II, pp. 199-200.
61) The third one in the New Version, the second one in Sport, New Version, p.6.
62) Ann Jellicoe, interview with the present writer, 20.9.68.
63) In her preface to the New Version (p. 6) Ann Jellicoe writes: "I used to think that the play was about the conflict between GRETA and CALDARO, and while this remains superficially true I find that, at a much deeper level, it is about the relationship between GRETA and CONE." In Sport this relationship is hinted

at in a very subdued way, and it remains obscure whether Cone killed himself immediately after his violent verbal attack on Greta which mirrors his
jealousy (II, 209).

64) <u>Sport</u>, II, p. 199.
65) <u>Taylor</u>, p. 70.
66) Similarities suggested by Prof. R. Stamm.
67) T.S. Eliot, <u>Collected Poems 1909-1962</u>, London 1963, pp. 123-124.
68) ibid, p. 136.
69) Interview with the present writer, 20.9.68.
70) Cf. p.7o.
71) Cf. p. 248, annotation 134: John Arden was of a different opinion.
72) <u>Sport</u>, I,i, p. 163. Cf. p. 71.
73) <u>Sport</u>, I,i, p. 163. Cf. pp. 71-72.
74) <u>Sport</u>, I,i, pp. 168-169. Cf. pp. 72-73.
75) "The play is written to be acted: nothing is put into words that cannot be
shown in action." (<u>New Version</u>, p. 5).
76) <u>Sport</u>, I,i, pp. 169-170. Cf. p. 73.
77) Interview with the present writer, 20.9.68.
78) <u>Sport</u>, I,i, pp. 175-176. Cf. pp. 73-74.
79) <u>Sport</u>, I,ii, p. 178. Cf. p. 75..
80) <u>Sport</u>, I,ii, pp. 183-185. Cf. pp. 75-76.
81) Interview with the present writer, 20.7.67.
82) Cf. <u>New Version</u>, p. 5. " ... in the theatre it all surges over and around
one, a strange, disturbing pattern of sights and sounds ..." (John Russell
Taylor in <u>Taylor</u>, p. 66).
83) 2.3.58, title <u>Good Sportsmanship</u>.
84) <u>Sport</u>, I,ii, pp. 186-187. Cf. pp. 76-77.
85) Ann Jellicoe, interview with the present writer, 20.9.68.
86) <u>Sport</u>, I,ii, 187-192. Cf. pp. 76-77.
87) Interview with the present writer, 20.7.67; 20.9.68.
88) <u>Sport</u>, I,ii, p. 192.
89) Ann Jellicoe, interview with the present writer, 20.9.68.
90) <u>Sport</u>, II, p. 125. Cf. p. 78.
91) <u>Sport</u>, II, p. 195. Cf. p. 79.
92) "The audience were too well bred to do anything about it. There was just
irritation floating up to Cone" (Ann Jellicoe, interview with the present writer, 20.9.68).
93) <u>Sport</u>, II, p. 195. Cf. p. 79.
94) <u>Sport</u>, II, pp. 199-200. Cf. pp. 79-80.
95) <u>Sport</u>, II, p. 200. Cf. p. 80.
96) <u>Sport</u>, II, p. 207. Cf. pp. 81.82.
97) Ann Jellicoe, interview with the present writer, 20.9.68.
98) <u>Sport</u>, II, pp. 215-216. Cf. p. 82.
99) 8.3.58.
100) <u>Daily Herald</u>, 26.2.58 (Harry Weaver): "In fairness one must admit that the
cast gave devoted performances." <u>The Financial Times</u>, 26.2.58 (Derek
Granger): " ... very well acted and mimed ...". <u>Westminster and Pimlico</u>

News, 7.3.58: "... there is no doubt about the acting. This on the whole is
excellent with Philip Locke, Wendy Craig and Sheila Ballantine just a few
marks ahead of the remainder of the cast ..."
101) Ann Jellicoe, interview with the present writer, 20.9.68.
102) Sport, I, ii, 192.
103) 26.2.58.
104) see also review in the Westminster and Pimlico News, 7.3.58.
105) Ann Jellicoe, interview with the present writer, 20.9.68.
106) Sport, I, i, 166.
107) Sport, I, i, p. 160.
108) "... Steve should be the link between Greta and the audience and the means
whereby she may, perhaps, be controlled." (Ann Jellicoe, New Version, p.6).
109) Sport, I, i, 160.
110) The Financial Times, 26.2.58 (Derek Granger).
111) The Observer, 2.3.58.
112) Ann Jellicoe, interview with the present writer, 20.9.68.
113) 26.2.58.
114) Richard Widmark, film actor.
115) 26.2.58.
116) Interview with the present writer, 20.9.68.
117) The Observer, 2.3.58.
118) Cf. Sport, I, i, 172.
119) Interview with the present writer, 20.9.68.
120) "The script of The Sport of My Mad Mother, in fact, makes very little sense
just read cold: it is simply the short score from which a full orchestral sound
can be conjured by a skilled musician, or the scenerio for a ballet waiting for
a composer to write the music and a choreographer to stage it ..." (J.R.
Taylor in Taylor, p. 66).
121) Interview with the present writer, 20.7.67.
122) Programme note.
123) Sport, I, i, 168-169; I, i, 169-170; I, i, 175-176; I, ii, 192.
124) Cf. pp. 89-91.
125) Sport, II, pp. 199-200.
126) Cf. p. 84.
127) "... Miss Jellicoe's direction frequently underlines what is already written
in italics: it is strident, overpaused, and hyper-agonized. One hoped for a
cooler tone, as trim and casual as that of the Modern Jazz Quartet." (2.3.58).
128) Jane Howell, who directed a revival of the play at the Royal Court on May 1st
1960, declared: "The third act is difficult to rehearse. There is not that
amount of improvisation in it as in the first two acts - to me it appears muddled." (Interview with the present writer, 27.7.67. Jane Howell refers to the
act division of the New Version).
129) New Version, I, p. 11.
130) Interview with the present writer, 20.7.67.
131) In the production of the same play directed by Jane Howell at the Court on
May 1st 1960, the set, designed by Kenneth Jones, was much better: it had a
claustrophobic quality about it and one got the feeling that the characters in

the play were being trapped.

132) Interview with the present writer, 20.7.67. "I think the word 'meaning' shows exactly what is wrong with people's attitudes. If they were to ask 'What is the play about?' it would be a better approach. This is a new kind of play, which demands a new approach. Most playgoers today are not used to taking anything direct in the theatre. What they do is transform it into words and put it through their brain." (Ann Jellicoe; Taylor p. 67).

133) New Version, p. 5.

134) The reason for this could be the same as John Arden mentioned when asked about the production of one of his plays at the Court. "I suspect that one of the reasons why 'The Happy Haven' did not do so well in Bristol is simply that the audience was frozen off by the proscenium arch, and the parts of the play that were meant to come out at the audience completely failed to do so." (John Arden in an interview with Tom Milne and Clive Goodwin, first published in Encore in 1961. Reprinted in Theatre at Work, ed. Charles Marowitz and Simon Trussler, London 1967, p. 47).

135) The Financial Times, 26.2.58 (Derek Granger).

136) P. 200; cf. p. 80.

137) 7.3.58.

138) 26.2.58.

139) 27.2.58.

140) 26.2.58.

141) 27.2.58.

142) 1.3.58.

143) 7.3.58.

144) "£ 1,000 towards the cost of its production has been paid by Schweppes - the first time a commercial firm has ever backed a play" (Daily Express, 26.2. 58).

145) 26.2.58.

146) Cf. pp. 75-76, 76-78.

147) 2.3.58.

148) 26.2.58.

149) Daily Mirror, 26.2.58 (Frank Entwisle).

150) Oxford Mail, 1.3.58.

151) News Chronicle, 26.2.58 (Alan Dent).

152) Daily Mail, 26.2.58 (Cecil Wilson).

153) The Morning Advertiser, 1.3.58.

154) The Scotsman, 27.2.58.

155) Plays and Players, April 1958 (Richard Buckle).

156) 26.2.58.

157) Cf. Shelley, pp. 13ff.

158) April 1958.

159) Cf. pp. 92-93.

160) It was for this reason that no music was used in the original production (except the sounds and noises produced by Flim). Jane Howell, in her production on May 1st 1960, had the plot accompanied by subtle jazz music to emphasize - perhaps unnecessarily - the musical effect of the dialogue.

161) 27.3.62.
162) 18.10.65. The dates refer to the official first nights.

IX John Arden: Serjeant Musgrave's Dance

1) Cf. Chapter V passim.
2) Press Office Royal Court.
3) John Arden, Serjeant Musgrave's Dance, Methuen & Co. Ltd., London 1960; Introduction, p. 7. This text is used for all the quotations throughout this chapter. Subsequently referred to as Musgrave.
4) Unfortunately I did not get the chance of talking to Arden about the play. When I rang him in September 1968, he answered that he was busy with new work and did not have the time to talk about his old plays. On the other hand, I had the opportunity of listening to a tape recording of Lindsay Anderson's original 1959 production at Anderson's London home (28.9.68).
5) Musgrave, I, i, 10.
6) Musgrave, I, i, 10.
7) Musgrave, I, i, 10-11.
8) Musgrave, I, i, 14.
9) Musgrave, I, ii, 16-17.
10) Musgrave, I, ii, 17.
11) Musgrave, I, ii, 17-18.
12) "The ballad tradition is useful when it enables characters to state simple emotions with a directness which might otherwise be difficult to take." (Ronald Hayman, John Arden. Contemporary Playwrights, Heinemann Educational Books Ltd., London 1968; p. 29). Subsequently referred to as Hayman/Arden.
13) Musgrave, I, i, 14; cf. p. 101.
14) "No work in the colliery. The owner calls it a strike, the men call it a lockout, we call it starvation." (Musgrave, I, ii, 20).
15) Musgrave, I, ii, 22.
16) Musgrave, I, ii, 23.
17) Musgrave, I, ii, 24.
18) Musgrave, I, ii, 26.
19) Musgrave, I, ii, 26.
20) Musgrave, I, ii, 26-27.
21) Musgrave, I, iii, 28-29.
22) Musgrave, I, i, 10; cf. p. 100.
23) Musgrave, I, iii, 29.
24) I, iii, 30-31.
25) Musgrave, I, iii, 33-34.
26) Cf. Musgrave, I, iii, 30-31; p. 105.
27) Musgrave, I, iii, 35-36.
28) I, iii, 36.
29) I, iii, 37.
30) Cf. I, iii, 33-34; p. 105.
31) Musgrave, II, i, 49.

32) Cf. Musgrave, II, i, 51.
33) "Our Black Jack'd say it's not material. He'd say there's blood on these two hands ... You can wipe 'em as often as you want on a bit o' yellow hair, but it still comes blood the next time so why bother, he'd say. And I'd say it too." (Musgrave, II, iii, 61).
34) Cf. Musgrave, I, i, 10; p. 100.
35) Musgrave, II, iii, 62.
36) Musgrave, II, iii, 63.
37) Musgrave, II, iii, 64.
38) Musgrave, II, iii, 65.
39) "MUSGRAVE. ... Look, if you're the right-marker to the Company and you're marching to the right, you can't see the others, so you follow the orders you can hear and hope you hear them true. When I was a recruit I found myself once half across the square alone - they'd marched the other way and I'd never heard the word!" (II, iii, 66).
40) Musgrave, II, iii, 64.
41) Cf. Musgrave, II, iii, 68.
42) In an interview with Tom Milne and Clive Goodwin Arden commented on this episode as follows: "Oddly enough, the death of Sparky is one of the things I had not anticipated. I didn't really decide that any of them were to die until I had started the second act. Then it suddenly struck me. I already had the concept of the scene in the stable, with the girl coming and playing a scene with each soldier in turn - given a situation of high tension such as exists in the play, one girl and three men is going to result in something. In this case Sparky's death ... I knew Annie had to be in the centre at the end, but I did not know how I was going to get her there. I also knew she had to be in the centre in the stable scene. To find a connection between the two scenes led me to the death of Sparky. I then went back and rewrote some of the earlier scenes to prepare for it." (First published in Encore in 1961; reprinted in Theatre at Work, ed. by Charles Marowitz and Simon Trussler, London 1967; pp. 49-50. Subsequently referred to as Theatre at Work). Despite Arden's explanation there remains something artificial about this murder. Ronald Hayman expressed it like this: " ... the death of Sparky falls ... flat. It's a key point in the action, the turning point in the relationship between the three surviving soldiers, and it ought to be an effective climax in itself, but in fact it has very little emotional impact. The reason is that the act of killing him is an action without an intention behind it ... The question of why Hurst kills Sparky is never seriously asked or answered. Arden goes along with Musgrave who says that it isn't material." (Hayman/Arden, p. 25).
43) Musgrave, II, iii, 72.
44) Musgrave, II, iii, 74.
45) Cf. Musgrave, III, i, 76.
46) Musgrave, III, i, 79.
47) Musgrave, III, i, 84. The pulling out of the skeleton, because of the timing, remains a shock. "I rather intended the skeleton to remain something of a surprise. There is some dramatic effect to be gained by pulling it out." (Arden, Theatre at Work, p. 48).

48) <u>Musgrave</u>, III, i, 84-85.
49) <u>Musgrave</u>, III, i, 90.
50) Cf. <u>Musgrave</u>, II, ii, 53f.
51) <u>Musgrave</u>, III, i, 91.
52) "MUSGRAVE. ... Now then, who's with me! Twenty-five to die and the Logic is worked out. Who'll help me? You? (<u>He points to WALSH</u>) I made sure that you would: you're a man like the black Musgrave, you: you have purpose, and you can lead. Join along with my madness, friend ..." (III, i, 92). "HURST ... We've earned our living by beating and killing folk like yourselves in the streets of their own city. Well, it's drove us mad - ..." (III, i, 94).
52) <u>Musgrave</u>, III, i, 94.
53) <u>Musgrave</u>, III, i, 99.
54) "The community's been saved. Peace and prosperity rules. We're all friends and neighbours for the rest of today. We're all sorted out. We're back where we were. So what do we do?" (III, i, 99).
55) "BARGEE. Free beer. It's still here./ No more thinking. Easy drinking. /End of a bad bad dream. Gush forth the foaming stream." (III, i, 99).
56) <u>Musgrave</u>, III, ii, 102.
57) <u>Musgrave</u>, III, ii, 102.
58) <u>Musgrave</u>, Introduction, p. 7; cf. pp. 99-100.
59) <u>Musgrave</u>, Introduction, p. 7; cf. p. 99.
60) <u>Musgrave</u>, Introduction, p. 7; cf. p. 99.
61) "Complete pacifism is a very hard doctrine: and if this play appears to advocate it with perhaps some timidity, it is probably because I am naturally a timid man - and also because I know that if I am hit I very easily hit back: and I do not care to preach too confidently what I am not sure I can practise." (<u>Musgrave</u>, Introduction, p. 7; cf. pp. 99-100.
62) "I have endeavoured to write about the violence that is so evident in the world, and to do so through a story that is partly one of wish-fulfilment." (<u>Musgrave</u>, Introduction, p. 7; cf. p. 99
63) "As with Brecht, part of his reason for going to history is to achieve a distance from the contemporary scene that enables him to comment on it all the more pointedly ... one of the things that sparked off <u>Serjeant Musgrave's Dance</u> was an incident in Cyprus." (<u>Hayman/Arden</u>, p. 4). Arden related this incident during his interview with Tom Milne and Clive Goodwin: "A soldier's wife was shot in the street by terrorists. And according to newspaper reports - which was all I had to work on at the time - some soldiers ran wild at night and people were killed in the rounding-up. The atrocity which sparks off Musgrave's revolt, and which happens before the play begins, is roughly similar." (<u>Theatre at Work</u>, p. 44).
64) <u>Musgrave</u>, III, i, 99.
65) pp. 17-18; cf. p. 102.
66) <u>Musgrave</u>, p. 7; cf. p. 99.
67) <u>Musgrave</u>, Introduction, p. 7; cf. p. 99.
68) " ... there <u>are</u> structural faults in it ..." (John Arden, <u>Theatre at Work</u>, p. 50).
69) <u>Hayman/Arden</u>, p. 27.

70) "He tends to use three words when one would suffice" (Lindsay Anderson, interview with the present writer, 26.9.68).

71) "He was killed, being there for his duty, in the country I was telling you about, where the regiment is stationed, It's not right a colony, you know, it's a sort of Protectorate, but British, y'know, British. This, up here, he was walking down a street latish at night, he'd been to the opera - you've got a choral society in this town, I daresay - well, he was only a soldier, but North Country, he was full of music, so he goes to the opera." (Musgrave, III, i, 86).

72) As to the similarity to Brecht in this point Ronald Hayman comes to the following conclusion: "Both playwrights have their characters sliding in and out of songs and rhymes in a way that makes us look at them as if through the wrong end of a telescope. In Brecht this is a deliberate alienation effect; in Arden it is a deep-seated habit, corresponding to the way he thinks." (Hayman/Arden, p. 5).

73) Theatre at Work, pp. 42-43.

74) Cf. Representative English Comedies, vol. IV, ed. by Charles Mills Gayley and Alwin Thaler, The Macmillan Company, New York 1936; The Recruiting Officer, I, i, p. 687. "What I needed was an ordinary recruiting speech, written in almost a pastiche style, which then gradually, without the audience quite realizing when, takes on a different meaning." (Arden, Theatre at Work, p. 43).

75) Hayman/Arden, pp. 4-5.

76) " ... all the time I write I find I am writing, partly indeed to express what I know, feel, and see, but even more to test the truth of my knowledge, feelings and visions. I did not fully understand my own feelings about pacifism until I wrote Serjeant Musgrave ..." (Arden, Theatre at Work, p. 46).

77) Theatre at Work, p. 47.

78) Cf. Sport, p. 158; cf. chapter VIII, p. 70 and p. 86.

79) Cf. chapter VIII, p. 86.

80) "The play is set in a mining town in the north of England eighty years ago. It is winter ... A canal wharf. Evening ... A few yards away SPARKY stands, as though on guard, clapping himself to keep warm." (Musgrave, pp. 8-9).

81) Theatre at Work. p. 48.

82) Cf. pp. 126-127.

83) Musgrave, p. 38.

84) Musgrave, II, ii, 53.

85) Musgrave, II, iii, 75.

86) This is most certainly one of the scenes for which Arden would have liked to have an open stage at his disposal (cf. p. 116). As the speeches were, according to the stage direction, "delivered straight out to the audience" (III, i, 76), a closer contact would have resulted in a greater impact on the spectators.

87) Musgrave, III, i, 79.

88) The high sustained organ sound was also used every time Billy Hicks was mentioned.

89) " ... in the production it was hardly a dance, but a physical and verbal 'demonstration'." (Arden, Theatre at Work, p. 43).

90) Musgrave, III, i, 90; cf. p. 110.

91) Lindsay Anderson, interview with the present writer, 26.9.68.
92) "MRS. HITCHCOCK: ... And it's not a dance of joy. ..." (Musgrave, III, ii, 102).
93) Theatre at Work, p. 45.
94) Interview with the present writer, 26.9.68.
95) 30.10.59.
96) Cf. Musgrave, p. 36.
97) 30.10.59.
98) Ian Bannen.
99) December 1959.
100) 29.10.59.
101) 23.10.59.
102) I, iii, 29f.; cf. pp. 104, 116.
103) I, iii, 31.
104) 30.10.59.
105) Interview with the present writer, 24.9.68.
106) Sparky's.
107) Court Press Office
108) Musgrave, I, i, 9-10.
109) II, i, 38-39.
110) II, iii, 58.
111) Faithful to Arden's stage direction: "The songs are to be sung to available traditional tunes." (Typescript).
112) Interview with the present writer, 26.9.68.
113) Typescript Court Press Office.
114) Musgrave, I, ii, 17-18; cf. p. 102.
115) I, ii, 18.
116) December 1959.
117) Cf. Musgrave, III, ii, 102.
118) December 1959.
119) Interview with the present writer, 26.9.68.
120) Musgrave.
121) December 1959.
122) 30.10.59.
123) Typescript Court Press Office.
124) Typescript.
125) " ... a minor character who looms large in my recollection was a pugnacious but understandably bemused collier, played with gusto by Colin Blakely ..." (Westminster and Pimlico News, 30.10.59.
126) "They (the colliers) don't stand out as individuals but most of the time they don't need to. Dramatically, they're at their most effective as members of a crowd in the pub or as dark, silent, threatening figures, with picks on their shoulders, looking suspiciously at the red-coated soldiers. Without saying a word, they sum up the unrest and victimization in the town, frozen in a movement, like people in a Lowry painting." (Hayman/Arden, p. 28).
127) Deposited in the Royal Court press office. Writing about Freda Jackson and Patsy Byrne, Alan Brien in The Spectator (30.10.59) observed that "They,

too, willingly sacrifice a showy solo turn to obtain those balanced ensemble effects at which Mr. Anderson aims ..."

128) The Waiting of Lester Abbs by Kathleen Sully (30.6.57); Progress to the Park by Alun Owen (8.2.59); Jazzetry by Christopher Logue (26.4.59).

129) The Long and the Short and the Tall by Willis Hall (7.1.59).

130) Interview with the present writer, 26.9.68.

131) The soldiers, e.g., got their final form during the rehearsals only: "I started off calling them 'One Soldier', 'Two Soldier', and 'Three Soldier', wrote a few scenes, decided they were developing certain characteristics of their own, went back and renamed them 'The Joking Soldier', 'The Surly Soldier', and 'The Grey-Haired Soldier'. I finished the play and when we went into rehearsal decided they had better have names - this was really Lindsay Anderson's idea. He maintained that if you call a character 'The Surly Soldier', it is going to make an actor think he has got to be surly all the way through. It was not until they had names that the soldiers really came alive as people." (John Arden, Hayman/Arden, p. 2).

132) Interview with the present writer, 26.9.68. "I have been very fortunate on the whole with the directors I have worked with. In nearly every case I have had very close consultations. I have been to rehearsals and there are certain scenes in some of my productions that really I can say without conceit I directed myself. I do believe very strongly in the importance of the author's presence for the first production of the play ..." (Arden, interview with Walter Wager, Tulane Drama Review, vol. 11, number 2, Winter 1966, pp. 41-53).

133) Anderson, interview with the present writer, 26.9.68. In the printed version of the play Arden re-inserted the cuts, which in Anderson's view is a pity, as they both worked out a text fit for performance.

134) "Arden tends to use three words where two or even one would be sufficient." (Anderson, interview with the present writer, 26.9.68).

135) Musgrave, pp. 91, 93-94. Further cuts included lines in Sparky's song in I,i, 9-10; in Musgrave's speech in the churchyard (I,iii, 31-37 passim); in the chorus Sparky leads in II,i, 39; in the stable scene (II,iii, 57), where there are certain repetitions in the dialogue between Sparky and Hurst; in Musgrave's speech in the market-square (III,i, 81-92 passim). Throughout the play there were minor cuts made: single words, and every now and then changes of position within sentences, as well as a few insertions.

136) Interview with the present writer, 26.9.68. "The play starts in a kind of poetic realism and ends in a kind of expressionism: one has to find a style to do them both." (Anderson, interview with the present writer, 26.9.68).

137) Theatre at Work, p. 39.

138) 31.10.59.

139) 6.11.59.

140) Bernard Levin in the Daily Express (23.10.59) confirms this: "Mr. Lindsay Anderson's overwhelming production, which treats the whole play as one huge crescendo from the slow start to the terrifying climax ..."

141) Further critics who thought that the production lacked lucidity included Ronald Bryden: "The difficulties in the play became more so" (Interview with the present writer, 24.9.68) and T.C. Worsley: "He establishes the atmos-

phere for us, but he certainly does not lead us through the fog ..." (The Financial Times, 23.10.59). Caryl Brahms in Plays and Players (December 1959) defended the director: "... Anderson ... must not be blamed for the obscurities of this play. For he has allowed the piece to gather his own pace and given it time to roar its thunder; and he has let his actors find their strength and speak with it."

142) 23.10.59.
143) 24.10.59.
144) Ronald Bryden, in an interview with the present writer (24.9.68), was of the same opinion: "Lindsay Anderson's production was a very faithful one which did not falsify the play ... a wonderful and fine production." With regard to the pace, he even thought that "the last scenes were done too quickly."
145) December 1959.
146) From the General Notes in Arden's typescript (Court Press Office). In the official version of the play published by Methuen the directions are given in greater detail (Musgrave, Introduction, pp. 5-7).
147) "At first I grew a bit alarmed when she removed more and more, but then it worked. I like to use space on a stage. Jocelyn wanted to confine the action." (Anderson, interview with the present writer, 26.9.68). "I hate scenery which is more important than the play." (Jocelyn Herbert, interview with the present writer, 18.9.68).
148) Ronald Bryden hinted at this possibility (Interview with the present writer, 24.9.68).
149) Theatre at Work, pp. 47-48.
150) Musgrave, I, i, 9.
151) Musgrave, I, ii, 14.
152) Musgrave, II, iii, 56.
153) Musgrave, III, i, 76.
154) The Spectator, 30.10.59.
155) Musgrave, Introduction, p. 5.
156) The defensive reaction obviously set in at the very beginning: Jocelyn Herbert overheard somebody in the audience commenting on the set as follows: "Oh, it's going to be one of these bare-stage productions." (Interview with the present writer, 18.9.68).
157) The Waters of Babylon (1957), Live Like Pigs (1958).
158) 23.10.59.
159) Cf. p. 117.
160) 25.10.59.
161) 23.10.59.
162) 23.10.59.
163) 23.10.59.
164) 30.10.59.
165) 30.10.59.
166) 11.11.59.
167) 25.10.59.
168) 24.10.59.
169) 23.10.59.

170) 30.10.59.
171) "The production by Jane Howell was badly directed" (Anderson, interview with the present writer, 26.9.68), It was. The present writer saw the production in Zürich, in the summer of 1966.
172) Lindsay Anderson, interview with the present writer, 26.9.68.
173) The Happy Haven (Royal Court 1960); The Business of Good Government (Brent Knoll, Somerset 1960); Ironhand (Bristol Old Vic 1963); The Workhouse Donkey (Chichester 1963); Ars Longa, Vita Brevis (together with Margaretta D'Arcy, New Lamda Theatre 1964); Armstrong's Last Goodnight (Glasgow Citizens' Theatre 1964 and National Theatre 1965); Left-Handed Liberty (Mermaid 1965); The Royal Pardon (together with Margaretta D'Arcy, Beaford Entertainment Devon 1966); Friday's Hiding (together with Margaretta D'Arcy, Lyceum Edinburgh 1966); Harold Muggins is a Martyr (Unity Theatre 1968). Two TV-plays: Soldier, Soldier (1960); Wet Fish (1961).

X Norman Frederick Simpson: One Way Pendulum

1) Cf. brochure English Stage Company 1958-1959, p. 7. Subsequently referred to as ESC 58/59.
2) Simpson was co-winner of the third prize in the Observer competition 1956, together with Ann Jellicoe and Richard Beynon.
3) Act I, pp. 11-12. Quotations throughout this chapter are taken from N.F. Simpson, One Way Pendulum. Faber & Faber, London 1960. Subsequently referred to as Pendulum. "The Faber text is the one used in the production" (N.F. Simpson, letter to the present writer, 7.8.69).
4) Pendulum, I, 12-14 passim.
5) I, 13.
6) I, 14.
7) "(colloq.). Foolish, lacking sense." (The Concise Oxford Dictionary of Current English, Oxford 1964).
8) Weighing machines.
9) I, 15.
10) Pendulum, I, 15.
11) Cf. I, 16.
12) I, 17.
13) I, 17.
14) Cf. Pendulum, I, 18-19.
15) I, 21-22.
16) Pendulum, I, 22-23.
17) I, 23.
18) Pendulum, I, 26.
19) I, 25.
20) I, 26.
21) I, 30.
22) Pendulum, I, 31.
23) I, 32-33.

24) <u>Pendulum</u>, I, 32.
25) I, 35-36.
26) I, 37.
27) I, 38-39.
28) <u>Pendulum</u>, I, 39.
29) I, 40.
30) I, 43-44 passim.
31) <u>Pendulum</u>, I, 45.
32) I, 50.
33) II, 56.
34) <u>Pendulum</u>, II, 57.
35) ibid.
36) <u>Pendulum</u>, II, 58.
37) ibid.
38) II, 60-61.
39) II, 61.
40) II, 62.
41) Cf. <u>Pendulum</u>, II, 62-63.
42) II, 63-64.
43) <u>Pendulum</u>, II, 64-65.
44) <u>Pendulum</u>, II, 69-70
45) <u>Pendulum</u>, II, 72-73.
46) pp. 38-39; cf. pp. 137-138.
47) <u>Pendulum</u>, II, 78.
48) ibid.
49) II, 79.
50) II, 80.
51) II, 81.
52) <u>Pendulum</u>, II, 85.
53) II, 86.
54) <u>Pendulum</u>, II, 88-89.
55) II, 90.
57) II, 91.
58) ibid.
59) ibid.
60) <u>Pendulum</u>, II, 92.
61) II, 93-94.
62) II, 94.
63) ibid.
64) <u>Pendulum</u>, I, 29.
65) "PROS. COUN.: Where were you, Mr. Groomkirby, before you came here today? MR. G.: I was living in a world of my own, sir." (II, 67).
66) Cf. <u>Taylor</u>, p. 63.
67) Simpson, in his preface to <u>Some Small Tinkles</u> (Television plays; Faber and Faber, London 1968) considers this attitude positive: "As for the overall moral tone of these plays, I would like to think it was set by the attitude of life of the two main characters, Bro and Middie Paradock. For them, there is nothing so

outrageous but what it may well have happened somewhere only last week; and
nothing so preposterous that it may not happen here before the day's out - in
all probability at a moment's notice and ringing a handbell. Consequently they
treat life very much like the weather, and organize themselves around its vaga-
ries as best they can with such means as come to hand. And in doing so, let me
say, they are to my mind on far solider ground than those who succumb to the
ludicrous delusion that life is something they have some kind of edge on. It
makes for cautious resignation - and a simple faith in the axiom that for those
to whom life is an exercise in survival, the secret is in knowing how to ride
with the punch. "

68) "Non-sequitur (it does not follow), illogical inference, paradoxical result."
(The Concise Oxford Dictionary of Current English, Fifth Edition, Oxford 1964).

69) Taylor, p. 63.

70) Taylor, p. 64.

71) "MRS. GROOMKIRBY: ... Oh, it's you. Mr. Barnes. I wondered who it was."
(I, 14). "MR. GROOMKIRBY: ... Oh, it's you, Bob, is it? Wondered who it
was." (I, 30). "MRS. GROOMKIRBY: ... I thought you weren't seeing Stan any
more." (I, 19). "MRS. GROOMKIRBY: ... I thought you weren't seeing Stan."
(I, 24). "MRS. GROOMKIRBY: You know very well he's busy up there." (I, 19).
"MRS. GROOMKIRBY: ... You know perfectly well it hasn't come yet, Aunt
Mildred." (I, 20). "MRS. GROOMKIRBY: ... You know that, Sylvia, as well
as I do." (I, 22). "MRS. GROOMKIRBY: ... You know perfectly well she got
on the wrong train, Sylvia." (I, 23). "MRS. GROOMKIRBY: ... You know he
won't start eating ..." (I, 23). "MRS. GROOMKIRBY: ... Surely you know by
now, Sylvia ... " (I, 23). "MRS. GROOMKIRBY: ... I suppose he's all right."
(I, 27). "MRS. GANTRY: Showing off, I suppose." (I, 32). "MRS. GROOMKIRBY:
... Missed his footing, I suppose?" (I, 33). "MRS. GANTRY: ... I don't suppose he even knew what it was." (I, 33). "MRS. GANTRY: I think that's more
or less everything, Mabel. (Rising) I haven't touched the gherkins, but I can
attend to those when I come in in the morning. MRS. GROOMKIRBY: Oh, don't
worry about those, Myra ... It's the other things I can't manage." (I, 40).
"MRS. GANTRY: (rising as at exit in Act One). I think that's more or less
everything, Mabel. ... I haven't touched the asparagus, but I can attend to
that first thing in the morning. MRS. GROOMKIRBY: ... Don't worry about
the asparagus, Myra. I can see to that. It's those great packets of cereals
they send us." (II, 53).

72) "JUDGE: Cold, blind, deaf - and now dumb! ... MR. GROOMKIRBY: You think
I'm paralysed, don't you?" (II, 75).

73) Strikingly enough, weighing machine Number One Gormless retains its individuality and refuses to sing as the others do. It shows a will of its own.

74) Martin Esslin, The Theatre of the Absurd. Eyre & Spottiswoode, London 1962;
pp. 228-230 passim.

75) "The division of Act One and Act Two points to an inherent fault of Simpson's
writing - actually, it is not really a fault. He is interested in social attitudes
and does not have the feeling of a whole." (William Gaskill, interview with the
present writer, 18.9.68).

76) Cf. the non-sequiturs in scene eleven.

77) ITMA (It's That Man Again) was a wartime show. Its main star was Tommy Handley. It made fun of anybody and particularly the government departments. The Goon Show was a crazy affair (a radio programme) featuring Peter Sellers, Harry Secombe and Spike Milligan. (For these informations I am indebted to Norman J. Akers).
78) Taylor, p. 58.
79) Mr. Shandy and his wife.
80) Walter Allen, The English Novel. A Short Critical History, London 1954; p. 75.
81) Pendulum, I, 39.
82) Letter to the present writer, 7.8.69.
83) "It was a marvellous effect, and the reaction of the audience was immediate." (William Gaskill, interview with the present writer, 18.9.68).
84) Daily Mail, 23.12.59.
85) The Tribune, 1.1.60.
86) Interview with the present writer, 18.9.68.
87) 18.9.68.
88) Letter to the present writer, 7.8.69.
89) Letter to the present writer, 16.6.67.
90) Interview with the present writer, 18.9.68.
91) Pendulum, p. 7.
92) 23.12.59.
93) Financial Times, 23.12.59.
94) 28.12.59.
95) Pendulum, I, 32-34; cf. pp. 136-138.
96) Plays and Players, February 1960.
97) Pendulum, p. 8.
98) Interview with the present writer, 18.9.68.
99) 23.12.59.
100) The Times, 23.12.59.
101) Kirby Groomkirby: Roddy Maude-Roxby; Robert Barnes: John Horsley; Sylvia Groomkirby: Patsy Rowlands; Aunt Mildred: Patsy Byrne; Myra Gantry: Gwen Nelson; Arthur Groomkirby: George Benson; Stan Honeyblock: Douglas Livingstone; Policeman: Alan Gibson; Usher: Jeremy Longhurst; Clerk of the Court: Robert Levis; Defending Counsel: Graham Armitage. "Mr. George Benson is excellent as the hobby-ridden man ..." (The Times, 23.12.59). "Alison Leggatt's Mrs. Groomkirby is a beautiful performance; and Douglas Wilmer's judge, George Benson's Mr. Groomkirby, Roddy Maude-Roxby's son, Patsy Rowlands' daughter, and Graham Crowden's prosecutor are all out of the top comic drawer." (Punch, 6.1.60). "Otherwise the comic gem of the evening was Alison Leggatt, who magnificently handled the mother's dead-pan matter-of-factness in face of the oddest odds." (Daily Mail, 23.12.59).
102) Gaskill, interview with the present writer, 6.7.67.
103) Interview with the present writer, 18.9.68.
104) 1.1.60.
105) Letter to the present writer, 7.8.69.
106) Interview with the present writer, 18.9.68.
107) Letter to the present writer, 7.8.69.

108) Interview with the present writer, 18.9.68.
109) A Resounding Tinkle, The Hole, One Way Pendulum.
110) Letter to the present writer, 16.6.67.
111) 23.12.59.
112) 31.12.59.
113) 6.1.60. "... production ... builds this suburban madness into riotous fun
    ..." (Yorkshire Evening Post, 2.1.60). "... production was wittily inventive
    ..." (Plays and Players, February 1960).
114) The whist-game between Mr. Groomkirby and the Judge (II, 73-74; cf. p. 141.
115) 2.1.60.
116) Cf. p. 151.
117) "A door Back opens inwards. Part of a kitchen can be seen through it./ A
    door Right opens inwards giving a view of the hall, and part of the staircase.
    /Against the wall Right, and Right of this door, stands a cash register, cov-
    ered and so unrecognizable./ Leading inconspicuously up the wall from the
    cash register is a tube which disappears into the ceiling./ The fireplace is
    on the left. On the mantelpiece above it, almost lost among other oddments,
    stands a small replica of a skull, where a clock might normally be. ..."
    (Pendulum, I, 11).
118) "The early idea was to have a two-dimensional set for the whole play. At
    first we wanted real weighing machines, but then we decided to have card-
    board ones. Simpson thought they should have been real." (Gaskill, interview
    with the present writer, 18.9.68).
119) Doncaster managed an impressive counterpart to Simpson's description:
    "Furniture has been crowded to one side by the courtroom which dominates.
    Part of one wall has had to go in order to make room for it. Access to vari-
    ous parts of the room, and to cupboards, involves squeezing with difficulty
    round some part of the Court. Table, with two chairs, is now downstage.
    ..." (Pendulum, II, 53).
120) Cf. II, 53.
121) A Resounding Tinkle, Penguin Plays P 149, 1964; Act II, 191.
122) Letter to the present writer, 16.6.67.
123) ibid.
124) Interview with the present writer, 18.9.68.
125) 23.12.59.
126) Mr. Groomkirby.
127) 1.1.60.
128) 16.1.60.
129) 2.1.60.
130) 23.12.59.
131) 23.12.59.
132) 23.12.59.
133) 27.12.59.
134) Daily Sketch, 23.12.59.
135) 23.12.59.
136) 1.1.60.
137) 23.12.59.

138) 1.1.60.

XI Arnold Wesker: The Kitchen

1) Performed on 14.7.58 and 7.6.60.
2) Performed on 30.6.59 and 28.6.60.
3) Performed on 27.7.60 (the dates refer to the first nights).
4) Arnold Wesker, The Kitchen. Jonathan Cape, London 1961; p. 5. Subsequently referred to as Kitchen.
5) Kitchen, I, 16.
6) I, 18.
7) I, 18.
8) I, 19.
9) I, 19.
10) Kitchen, p. 7.
11) I, 22.
12) Cf. Kitchen, I, 23.
13) Cf. I, 26.
14) Kitchen, I, 27.
15) I, 28.
16) I, 30.
17) Kitchen, I, 34-35 passim.
18) Cf. I, 35.
19) Kitchen, I, 36.
20) I, 38-39.
21) I, 39.
22) Kitchen, I, 42.
23) ibid.
24) I, 43.
25) Kitchen, I, 48.
26) I, 49.
27) Kitchen, I, 50-51.
28) Kitchen, Interlude, 55.
29) Kitchen, Interlude, 57.
30) Interlude, 59.
31) ibid.
32) Interlude, 60.
33) Kitchen, Interlude, 60.
34) II, 63.
35) ibid.
36) II, 66.
37) ibid.
38) Kitchen, II, 69.
39) II, 70.
40) ibid.
41) ibid.

42) <u>Kitchen,</u> II, 76.

43) II, 78.

44) <u>Kitchen,</u> II, 78-79.

45) p. 5.

46) " ... it is to show what happens when people are cooped up, constantly frustrated and limited entirely to the dreariest, least stimulating practicalities." (<u>Taylor</u>, p. 155).

47) <u>Taylor,</u> pp. 156-157.

48) <u>Taylor</u>, p. 158 (quoted from <u>The Transatlantic Review.</u>)

49) "Als Stückschreiber hielte ich meine Aufgabe für durchaus erfüllt, wenn es einem Stück jemals gelänge, eine Frage dermassen zu stellen, dass die Zuschauer von dieser Stunde an ohne eine Antwort nicht mehr leben können - ohne ihre Antwort, ihre eigene, die sie nur mit dem Leben selber geben können." (Max Frisch, <u>Tagebuch 1946-1949,</u> Droemer Knaur, München/Zürich 1965, p. 108).

50) <u>Daily Express,</u> 28.6.61.

51) <u>Hampstead and Highgate Express,</u> 7.7.61.

52) Letter to the present writer, 30.9.69.

53) "The author would prefer there to be no interval at this point but recognizes the wish of theatre bars to make some money." (<u>Kitchen</u>, p. 51.)

54) Interview with the present writer, 14.9.67.

55) <u>New Statesman,</u> 7.7.61.

56) 3.7.61.

57) Letter to the present writer, 30.9.69.

58) 28.6.61.

59) <u>The Financial Times</u>, 28.6.61.

60) 7.7.61.

61) 5.7.61.

62) 7.7.61.

63) Letter to the present writer, 30.9.69.

64) Interview with the present writer, 14.9.67.

65) <u>The Yorkshire Post</u>, 20.6.61 (referring to the production at the Belgrade Theatre, Coventry).

66) 7.7.61.

67) August 1961.

68) In the 1959 Sunday night production.

69) 19.7.61.

70) 15.7.61.

71) <u>The Observer</u>, 2.7.61.

72) Letter to the present writer, 30.9.69.

73) Letter to the present writer, 5.9.69.

74) " ... there's a notable performance by Robert Stephens ..." (K.A. Hurren in <u>What's On in London</u>, 7.7.61). " ... piece of bravura acting by Mr. Robert Stephens ..." (T.C. Worsley in <u>The Financial Times</u>, 28.6.61). "Robert Stephens is outstanding as the German chef" (<u>Daily Herald,</u> 28.6.61). "Robert Stephens gets under the skin of this man and evokes a sympathy hardly deserved by his behaviour ..." (<u>Reynolds News,</u> 2.7.61). "Robert Stephens gives a clever

performance as the hysterical German ..." (<u>Punch</u>, 5.7.61). "I do not think that Robert Stephens could make more of the part of Peter as it is at present written ..." (<u>The Tribune</u>, 7.7.61).

75) <u>Plays and Players</u>, August 1961.
76) 28.6.61.
77) 28.6.61.
78) August 1961. "There are many excellent small character-studies, and outstanding performances in key parts by Robert Stephens ..., Martin Boddey, Harry Landis and Mary Peach." (<u>The Stage</u>, 29.6.61).
79) The remainder of the cast: Tommy Eytle (Magi), Martin Boddey (Max), Jane Merrow (Molly), Ida Goldapple (Winnie), Marcos Markou (Mangolis), Harry Landis (Paul), Andre Bolton (Raymond), Rita Tushingham (Hettie), Gladys Dawson (Anne), Jeanne Watts (Gwen), Shirley Cameron (Daphne), Sandra Caron (Cynthia), Dimitri Andreas (Dimitri), Tarn Bassett (Betty), Charlotte Selwyn (Jackie), Wolf Parr (Hans), Reginald Green (Alfredo), Andreas Markos (Gaston), Brian Phelan (Kevin), Andreas Lysandrou (Nicholas), Ken Parry (Frank), Arnold Yarrow (Chef), Charles Workman (Head Waiter), Andreas Malendrinos (Marango), Patrick O'Connell (Tramp).
80) <u>Kitchen</u>, p. 6. "Dexter needs a central idea in physical terms: as soon as he has this, he knows how to proceed." (William Gaskill, interview with the present writer, 11.7.67).
81) Desmond Pratt in <u>The Yorkshire Post</u>, 20.6.61.
82) <u>Evening Standard</u>, 28.6.61.
83) <u>The Sunday Telegraph</u>, 2.7.61.
84) <u>Liverpool Daily Post</u>, 1.7.61.
85) <u>The Tablet</u>, 8.7.61.
86) <u>Taylor</u> (revised paperback edition, Pelican A 641, 1963), p. 145.
87) Letter to the present writer, 30.9.69.
88) <u>The Observer</u>, 2.7.61.
89) Letter to the present writer, 5.9.69.
90) 7.7.61.
91) <u>Time and Tide</u>, 6.7.61.
92) 19.7.61.
93) 28.6.61.
94) 2.7.61.
95) <u>The Guardian</u>, 29.6.61.
96) Letters to the present writer, 30.9.69 and 5.9.69 respectively.
97) Wesker, letter to the present writer, 30.9.69.
98) ibid.
99) <u>Kitchen</u>, p. 6.
100) "Whenever Dexter asked Wesker because of some cut he wanted to make, Arnold's face was like Christ's when the nails went in." (William Gaskill, interview with the present writer, 11.7.67).
101) 7.7.61.
102) August 1961.
103) "An excellent production" (Wesker, letter to the present writer, 30.9.69). "A marvellous production" (Robert Stephens, interview with the present

writer, 14.9.67). "Such places are obviously highly organized hives of toil, and in reproducing the essence of their activity on the stage, the director ... has accomplished a small miracle ... " (K.A. Hurren in What's On in London). "A real virtuoso production" (Keith Johnstone, interview with the present writer, 12.7.67). "Dexter has produced with consummate, juggling skill; he catches the play's heartbeat and never lets go." (Bernard Levin in The Daily Express, 28.6.61). " ... strikingly well directed ... Mr. Dexter's direction is, as I have implied, a work of art in itself" (T.C. Worsley in The Financial Times, 28.6.61). "John Dexter directs - well, dexterously. Except at the end, where he forces a silent climax out of the audience's view." (David Nathan in the Daily Herald, 28.6.61). " ... remarkably effective production by John Dexter ..." (R.B. Marriott in The Stage, 29.6.61). "John Dexter's orchestration of this madhouse documentary is very skilful." (Punch, 5.7.61). "Mr. John Dexter's direction can hardly be faulted." (The Tribune, 7.7.61).

104) 28.6.61.
105) 28.6.61.
106) Letter to the present writer, 5.9.69.
107) Letter to the present writer, 30.9.69. "Miss Jocelyn Herbert's stark décor is all we want ... " (T.C. Worsley in The Financial Times, 28.6.61).
108) Letter to the present writer, 5.9.69.
109) Letter to the present writer, 5.9.69.
110) Letter to the present writer, 30.9.69.
111) 3.7.61; cf. p. 170.
112) 2.7.61.
113) 14.7.61.
114) 28.6.61.
115) 2.7.61.
116) August 1961.
117) 2.7.61.
118) Cf. p. 176.
119) 2.7.61.
120) 28.6.61.
121) 1958.
122) From Biographical Details of Arnold Wesker, a leaflet which Wesker sent to the present writer.
123) Interview with the present writer, 11.7.67.

XII John Osborne: Luther

1) 26.6.61. (first night).
2) Performed on 6.7.61.
3) Cf. Act I, scene i, pp. 13-14. Text quotations throughout this chapter are taken from John Osborne, Luther, Faber and Faber, London 1961. Subsequently referred to as Luther.
4) Luther, I, i, 19.
5) I, i, 19-20.

6) I, i, 20.
7) I, i, 22.
8) <u>Luther</u>, I, i, 23.
9) I, ii, 24.
10) I, i, 21.
11) I, ii, 24.
12) <u>Luther</u>, I, ii, 26-27.
13) I, ii, 27.
14) I, ii, 28.
15) I, ii, 29.
16) <u>Luther</u>, I, ii, 29.
17) Cf. I, ii, 30.
18) I, ii, 30.
19) I, iii, 31-32.
20) <u>Luther</u>, I, iii, 38.
21) I, iii, 40.
22) Cf. <u>Luther</u>, I, iii, 42-43.
23) I, iii, 44.
24) ibid.
25) <u>Luther</u>, I, iii, 45.
26) II, i, 47.
27) II, i, 47.
28) II, i, 48.
29) <u>Luther</u>, II, i, 49.
30) II, i, 50.
31) <u>Luther,</u> II, i, 50-51.
32) "(The sound of coins clattering like rain into a great coffer as the light fades.)"
    (II, i, 51.)
33) II, ii, 53.
34) II, ii, 55.
35) II, ii, 56.
36) <u>Luther</u>, II, ii, 58.
37) II, ii, 60.
38) <u>Luther</u>, II, iii, 61.
39) II, iii, 62-63.
40) II, iii, 63.
41) Cf. <u>Luther</u>, II, iii, 63.
42) <u>Luther</u>, II, iv, 68.
43) II, iv, 69.
44) II, iv, 71.
45) Cf. II, iv, 71-72.
46) <u>Luther</u>, II, iv, 72.
47) II, iv, 72.
48) II, iv, 73.
49) II, iv, 73-74.
50) II, v, 76.
51) Cf. <u>Luther</u>, II, v, 76.

52) II, v, 77-78.
53) _Luther_, II, vi, 79.
54) Cf. II, vi, 80.
55) III, i, 81.
56) Cf. III, i, 83-84.
57) Cf. III, i, 85.
58) _Luther_, III, i, 85.
59) _Luther_, III, ii, 86.
60) III, ii, 86-87.
61) III, ii, 87.
62) _Luther_, III, ii, 89.
63) III, ii, 89.
64) Cf. III, ii, 90-91.
65) III, ii, 91.
66) "What Osborne's Luther feels more than anything is a nostalgia for childhood, with its combination of innocence and dependent love on a strong protecting father. It is because he never experienced this love himself that he hankers after it so much and he expresses his fantasy of what it would be like in the description of Abraham and Isaac ..." (Ronald Hayman, _John Osborne_. Contemporary Playwrights Series. Heinemann Educational Books Ltd., London 1968, p. 45. Subsequently referred to as _Hayman/Osborne_).
67) _Luther_, III, iii, 97.
68) _Luther_, III, iii, 99.
69) Cf. III, iii, 100.
70) III, iii, 102.
71) " ... the historical material is straightforwardly presented on the whole, with Luther's own words used whenever possible (as Osborne and his supporters rapidly pointed out to the tender-minded who quailed at the dramatist's apparent obsession with constipation and defecation)." (John Russell Taylor, _Anger and After. A Guide to the New British Drama_. Methuen & Co. Ltd., London 1962, pp. 54-55. Subsequently referred to as _Taylor_.
72) "The best act is the first and this is the one which is intended as an investigation of the internal and unconscious conflicts. Osborne never quite succeeds in getting a clear focus on the relation between Luther's rejection of his father and his rejection of the Church, but the long argument with the father which is the climax of the act gives a good pointer to Luther's memories of the boy's frustrated love for the man. ... We see how this could lead to a projection of the same combination of emotions towards God: a sense of desperate need and a sense of being singled out for special victimization." "The growing isolation of Luther in the monastery is shown very well. The intensity of the internal pressure leads to an exorbitant guilt for which confession is an inadequate safety-valve." (_Hayman/Osborne_, pp. 43-44).
73) _Hayman/Osborne_, p. 48.
74) "The monastery sequences are easy to follow but the story-line gets very muddled afterwards, especially in Act Three. ... After the Diet of Worms scene, the narrative goes completely to pieces. With a leap of four years to 1525, one dead peasant on a cart, an anachronistic marching hymn and some off-stage

cannon shots and shouting, we have nothing except a long monologue from the
Knight to tell us what happened and it's extremely difficult either to understand
what the Knight is meant to stand for or to make sense of his monologue ... The
colloquial language and the twentieth-century speech patterns don't make it any
easier to tune in to what he's on about. No audience could possibly guess from
this scene why or how the peasants rebelled or in what sense Luther let them
down." Hayman/Osborne, pp. 49-51).

75) "The dependence on Erikson (author of Young Man Luther) explains why the parts
of the play dealing with Luther's private conflicts are so much better than the
parts dealing with public conflicts. He is convincing as an individual rebel, but
not as a leader capable of getting half Germany on his side. When Staupitz sums
up Luther's achievement at the end of the play we feel incredulous and bewildered.
... The play as a whole hasn't contained anything to substantiate this dramatically and Osborne's Luther hasn't established himself as a personality capable
of doing what the historical Luther did." (Hayman/Osborne, p. 43).

76) "Like the language, the whole characterization consists of jig-saw pieces which
don't fit together. Osborne leans heavily on a psycho-analytical interpretation,
Young Man Luther by Erik H. Erikson, which was published in 1959, and it is
from this that he derives his emphasis on psycho-physiological factors, explaining Luther's revolution against the Church in terms of a persistent identity
crisis in which the constipation, the epilepsy and the conflict with the father are
all inter-related." (Hayman/Osborne, pp. 42-43). Cf. Bill Maitland's headache
and taking of pills in Inadmissible Evidence by John Osborne.

77) Luther, I, i, 15.

78) I, iii, 32. "But with historical characters, like Holyoake and Luther, Osborne
doesn't have the basic confidence in his writing of the part to let a speech-pat-
tern emerge naturally. The only distinctive characteristic of Holyoake's way
of speaking is his stammer, and this disappears in his big speech to the court
in Act Two. Otherwise, his language varies, as Luther's does, between passages of quotation, which sound like what they are, and passages of Osborne,
which sound very modern." (Hayman/Osborne, p. 42).

79) "The subtlest writing comes in the scene with Cajetan, but this is made up
more of interlocking monologues than of dialogue, while many of Cajetan's
speeches are explanations of Luther to Luther, an extra interpretative gloss
on his personality, thinly disguised as a scene between two characters." (Hay-
man/Osborne, p. 52). " ... a rather feeble scene of disputation between Luther
and Cajetan, the papal legate (which again demonstrates Osborne's deficiencies
when a conflict of equals rather than a tirade to a captive audience is called for,
since, though apparently engaging in a discussion, Luther and Cajetan never
really interlock so that one answers the other; their 'dialogue' turns out, in
fact, to be two monologues skilfully intercut) ..." (Taylor, p. 55.)

80) E.g. I, i, 19-20; I, iii, 43-44; II, ii, 58-59; II, iii, 63; III, ii, 92.

81) "He was in love, as always, with the idea of defiance of authority, and the main
attraction of Luther as a subject must have been his success in flouting the authority of the Establishment - one man who divided the world into two camps.
But Osborne's Luther is a man whose motivations have very little to do with ex-
terior reality. The characters in the play who are meant to stand for the various

authorities against which Luther rebelled are mere <u>papier maché</u> figures. ...
The Pope and von Eck are typical Osborne Aunt Sallies and Katherine, Luther's
wife, is extremely shadowy." (<u>Hayman/Osborne</u>, pp. 51-52).

82) "But the most positive new discovery about Osborne it offered us was that he
was not just the primitive we had feared he might be - inspired or nothing; he
could turn his hand to play-writing simply as a craft and turn out something
perfectly presentable. But equally, taken in conjunction with the two previous
plays, it did make us wonder whether, barring any sudden unforeseen transformation, we would have to say good-bye to Osborne the innovator and greet
instead Osborne the careful craftsman." (<u>Taylor,</u> p. 57).

83) <u>Hayman/Osborne</u>, p. 46.

84) ibid., p. 47.

85) <u>Luther</u>, p. 11.

86) Cf. p. 210.

87) Among others Jocelyn Herbert, William Gaskill and some of the staff in the
Royal Court Press Office. "The shadowy cloisters and chapel, the incense-
laden air, the procession of chanting monks, the solemnity of the ceremony,
the depth of feeling marking the taking of vows under an agonised representation of Christ crucified give the scene a sombre but moving beauty, and unforgettable serenity ..." (<u>The Morning Advertiser</u>, 14.8.61). " ... some memorable scenes - especially the opening one with the monks chanting and singing
beneath a gigantic, distorted figure of the crucified Christ ..." (<u>Liverpool
Daily Post</u>, 29.7.61).

88) <u>Luther,</u> I, i, 23; cf. p. 184.

89) 30.7.61.

90) To the present writer, 14.11.67.

91) 7.9.61.

92) Letter to the present writer, 14.11.67.

93) Cf. <u>Evening News</u>, 28.7.61; <u>Press and Journal</u>, 5.8.61.

94) 3.8.61.

95) Their names: Champion Rifka's; Tarquin of Carloway; Flamenco Ben Rifka.

96) <u>Luther</u>, II, vi, 78.

97) "One remembers the sudden appearance of the Pope with his hunting party -
sulky, sensual, elegant, childishly proud and brusquely decisive. It was an
arresting indication that the Reformation was up against the subtlety and grace
of princes." (V.S. Pritchett in the <u>New Statesman,</u> 4.8.61).

98) 4.8.61.

99) Cf. pp. 211-212.

100) Cf. <u>Luther</u>, III, i, 81.

101) Anachronistic?

102) " ... the far, staccato singing of 'Ein Feste Burg' suddenly became the loud,
frightening chorus of a revolutionary rabble." (<u>New Statesman</u>, 4.8.61).

103) Luther.

104) 4.8.61.

105) Interview with the present writer, 5.10.67.

106) Interview with the present writer, 5.10.67. "Albert Finney's performance is
superb ..." (Bamber Gascoigne in <u>The Spectator,</u> 4.8.61).

107) September 1961.
108) "Mr. Albert Finney plays the 'foul-mouthed monk' with a mask of pallor and an expression of doubting anguish but gradually assumes the peaceful mien of one who has gone through life's fires and been toughened by them. His regional accent is native and proper to him just as is his homely Anglo-Saxon vocabulary." (The Times, 7.7.61; Paris production).
109) 30.7.61.
110) 30.7.61.
111) 28.7.61. " ... brilliantly brought to life by Albert Finney in a performance of extraordinary concentration and depth. I cannot remember ever having seen an actor age and alter so convincingly - not by means of elaborate make-up but simply by masterly muscular control ..." (Robert Muller in the Daily Mail, 28.7.61.)
112) 4.8.61.
113) 3.8.61.
114) 28.7.61.
115) Interview with the present writer, 24.9.68. A slight criticism is implied in Anthony Merryn's statement in a later issue of The Stage (7.9.61) dealing with the production after its transfer to the West End, although this time the overall impression is more positive: "Albert Finney, who, nevertheless, reveals great resources in variety of mood, and manages, through graduating diction from the quietly restrained to the ferocious (though calm force instead of shouting would impress more), to focus a nearly constant attention on the man." Some further criticism is expressed in two reviews concerning the productions in Nottingham and Edinburgh respectively: " ... although his performance is always sensitive and sincere Albert Finney is at his best when portraying Luther's spirits at their lowest ebb. ... It is, nevertheless, a great and almost unnerving performance, reducing all the other characterisations in the play to little more than shadows or charades." (Nottingham Evening News, 27.6.61). " ... Mr. Finney too frequently adopts, notably in long speeches, where modulation, pauses and variety of inflection are all important, an agonisingly persistent monotony ..." (South Wales Argus, 24.8.61).
116) 30.7.61.
117) 14.8.61.
118) "Albert Finney demonstrates ... that ... he is an artist at the top of the junior league ..." (Time and Tide, 10.8.61.) "Mr. Finney gives a fine study of a completely honest and sincere man fighting against impossible odds and somehow winning through ..." (W.A. Darlington in The Daily Telegraph, 28.7.61). "Finney, at times towering above all with his personality, and at other times trying to do something with banality, is a wonder." (Yorkshire Evening Post, 5.8.61). "Albert Finney's Luther is a brilliant combination of tortured innocence, spiritual frustration, righteous indignation, and physical handicap ..." (Norman Phelps in the Liverpool Daily Post, 29.7.61).
119) 11.8.61. "I enjoyed 'Luther'. That was very demanding." (Finney in an interview with Hunter Davies; The Sunday Times, 26.11.67).
120) The Financial Times, 28.7.61.
121) Luther, II,i, 47.

122) <u>Yorkshire Evening Post</u>, 5.8.61.
123) 10.8.61.
124) 16.8.61.
125) September 1961.
126) 4.8.61.
127) 30.7.61.
128) "Peter Bull has a glorious ten minutes as the bullying Tetzel when he comes on the stage escorted by drummers and banner wavers to frighten the audience into buying indulgences ..." (<u>Nottingham Evening News</u>, 27.6.61). "Peter Bull is brilliant in the extrovert caricature of the indulgence-monger Tetzel ..." (<u>The Stage</u>, 7.9.61).
129) 5.8.61.
130) 7.9.61.
131) September 1961.
132) 28.7.61.
133) <u>The Financial Times</u>, 28.7.61.
134) <u>New Statesman</u>, 4.8.61.
135) 10.8.61.
136) Cf. chapter VI, pp. 55-56.
137) 28.7.61.
138) 3.8.61.
139) 4.8.61.
140) "The play is admirably served by its actors." (<u>The Sunday Telegraph</u>, 30.7.61). The rest of the cast: Knight: Julian Glover; Prior and Von Eck: James Cairncross; Lucas: Peter Duguid; Weinand: Dan Meaden; Miltitz: Robert Robinson; Katherine: Meryl Gourley; Monks, Lords, Peasants etc.: Stacy Davies, Murray Evans, Derek Fuke, Malcolm Taylor; Singers: Ian Partridge, Frank Davies, Andrew Pearmain, David Read; Children: Roger Harbird, Paul Large.
141) 16.8.61.
142) 5.8.61.
143) <u>New Statesman</u>, 4.8.61.
144) <u>Evening Standard</u>, 28.7.61.
145) ibid.
146) <u>The Morning Advertiser</u>, 14.8.61.
147) <u>The Stage</u>, 3.8.61.
148) <u>The Daily Telegraph</u>, 28.7.61.
149) <u>The Daily Mail</u>, 28.7.61. "Tony Richardson tried hard to reinstate the sixteenth century in the production but, encouraged perhaps by references to Holbein and Dürer in the stage directions, he presented it in a very static visual way, much more in terms of groupings and backdrops than of life or movement. He gave us plenty of vivid scenic detail ... but history remained obstinately on the backcloth." (<u>Hayman/Osborne</u>, p. 46).
150) <u>The Financial Times</u>, 28.7.61.
151) 28.7.61.
152) Cf. p. 201.
153) 30.7.61.

154) The critic of <u>Plays and Players</u> was mistaken as well: "Rarely can a good play have owed more to its director ..." (September 1961).
155) 7.7.61. (Paris production).
156) <u>West London Press</u>, 11.8.61.
157) Jocelyn Herbert, interview with the present writer, 18.9.68.
158) Cf. <u>Luther</u>, p. 79; cf. p. 203.
159) <u>Luther</u>, p. 81.
160) ."Jocelyn Herbert ... has brought the outer aspects of the play to life with that striking economy which is so strong a feature of her settings, once again proving that as a stage designer she comes near to genius ..." (<u>John O'London's</u>, 10.8.61).
161) 4.8.61.
162) Autumn 1961.
163) 10.8.61.
164) <u>The Sunday Times</u>, 30.7.61.
165) 30.7.61.
166) 28.7.61.
167) 29.7.61.
168) 5.8.61.
169) 28.7.61.
170) 4.8.61.
171) 28.7.61.
172) 1.8.61.
173) 10.8.61.
174) Tony Richardson, interview with the present writer, 5.10.67.
175) " ... author, director, designer and actors weld themselves into a single image." (<u>The Sunday Telegraph</u>, 30.7.61).

XIII Conclusion

1) Cf. <u>The Stage,</u> 28.7.66; cf. chapter IV, p. 37.
2) Interview with the present writer, 5.10.67.
3) Cf. chapter IV, p. 37.
4) The Sunday Night Productions also proved an effective means to fight the Lord Chamberlain. "The Sunday Night Club is an organization to cunteract legal problems." (Gaskill, interview with the present writer, 18.9.68). "In the last ten years, the Society has mounted over fifty productions, including John Osborne's 'A Patriot For Me' and Edward Bond's 'Saved', which could not otherwise have been presented in a main bill at this theatre as they were written." (<u>Ten Years</u>, p. 35).
5) Cf. chapter IX, pp. 122-123; X, 152; XI, 176-177; XII, 210. Ann Jellicoe directed <u>The Sport of My Mad Mother</u> herself (cf. VIII, 91-92.
6) Jellicoe: <u>The Knack</u> (1962), <u>Shelley</u> (1965). Johnstone: <u>Eleven Men Dead at Hola Camp</u> (together with Gaskill, 1959), <u>Clowning</u> (1965). Soyinka: <u>The Invention</u> (1959). Howarth: <u>Lady on the Barometer</u> (together with Miriam Brickman, 1958), <u>Ogodiveleftthegason</u> (1967).

7) Cf. chapter VIII, 92-93.
8) Gaskill directed A Resounding Tinkle (1957, 1958), The Hole (1958), One Way Pendulum (1959).
9) Richardson directed Look Back in Anger (1956), The Entertainer (1957), Luther (1961).
10) Dexter directed The Kitchen (1959, 1961), Chicken Soup with Barley (1958), Roots (1959), I'm Talking About Jerusalem (1960), Chips with Everything (1962).
11) Cf. chapters IX, 122-123; X, 152; XI, 176-177.
12) Cf. chapter IV passim.
13) Cf. chapter V, p. 43.
14) Cf. chapter IV, p. 37.
15) Cf. chapters VIII, 96; IX, 131; XI, 181.
16) "It seems to me obvious that, whatever his private political views might be, George Devine never wanted to found a politically-oriented theatre, and never had any clearly defined idea of what function his company ought to exercise in society beyond providing all playgoers with the best drama it could lay its hands on in whatever shape or form interesting writers liked to write it ..." (John Russell Taylor, "Ten Years of the English Stage Company". In: Tulane Drama Review, Vol. II, number 2, Winter 1966, pp. 120-131).
17) "But the impact of our policy is beginning to be felt in the West End and the provinces. Openings for new dramatists are greater than at any time in my 30 years of experience. Theatre is slowly beginning to be a force in society." (Devine in ESC 58/59; p. 26).
18) "Beyond Sloane Square I think we exercised the greatest influence in the field of designing, especially through the work of Jocelyn Herbert." (William Gaskill, interview with the present writer, 18.12.69).
19) John Dexter went to the National Theatre, where he directed Shakespeare's Othello, Arden's Armstrong's Last Goodnight, and Shaffer's Black Comedy and The Royal Hunt of the Sun. Gaskill directed Farquhar's The Beaux' Stratagem for the same theatre (1969). Robert Stephens and Joan Plowright joined the National Theatre Company. Tony Richardson went into filming: Look Back in Anger, Tom Jones (with Albert Finney), The Charge of the Light Brigade, etc. So did Lindsay Anderson. Ann Jellicoe directed her play The Giveaway at the Garrick Theatre (1969).

XIV Gaskill and After: Outlook

1) Plays and Players, March 1966.
2) Among others A Resounding Tinkle, Epitaph for George Dillon, The Hole, One Way Pendulum (cf. chapter X), The Happy Haven, Saved.
3) Gaskill in the Telegraph & Argus, Bradford, 4.2.65. To encourage young dramatists, the so-called George Devine Award has been established: "The George Devine Award has been set up as a Memorial by his friends and colleagues. It is not simply the English Stage Company, but the English theatre as a vigorous force in the life of this country, that owes a special and unique debt to the work of George Devine. To acknowledge this historic fact in a permanent way, it has

been decided to create a memorial in the form of an Award. It was felt that the only memorial of which George would have approved would have to be practical and useful as well as permanent. To do this we shall set up a fund and intend to raise at least £ 20,000 which would produce an annual award of at least £ 1,000. This Award will be made to any promising or unproved playwright, director or designer. The money may be used in whatever way is most beneficial to the recipient who may need a special kind of encouragement at a crucial point in his career. The Trustees of the Fund will be Neville Blond, CMG, OBE, Miss Jocelyn Herbert and Robin Fox, MC." (Programme note to a performance in aid of the George Devine Award at the Old Vic; 13.6.66).

4) Gaskill, interview with the present writer, 6.7.67.

5) "The present policy at the Court is the only one possible. They continue the same thing. But it is getting more and more difficult to find new plays. Now everybody wants new plays, and that makes it difficult. There is a competition today which was not there around 1956 ... Beyond being a forum of new writers the Court had a historical role which it fulfilled, and inevitably it has a less important position today than it used to have in its beginning." (Tony Richardson, interview with the present writer, 5.10.67).

6) Jellicoe: Shelley (1965); Simpson: The Cresta Run (1965); Wesker: Their Very Own and Golden City (1966); Osborne: Time Present, The Hotel in Amsterdam (1968).

7) "I want to look after writers over a long period. We'll give them a chance to develop without pressures from outside ... I want them to speak with their own voices, not with the voice of fashion." (Gaskill, interview with Kenneth Pearson, The Sunday Times, 10.10.65). "I am very proud that we shall have presented, in this season, new plays by Ann Jellicoe, N.F. Simpson, Edward Bond, Keith Johnstone, David Cregan and Arnold Wesker and so have been able to maintain the continuity of their work regardless of financial failure and critical disapproval, but we must develop more new writers if the Court is to continue to serve its function." (Gaskill in Ten Years, p. 30). "There is a kind of 'nursing process' going on at the Court which is, in my opinion, very crucial." (Gaskill, interview with the present writer, 6.7.67).

8) "I try to follow the text very exactly. I like to follow the author, I am a 'textman'." (Gaskill, interview with the present writer, 6.7.67).

9) "There are surprisingly few differences between authors and directors." (Gaskill, 6.7.67). "I work especially closely with the respective designer ... Experiment and team-work and rehearsals lead to the final production ..." (Gaskill, 6.7.67).

10) "The playwright is treated with respect." (Gaskill, 6.7.67). A letter to the New Statesman, (16.1.70) by dramatist Frank Norman raises serious doubts against the assertion that this principle is still adhered to: on the occasion of rehearsals of his play Insideout Norman maintained that his text was mercilessly cut and distorted by Lindsay Anderson's and Anthony Page's dictatorial interventions. Playwright Donald Howarth however, in a letter published in the New Statesman on January 30th, 1970, expressed himself very positively about the team-work at the Court (his new play Three Months Gone had its first night there on January 28th 1970).

11) "The Royal Court has a style, but this style is not based on a theory. It is a natural style. We try to give each play its real face." (Gaskill, interview with the present writer, 6.7.67). Lindsay Anderson was somewhat sceptical about the development of the Court: "The tradition of the Court at its best was the integration of theatre elements in the service of the script. The author was given an important place. Acting and design were felt to be very important, and that made the Court. After George's death there was a marked decline in the arts of direction, acting and décor. This has been excused with the Court being a writer's theatre - an excuse which implies a complete misunderstanding of the term." (Interview with the present writer, 26.9.68).

12) Cf. chapter VII, p. 66.

13) Cf. Appendix, p. 289.

14) "I have often come out of the Royal Court irritated, or angry, or even disappointed. But I have never left it depressed by a sense of wasted hours. ... Coining money in the theatre is not easy but none of us regular Courtiers would allow the English Stage Company to get away with any chore as simple as that. We insist that they should present only the best plays, and not only the best plays but the best new, original, honest, alive, young plays. We treat them like a schoolmaster might treat a bright, wayward sixth former. We are always awarding them marks for courage, and taste, and intelligence, and concentration. Then we tot up the marks and compare with the totals of our friends. We are always arguing about the Royal Court - at parties and in pubs, in little magazines and Sunday paper essays, in statements to the press and letters to the weeklies. We are never entirely satisfied with them whatever they do. And we never allow them to become self-satisfied. ... However, some of its productions may miss the target at times, they stimulate the flow of ideas and opinions among those who are professionally concerned with the theatre. It has never had a failure which did not possess some quirks in the viewpoint, some pungency in the language, some explosive flare-up in the acting which made the evening memorable when many a better-organised, slicker-mounted commercial success had faded from the memory like an old photograph." (Alan Brien in ESC 58/59, p. 4).

15) Interview with the present writer, 6.7.67.

16) "The Court has still no audience of any size - at least within these four walls. ... Our only hope, and I think this is the conclusion that many provincial theatres are arriving at, is that we have to create a new audience drawn from schools, training colleges, universities and student organisations - an educated audience, if you like, who will be prepared to take a risk on something new. The West End theatre is, once again, full of Edwardian revivals, Chekhov, Shaw, Oscar Wilde that were the mainstay of the theatre ten years ago and the same public is going to them. If the theatre is to change, we have to ignore that need because, perhaps in another ten years, that audience will have dwindled. Already the concept of subsidised theatres is accepted and very soon one hopes new civic theatres will be started in provincial centres. If we are to serve any useful purpose, we must look to the audiences of twenty to thirty years time to see how best we can stimulate and satisfy them." (Gaskill, Ten Years, p. 30). "Yet I should have to be convinced that the Court, or for that

matter the National or the Aldwych, have in any considerable way changed the pattern of theatregoing, substantially increased the size of the audiences or remade its composition." (George Goetschius in <u>Ten Years</u>, p. 34).

17) Interview with the present writer, 6.7.67.

RECORD OF PRODUCTIONS

Date	Play	Author	Director	Designer	Music
2. 4. 56	The Mulberry Bush	Angus Wilson	George Devine	Motley	
9. 4. 56	The Crucible	Arthur Miller	George Devine	Stephen Doncaster and Motley	T. Eastwood
8. 5. 56	Look Back in Anger	John Osborne	Tony Richardson	Alan Tagg	T. Eastwood
15. 5. 56	Don Juan and the Death of Satan	Ronald Duncan	George Devine	John Minton and Richard Negri	T. Eastwood
26. 6. 56	Cards of Identity	Nigel Dennis	Tony Richardson	Motley and Alan Tagg	
31. 10. 56	The Good Woman of Setzuan	Bertolt Brecht (Trans: Eric Bentley)	George Devine	Teo Otto	P. Dessau
12. 12. 56	The Country Wife	William Wycherley	George Devine	Motley	T. Eastwood
5. 2. 57	Member of the Wedding	Carson McCullers	Tony Richardson	Alan Tagg and Stephen Doncaster	
10. 2. 57	Programme of Poetry*	Compiled by Stephen Spender			
3. 4. 57	Fin de Partie and Acte Sans Parole	Samuel Beckett	Roger Blin and Deryk Mendel	Jacques Noel	John Beckett
10. 4. 57	The Entertainer	John Osborne	Tony Richardson	Alan Tagg and Clare Jeffrey	John Addison
14. 5. 57	The Apollo de Bellac	Jean Giraudoux (Adapt: Ronald Duncan)	Tony Richardson	Carl Toms	

Date	Play	Author	Director	Designer	Music
14. 5.57	The Chairs	Eugène Ionesco (Trans: Donald Watson)	Tony Richardson	Jocelyn Herbert	
26. 5.57	The Correspondence Course*	Charles Robinson	Peter Coe		
9. 6.57	Yes-and After*	Michael Hastings	John Dexter		
25. 6.57	The Making of Moo	Nigel Dennis	Tony Richardson	Audrey Cruddas	T. Eastwood
30. 6.57	The Waiting of Lester Abbs*	Kathleen Sully	Lindsay Anderson		
22. 7.57	Purgatory (Devon Festival)	W.B. Yeats	John Dexter	Jocelyn Herbert	
5. 8.57	How Can We Save Father	Oliver M. Wilkinson	Peter Wood	Clare Jeffrey	
17. 9.57	Nekrassov	Jean-Paul Sartre (Trans: Sylvia and George Lesson)	George Devine	Richard Negri	T. Eastwood
20.10.57	The Waters of Babylon*	John Arden	Graham Evans		
26.11.57	Requiem for a Nun	William Faulkner	Tony Richardson	Motley	
1.12.57	A Resounding Tinkle*	N.F. Simpson	William Gaskill		
26.12.57	Lysistrata	Aristophanes (Adapt: Dudley Fitts)	Minos Volonakis	Nicholas Georgea-dis	T. Eastwood
11. 2.58	Epitaph for George Dillon	John Osborne and Anthony Creighton	William Gaskill	Stephen Doncaster	
16. 2.58	Love from Margaret*	Evelyn Ford	John Wood		
25. 2.58	The Sport of My Mad Mother	Ann Jellicoe	George Devine and Ann Jellicoe	Jocelyn Herbert	
9. 3.58	The Tenth Chance*	Stuart Holroyd	Anthony Creighton		

Date	Play	Author	Director	Designer	Music
23. 3.58	Each His Own Wilderness*	Doris Lessing	John Dexter		
25. 3.58	The Catalyst (Arts Theatre)	Ronald Duncan	Phil Brown	Stephen Doncaster	
2. 4.58	A Resounding Tinkle	N.F. Simpson	William Gaskill	Tazeena Firth and Stephen Doncaster	
2. 4.58	The Hole	N.F. Simpson	William Gaskill	Stanley Rixon and Stephen Doncaster	
21. 5.58	Flesh to a Tiger	Barry Reckord	Tony Richardson	Loudon Sainthill	Geoffrey Wright
18. 6.58	The Lesson	Eugène Ionesco	Tony Richardson	Jocelyn Herbert	J. Addison
22. 6.58	Brixham Regatta*	Keith Johnstone	William Gaskill		
22. 6.58	For Children*	Keith Johnstone	Ann Jellicoe		
7. 7.58	Gay Landscape (Citizens Theatre, Glasgow)	George Munro	Peter Duguid	David Jones	
14. 7.58	Chicken Soup with Barley (Belgrade Theatre, Coventry)	Arnold Wesker	John Dexter	Michael Richardson	
21. 7.58	The Private Prosecutor (Salisbury Arts Theatre)	Thomas Wiseman	Derek Benfield	Jean Adams	
28. 7.58	Dear Augustine (Leatherhead Repertory Theatre)	Alison Macleod	Jordan Lawrence	Gillian Armitage	
28. 8.58	Major Barbara	G.B. Shaw	George Devine	Motley	
14. 9.58	Lady on the Barometer*	Donald Howarth	Miriam Brickman and Donald Howarth		
30. 9.58	Live Like Pigs	John Arden	George Devine and Anthony Page	Alan Tagg	A.L. Lloyd

279

Date	Play	Author	Director	Designer	Music
5.10.58	Evening of Negro Poetry*	Black and Unknown Bards	Gordon Heath		
19.10.58	Actors Rehearsal Group	Mc Grath, Arden, Johnstone, etc.	Anthony Page, Miriam Brickman, Ann Jellicoe		
28.10.58	End-Game	Samuel Beckett	George Devine	Jacques Noel	John Beckett
28.10.58	Krapp's Last Tape	Samuel Beckett	Donald McWhinnie	Jocelyn Herbert	
2.11.58	Recital of Poetry*	Dame Edith Evans and Christopher Hassell			
30.11.58	Displaced Affections*	George Hulme	Phil Brown		
4.12.58	Moon on a Rainbow Shawl	Errol John	Frith Banbury	Loudon Sainthill	
7. 1.59	The Long and the Short and the Tall	Willis Hall	Lindsay Anderson	Alan Tagg	
25. 1.59	Recital of Poetry*	Louis MacNeice			
8. 2.59	Progress to the Park	Alun Owen	Lindsay Anderson		
8. 3.59	Recital of Poetry*	Dame Sybil Thorndike and Lewis Casson			
15. 3.59	A Resounding Tinkle (Cambridge A.D.C.)	N.F. Simpson	John Bird	John Bird	Temperance Seven
9. 4.59	Sugar in the Morning	Donald Howarth	William Gaskill	Sean Kenny	
19. 4.59	Leonce and Lena*	Georg Büchner	Michael Geliot		
26. 4.59	Jazzetry*	Christopher Logue	Lindsay Anderson		Tony Kinsey and Bill le Sage
14. 5.59	Orpheus Descending	Tennessee Williams	Tony Richardson	Loudon Sainthill	
17. 5.59	The Shameless Professor*	Pirandello	Victor Rietty		

Date	Play	Author	Director	Designer	Music
31. 5. 59	Contemporary American Opera*			Jocelyn Herbert	
30. 6. 59	Roots	Arnold Wesker	John Dexter		
19. 7. 59	Eleven Men Dead at Hola Camp*	Keith Johnstone and W. Gaskill	Keith Johnstone and W. Gaskill		
29. 7. 59	Look After Lulu	Noel Coward	Tony Richardson	Roger Furse	
6. 9. 59	The Kitchen*	Arnold Wesker	John Dexter	Jocelyn Herbert	
17. 9. 59	Cock-a-Doodle Dandy	Sean O'Casey	George Devine	Sean Kenny	Geoffrey Wright
11. 10. 59	Swiss Fortnight Programme including play by Dürrenmatt				
22. 10. 59	Serjeant Musgrave's Dance	John Arden	Lindsay Anderson	Jocelyn Herbert	Dudley Moore
1. 11. 59	The Invention*	Wole Soyinka	Wole Soyinka		
18. 11. 59	Rosmersholm	Henrik Ibsen	George Devine	Motley	
22. 11. 59	The Naming of Murderers' Rock*	Frederick Bland	John Bird		
29. 11. 59	Recital*	Ronai Segal	John Bird		P. Feuchtwanger
22. 12. 59	One Way Pendulum	N.F. Simpson	William Gaskill	Stephen Doncaster	Dudley Moore
24. 1. 60	Christopher Sly*	Thomas Eastwood and Ronald Duncan	Colin Graham		
27. 1. 60	The Lily White Boys	Harry Cookson	Lindsay Anderson	Sean Kenny	Tony Kinsey and Bill le Sage
8. 3. 60	The Room	Harold Pinter	Anthony Page	Michael Young	
8. 3. 60	The Dumb Waiter	Harold Pinter	James Roose Evans	Michael Young	
20. 3. 60	One Leg Over the Wrong Wall*	Albert Bermel	John Blatchley	Jocelyn Herbert	Thea Musgrave
30. 3. 60	The Naming of Murderers' Rock	Frederick Bland	John Bird	Motley	
10. 4. 60	Eleven Plus*	Kon Fraser	Keith Johnstone		
28. 4. 60	Rhinoceros	Eugène Ionesco (Trans: Derek Prouse)	Orson Welles	Stuart Stallard	Marc Wilkinson

Date	Play	Author	Director	Designer	Music
1. 5.60	The Sport of My Mad Mother* (Bristol Old Vic Theatre School)	Ann Jellicoe	Jane Howell	Kenneth Jones	
8. 5.60	Western Theatre Ballet*	Elizabeth West			
7. 6.60	Chicken Soup with Barley	Arnold Wesker	John Dexter		
11. 7.60	Sea At Dauphin and Six in the Rain*	Derek Walcott	Lloyd Reckord	Colin Garland	
27. 7.60	I'm Talking About Jerusalem	Arnold Wesker	John Dexter	Jocelyn Herbert	
14. 8.60	The Keep*	Gwyn Thomas	Graham Crowden		
22. 8.60	Wesker Repertory				
14. 9.60	The Happy Haven	John Arden	William Gaskill	Michael Ackland	Dudley Moore
13.10.60	Platonov	Chekhov (Trans: Dmitri Makaroff)	George Devine and John Blatchley	Richard Negri	Dudley Moore
23.10.60	You in Your Small Corner*	Barry Reckord	John Bird	Motley	
30.10.60	Political Theatre – Yes or No* (Discussion)				
23.11.60	Trials by Logue	Christopher Logue	Lindsay Anderson	Jocelyn Herbert	Bill le Sage
27.11.60	The Maimed*	Bartho Smit	Keith Johnstone		Marc Wilkinson
11.12.60	On the Wall*	Henry Chapman	Peter Duguid		B. Chapman
18.12.60	Song in the Theatre*		Bernard Shaktman		Dudley Moore
29.12.60	The Lion in Love	Shelagh Delaney	Clive Barker	Motley	Monty Norman
15. 1.61	Music Today*	John Carewe		Una Collins	
24. 1.61	The Importance of Being Oscar	Micheal Mac Liammoir	Hilton Edwards		
21. 2.61	The Changeling	Middleton and Rowley	Tony Richardson	Jocelyn Herbert and David Walker	Raymond Leppard

Date	Play	Author	Director	Designer	Music
22. 3.61	Jacques	Eugène Ionesco	R.D. Smith	Michael Young and Michael Ellis	
26. 3.61	Music Today*	John Carewe			
19. 4.61	Altona	Jean-Paul Sartre (Adapt: Justin O'Brien)	John Berry	Sean Kenny	
7. 5.61	The Departures*	Jacques Languirand	John Blatchley		
28. 5.61	The Triple Alliance*	J.A. Cuddon	Keith Johnstone		
30. 5.61	The Blacks	Jean Genet (Trans: Bernard Frechtman)	Roger Blin	André Acquart	Patrick Cowers
8. 6.61	Empress with Teapot*	B.R. Whiting	Nicholas Garland	Jocelyn Herbert	
27. 6.61	The Kitchen	Arnold Wesker	John Dexter		
16. 7.61	Brecht Film Evening arranged by Ronald Hayman*				
27. 7.61	Luther	John Osborne	Tony Richardson	Jocelyn Herbert	John Addison
13. 8.61	Humphrey, Armand and the Artichoke*	G. Roy Levin	Piers Haggard		
12. 9.61	August for the People	Nigel Dennis	George Devine	Stephen Doncaster	
24.10.61	The Death of Bessie Smith and The American Dream	Edward Albee	Peter Yates	Alan Tagg	
13.11.61	That's Us	Henry Chapman	William Gaskill	Stephen Doncaster	B. Chapman
22.11.61	The Keep	Gwyn Thomas	John Dexter	Ken Calder	Dudley Moore
26.11.61	Fando and Lis and Orison*	Fernando Arrabal (Trans: Barbara Wright)	Nicholas Garland		
3.12.61	The Scarecrow*	Derek Marlowe	Corin Redgrave		Inigo Kilborn

Date	Play	Author	Director	Designer	Music
21.12.61	The Fire Raisers and Box and Cox	Max Frisch (Trans: Michael Bullock)	Lindsay Anderson	Alan Tagg	Dudley Moore
24. 1.62	A Midsummer Night's Dream	Shakespeare	Tony Richardson	Jocelyn Herbert	John Addison
28. 1.62	Sacred Cow*	Kon Fraser	Keith Johnstone		
18. 2.62	Twelfth Night	Shakespeare	George Devine		A. Lockwood
25. 2.62	The Prisoners	A dramatic antho-logy by Tomorrow's Audience	John Duncan	Roger Furse	
27. 3.62	The Knack	Ann Jellicoe	Ann Jellicoe and Keith Johnstone	Alan Tagg	
27. 4.62	Chips with Every-thing	Arnold Wesker	John Dexter	Jocelyn Herbert	Colin Parrell
13. 6.62	Period of Adjust-ment	Tennessee Williams	Roger Graef	Seamus Flannery	
1. 7.62	The Captain's Hero*	Claus Hubalek (Trans: Derek Goldby)	Derek Goldby		
19. 7.62	Plays for England	John Osborne	John Dexter and Jonathan Miller	Alan Tagg	John Addison
11. 9.62	Brecht on Brecht	George Tabori (arr.)	John Bird		
16. 9.62	Day of the Prince*	Frank Hilton	Keith Johnstone	Jocelyn Herbert	
1.11.62	Happy Days	Samuel Beckett	George Devine		
3.12.62	Mime	Samy Molcho	Samy Molcho		
9.12.62	The Pope's Wedding*	Edward Bond	Keith Johnstone		
18.12.62	Squat Betty and The Sponge Room	Keith Waterhouse and Willis Hall	John Dexter	Ken Calder	
8. 1.63	Misalliance	G. B. Shaw	Frank Hauser	Desmond Heeley	

Date	Play	Author	Director	Designer	Music
1. 2.63	Jackie the Jumper	Gwyn Thomas	John Dexter	Michael Annals	Alun Hoddinott
24. 2.63	Discussion sponsored by 'Encore'*				
6. 3.63	Diary of a Madman	Gogol	Lindsay Anderson	Voytek	Carl Davis
17. 3.63	Home to Now*	Negro Sketches etc., Bari Jonson	Bari Jonson		
24. 3.63	In the Interests of the State*	Vanessa Redgrave (arr.)			
4. 4.63	Naked	Luigi Pirandello	David William	Henry Bardon	
7. 4.63	Skyvers*	Barry Reckord	Ann Jellicoe		
21. 4.63	Spring Awakening*	Frank Wedekind (Trans: Tom Osborn)	Desmond O'Donovan		
28. 4.63	First Results*	Mime, Clowning and Comic Improvisation	William Gaskill, George Devine, Claude Chagrin		
14. 5.63	Day of the Prince	Frank Hilton	Keith Johnstone	Sally Jacobs	
12. 6.63	Kelly's Eye	Henry Livings	David Scase	Alan Tagg	
15. 7.63	Poetry Festival*	Poetry Book Society			
23. 7.63	Skyvers	Barry Reckord	Ann Jellicoe	Jocelyn Herbert and Suzanne Glanister	
28. 7.63	Wiley*	Mary McCormick	Elaine Pranksy		Ernest Berk
12. 9.63	Exit the King	Eugène Ionesco	George Devine	Jocelyn Herbert	Michael Dress
15,12.63	Edgware Road Blues*	Leonard Kingston	Keith Johnstone		

WEST END SEASON (Queen's Theatre)

Date	Play	Author	Director	Designer	Music
12. 3.64	The Seagull	Chekhov (Trans: Ann Jellicoe)	Tony Richardson	Jocelyn Herbert	John Addison

Date	Play	Author	Director	Designer	Music
11. 6.64	St. Joan of the Stockyards	Bertolt Brecht (Trans: Charlotte and A. L. Lloyd)	Tony Richardson	Jocelyn Herbert	John Addison

ROYAL COURT (Re-opening after redecoration)

Date	Play	Author	Director	Designer	Music
9. 9.64	Inadmissible Evidence	John Osborne	Anthony Page	Jocelyn Herbert	Marc Wilkinson
22.10.64	Cuckoo in the Nest	Ben Travers	Anthony Page	Alan Tagg and Motley	
26.11.64	Julius Caesar	Shakespeare	Lindsay Anderson	Jocelyn Herbert	Marc Wilkinson
30.12.64	Waiting for Godot	Samuel Beckett	Anthony Page	Timothy O'Brien	
28. 2.65	The Sleepers'Den*	Peter Gill	Desmond O'Donovan	Brenda Briant	
11. 3.65	Happy End	Kurt Weill and Bertolt Brecht	Michael Geliot	Ralph Koltai	Francis Chagrin
19. 4.65	Spring Awakening	Frank Wedekind (Trans: Tom Osborn)	Desmond O'Donovan	Dacre Punt and Motley	Marc Wilkinson
2. 5.65	Miniatures*	David Cregan	Donald Howarth		
19. 5.65	Meals on Wheels	Charles Wood	John Osborne	Alan Tagg and Jocelyn Rickards	
30. 6.65	A Patriot For Me	John Osborne	Anthony Page	Jocelyn Herbert	John Addison
8. 8.65	A Collier's Friday Night*	D. H. Lawrence	Peter Gill	Ruth Myers	
29. 8.65	The World's Baby*	Michael Hastings	Patrick Dromgoole	Timothy O'Brien	

GASKILL SEASON

Date	Play	Author	Director	Designer	Music
18.10.65	Shelley	Ann Jellicoe	Ann Jellicoe	John Gunter	George Hall
27.10.65	The Cresta Run	N. F. Simpson	Keith Johnstone	John Gunter	

Date	Play	Author	Director	Designer	Music
3.11.65	Saved	Edward Bond	William Gaskill	John Gunter	
9.12.65	Serjeant Musgrave's Dance	John Arden	Jane Howell	Paul Mayo	Robert Long
12.12.65	Experiment*	Actors' Studio	Keith Johnstone		
20.12.65	Clowning	Keith Johnstone	Keith Johnstone		
13.1.66	A Chaste Maid in Cheapside	Thomas Middleton	William Gaskill	John Gunter	Robert Long
16.1.66	The Dancers and Transcending*	David Cregan	Jane Howell	Charles Knode	
	Instant Theatre*		Keith Johnstone		
6.2.66	The Knack	Ann Jellicoe	Desmond O'Donovan	John Gunter	
17.2.66					
3.3.66	The Performing Giant	Keith Johnstone	William Gaskill and Keith Johnstone	Charles Knode	
3.3.66	Transcending	David Cregan	Jane Howell	Charles Knode	Robert Long
27.3.66	Little Guy, Napoleon*	Leonard Pluta	Tom Osborn	James Heard	
27.3.66	The Local Stigmatic*	Heathcote Williams	Peter Gill		
11.4.66	The Voysey Inheritance	Harley Granville Barker	Jane Howell	John Gunter	Robert Long
19.5.66	Their Very Own and Golden City	Arnold Wesker	William Gaskill	Christopher Morley	
5./19.6.66	When Did You Last See My Mother*	Christopher Hampton	Robert Kidd		
26.6.66	Bartleby*	Herman Melville			
26.6.66	The Local Stigmatic*	Heathcote Williams	Peter Gill		
21.7.66	Ubu Roi	Alfred Jarry	Iain Cuthbertson	David Hockney	
21.8.66	It's My Criminal*	Howard Brenton			
21.8.66	The Ruffian on the Stair*	Joe Orton			

Date	Play	Author	Director	Designer	Music
30. 8.66	Natinal Youth Theatre	Michael Croft			
21. 9.66	Three Men for Colverton	David Cregan	Desmond O'Donovan	Christopher Morley	Marc Wilkinson
20.10.66	Macbeth	Shakespeare	William Gaskill	Christopher Morley	Marc Wilkinson
30.10.66	A Provincial Life*	Peter Gill (from Chekhov's short stories)			
12.12.66	The Lion and the Jewel	Wole Soyinka	Desmond O. Donovan	Jocelyn Herbert	
12. 1.67	The Soldier's Fortune	Thomas Otway	Peter Gill	John Gunter	John Dankworth
23. 2.67	Roots	Arnold Wesker	Jane Howell	Jocelyn Herbert	
5. 3.67	A Touch of Brightness*	Partap Sharma			
16. 3.67	The Daughter-in-Law	D.H. Lawrence	Peter Gill	John Gunter	
19. 3.67	A View to the Common*	James Casey			
18.4 67	Three Sisters	Chekhov	William Gaskill	Abd' Elkader Farrah	
6. 6.67	Crimes of Passion	Joe Orton	Peter Gill	Deirdre Clancy	
20. 6.67	A View to the Common	James Casey	Desmond O'Donovan	Harry Wastnage	
4. 7.67	The Restoration of Arnold Middleton	David Storey	Robert Kidd	Bernard Culshaw	
23. 7.67	The Rising Generation*	Ann Jellicoe	Ann Jellicoe		
23. 7.67	Dance of the Teletape*	Charles Hayward	Charles Hayward		
25. 7.67	Ogodiveleftthegason	Donald Howarth	Donald Howarth	Vanessa James	

Date	Play	Author	Director	Designer	Music
2. 8.67	America Hurrah	Jean Claude van Itallie	Jospeh Chaikin, Jacques Levy		
11. 9.67	Fill the Stage with Happy Hours (Vaudeville Theatre)	Charles Wood	William Gaskill	Harry Waistnage	
8.10.67	The Journey of the Fifth Horse*	Ronald Ribman			
19.10.67	Marya	Isaac Babel	Robert Kidd	John Gunter	Julian Dawes
15.11.67	Dingo	Charles Wood	Geoffrey Reeves	Charles Wood and Bernard Culshaw	
7.12.67	The Dragon	Yevgeny Schwarz	Jane Howell	Abd' Elkader Farrah	
21.12.67	The Paper Bag Players (Group Soup/ My Horse is Waiting				
31. 1.68	Twelfth Night	Shakespeare	Jane Howell	Patrick Procktor	
11. 2.68	Backbone*	Michael Rosen			
29. 2.68	A Collier's Friday Night	D.H. Lawrence	Peter Gill	John Gunter	
7. 3.68	The Daughter-in-Law	D.H. Lawrence	Peter Gill	John Gunter	
14. 3.68	The Widowing of Mrs. Holroyd	D.H. Lawrence	Peter Gill	John Gunter	
	(The above three plays ran in repertory until 4th May, 1968)				
31. 3.68	Early Morning*	Edward Bond	William Gaskill		
28. 4.68	Funnyhouse of a Negro*/A Lesson in Dead Language*	Adrienne Kennedy	Rob Knights		
8. 5.68	Backbone	Michael Rosen	Bill Bryden	Kenneth Bridgeman	
23. 5.68	Time Present	John Osborne	Anthony Page	Tony Abbott and Donald Taylor	
3. 7.68	The Hotel in Amsterdam	John Osborne	Anthony Page	Tony Abbott and Donald Taylor	

Date	Play	Author	Director	Designer	Music
4. 8.68	Changing Lines*	Nicholas Wright	Nicholas Wright	Hayden Griffin	
21. 8.68	Trixie and Baba	John Antrobus	Jane Howell	Patrick Procktor	
11. 9.68	Total Eclipse	Christopher Hampton	Robert Kidd		
2.10.68	The Houses by the Green	David Cregan	Jane Howell	Deirdre Clancy	
13.10.68	The Tutor adapted by Brecht translated by Richard Grunberger	Jakob Lenz	Barry Hanson		
29.10.68	Look Back in Anger	John Osborne	Anthony Page	Tony Abbott/ Donald Taylor	
4.11.68	The Beard	Michael McClure			
11.12.68	This Story of Yours	John Hopkins	Christopher Morahan	Tony Abbott D. Taylor	
13. 1.69	Life Price	Michael O'Neill and Jeremy Seabrook	Peter Gill	Jocelyn Herbert	
7. 2.69	Saved	Edward Bond	William Gaskill	John Gunter	
19. 2.69	Narrow Road to the Deep North	Edward Bond	Jane Howell	Hayden Griffin	
13. 3.69	Early Morning	Edward Bond	William Gaskill	Deirdre Clancy	
22. 4.69	In Celebration	David Storey	Lindsay Anderson	Peter Docherty	
24. 6.69	The Cry of the People for Meat	The Bread and Puppet Theater)	directed by Peter Schumann		
30. 6.69	Blue Raven Beauty & Theater of War	The Bread and Puppet Theater)			
22. 7.69	The Double Dealer	William Congreve	William Gaskill	John Gunter	
1. 9.69	Saved	Edward Bond	William Gaskill	John Gunter	
8. 9.69	Narrow Road to the Deep North	Edward Bond	Jane Howell	Hayden Griffin	

Date	Play	Author	Director	Designer	Music
25. 9.69	Oh! Les Beaux Jours	Samuel Beckett	Roger Blin	Matias	
25. 9.69	L'Amante Anglaise	Marguerite Duras	Claude Regy	Jacques Lemarquet	
20.10.69	The Contractor	David Storey	Lindsay Anderson	John Gunter	
1.12.69	Insideout	Frank Norman	Ken Campbell	John Gunter	

Plays marked with an asterisk (*) denote Sunday Night
Productions without Décor for the English Stage Society.

HOW PROFITABLE IS THE ROYAL COURT?

Date	Operating Deficit Royal Court	Theatre re-construction Costs less Special Receipts	Arts Council Grant	Income from Other Grants and Donations	Income from Transfers Tours Film Rights etc.	Deficit	Surplus
	£	£	£	£	£	£	£
1956 Pre-Production	4092		2500	2397			805
1957 1st Year	11327		7000	1067	8505		5245
1958 2nd Year	20448		5000	1917	39631		26100
1959 3rd Year	31154		5500	1943	18507		
1960 4th Year	28466		5000	991	19653	5204	
1961 5th Year	27839		8000	1077	7888	2822	
1962 6th Year	45434		8000	4880	26724	10874	
1963 7th Year	46965		20000	4567	20038	5830	
1964 8th Year*	25743	17594	20000	6130	16801	2360	
1965 9th Year*	35439	878	32500	3188	12076	406	11447
	£ 276907	£ 18472	£ 113500	£ 28157	£ 169823	£ 27496	£ 43597 27496
Average over nine years	£ 30765		£ 12611	£ 3126	£ 18869		£ 16101

Note 1964 and 1965* The theatre was let to visiting companies for five months to March 1964 after which it was closed for re-construction until September 1964.

These figures were compiled by Frank Evans, who was Accountant to the English Stage Company for its first ten years.

(from the brochure Ten Years at the Royal Cour 1956/66, p. 5.)

BIBLIOGRAPHY

Ann Jellicoe, The Sport of My Mad Mother. In: The Observer Plays, Faber & Faber, London 1958 (pp. 157-217).

Ann Jellicoe, The Sport of My Mad Mother. New Version. Faber Paper Covered Editions, London 1964.

Ann Jellicoe, Shelley, or The Idealist. Faber & Faber, London 1966.

John Arden, Serjeant Musgrave's Dance. Methuen & Co. Ltd., London 1960. Reset and reprinted 1966, reprinted 1967. The original typescript is deposited in the press office of the Royal Court Theatre.

Norman Frederick Simpson, One Way Pendulum. Faber & Faber, London 1960. The original typescript is deposited in the University of London Library.

Norman Frederick Simpson, Some Small Tinkles. Television Plays. Faber & Faber, London 1968.

Arnold Wesker, The Kitchen. Jonathan Cape, London 1961, reprinted 1962 and 1966. The original typescript is deposited in the University of London Library.

John Osborne, Luther. Faber & Faber, London 1961.

John Osborne, Inadmissible Evidence. Faber & Faber, London 1965.

T.S. Eliot, Collected Poems 1909-1962. Faber & Faber, London 1963.

George Farquhar, The Recruiting Officer. In: Representative English Comedies, Vol. IV. Ed. by Charles Mills Gayley and Alwin Thaler, New York 1936.

Max Frisch, Tagebuch 1946-1949. Droemer/Knaur, München/Zürich 1965.

John Russell Taylor, Anger and After. A Guide to the New British Drama. Methuen & Co. Ltd., London 1962.

Charles Marowitz/Simon Trussler, Theatre at Work. Playwrights and Productions in the Modern British Theatre. Methuen & Co. Ltd., London 1967.

Martin Esslin, The Theatre of the Absurd. Eyre & Spottiswoode, London 1962.

Ronald Hayman, John Arden. Contemporary Playwrights Series. Heinemann, London 1968.

Ronald Hayman, John Osborne. Contemporary Playwrights Series, Heinemann,

London 1968.

William A. Armstrong (ed.), Experimental Drama, London 1963.

Horst Oppel (Hrsg.), Das moderne englische Drama. Erich Schmidt Verlag, Berlin 1963.

Robert Fricker, Das moderne englische Drama, Göttingen 1964.

Marianne Kesting, Panorama des zeitgenössischen Theaters. 50 literarische Porträts. Piper & Co., München 1962.

Desmond MacCarthy, The Court Theatre. 1904-1907. London 1907.

C.B. Purdom, Harley Granville Barker, London 1955.

Konstantin Stanislavsky, Stanislavsky on the Art of the Stage. Translated with an introductory essay by David Magarshack. Faber & Faber, London 1967.

Raymond Mander/Joe Mitchenson, The Theatres of London, New York 1961 / London 1963.

Rudolf Stamm, Geschichte des englischen Theaters. Francke, Bern 1951.

Oscar James Campbell/Edward G. Quinn (ed.), A Shakespeare Encyclopaedia. Methuen & Co. Ltd., London 1966.

Walter Allen, The English Novel. A Short Critical History, London 1954.

Brochures

English Stage Company. A Record of Two Years Work. London 1958.

English Stage Company 1958-1959. London 1960.

Ten Years at the Royal Court 1956/66.

Articles

"British Theatre 1956-66". Ed. by Charles Marowitz. In: *Tulane Drama Review*, Vol. 11, Number 2 (T34), Winter 1966.

Penelope Gilliatt, "A Decade That Destroyed 'A Stuffed Flunkey'". In: *Life Magazine*, 13.6.66.

George Devine, "The Right to Fail". In: *The Twentieth Century*, February 1961, pp. 128-132.

Lawrence Thompson, "Can this man save the British Theatre?" In: *News Chronicle*, 8.10.57 (about George Devine).

William Gaskill, "Man for the Future". In: *Plays and Players*, March 1966, p. 55 (about George Devine).

Biographical Details of Arnold Wesker. A leaflet.

Radio Programmes

George Devine 1910-1966. Broadcast on BBC-3 on December 4th 1966. Compiled and narrated by Leigh Crutchley. Produced by Robert Pocock.

Tapes

Tape recording of the original 1959 production of *Serjeant Musgrave's Dance.* The tape is in the possession of Lindsay Anderson.